BORDELLO

Other books by the author

❀

The first three books listed below, comprise the trilogy of the O'Kelleher family:

"Seanachie"
'A Story of the Irish'

"To Shed a Tear"-
'A Story of Irish Slavery-
in the British West Indies'

"The Wind is Rising"
'A Story of Revenge'
****

In Addition,

"The Lads"
'Erin's Far-flung Exiles'

and

"Bordello"
'A Story of Love and Compassion'

Lawrence R. Kelleher

BORDELLO

A Story of Love and Compassion

Lawrence R. Kelleher

iUniverse, Inc.
New York Lincoln Shanghai

Bordello
A Story of Love and Compassion

Copyright © 2005 by Lawrence Kaliher

All rights reserved. No part of this book may be used or reproduced by any means, graphic, electronic, or mechanical, including photocopying, recording, taping or by any information storage retrieval system without the written permission of the publisher except in the case of brief quotations embodied in critical articles and reviews.

iUniverse books may be ordered through booksellers or by contacting:

iUniverse
2021 Pine Lake Road, Suite 100
Lincoln, NE 68512
www.iuniverse.com
1-800-Authors (1-800-288-4677)

This book is a fictional story, based on fact. Aside from actual historical figures, places and historical events, all other names, characters, places and incidents, are products of the author's imagination, or are used fictitiously. Any resemblance to actual events, or locales, or persons, living or dead, is entirely coincidental.

ISBN-13: 978-0-595-37046-7
ISBN-10: 0-595-37046-2

Printed in the United States of America

Dedication

To those of us who had to endure the pain of poverty, with little sustenance, ill housed, and the shameful finger of blatant bigotry, always pointing at us during the 'Great Depression', I salute you. Is it any wonder that they refer to us, as the 'Greatest Generation'? It was circumstances such as I describe herein, that molded us into what we are.

That time in America, certainly proved the maxim, *'the survival of the fittest.'*

Lawrence R. Kelleher

"I wonder, shall ye' judge, and yet, not yourself?"

—**Anonymous**

-Acknowledgement-

To those residents of the Chicago South-side and to the Park Manor neighborhood in particular, who unwittingly provided me with the foundation for my life, with their many stories and experiences, that I was so fortunate enough to have shared and remembered, having grown up during the 'Great Depression', I shall be forever grateful.

Lawrence R. Kelleher

-Introduction-

My story involves two unlikely people who fell in love, under most unusual circumstances. They both came from somewhat different childhood backgrounds. Both shared some of the same pain, knowing that they were different, caused by painful wounds, both physical and physiological. Wounds which had been inflicted on them by others and yet, they somehow found in each other, a compassion and an understanding, which developed into a life-long, love affair

One shunned society, choosing to live in the shadows while the other, sought approval from that same society, with its fickle and judgmental, 'better than thou', self-righteous attitude.

Society looked upon them both, as being different, not seeing their inner beauty.

Love will always find a way!

Lawrence R. Kelleher

CHAPTER 1

❀

Chicago
-Erin O'Hara-

I have had several pleasant encounters with Mademoiselle Adrienne de la Durequex, or Erin O'Hara, which was her birth name, and again several years ago, when we both worked in Chicago at the 1933-34, World's Fair. The fair was billed as, 'A Century of Progress', at the height of the 'Great Depression', although; we had met, as I said, in a rather serendipitous manner, several other times and I was more than fascinated with her, fact is, I was in love with her, in a sort of on and off again relationship.

Erin O'Hara, as I said, was her birth name, but she was now billed as, Mademoiselle Adrienne de la Durequex, the famous French chanteuse, at the French Pavilion, where she sang in the world famous Café; Toulouse-Lautrec exhibit, at the Chicago-'A Century of Progress'-World's Fair. Mademoiselle de la Durequex was a chanteuse, a singer of ribald French café songs and ballads. However, Mademoiselle de la Durequex also sang classical and Broadway show tunes. Erin grew up in Canaryville, a miserable Irish ghetto, where death was the easy way out. It was located on the south eastside of Chicago, just about a half-mile from the Union Stockyards.

She had a brutal young life, as a child of an abusive, tyrannical father, who was hardly ever sober. When he wasn't too drunk to stand, he butchered cattle at the Union Stockyards. Erin had to leave school when she was just eight years old; as her father needed money for booze and so, he got her a job, washing floors in the offices of the Union Stockyards; a job, whose hours were, from eleven p.m., until six a.m. She was the youngest child in an Irish-American family of six boys and five girls and probably, the most beautiful. Her hair was jet black and her eyes were an emerald-green with one sweet dimple in her right cheek. She had a peaches and cream complexion, with a few freckles on her petite nose.

Even at eleven years old, Erin was showing the promising physical attributes, of a mature woman. Although she was forced to quit school in the fourth grade, at St. Teresa's parochial school, her teacher, Sister Angela Clare, never gave up on her, as Erin had what the Sister described as a voice, that only God gives to someone, once every hundred years or so, and Erin was also, her brightest pupil. So unbeknownst to her father, Sister Angela Clare would continue to give voice lessons to little Erin, during her lunchtime, at St. Teresa's parochial grammar school, until that is; Erin left her father's home, a scared, eleven year old runaway.

As each of her older brothers and sisters reached the ages of ten or eleven, they one by one, left the home where they were reared, as none could tolerate the brutality of their father. He was constantly bemoaning his lot in life and of course, he would seek to depreciate theirs, in order to kind of lift his own low self esteem, telling them all, that they would never amount to anything. He would become violent when he was drunk, which was most of the time, with his Irish, hair-trigger temper. He showed no favoritism when it came to laying down the law in his home. He would deliberately find some petty fault, which one of his children did or didn't do, so that he could demonstrate his ironfisted rule over his children. The children lived in terror of their father's many dark moods, especially when he was drunk.

While the boys would fight back with their little fists, as best they could, the girls were almost helpless. Fact is; Mr. O'Hara usually enjoyed fist fighting with his sons, who were less than half his size. A vicious brute he was, make no bones about that. He would then use his belt on both the girls and the boys. What little food there was on the table, the children would gobble down what was served to them, as fast as they could, so that they could leave the table and try and get away from his wrath. When they finished their meal, they one by one said,

"Pa, may we be excused please?"

The rationale was, that if you left the table quickly, after you had gulped down your meager meal, he then wouldn't observe you long enough, for him to think of some petty complaint about you. Such complaints were mostly what he in his drunken stupor, made up. His individual tirades and these fits of anger, were for the most part, endured by the younger children, as they were the slowest eaters and they also were forced to sit, closest to their father by their older brothers and sisters. The older children, tried to put as much distance between themselves and their ogre of a father, as they could.

He would always think of something, that one or more of the children didn't do, to meet his never ending list of chores, whatever they were, as the children certainly didn't know what he wanted them to do. As most times, he was too drunk to tell them what he wanted and most of the time, he couldn't remember what he had said the night before anyhow.

If a child might have stupidly lingered, for a more normal time period, and tried to converse with him at lunch or supper, out of compassion and nothing else, which of course was stupid, as none of the children, really cared to converse with their cantankerous father, it was then, that you would most likely, get a whipping. He had a way of studying the faces of each of his children and he would find a reason first to berate, and then to beat the poor child with his belt. Thus, the children tried to avoid eye contact with him, for that reason. His motto was, *'children should be seen, and not heard'*!

Erin's mother had died in childbirth; actually, she died while giving birth to her, as Erin was a breech baby and Mrs. O'Hara died, from loss of blood and little Erin, had always felt that she had caused her mother's death, an awful burden for a little girl, to have to carry around.

Finally, at eleven years of age, Erin could no longer, endure the unfair and vicious beatings from her father, even though she still felt as the only child left at home, that she had a certain responsibility to him, and a normal child's compassion for her pa. This confusing feeling was further magnified, by her troubled conscience. Neither her brothers, nor her sisters, shared this same compassion, normal or otherwise, and so, she too, finally left home and wandered the streets for a few weeks, trying to figure out how to survive and what to do with her life; a major problem for an little eleven-year-old little girl, alone in the big city.

She ate out of garbage cans and waited in long food lines, which sometimes, wrapped around a full city block. She had to endure, the unwanted touching and the many lewd sexual comments she had to listen to, by the many bums, who lived on the streets, surrounding the Union Stockyards, while waiting to get some scraps of food and some watered-down soup. It was the height of the 'Great Depression' and Chicago was feeling the worst of it. Both the Salvation Army and the Catholic Church, had set-up food kitchens throughout Chicago, to feed the hungry and the poor.

She had lost track of her brothers and sisters, as they left no forwarding addresses, of where they were now living, as they didn't want their father, to come looking for them, or the authorities. It was one month to the day, that little Erin left home, when word had some how reached her, that her father was found frozen to death along a curb, after he left one of the local saloons and he had evidently slipped on some ice, and fell, hitting his head on the pavement. Erin could shed no more tears for her father, or for herself, as from her standpoint, he was worse than a nightmare from hell and she now knew, that expressing her own grief outwardly, only made things worse. She knew though, that with her bitter feelings toward her father, even though she felt they were justified, that she too, would probably burn in hell, for leaving him and thinking such ill thoughts of him, but she thought, 'could hell be any worse than what I now have to endure'?

It was two weeks later, after learning of her father's death, when a vagrant, a black man, discovered her sleeping in an alley, where he beat her and raped her, savagely. She had been sleeping, underneath some cardboard boxes and old rags, when he found her, and he raped her repeatedly, breaking her arm and her leg and several ribs, as she unwittingly succumbed to his assault, as he continued to club her viciously, with a broken two by four, as she tried to defend herself from her attacker. She ended up with two black eyes, with one eye, completely swollen shut, a broken leg and her mouth was badly cut and swollen. Some other vagrants had found her and notified the police. She was taken to Cook County Hospital to the indigent ward, for medical help.

After she recovered somewhat, she was taken to a Catholic orphanage, St. Agnes, by the juvenile authorities. St. Agnes was located in Lemont, Illinois, a suburb of Chicago. Because the doctor attending her at Cook County Hospital was careless, as he didn't set her leg bone properly where it had been broken, she now walked with a noticeable limp, like one leg was shorter than the other, which it was.

Erin was both bitter and frightened, at how her young life had become, these past few years. She thought that her dreams of being a famous singer, had all but disappeared, considering her circumstances, with her crippled leg, her shattered confidence and her lost innocence.

She now had to undergo additional suffering, at the hands of two bitter and frustrated nuns, whose convent life was not what they had thought it would be, who would beat her with a broom handle, if she didn't do what they wanted, to ease their frustration, with convent life. She washed the orphanage floors, from sun-up to sundown on her knees, with both nuns standing over her, commenting on what portion of the floor, they felt she had not been cleaned properly, and forcing her to re-wash this same area, over and over again. Becoming fed up with the brutal treatment she was receiving at the hands of the nuns, and seeing in their eyes, the bitterness and frustration, of convent life, she finally ran away from the orphanage. Erin was now fifteen years old.

She hitchhiked her way back into Chicago, figuring that she could more or less, blend in with the crowds of people who were going to and fro', conducting their daily business and running errands here and there, and not be noticed. The delivery truck driver, who picked her up hitchhiking, had to leave her off, on South Michigan Avenue, a mile from the tenderloin or Red-light district, of Chicago.

Walking toward the bright lights of the city, she happened to pass what to her, looked like a nightclub or cabaret of some sort, on South Michigan Avenue; the Kit-Kat Club. The sign in the window said, **"Singer wanted, good wages and meals included."** So she thought, *'what have I got to lose, I've got nothing to my name and perhaps, I can still sing, although it's been a few years, since I last sung the Ave Maria, for Sister Angela Clare.'*

She opened the front door and the first thing she noticed, was the smell of stale beer. The front part of the cabaret was dimly lit, where in the rear of the establishment, a single light bulb hung down, shedding a small amount of light, over an old beat-up, upright piano, which sat on a raised platform or stage. Seated at the piano was a black man with his shiny and slicked back, pomaded black hair, parted in the middle and smoking a cigarillo.

The piano player was stylishly dressed. He wore a white yellowing, celluloid collar, affixed to his pale blue shirt. His suspenders were a bright yellow and covering his dark brown high button leather shoes, were white spats, trimmed with gold buttons. On his little finger, he sported a flashy rhinestone, fake diamond ring, and a similar stickpin, the kind you could buy from some street vendor, over on Maxwell Street, a primarily Jewish, mercantile district, for fifty cents. His gold front teeth glittered, as he smiled at Erin, as she walked toward the back of the club, where a tall voluptuous blonde was attempting to sing a popular torch song of the day, *'Some of these Days'*. The blonde girl was struggling to sing, as she tried to meet the tempo of the song, which was a sort of a lament, or a tearjerker.

Standing behind the bar, was a short stocky man with a derby hat on, smoking a large Havana cigar. He had a thin moustache and perspiration shown on his greasy forehead. His fat belly, covered with greasy black hair, was visible, where the lower two buttons on his candy stripped shirt, were missing. Fact is;

he had more hair on his belly, than he did on his head. His belly hung over the front of his faded gray-stripped black pants, and he showed whisker stubble on his chin. His multi-colored vest was too small for him. Finally after listening to a few bars of the song, the man behind the bar whose voice sounded like gravel, being jiggled in a pail, said,

"I'm sorry doll, but I'm looking for someone, who can really belt out a song, I mean after all, this song is not a lullaby, it's a torch song." The blonde girl was visibly disappointed, as she needed the job badly and on her face, she showed the hurt of one, who had come to the big city, to make her fame and fortune.

Most of these young girls would end up as prostitutes, working in some seedy Bordello, over on south Wabash, after being brutalized and used for sexual purposes, by the proprietors of these seedy bars and clubs, in the tenderloin district, who generally plied them with drugs, in order to break down any resistance they might have, to engage in prostitution. The tenderloin-district ran from south Twelfth Street, to approximately south Thirty-first Street, from South Michigan Avenue to Wentworth Avenue.

"But Mr. La Rocco sir, couldn't I please sing another song, perhaps one with a different tempo?" Mr. Tony La Rocco, who was a Capo in the Sicilian/Italian Mafia, under the Don, 'il capo, il signore Al 'Scarface' Capish, said,

"No doll, ya' just don't have, the kind of a voice, I'm a looking for," as he undressed the blonde with his eyes. "But", he said, "I might be able to use ya' in the chorus, if yous' show yous' gratitude to me."

"Anything Mr. La Rocco sir, anything."

"Here" he said, "Pull your dress up to your hips, as I'd like to see your 'gams'." The blonde was embarrassed; her pretty face turned crimson, as no one had ever asked her to pull her dress up before, not even her boyfriend Freddie Klein, back in Elvira, Iowa. She now knew, that she should have married Freddie when he asked her to, but she didn't want to be tied down in a small Iowa town for the rest of her life, married to a grocery clerk, and never having fulfilled her dreams and wondering, what might have been. Elsie Saunderson, her friend, however, did marry Freddie Klein and she had a premature baby, or so they said.

Nevertheless, her stomach reminded her, that she hadn't eaten in two days and so she did as she was told. Mr. La Rocco smiled, as he licked his fat lips and then he said, "Aw right babe, I'll put ya' in the chorus line, but wait for me in my office for a few minutes, as I would first like to see this other young doll, to see what she wants." The blonde gave Erin a kind of watch-out look, as she walked back to Mr. La Rocco's office in the rear of the club. Mr. La Rocco then said,

"Aw' right doll, what can I do for ya'?" Erin didn't like what she had seen with the blonde and the suggestive sexual treatment, she was receiving from Mr. La Rocco, with his lecherous black eyes, but she too, was hungry and scared, and so she figured, *'Well, I believe that I can handle Mr. La Rocco, should he get fresh.'* Erin O'Hara, had no idea just what kind of violent animals, these Mafioso 'dagos', were.

"Well sir, I'm a singer, I've been classically trained in all kinds of songs, both in the classics, as well as the more popular ballads." Mr. La Rocco was sort of put off for a moment, as he looked at this gorgeous creature that was standing before him, as he said, "Aw' right doll, lets hear ya' sing." Erin then said,

"Sir I'm not familiar with the song the young lady before me was singing, however, if you would allow me to read the words from the sheet music on the piano, I believe that I could capture the essence of this song, for your approval." Mr. La Rocco studied Erin for a moment longer and then he said,

"Yeah, yeah, okay sister, let's see what ya' got." The piano player started to play the introduction to the same song that the blonde had tried to sing and after the intro', Erin began to sing. She started to belt out, *'Some of these day, you're goin' a miss me honey, some of these days-—'*. Erin through her classical voice training, could reach the depths of emotion that was required, in interpreting this torch song, as she continued singing, with her body swaying from side to side, and with her beautiful and sensual emerald green eyes, flickering slightly, with a sort of come hither expression on her beautiful face. Mr. La Rocco was enthralled with her voice and the sensual movement of her body, as he too, was moving his body in time with the music, mimicking Erin's sexual body language, to the music.

After Erin had finished her song, she waited for Mr. La Rocco to say something. Finally, after a minute or two, of sizing Erin up and down, and licking his fat lips, with a small amount of drool, appearing on his lower lip, Mr. La Rocco said, "What's your name doll?" Erin answered,

"My name is Erin O'Hara." Mr. La Rocco had all but forgotten about the blonde, who was cooling her heels in his office, as he said,

"Your name is fine for now, but if you are going to sing in my club, you'll need a more fancy name, perhaps a French name, a name that these French chanteuse singers use and not a 'Mick's' name, you catch my drift, doll?" Erin then said,

"Yes sir, and I do." Mr. La Rocco then asked Erin where she was staying.

"Well sir, since I just got into town, off of the Greyhound bus, and I really haven't had time, to look for lodgings, as I saw your sign in the window."

Mr. La Rocco picking his rotten teeth with his penknife, then said,

"Well doll, I just happen to have friends in the hotel business, who own and operate the New Michigan Hotel, which is located just about four blocks north of here and when you go in, tell the desk clerk, Sammy Di Salvo, that Big Tony La Rocco, said to fix you up with a room." Erin thanked Mr. La Rocco and as she turned to leave, he patted her on her ass. She turned as though she might have ideas of hitting him, as her face was beginning to turn red, but thinking better of it, she kind of smiled and then she left.

The New Michigan Hotel was a semi-high-class brothel, and the headquarters, for the number one gangster in America, Al 'Scarface' Capish.

CHAPTER 2

❦

Chicago

-Jimmy O'Brien-

I had been working in various carnivals around the United States and Canada, since I was wounded in France in 1917, in the 'war, to end all wars', or so they said. I was a roustabout in that I handled all sorts of manual labor jobs, from setting up the main tent, to handling the animals, if there were any, and repairing the equipment. I guess you could say, that I did everything.

I was a graduate of the University of Chicago, with an undergraduate degree in sociology and I graduated from the U.of C. School of law, Summa Cum Laude, class of 1916. My father, Cornelius O'Brien was the Alderman for the Hyde Park community and of course, it was through his political connections, that I was allowed to enter the University of Chicago in the first place. While my father had picked up certain airs, believing that he was a 'lace curtain' Irishman, when really he was nothing but, a 'Shanty' Irishman, the academic community at the U. of C. was not fooled by his affected pretense and of course, the university was controlled by the w.a.s.p.s, whose board of regents, were all prominent Chicago business men. Therefore, but for my father's political clout, I wouldn't have been allowed to enter such a prestigious university in the first place, being an Irish Catholic.

When the war broke out in 1914 in Europe, I was entering my second year of law school. However, when the United States entered the war, I had by then, graduated as a lawyer and I had opened up a law office at 55th, and Lake Park Avenue, practicing corporate and divorce law. My law practice was just beginning to show promise, but I knew that with President Woodrow Wilson as President, the democrats were chopping at the bit, and couldn't wait for the United States to become involved in this European war. That, together with the German's refusal to give up it's brutal submarine warfare, against allied shipping to England, by several neutral powers, including the United states, and was sinking, hundreds of thousands of tons of cargo each month and of course finally, their sinking of the British luxury ocean liner, the Lusitania. That was all that was needed, for the United States to declare war on Germany.

When war was declared by congress on April 6th. 1917, against the axis powers, I was chopping at the bit so to speak, to enlist. I finally enlisted and I received my commission as a First Lieutenant, in the 155th, Regiment of the Fifth Division, of General John J., 'Black Jack' Pershing's, American Expeditionary Force. I received my basic training both at Camp Grant, Illinois and my officer's training, at Camp Fort Leonard Wood, Missouri.

My unit shipped out by train, on the New York Central railroad, for New York, in the fall of that same year. When my unit disembarked in the great French harbor of Le Havre, France, after our long ocean voyage, I felt that destiny was calling me to new places and to new adventures, that I had only dreamed about as a small boy, growing up behind the Union Stock Yards in Chicago, in an Irish ghetto, called Canaryville. Of course, when my father was elected alderman in the Hyde Park district of Chicago, he really wasn't living in that district, but with a few favors given to some of the Democratic Party's bosses and to his other political cronies, that minor glitch, was soon overcome. 'Gerrymandering', wasn't new to the Democratic Party, I guess they invented it, but it wasn't necessary in my father's case. After all, the Democratic Party never allowed such trifling problems, to interfere with it's benevolent approach to the folks, and it's heartfelt theme, of looking out for the 'workingman' and the hordes of illiterate immigrants, pouring into Chicago, who in essence, were beholden to them for patronage jobs, and who received their votes. Therefore, my father carried out his aldermanic duties for Hyde Park, for almost a full year, while still living in Canaryville, behind the Union Stock Yards.

After about a year, my father had found a flat in a Hyde Park neighborhood; a run down, four bedroom, stove heated flat, and so we moved. All of our furniture and bedding, we managed to fit on a horse-pulled, flat bed, wooden, stack-sided freight wagon. My mother was so embarrassed by the means, by which we moved; with all of our nosy Irish neighbors, peering out from behind their old faded lace curtains, and snickering, well, she wasn't speaking to my father. I mean, after all, what would the neighbors say? I can still remember my mother yelling at my father as she said,

"God Damn it Con, what will the neighbors say about the way you're making us move and the 'Ladies Altar and Rosary Society', of St. Catherine's; I mean, and getting that old drunken bum, Joe McCarthy, to lend you his filthy old, coal hauling wagon and his flea bitten horse Nellie, to put our nice furniture in?" My mother didn't talk to my father for a month.

CHAPTER 3

❀

World War 1
-Marne, France-

It had been discovered, through allied spies, that the German army was about to open up an offensive front, in order to drive the French army from its positions, over looking the Meuse valley, a strategic location.

My regiment, along with several others, was ordered to attack the German positions, in an effort to thwart their predicted offensive. We had charged the German lines with heavy allied machine gun fire, which fired over our heads, as we crawled on our bellies, so as not to get hit by our own fire, when I felt a hot searing pain, crawling up my left leg. A German machine gunner, had riddled my left leg with bullets, breaking my leg. I lay in the yellowy brown muck, which covered no-man's land, bleeding profusely, with large rats, the size of squirrels, feasting on the dead and dying, in an orgy of agony and death. The screams of the wounded and dying men were ringing in my ears.

I was semi-conscience, on the battlefield at Marne, France. Shortly, thereafter, a howitzer shell, landed within fifteen feet of where I lay, and that shell, further wounded me. It took off, my left ear, and part of my scalp and face, on that same side, plus I received some shrapnel in my left shoulder and adding to this, was the concussion, which caved-in, all of my ribs and my chest, on my left side. I wasn't a pretty sight to say the least. After the battle, the Germans retreated, and a French medic found me and after applying a tourniquet to my left leg, he managed to stop the bleeding. After convalescing in a French hospital for over a year, I returned to the United States. By that time, the Germans had sued for peace and the Armistice was signed on November 11, 1918.

Upon arriving home in 1919, my mother and father were stunned by my grotesque appearance. I guess they made me finally realize without saying anything, just by the look of horror and revulsion on their faces, which convinced me, that I couldn't resume my law practice, looking like I did. Therefore, in order to make a living and not to cause myself to be an embarrassment to either my parents or others, I left home and joined a small carnival, which was operating in our neighborhood at the time.

I guess that is why I chose to work in these many carnivals and circuses, which toured the country. I could kind of remain out of the public's eye, as some sort of a sorrowful and disfigured war veteran, to the public, with their prying ignorance, coupled with their never-ending stares, and worse of course, my own personal feelings, about my condition. As many of the performers in these carnivals and circuses, were freaks so to speak, so I wasn't particularly noticed, as I sort of fit in. I walked with a decided limp, which got considerably worse, in the damp and wet weather, although I was still able to perform my many rigorous duties with the carnival. I wore a stocking hat, pulled down over the left side of my head and face, to partially hide my disfigurement.

CHAPTER 4

❈

A Mafia Courtship
-Tony La Rocco's Son-

Erin had noticed an inordinate amount of well dressed men entering and leaving the New Michigan Hotel, at all hours of the night and day, as she sang in the Kit-Kat Club from around nine p.m. each evening, usually, until four in the morning, except on week ends, when she sang until six a.m. She could see them, coming and going. In addition, she couldn't help but notice the many girls, who were made up like show girls, with their bright red lips, and rouged cheeks, and their short frilly skirts, worn above their knees. Most wore felt chapeau's, in many different colors. Some of the girls even wore rouge, above their knees, which Erin thought was a bit risqué. But she figured, as show girls, they had to more or less, dress the way they did, as well as use the heavy rouge and bright lipstick colors, as they had to be noticed, behind the bright footlights of the stages, which tended to mute their normal facial complexions somewhat she thought; otherwise, the patrons, couldn't see their faces. Most of the girls Erin thought, were cute, some she thought were pretty enough to have been models. She also noticed, that all the girls, wore exposed dress tops, revealing most of their gorgeous, milky-white breasts.

They all, she thought, *'had faces, that behind their makeup, showed some premature aging, which kind of belied their true ages, as though they were living life, like it would be over shortly, burning the candle at both ends, so to speak'*? Perhaps she thought, *'that it was the evening and the early morning hours, that showed on their pretty young faces, when such show girls performed'*. Erin hadn't yet realized, that most of these so called show girls, were really prostitutes, either returning from their nightly rendezvous, or else, were taking a so called, in-house coffee break and had for the moment, stepped out of their rooms, with their lovely revealing silk robes, barely covering their nude bodies.

Booze, drugs and the horrific lifestyle they were living, most, certainly didn't choose, but circumstances beyond their control, gave them no other choice. Carefully administered drugs by their pimps or Mafiosi handlers, controlled their every movement.

They in essence, were hooked on drugs, as their snorting of cocaine, or shooting heroin, was like a warm and intoxicating caress, a caress that few could resist, once they sampled its euphoric promise. Cocaine initially was thought to be a recreational, or a party activity drug, during the so called, 'Roaring-Twenties'. It for a while, would give temporary relief from the terrible pain, which these girls had to endure, both night and day.

Some tried to fight it's disastrous consequences, but few could overcome their insatiable appetite for more drugs, in a never-ending cycle, where the craving for more, never really subsided, as each fix or snort, seemed to last, a shorter and shorter time. Thus, the cravings could only temporarily be satisfied. Violent mood swings with suicidal thoughts, coupled with vomiting, were just some of the withdrawal symptoms these girls had, whenever they tried to kick their habit. Few were successful.

Opium however, was the drug of choice, as it was so easy to obtain through the Mafia's long over seas reach, and the most potent. Many a poor girl died overdosing from mixing these drugs, with the rotgut booze, they had to drink, night after night, in these sleazy speakeasies, as a sort of incentive to charm their customers and to break down, the customer's will, with the lure of sex, the main ingredient in such love trysts. Many of their once lovely bodies, old before their time, lay in potter's field, outside the Cook County Hospital, as 'Jane Doe's', unclaimed and known, only to God. Such beauty was so wasted.

Most of these girls, were from small towns, in Middle America, lured by the promise of a bright career, and the excitement of city life, which had the inducement of taking them away from their rather humdrum lives, on the farms, where they mostly came from.

It was Friday night and Erin was sort of making her debut at the Kit Kat Club and so, without any so called stage name as yet, to identify her, Tony La Rocco was advertising her as a mystery singer. Mr. La Rocco had given Erin a few dollars, for her to buy a couple of so-called 'flapper' dresses, which were rather revealing for her singing debut. One was bright red and the other, a slinky black dress, with slits, cut above the knee, to her waist, revealing her black silk, lace panties. Both dresses hung, several inches above her knees, flapper style. For now, that would be her only wardrobe.

The house lights dimmed, as Erin walked out onto the stage. A spotlight shown on her, as she began her introductory number; *"Some of These Days."* Her face was radiant and she had thrown some bits of multi-colored glitter over her hair and on her bare shoulders. She had a very stylish headband, with a jeweled broach set in the middle of it, above her forehead, which was the style of that era. The glitter sparkled under the one spot light. As the piano player, Art 'Fingers' Washington, played the introduction to her song, she began to sing. For a moment, given her striking beauty, the crowd forgot about her singing, but then, they seemed taken by her voice. Her range for the song she was singing, was incredible. It ranged from the very low to the very high octaves. The crowd was electrified.

Encore after encore, she went on with her program. While she was singing under the spotlight, she couldn't see the audience, as the spotlight blinded her. However, sitting on a bar stool at the crowded bar, was a rather tall and good-looking suave gentlemen, smoking a cigarette. His name was Enrico La Rocco, son of the owner. He was dressed in the style of the day. His shiny black hair was parted in the middle and he was impeccably dressed. A thin moustache adorned his upper lip. His father had told him, that he had hired a torch singer and that she would be making her debut this very evening; a very, very, beautiful torch singer, he added.

Mr. La Rocco senior had placed a small advertisement in the Chicago Tribune newspaper, in Thursday's Art and Music section. Enrico was quite taken by Erin; aside from her beautiful and sensual voice, she was a knockout, with a body, that was bursting to leave her confining garment, which held her, in a close lover's embrace. He had never before in his life, had ever seen such a beautiful woman and one who was so vivacious.

After Erin walked off of the stage, after responding to seven curtain calls, she walked to her dressing room. As she opened her dressing room door, there stood a tall gentleman, who was standing next to her dressing table, and he startled her. Enrico La Rocco then said,

"Excuse me, I didn't mean to frighten you, but I am the owner's son, Enrico, and my father had told me something's about you. However, nothing that he told me, no matter how flattering his comments were, could do you justice, his comments were trite, when compared to your beauty, as I stand here before you. Fact is doll, you are one gorgeous broad."

The words gorgeous or beautiful are probably the most flattering comments; a girl or a woman can receive, unless it would be; hi mom, especially coming from a very handsome man. A man with the most sensuous black eyes, that Erin had ever seen. His skin was smooth and it had an olive cast to it. His teeth were snow white and he was dressed in the fashion of the day. Erin was a bit taken, by this man's flattering remarks, but she tried to pull herself together and trying not to act like a schoolgirl, she said in a very cool voice,

Mr. La Rocco sir, I'm not used to anyone, especially a man, coming into my dressing room unannounced; please don't let it happen again." Enrico smiled at this feisty Irish beauty as he said,

"Once again, I'm so sorry for my careless and assuming manners. I guess I'm not used to anyone with the charm and bearing that you possess. Erin; eh', may I call you Erin?" Erin answered,

"That's my name sir." He went on,

"For the most part, most of the singers and chorus girls that my dad employs, are pretty rough and I guess, I just assumed that you were also."

So after Erin kind of relaxed, she and Enrico had a nice long conversation about Erin's early life, her aspirations and her other personal talents if any, other than singing. Erin asked him about his life and his personal goals and he, being somewhat evasive, tried to answer her questions, without of course, revealing his Mafia ties. Erin then said,

"If you don't mind Mr. La Rocco, I would like to get dressed in my street clothes and I don't need you gawking at me like some monkey, so please let me have some privacy." Enrico kind of smiled, as he had never had any employee of his father's, ever talk to him like that and get a way with it. However, he was taken by Erin, her beauty, and her feisty charms, and of course, this further enticed him. Therefore, he made a sort of a bow and he walked out into the hall and closed Erin's dressing room door behind him. Erin who was also quite intrigued by Enrico, had a smile on her face, as she went about taking off her 'Flapper's' dress and putting back on, her only other dress, a rather plain cotton dress, she had purchased in Lemont, Illinois. She had purchased the dress in a small neighborhood second-hand, dress shop, before she ran away from the Catholic orphanage, St. Agnes. Erin figured that Enrico would be waiting for her in the hall, though; she still acted surprised, when he appeared in front of her as he said,

"Erin, may I buy you breakfast?" She was hungry and so she said, "That would be nice Mr. Enrico." They walked north from the Kit-Kat Club for about a block and on the corner was a small cafe, called Big Mama's, Pasta Joint. They entered and as they did, it appeared to Erin that the recognition Enrico was getting from the customers, indicated to her, that he was somebody they all knew and/or, he was some kind of a big shot.

They both sat in a small booth in the rear of the cafe. After they ordered breakfast, Enrico said, "Erin, I hope you don't mind me asking, but I noticed a slight limp when you walk, is that from an injury." Erin became red in the face, as she had always tried to hide her gimpy leg, as it embarrassed her and so now, she didn't exactly know what to say in answering Enrico's inquiry. Finally, after a moment's hesitation, she said,

"Not that's it's any of your business, but I was beaten rather severely a few years ago, buy a bum and the doctor who repaired my leg, didn't do a very thorough job of setting my leg bone and so, that is why I have a slight limp." Enrico studied Erin's beautiful face with her pained look and then he said,

"I'm so sorry about you leg, but after our breakfast is finished, I'd like you to accompany me to a store in a place called 'Little Italy'. It's a neighborhood over on Taylor and Halsted Streets, and it sits on the south edge of downtown Chicago, where most of the Sicilian/Italian immigrants live, and it's where I grew up," Erin then said,

"Why would we want to go to that store, does your family own it?" Enrico laughed as he said,

"No Erin, my family doesn't own it, but there is someone there, I would like you to meet." Erin sort of shrugged her shoulders, as she said,

"It's okay with me Enrico, but as you know, I really do have to get back to my hotel room soon, to get some sleep, as I'm exhausted from my opening night's performance." Enrico paid the bill, he hailed a cab, and they left for 'Little Italy'. As the cab pulled up in front of the store, Erin saw the sign out front, which read, in Italian, *"Lo Stivale di Tostelli-Padrone di Luigi & il Fabbricante di Scarpa e la Riparazione"*, and underneath in English; 'Luigi Tostelli-Master Boot & Shoe Maker and Repair.' Erin was somewhat curious as to why, Enrico stopped at a shoe repair shop. Anyhow, they both got out of the cab and went into the store. Standing behind the counter was a young boy who first greeted Enrico with *"Buon giorno La Rocco di Signore, il signore",* 'Good morning, Mr. La Rocco, sir', and what can I do for you. Enrico then said,

"il figlio," 'son, where is your father, Luigi?' The young boy answered,

"He's in the back Mr. La Rocco. I will call him." The young boy hollered,

"Pa, Pa, Mr. La Rocco is here to see you." It was but a moment later, when a short stocky man appeared, wearing a leather apron and he had a leather cap on his head. After they, all greeted one another, Enrico said,

"Mr. Tostelli, I have a young customer for you, who needs a new pair of shoes with a thicker sole on her right foot." Mr. Tosteilli examined Erin's foot and he asked her, to walk around his shop. He verified what Enrico had told him and then he said to her.

"A young lady, please a take a seat a, while I examine the shoe a, you have on a." After examining Erin's foot and shoe, he had her stand against a marked wall, which had a ten foot ruler, nailed to it. She first stood on one foot and then on the other, while Mr. Tostelli wrote down her measurements. He looked at Erin and then at Enrico, as he said,

"I fix a, but give me a week, to be a sure a, that I am able to correctly make her a shoe, which will compensate for her a one a leg, a being a shorter than her other one." Enrico smiled as he said,

"That will be just fine Luigi, we'll be back in a week." Erin then spoke up,

"Enrico, while I appreciate what you are doing, but I can't afford to have a special shoe made for my bad leg, not yet anyway, that is, until I get paid, as the cost would be too much." Enrico said,

"Erin, please, let me do this for you, as it will make a big difference in your stage presence and it will give you much more confidence in your singing and in your walking, please, Erin." Erin really didn't know what to say, as she didn't want to be obligated to Enrico, but she did agree with him, that it would make a tremendous difference in her stage presence and so she finally agreed.

"Thank you, thank you, Enrico, but I'm afraid that it will cost you too much." Enrico then said,

"Forget it, Mr., Tostelli owes me a favor, as he looked directly at Mr. Tostelli." Mr. Tostelli nodded his head in agreement. After they both said goodbye to Mr. Tostelli, they left the shop and walked down the street to the corner. There was a cabstand on the corner and a cab was sitting there. They both got into the cab and Enrico said, "New Michigan Hotel;" and away they went.

CHAPTER 5

The Party
-Seduction-

Erin took the elevator to the floor, her room was located on and Enrico accompanied her. She put the key in the doorknob and as she entered, Enrico was right behind her. Erin turned and she said, "Please Enrico, I am so tired; I'm just exhausted and I must get some sleep." Enrico didn't like what he was being told and he was just about to grab Erin by her arm, and force himself on her, when reluctantly, he backed away.

The look on his face was not pretty, as he was seething mad inside, as no girl had ever rebuffed his so called charms. Therefore, it was all he could do to restrain himself. Finally, he relaxed somewhat, and he leaned over and kissed Erin on her cheek and she kissed him back. He thought to himself, *'they'll be time for Erin to accept my charms, if I have anything to say about it and I will.'* They both parted and as Enrico was about to walk out, he turned and said,

"Erin, I'm throwing a small dinner party Monday evening at a friends supper club and I would like very much, for you to accompany me as my guest. It will be just a small gathering of some of my associates, or *Consigularies*, as their sometimes called, and their girl friends." Erin said,"

"Sure, I would very much like to go with you and to meet some of your friends." Enrico then said,

"Fine, I'll pick you up at seven p.m." Erin thought a moment more and then she asked,

"You only mentioned your associates or *Consigularies* as you called them, and their girl friends, don't any of them have wives?" Enrico was caught kind of flat footed, as he didn't have a ready answer for Erin's innocent question, Finally he said,

"Well Erin, we hold what is commonly referred to, as a sort of stag party, where wives are not invited, its kind of a men only affair." Erin thought about what Enrico had just said, but she wasn't satisfied with his answer, and so she said to Enrico,

"I still don't get it, a party of friends as you call them, and yet, no wives are invited, just their girlfriends, that's sounds strange to me." Enrico was getting a little irritated with Erin's questioning of him, as he never had any woman or girl, question him before. Finally, he said,

"Look Erin, I'm not used to being questioned by any lady friend of mine, on anything pertaining to business, and this is business, even though I called it a party." Erin became red in the face, as she was now becoming suspicious of Enrico and his so called party. Finally, Enrico said,

"Look Erin, I like you, I like you very much, so please, lets drop the questions, until we get to the party and if you for some reason, don't like it, you can leave." He then turned on his heel and left her standing in the doorway, with a puzzled look on her face. She was just about to close her door, when she saw a blonde woman, coming toward her, walking down the hall. Erin thought she looked familiar. As the woman came closer, Erin recognized her as the woman who was having a tryout, singing for Mr. La Rocco. Erin said, "Hi, how've you been and how is the chorus?"

The blonde woman looked at Erin, as she finally recognized her and she said, "Some chorus, why that lousy 'dago' son-of-a-bitch. Do you know what he did to me after you left your audition and he returned to his office for our discussion and my possibly becoming a chorus girl?"

"No I don't", answered Erin. She continued, "Well, when he came into his office, I had been sitting in a side chair and when he came in, he walked over to me and he kissed me full on the mouth. I kind of shuttered, as I really didn't like his manners, and I certainly didn't like his kisses, with his rotten garlic breath. Anyway, he had a cooler behind his desk and in it, he kept some champagne."

He then said, "Babe, lets you and I, sip a little of the bubbly, to celebrate you're becoming a chorus girl. Well, I was down and out, I needed the job, and so I said,

"Fine Mr. La Rocco. Well he must have slipped some kind of a drug in my champagne, as I became sort of dizzy and after a couple of glasses, I could hardly stand up. It was then, that he assaulted me" She went on,

"He lifted me up on his desk and he raped me over and over, until I could hardly walk. I had absolutely no resistance to his advances; I was like I was paralyzed. After he was through, he called that 'nigger' piano player, for him to take his pleasure with me also." She went on, "Believe me when I tell you this, I have never in my life before, had sex with any man, believe it or not, I was a virgin." Then the young blonde, started to bawl, like a baby, as Erin put her arms around her in an attempt to comfort her.

Between her sobbing and her wanting to tell someone, about her terrible ordeal, she continued with her sad story as she said, "I have had a strange feeling in the pit of my stomach ever since they assaulted me, and so I went to the doctor this afternoon and he said that I was pregnant." She once again began to cry, as she continued with her sad story,

"Now it's bad enough for me to be pregnant without a husband, but I don't know who the father is; is it Mr. La Rocco or that 'nigger' piano player?" She continued, "I went to see Mr. La Rocco about my condition and he said, "Go screw yourself, as how do I know, that you were not just having some fun, with all the guys, you whores like to play around with?"

Erin then said, "What is your name?" The blonde said,

"My name is Frieda, Frieda Anderson." Erin said,

"What will you do now, what are your plans?" Frieda answered, "I don't' know yet. However, I know one thing, I can't go home. I don't have any money for bus fare and even if I did, my folks would kill me, especially if I gave birth to a 'nigger' baby."

"Well", said Erin, "Why don't you try and get a good night's sleep and tomorrow, we'll talk about your predicament, some more." Erin gave Frieda a kiss on her cheek and then she said, "Goodnight." It seemed like only a couple of hours had gone by, when Erin was awakened by loud voices coming from the hall in front of her room. She put on her robe and she peeked out of her door. A policeman was just walking by when Erin said, "Officer sir, what is the problem, if I might ask?" The officer turned and he said,

"Oh lass, a young lady has just committed suicide in her bathtub, she slashed her wrists, poor girl and such a beautiful darl'n' too." Erin then said,

"Oh I see officer, do you know her name?"

"The name in her purse said, "Frieda Anderson," said the officer. He went on, "Aye' and we make several such calls to this hotel, each month, as another girl has taken her young life, tis' a shame it tis.'" Erin slowly closed the door and she lay on her bed crying. Erin thought to herself, '*is this what's going to happen to me?*'

It was Monday afternoon and Erin knew that Enrico would be stopping by to pick her up for his party at seven p.m. She didn't feel good, as she kept wondering about Frieda Anderson, with no one here to bury her, no family or relatives, nor anyone, who really cared about her, or knew what this tragedy was all about. '*It's a shame*', she thought.

Erin began to be concerned about this evening's party and Enrico's curt and evasive answers, to her questions, regarding the fact that no wives were invited; fact is, she thought, '*I wonder if Enrico might be married*'? She didn't know why she didn't think to ask Enrico, if he were married or not, but the thought never occurred to her, as he approached her as though he was single. He wore no wedding ring, but so what, many men didn't for reasons she supposed, was that a ring could stand in the way of a man, having some fun, with some innocent girl, who didn't realize that the man she was with, was married

It was just a quarter to seven and she was putting on the last of her make-up. She wore her red flapper dress for tonight's party, as she thought her black dress, was a little too somber for a party. There was a knock on her door and when she opened it, Enrico was standing there with a bouquet of roses in his hand. She smiled at him and he gave her a kiss on her cheek, all very proper she thought. Enrico was impeccably dressed in his tailor made suit. He smelled of after-shave lotion. Enrico said, "Are you ready?" Erin answered,

"As ready as I'll ever be." They entered a cab and Enrico told the driver, "Flamingo Club, driver."

"Yes sir," said the driver. The Flamingo Club was another fabulous show club in Chicago, with beautiful chorus girls and various vaudeville acts. The club was located over on Wabash Avenue and Roosevelt Road, and was owned by Al Capish. When they arrived, the Negro doorman who was dressed in a gaudy red outfit opened the cab door. Erin, and Enrico, got out. The doorman said to Enrico,

"Its nice to see you Mr. La Rocco, sa.'"

"Thanks," said Enrico. The hostess escorted them to a small room, adjoining the main dining room and stage. When the door was opened to, the small room, there seated around an oblong table, was several men and women. The men all wore tuxedos, their female companions all looked to Erin, like they might be showgirls, in that they were made-up with very heavy lipstick, rouge, and all wore low cut, short dresses. Erin wondered why the girls wore such heavy make-up, when they certainly weren't performing on stage. She would soon find out.

As they both entered the room, all of the men got up and kind of saluted Enrico, as each man came up to him and kissed him on both cheeks. Erin had never before seen a man kiss another man, even though the kisses weren't on Enrico's lips. She wondered to herself about such a strange custom. *Perhaps its done in Italy, she thought?* Enrico then introduced Erin to all of the guests. The girls all gave Erin the once over, from top to bottom, as they knew that this was another of Enrico's paramours, and they wondered just how long she would last as his, so called girlfriend?

The waiter's soon came out with the salads and then champagne was poured. Enrico gave a toast in Italian, which Erin didn't understand.

"*Ai miei soci di affari e la loro ragazza il loro miei di di amici ed amare.*" 'To my business associates, their girl friends and to love'. They all applauded Enrico's toast. The supper lasted about an hour, when to Erin's surprise, the girls started making love to their boy friends, right in front of each other. Erin was shocked at such conduct by these chorus girls. The girls were all giggling and their dates were drinking champagne, from their slippers.

Erin, who up to now had her wits about her, as she was afraid that she might be following the same path as Frieda, suddenly became kind of woozy. Evidently unbeknownst to her, one of the waiters had dropped a small pill in her champagne glass. Enrico had been watching Erin to see when the pill would affect her, as he reached over and kissed her on her neck. She instinctively tried to pull away, but she found that she could not; as it seemed like her, arms and legs were made of lead. Enrico continued to kiss her, with his mouth on hers, skillfully using his tongue, then he proceeded to undress her. By the time he was through, Erin was totally nude.

After brushing away the glasses and dishes in front of him, Enrico picked her up and placed her on the table in front of him, as he then raped her several times, to the applause of his dinner guests. Erin knew what was being done to her, but she didn't seem to care any longer, as she offered no resistance. The powerful drug had overpowered her will to resist. Now as was the custom at such Mafiosi gatherings, all of the associates or *Consigularies,* as they were referred to in the Mafia, started to gather around Enrico and Erin, as the so-called chorus girls who were giggling, watched what they all would see, would be a traditional gang rape. However, Enrico who normally enjoyed such orgies, suddenly raised his hand, as he said in Italian, "*No, i gentiluomini, posso lasciare questo per succedere alla mia ragazza, almeno no stasera.*"

'No gentlemen, I cannot let this happen to my girl, at least not tonight.' Enrico's associates were disappointed, as were the girls, as this had never happened before. Enrico normally enjoyed this unusual ceremony, as much as anyone else, as all of the prostitutes had gone through this ritual, several times in the past, some more than others. Meanwhile, Erin had passed out and was slumped in her chair. Enrico then said,

"Well, I think that is enough for one night, as I best take Erin to her room." He borrowed one of the girl's coats, putting it around Erin's shoulders, and they walked out a side door, to an awaiting cab. They went back to her room at the New Michigan Hotel where after a brief sleep, Erin awakened and sitting on the bed next to her, was Enrico, who had been snorting a white substance into his nose, that he had put on the night stand. It looked a lot like powdered sugar. Erin not remembering what had happened to her, was curious as she said,

"Enrico, what is that white powder?" Enrico said,

"Erin that is your trip to *'il paradiso'*." Without realizing what she was doing, Erin also, began to sniff and snort this white powder. She thought to herself, *'what a beautiful sensation, it was kind of like a feeling of euphoria, the sensation of warmth'*. After about fifteen minutes of both snorting the cocaine, they once again had sexual relations. Finally, after an exhausting hour, Enrico said,

"Erin my dear, I've must be going as I have some business to attend to, but I'll see you tomorrow morning." Enrico then gave Erin a passionate kiss and this time, Erin kissed him fully on his mouth.

CHAPTER 6

The Morning After
-The Road to Depravity-

Erin fell into a deep sleep and when she awoke, she felt sort of hungry, although she remembered, that she had eaten quite a lot of food at last night's party and she couldn't understand why she was so hungry? As she returned from the bathroom, she noticed a white powdery substance on her night stand. She seemed puzzled by what it was, and what it was doing there, as to her, it looked a lot like powdered sugar. She thought further, *'I wonder, could Enrico have spilled something on the nightstand last night?'* She wet her finger and touched the white powder with her wet finger and she tasted it. It tasted sort of sweet and yet it had a strange odor to it, and for some reason it had a familiar taste, like she might have tasted it before. She tasted more of it and her subconscience mind told her to snort it and so bending her head down to reach the white powder, she did.

By the time Enrico knocked at her door, Erin was already in an ecstatic state of mind. She heard the knock on her door, and in a sort of slow motion reflex, she finally reached the door and opened it. Enrico gave her a long and passionate kiss, which she more than returned. He noticed how she looked with her glazed eyes and for a moment, he couldn't figure out, what was wrong with her. Then he glanced over at the nightstand and he saw the residue of Erin's introduction to drugs from last night. He and Erin immediately undressed and as she lay on the bed naked, they became involved in a torrid sexual scene. Her passion seemed all-consuming. Finally, after it was over, Erin snuggled up against Enrico's bare and hairy chest, and fell fast asleep.

Enrico starred at the ceiling as the smoke from his cigarette, wafted up to the ceiling and curled around the ceiling fan, which was slowly turning, as though it was too tired to turn any faster, after witnessing last nights and this mornings, torrid sex scenes. Enrico's mind was racing, as he was plotting a scenario, whereby he thought, that after a few more months of having Erin become more and more hooked on drugs, she would be like putty in his hands. He in essence, would become her pimp and handler.

Enrico decided that each morning before Erin came home from her nightly singing at the Kit Kat Club, he would enter her hotel room and he would leave a small amount of cocaine powder, on Erin's night stand, unbeknownst to her. He hoped that she would continue to snort the white powder, as long as it was available on her nightstand and in time, she wouldn't be able to stop, this early morning ritual. Not realizing where the euphoric white powder came from, and not caring, until that is, it was no longer lying on her nightstand. Then in a frantic desire for more, she would eventually contact Enrico, and he would then, use the carrot and stick approach on her, as now, she would be so hooked on cocaine, that she would do anything he asked her to do.

He first introduced her to two visiting Mafia Dons, one, Al 'Big Nose' Salvatore, from New York and the other, Sal 'The Shark' Tratroviní, from Cleveland, who had business to conduct, with Al Capish. Erin now spent most every morning after her singing was through at the Kit Kat Club, with one or the other of these Sicilian Mafia Dons, and sometimes with both. They both had an almost endless supply of cocaine, and an almost insatiable appetite for sex. The hierarchy in the Mafia, (the Dons), were most always, of Sicilian origin.

Erin was now so hooked on cocaine, that she literally, would do anything that Enrico asked her to do. He had arraigned with several of his prostitute girl friends, to seduce Erin, which they willingly did. He had her become involved in many sex parties, which she attended with him. She now was nothing more than a very beautiful, high class prostitute, who wasn't able, to over come, her insatiable appetite for drugs and booze, and she had literally, become his sex slave and he, her handler, pimp and part time paramour. While Enrico enjoyed snorting cocaine, he was able to control his need for it, and therefore he was always in control of his faculties. He knew of its insidious hold, on whomever, indulged too much, in its role of seductress.

Enrico had thought for a time, about introducing Erin to opium. However, he knew that once he did, she would have become, totally useless to his business and as a singer at his father's Kit Kat Club, she wouldn't have been able, to perform. As opium is such a powerful opiate, that it renders the user, helpless and unable to perform any of her or his, normal day to day, tasks. Because of that, he had envisioned Erin someday in the not too distant future, as the Madam of a Bordello that he and a friend, had talked about opening and she getting hooked on opium wouldn't have allowed her to act in that capacity.

While Erin was under Enrico's control as far as cocaine was concerned, he also recognized her innate intelligence and her natural ability, to get along with the many chorus girls, who also acted as prostitutes, while living in, the New Michigan Hotel. The girls all looked up to her. Enrico knew that these natural qualities, which Erin possessed, that she would be able to control the girls, with their constant bickering and fighting, with one another, in the Bordello, over some 'john'.

He smiled to himself, as he now realized what a very good Irish friend of his, from the Bridgeport neighborhood of Chicago, Patrick Monahan, had been trying to get him to invest in as partners, in what would become, a very respectable and high-class Bordello, or whorehouse, catering exclusively to the richest, Chicago business men. Patrick Monahan, whose father was a state senator, the Honorable Chauncey Q. Monahan, wanted to buy a very beautiful mansion, in what was then known as, the South Gold Coast. Many years later, the name Gold Coast, would move north, off of North Michigan Avenue, along Lake Michigan itself, where the old money had gradually moved, from the Southside, to the North side of Chicago, as the Negroes, were encroaching on this wealthy Southside neighborhood.

The mansion's former owner, was one of the great steel magnates, who along with several meatpacking giants, made unbelievable wealth. He owned a steel mill in South Chicago, and they owned several large meatpacking businesses, in the Union Stockyards. They all had lived in mansions, off of Lake Park Avenue, in what was then known, as Washington Park. It was through their wealth, and other wealthy businessmen, that Chicago became the number one wealthiest city in America at that time, and developed the finest cultural and aristocratic society, in America. Entrepreneurs flocked to Chicago, as it's opportunities were seemingly endless.

New York couldn't compare with Chicago at that time, for wealth and the number of people that possessed it. Chicago also became home, to the nation's very first skyscraper, which was designed by an Irishman, Louis Sullivan, and the city laid claim to many other notable firsts. After all, it was the city of the 'Big-Shoulders'. Patrick had told Enrico at a luncheon meeting they had, that he wanted some very beautiful woman, who of course would be a prostitute, with a good head on her shoulders, to run the brothel. He thought that the name, The Bombay Club, would make it unique to some other sex clubs in Chicago, and yet, so sophisticated, that the name and it's reputation, for what it stood for, would make it a lure for the wealthiest Chicago clientele. It would be a very private club with membership starting at ten thousand dollars annually.

Enrico and Pat envisioned scantily clad women, mostly showgirls, who had the looks, poise and the sophistication, to mingle with the wealthy patrons, in seductive poises, as they wandered about the premises, in their negligees. They didn't want any so-called street hookers, in their establishment, with their filthy mouths, their cheap gaudy clothes, their tattoos, and their lack of manners.

Several piano bars, would entertain the clientele and perhaps, a torch singer or two, would also entertain. The wealthiest members could hold board meetings and other business and/or social gatherings, in several large private rooms on the main floor. The sexual activity would take place in smaller rooms or boudoirs, as they were sometimes referred to, located on the second floor of the mansion. The girls and the Madam would have their own rooms, on the third floor, a suite for the Madam and a bedroom for the girls. These rooms were constructed, where there was once a ballroom for the former owner and his family. All such mansions at that time had large ballrooms on the second or third floors, depending on the size of these private mansions.

All of the girls would be tested monthly for any social diseases; they might have caught, from some infected customer. The club's reputation would be the draw, to lure the wealthiest clientele not only from Chicago, but eventually, worldwide. It would have a policy of strict confidence, in order to, protect their clientele, from suspicious wives, jealous lovers, or newspaper reporters. There was adjoining the mansion, an empty lot, which Pat said they could buy, for a reasonable price. They would fence it in, pave it, and it would be gated, to allow cars to enter and park, with valet parking only. Members would have ingress and egress, to and from the mansion itself, via a side door, with a one hundred foot canopy, attached to the mansion, from the parking lot, in order to, offer privacy, and protection from the weather, so necessary in an operation, such as Pat envisioned. Enrico would tell Pat in the morning, to offer the owner, earnest money, with the condition, that they would purchase the mansion and the adjoining lot, within three months, from tomorrow's date.

To begin with, the Bombay Club would be advertised in certain large city newspapers and certain magazines initially, as an exclusive men's club. A place to shed the cares of the day and to be pampered by the world's most glamorous and understanding attendants; a place suitable to hold business meetings and social affairs of all sorts.

Pat felt that within one year of such advertising, the club would then advertise itself only, by word of mouth, and he would no longer need to place advertisements anywhere.

CHAPTER 7

❀

The Carnival
-Roustabout-

It was now 1928 and I had been working in circuses and carnivals, for almost ten years. I'll admit I didn't have much to show for these past nine years or so, other than it kept my sanity, such as it was, although, I've been trying to drown my self-pity, in booze, most every night and I haven't had much luck. My Indian friend and I had developed a strong bond over the years and I guess in a way, we were inseparable. In all of the years I've known Bill, he never once ever looked at my face in any disparaging way, other than in just a matter of fact kind of a look, that one friend gives to another.

Otto the owner of the carnival, said to both of us, "Vell boys, our next shtop', vell' be Zinn-zinnati', Ohio, "*Seines wo mein Familie Lebe*", 'its where my family lives'.

Why Cincinnati I had wondered, when it seemed so far from our Chicago headquarters. But I found out later, that the boss had originally came from there and as he still had family living there, he always made it a point to schedule his carnival in Cincinnati, either during the spring, summer, or fall, depending on our schedule of neighboring cities. In addition, the owner was a German, by the name of Otto Mueller and the majority of Cincinnatian's settlers were of German descent at that time. I guess the steep bluffs, fronting on the Ohio River, reminded the German settlers, of the Rhine River in Germany, where many German immigrants came from and of course, the river was the most used means, for travel and for commerce.

Otto loved the German food and the 'ump pa-pa' music of the many German bands and orchestras, which performed, either in the many saloons in the city, or in the outlying roadhouses, which were primarily brothels, as well as the Sunday band concerts, held in University Park.

Many of the girls who were prostitutes in these roadhouses, came from Kentucky, across the Ohio River from Cincinnati, in a small town called, Covington, and other, small rural villages, such as, Ft. Thomas and Ft. Mitchell. Most of these girls who were trying to escape their dead-end lives, came from scrubland farms, which barely kept a family of three alive, when most times; there were ten or more children living in a one or two room cabin. So one by one, as the girls reached the ages of twelve or thirteen, they left home. A drunken father of course, had abused many, both physically and sexually, and that more or less, led them down the path to prostitution, where they could make some money and charge for being manhandled, at the same time. They, I'm sorry to say, learned at an early age, what men enjoyed, no matter what the fairy stories their mother's had read to them, said to the contrary.

With Prohibition still being enforced by the Federal Government, the manufacture of bathtub gin and rotgut whisky, kept these places alive. The many farms around Northern Kentucky and Ohio, all had stills, with most operating, twenty-four hours a day. The money from producing illegal alcohol, made farming much less attractive, as a source of income for these farmers. Actually, the farm itself was merely a cover, for this most lucrative business.

The location the owner of our carnival liked to set-up his yearly carnival in Cincinnati, was along the Ohio River, in a place called, the Riverfront. Like most Carnivals in those days, the owner was not adverse, to providing prostitutes, along with the many sideshows and amusement rides, such as the merry-go-round and the Ferris wheel and other assorted rides for both children and adults. Having prostitutes in our carnival, made life a lot easier for the many younger men of our carnival, including myself, to ease our frustrations and to enjoy the company of a young woman, no matter what society thought of them and their despicable business. Speaking for myself, none of the prostitutes I had any relations with, ever seemed to notice my disfigured face, and if they did, none said a word about it. I guess girls such as these, had seen the worst of humanity and they were just insensitive to any kind of physical disfigurement.

From a practical standpoint, old Otto also knew, that if he didn't have these girls in his carnival, the younger lads would end up in some small town, looking for such pleasures and more than likely, get rolled and/or beaten-up. Moreover, the going rates for the prostitute's services were generally much cheaper in the carnival, especially if one of the girls took a liking to you. Also, Otto didn't have to nurse these young lads, back to health, after they were either beaten up, or were recovering from a ferocious hangover, if they had ventured into town, The carnival was much safer and cheaper in the long run. Many a 'carny' however, ended up marrying one of these prostitutes, as true love is blind.

Otto had found out through one of my roust-a-bout friends in the carnival, that I had at one time, had a law practice in Chicago, and so, it wasn't too long, before I handled all of Otto's business dealings. They included, various contractual matters, personnel and business leases. I also did his payroll and any other business transactions, where he needed legal advice. Of course, I didn't mind, as this work not only added to my income such as it was, but it gave me the necessary assurance, that I could still handle legal matters and even if necessary, handle any court cases, where law suits, might have been brought against the carnival, or one of it's performers.

While I didn't like to appear in court, because of my facial disfigurement, as I always hid the left side of my face, by wearing a small cap, one of the girls had made for me. It had on it's left side, an earflap, which would cover the left side of my face, and it tied under my chin, in court, so it wouldn't fall off. Any other lawyer, in a court of law, would never have been allowed to wear a hat of any kind in court, but after I showed my disfigured face to the many judges, I practiced before; they all agreed that it was necessary in the interest of not offending the public tastes, or the court itself.

CHAPTER 8

❦

A Life Saved
-Bill John-

While serving In France during the Great War, I met a couple of American-Indians, who I befriended, as I kind of felt sorry for them both, as no one seemed to want to be friendly toward them. As a young boy, my brothers and myself, had always taken the side of the underdog, who we thought was the Indian, in our many 'cowboy and Indian' games, we often played, in the alleys of Canaryville, behind the Union Stock Yards, while growing up in Chicago.

My one Indian friend's name was Bill John. The other Indian's name was Smith Jesse. Both Bill and Smith were Crow Indians, having grown up on an Indian reservation, in Montana. Originally, the Crow people ranged along the Wyoming River, in what is now the state of Wyoming, along with the Arapaho, Sioux, Blackfoot and Shoshone. The Crow, after the Civil War, were used as scouts by the U.S. Army in battles against the Sioux, they're most hated enemy.

Before I was so badly wounded, Bill John, had saved my life, when I was about to be bayoneted by a German soldier, who I had my back to, while I was in a hand to hand fight, with another German soldier. Bill John, shot the German soldier through the heart. It was in our regiment's first battle, as part of the U.S. Fifth Division, at Château-Thierry, France, before I was so badly wounded at the battle of the Marne, several months later.

Since leaving the army, Bill John had re-grown his ponytail, as the army had cut it off, during basic training. Long hair was not allowed in the U.S. Army. However, a ponytail for an Indian was part of who he was, as a brave and a warrior and of course, his religion, the Great Spirit. Bill was quite tall, as most of the plains Indians were. After the war, Smith Jesse returned to his reservation in Montana, while Bill stayed with me, where we both joined a carnival, which was performing in Chicago, in Canaryville, my old neighborhood.

Many roust-a-bouts within the carnivals and circuses that toured the United States and Canada were criminals, wanted by the law. They, like myself, were trying to hide themselves in an environment, which criticized no one, for his or her past societal problems, or their physical impairments, as there were no acceptable or unacceptable standards, to measure oneself by, only the shared environment of the carnival. There seemed to be a sort of common bond, which existed within these traveling road shows. After all, most of these carnivals had what were called freaks, persons who couldn't help how they looked, but were dealt a bad hand by the good lord for some reason.

To make a living, they had to show to society, their imperfections and suffer, the cruel stares and the open laughter of people, who had not one ounce of empathy for their physical problems. Once you peeled back the fragile veneer of these creatures, one would find in most cases, vary sensitive and caring human beings

CHAPTER 9

The Kit Kat Club
-Scarface & the Mayor-

Erin O'Hara alias, Mademoiselle Adrienne de la Durequex, had been an instantaneous smash hit in the Kit Kat Club. Patrons had to wait for over two hours some nights, just to gain entrance to the sleazy club. Her fame throughout Chicago and the United States grew and grew. She had been offered contracts in some of the largest show clubs in New York City, and even, the world famous Parisian club, the Moulin Rouge made a bid for her, but she refused them all. She had fallen in love with Enrico La Rocco, in spite of his often public and private cruelty, but really, she had fallen in love with cocaine, her secret paramour, as she couldn't live without it.

It was on a Thursday night, when late word had been received, that Al Capish and the Mayor of Chicago, the Honorable 'Big' Bill Thompson, would be paying a visit to the Kit Kat Club, to see this Irish beauty, whose fame had now spread far and wide. It was just about nine-thirty that evening, when the front door of the Kit Kat Club opened and eight bodyguards of Al Capish's entourage arrived, followed by Scarface himself, the Chicago mayor, and several of his plain-clothes detectives.

Both Al Capish and the mayor sat at a front table; while being close to the stage, it was not in the center of the audience, but rather, they both sat in what was called the loge. These loges could be curtained off, so that the occupant's of the loge couldn't be seen or bothered. Gangsters and the many politicians, who needed a little privacy for their love trysts, mostly used these loges.

With the small band playing, it's introductory music for Mademoiselle Adrienne de la Duerquex. The world famous chanteuse, walked out on the stage. She looked to her right, as she made a slight bow to both Al Capish and the mayor, who was sitting on Al Capish's left. Al was smoking a large Cuban cheroot, as was the mayor. She flashed her most beautiful smile at Mr. Capish, and with the band beginning to play, *'Some of these Days'*, she began her song. Mademoiselle Duerquex was dressed in an emerald green sequined floor length gown, which hid her built up shoe. She sang four more torch songs and then in a tribute to Al Capish, she sang in her operatic voice, a favorite song of his, from a famous Italian opera; by Puccini, titled *'O mio babbino Caro'*, from his opera; *'Gianni Schicchi'.*

If you could have seen the expression on Al Capish's face, you wouldn't have believed your eyes, in what you saw. As the hardened animalistic-psychopathic leader of the Mafia, the gangster who would kill on a whim and think nothing of it, who had bashed in the skull of a suspected mob squealer with a baseball bat, the previous week, literally had tears flowing from his eyes, he was so touched.

Mademoiselle Duerquex used all of her superb, operatic singing talents, plus her innate charm, as she literally brought the house down. Her voice was angelic and flawless in its range and power. The crowd was enthralled with her. Not only for her operatic singing, but also her stage presence, which was stunning to see. Behind the footlights, with bits of sparkle strewn about her jet-black hair, she looked like a picture, with her white teeth shinning and her peaches and cream complexion.

Mademoiselle Duerquex wore just the right amount of makeup, only enough though, to accentuate her emerald green eyes and a small amount of blush on her cheeks. She certainly didn't use make-up like the chorus girls and the prostitutes used, who were overly made-up, to look almost like store mannequins or cadavers. Her gown was cut very low in front, to reveal, a certain amount of cleavage, and a portion of her milky-white breasts, which of course, Mr. La Rocco demanded of all his performers. Without question, Mademoiselle Duerquex had no rival in the entertainment world at that time. She was as they say, on top of her game. She took fifteen curtain calls and even Al Capish, blew her a kiss, before he and the mayor left.

When she got back to her dressing room, Enrico was standing beside her dressing table and after giving her a big hug and a passionate kiss, he handed her an envelope. She opened the envelope with deliberate caution, as she guessed whom it might be from and yes; it was from Al Capish himself. He thanked her for her performance and especially for her singing of one of his favorite Italian operatic arias and he closed his message with these words. *"Finché lo tengo nelle mie braccia e lo bacia appassionatamente, il suo ammiratore, Al".* 'Until I hold you in my arms and kiss you passionately, your admirer, Al."

Enrico snatched the note away from Erin and read it. His face went from surprise to shock, as he never anticipated that Mr. Capish would be interested in Erin, other than to hear her sing. Erin's face was turning red, as she didn't feel that Enrico had any right, to read a note addressed to her, from Al Capish and she told him so. Enrico didn't quite know what to say, and of course, he didn't' like Erin's reaction to his reading of Mr. Capish's note on the one hand, but he was also afraid, that Erin might tell Mr. Capish of what he did and he dreaded the possible consequences. So, he said to Erin,

"I'm sorry I read your note, I had no right to do so and you have every reason to be mad." Erin had cooled down some and she said,

"I would say that you should be sorry Enrico, I wouldn't have read any mail you might have gotten from anyone, I respect your privacy, but you don't seem to respect mine."

Erin had noticed ever since she received that note from Al Capish, that Enrico was becoming more and more, standoffish. She wasn't sure exactly why, unless he was afraid of what Mr. Capish might do to him, if Mr. Capish, found out about her and Enrico as lovers. However, Mr. Capish had sent for Erin on more than one occasion and I guess, the obvious question was, was Erin and Mr. Capish lovers, or was she just another of his many sexual playthings? No one seemed to know and if they did, it was doubtful that they would have disclosed such information, for fear for their lives.

Of course, Erin knew that Enrico and Pat were very busy with their involvement in the construction of the Bombay Club and this project, consumed most of their time. Erin had yet to meet Pat, as she sensed rightfully, that Enrico was very jealous of Pat, as he was afraid that Erin might take a liking to Pat. However, Erin would soon insist, that she meet Pat, as Enrico had said that Pat was his partner in this business venture and his best friend, as they both went to St. Patrick's parochial school and palled around together as children.

CHAPTER 10

❀

The Bombay Club
-Silent Partner-

The Bombay Club's exterior or the facade, of the mansion's construction, which fronted on Lake Park Avenue, was nearing completion. Neither Enrico nor Pat liked the facade of the mansion, as it was. It wasn't in their minds, ornate enough, or perhaps gaudy, would have been the better choice of words. The lot next to the club had been cleared of weeds, debris, and its red brick pavement, was just about complete. A six-foot high, wrought iron fence that enclosed the parking lot, was also nearing completion. It had a wooden covering, facing from the inside, so that the public couldn't see who was coming and going, via motorcar.

Expensive motorcars in those days of the very wealthy had pull-shades, to shield the occupants from the nosy public. Lincolns, Cadillac's, Duesenbergs, Packard's, Pierce Arrows and other fine motorcars, would soon be seen, coming and going, from the parking lot, next to the Bombay Club, and many of these cars, were built to accommodate, summer and winter bodies. The younger wealth, the sons of the older patrons, would drive their Stutz 'Bearcats', their Cords, their Auburns, Cabriolets, Duesenbergs' and other expensive sport motorcars, and they really didn't care who saw them. After all, this was the 'Roaring Twenties', with 'bootleg' Gin, hipflasks, raccoon coats, flapper girls and the 'Black-bottom' dance. The girls all wore their hair in a bobbed fashion, with flowered garters, which could be seen, when the girls sat crosslegged. Their dresses were worn well above their knees, with a kind of reckless abandon, as though the young people were trying to escape their parent's, Victorian mores and proper behavior, which seemed to have suffocated, even their own mothers. After all, women's rights were now high on the agenda of the public's conscience.

Pat Monahan had asked Enrico, how he was able to obtain the financial backing, necessary to complete this project. Enrico would never tell him, only to say that an anonymous backer was involved and he didn't want his name associated with this enterprise. Pat was no dumb Irishman and putting two and two together, he figured that Al Capish was the anonymous financial backer. However, he shrugged his shoulders, as he knew, that regardless of who was the financial backer, Al Capish would have muscled his way in, one way or the other.

Pat had expected that the club would be completed no later than two months from now and then would come, the process of hiring staff, miscellaneous help, and the prostitutes themselves. Enrico had told Pat, that he had a girl already lined up, who would be the Madam. Pat had heard about Erin through the grapevine, but he hadn't yet seen her perform at the Kit Kat Club. *'Perhaps'*, he thought, *'Enrico doesn't want me to meet this Irish beauty, this woman of mystery, as I might cramp his style'*?

Finally, Pat thought, seeing as how he was a partner in this venture, he had better take a look at whom Enrico had chosen as the Madam, of the Bombay Club, as he knew from experience with Enrico, that he sometimes got his personal life, mixed up with his private life, and that always leads to trouble. Pat checked his schedule and he found that he had this Friday night open, at least the early part and so, he thought that he would pay a visit to the Kit Kat Club.

Pat made much of his living, as a professional gambler and between him and his father; they owned a dozen or more, rundown apartment buildings or tenements, on the Southside of Chicago. His father had a business interest in a Chicago baseball team and he owned, a part of a steel company in South Chicago. Pat's father now lived in a high-class neighborhood, in an area called South Shore. There were seven children in the Monahan family, four boys and three girls. Pat was the oldest, and he had received a high school football scholarship, from Mt. Carmel High School, to the University of Notre Dame, where he graduated at the head of his class, in economics.

Pat operated a small, but very profitable investment brokerage office, on North Michigan Avenue during the day. However, while he was successful in his business enterprise, his first love was gambling and betting on the horses—Pat loved to bet on the horses.

CHAPTER 11

Cincinnati
-Herr Mueller's Daughter-

Frieda Mueller was the apple of her pa-pa's eye, when she wasn't in the carnival's kitchen, helping her mother with the cooking and the other chores, so necessary in feeding the many mouths in the carnival, she was out trying to seduce every man in the carnival. Frieda was a buxom blonde, who had her father's; stocky build, but she had her mother's looks.

Frieda had been going steady with Harry Stockton, the carnival's strong man, but they had an argument as couples sometimes do, and their relationship grew strained and finally, they stopped seeing one another all together. Frieda tended to flirt with almost every man in the carnival, and she was not averse to having an occasional romp in the hay, so to speak, which gave her the nickname of, 'Frigg'n' Frieda.

Harry Stockton was now seeing another performer in the carnival, a Maude Silverstein, who was a bearded contortionist. As I said earlier, carnival and circus life, seems to make the unusual and the bizarre, seem normal and so, for the carnival people, life was a bit myopic, in that they tended to perceive one another as normal, but nevertheless, they made strange, bedfellows.

Now that's not saying that they weren't insensitive to the gawking of the crowds, the jeers, the cruel laughter, and the hurtful comments of these ignorant customers, who paid ten cents, to observe these freaks of nature.

Man has a need to be seen by others, as something more than what he really is, and so, the incongruity of life, that these poor unfortunate souls provided, tended to inflate what little ego, the carnival patrons had. Nevertheless, the people of the carnival knew, no other way of making a living in an intolerant society, and so, they had to tolerate this freak show atmosphere, in which they themselves were the main attraction.

How else can one explain, the many unusual marriages, which have occurred over the years, within these two traveling amusement shows, the carnivals and the circuses? Life can be so cruel sometimes.

Jimmy O'Brien however, never seemed to be interested in the females in the carnival, as I guess he felt that his disfigurement, was not the cruel fate of being born with a deformity, but rather, Jimmy was an accident so to speak, of a war, a World War, a war that was supposed to end all wars. Therefore, Jimmy found his female pleasures, outside of the grotesque self-imposed, boundaries of the carnival, and his friend, Bill John, felt the same way

Jimmy O'Brien besides being very well educated in both sociology and law, was on the University of Chicago's Big Ten boxing team, and was middleweight champion in his senior year. While Jimmy grew up in probably the toughest neighborhood in Chicago, 'Canaryville', as a young man and he had to survive with his fists. His boxing training however, gave him a decided edge, when it came to being able to defend himself. Boxing was not a sport where the ability to take punishment was a prerequisite to success, as it was in fighting the hoodlums and gangs in the back alleys and streets of Canaryville, plus of course, having a good right hand.

Boxing as a sport rose above such toe-to-toe bare-knuckled fistfights, where skill was mostly the ability to avoid your opponent's fists, or his weapons. So Jimmy having survived in this toughest street environment, as a young boy and now, given the experiences of his street life, and using all of his skills as a good boxer, this would give him the advantage, when it came to fighting the street toughs. This combination, would allow Jimmy to survive in situations, where other men might not have survived.

Jimmy and Bill, had just left a whorehouse on Jepson Street in Covington, Kentucky, when four hoodlums who were intent on robbing them, attacked. Now Bill John was also very good in hand to hand fighting, as his ancestors had been and he was taught, many survival skills, by both his grandfather and his father, so necessary in a bigoted white man's society. Jimmy O'Brien never carried any sort of a weapon, as he didn't think that it was necessary, however, Bill John, always carried a small hunting knife under his shirt in a leather sheath, as carnival life could sometimes turn violent and unpredictable.

From what Jimmy could see in a quick assessment, under the gas lit street lamp was, that these four were rednecks, all wore bib-overalls and none had shoes. The first redneck spoke, "Wa'll' I'll be a dam'ed polecat, what has we hea'a', looks ta' me lik' we don'd' getch'd ourselves a couple of good ole' Yankee boys."

Evidently, this redneck was the leader of the foursome. The other three rednecks laughed, as they swung without warning, their heavy wooden clubs at Jimmy and Bill's heads. Jimmy right after the leader spoke, stepped forward and hit the leader in the nose and he fell to the ground.

His nose was now located on the far side of his left eye. At just about the same time, Bill ducked under the club of the second rushing redneck, as he hit the redneck in the stomach, and then he brought the heel of his hand down across the redneck's neck, paralyzing his left side. He too, fell to the ground. The third redneck, who had also swung his club at Bill, now found himself lying on the ground, as Bill had hit him twice in the nose and then with a terrific uppercut, knocked him out cold. The fourth redneck wisely decided, that these two Yankee boys, were just too much for him, to foolishly continue fighting, so he took off, retreating down Jepson Street, as fast as his bony legs and bare feet could take him. Jimmy then said to Bill,

"Well Bill, we best be a hurrying along, as the last ferry boat from Covington to Cincinnati, leaves in just about a half-hour." Both lads ran down to the Kentucky waterfront, where the ferry was tied up and paid their penny each, for the ride back across the Ohio River. After reaching the Ohio side of the river, they still had about a five-mile walk to get back to the carnival. As it was a nice fall night with a full moon shinning overhead, their walk was pleasant and amenable. As they walked and were within a half-mile of where the carnival was situated, they could see in the night sky, a red glow. As they walked further, they could now see, that the carnival was on fire. Huge plumes of smoke and red flames lit the night sky. They both began to run and as they reached the perimeter of the carnival, they could see a crowd gathered around someone lying on the ground. It was Herr Muller. From what Jimmy could see, it looked like someone had beaten Mr. Muller savagely, as his face was a swollen pulp and was not easy recognizable. Mrs. Mueller and her daughter were kneeling on the ground next to Mr. Mueller, cradling his head. Upon seeing Jimmy, Frieda got up from where she had been kneeling and she fell into Jimmy's arms. Jimmy not knowing quite what to do, but rather out of instinct, cuddled her in his arms, while stroking her hair. Jimmy then asked,

"What happened Frieda?" Between sobs, Frieda said,

"They came just after midnight and after robbing pa-pa, they beat him with a two-by-four and set fire to the carnival." She went on, "Why didn't they just take the money and leave, why did they have to beat him so, he never done anything to deserve this?" Jimmy noticed that while the main tent and some smaller booths on the mid-way were in flames, the worker's trailers were mostly intact, as they sat, quite a ways away from the carnival itself. Mrs. Mueller finally said,

"I don't know what is going to happen to the carnival, I kind of doubt, that even if Otto survives, he will ever again, be in the carnival business. So, in the morning, I would like to talk to you all, about what our future looks like."

Finally, the fire department arrived with an old pumper truck, but by the time it got there, the main tent and all of the booths were destroyed. A medical ambulance soon arrived and took Otto, Mrs. Muller and Frieda to the hospital. However, Mr. Mueller died en route to the hospital. Funeral arrangements were made to have Mr. Mueller buried in his families plot, up on University Hill. The funeral wouldn't take place for several days, as Mr. Muller's relatives had to be notified and many lived outside of Cincinnati and outside of Ohio itself. Mrs. Mueller planned on having a three-day wake, prior to the funeral itself.

In the morning, Mrs. Mueller addressed the entire carnival saying, "I'm so sad about pa-pa's death. Pa-pa was the affectionate name Mrs. Mueller called her husband. Mrs. Mueller then said, "I'm afraid that I will have to close the carnival and of course, that will mean the loss of jobs." "However", she went on,

"The robbers only got yesterday's receipts and after the funeral, I will pay all the employees, one month's severance pay, to help you all get started somewhere else." Both Jimmy, Bill, returned to their trailer, to make sure that their small cache of money was still hidden, it was, and then they discussed their future. Bill said to Jimmy,

"What are your plans, or have you even thought about what you would like to do?"

"Well", said Jimmy," I've given it some thought and while we were over in Covington yesterday evening, I happened to notice a couple of those huge paddle-wheelers, which were docked along the Cincinnati piers." Bill seemed puzzled by Jimmy's comments and so he said,

"So, what's that got to do with us, finding work?" Jimmy thought for a minute before he answered Bill, and then he said,

"Well it seems to me, that being so huge and all, they might have some job openings and I had thought that perhaps you and I, might like to work and travel on these huge paddle-wheelers, and see some of America, from the Ohio River." Bill then said,

"Fine Jimmy, but what kind of work do you expect to find on a paddled-wheel boat such as the two, that are moored along the Cincinnati waterfront?"

"Well," said Jimmy, "If I'm not mistaken, these river boats are traveling theatres and gambling parlors combined and they cater to a wealthy clientele, and I'm sure that persons such as us, might be able to find work either below decks in the engine room or perhaps, in some other laboring or semi-skilled capacity." Bill John thought about what Jimmy had said for a few minutes before he said,

"Well, unless or until, we find another carnival, perhaps your idea might be a good one, as we both need to find work in order to survive." They shook hands and each climbed into their respective bunks, to rest and to ponder their future.

Three days had gone by and finally Mrs. Mueller came back to the carnival after burying her husband. She had Frieda knock on all of the trailer doors, in order to awaken those persons, who might still be asleep, as she wanted to give each of the employees, their severance pay, personally. Mrs. Mueller had already lined up a buyer for the remainder of the carnival's assets, a Mr. Justin Schneider. He bought and sold, used carnival and circus equipment, where former owners, either because of ill health, or bankruptcy, and foreclosure, needed to sell their carnivals and or circus equipment.

CHAPTER 12

❦

The Irish Beauty
-Erin & Pat-

It was nine p.m. when Pat Monahan walked into the Kit Kat Club. He knew Mr. La Rocco, as he often had supper in the La Rocco home, as a young schoolboy with his pal, Enrico La Rocco, eating the many scrumptious Sicilian-Italian dishes, that Mrs. La Rocco served. Mr. La Rocco was behind the bar and when he spotted Pat, he hollered, "Who in the hell, let this shanty Irishman in?" Pat shook Mr. La Rocco's hand, as he sat on a barstool. Mr. La Rocco then asked Pat, "What brings you out here in my neck of the woods?"

Pat smiled and said,

"Well Mr. La Rocco, that son of yours, tells me that you have a young Irish beauty singing here, and he thinks that she would be just fine, working for us in our new business and I thought knowing Enrico, and how easily he can mix business with pleasure, I had better check out the merchandise." Mr. La Rocco laughed as he said,

"You're so right Pat, Enrico sometimes forgets his business interests and falls in love with many of these chorus girls."

The small intimate club had already filled all of its available tables and chairs and an overflow crowd was standing on the periphery of the darkened club. It was but a minute more, when a drum roll was heard and the small orchestra began Erin's introductory number, 'Some of These Days'. Erin came on stage from behind the curtain and she was dressed in her favorite emerald green dress, which reached to the floor. Her raven black hair was once again, sprinkled with glitter.

Pat watched Erin from the bar and as she began to sing. Her beauty and her stage presence immediately intrigued him. He thought to himself, *'And this Irish beauty is what Enrico wants to use as a Madam in the Bombay Club'*? He scratched his chin and continued to watch Erin, who by now had captivated Pat. Her singing seemed so effortless, as she belted out both torch songs and sentimental ballads. Her singing range was phenomenal, as was her ability to put herself personally, into each of the songs she was singing, as though, she too, was caught up in capturing the mood, of the song writer.

An audience, no matter how unsophisticated, responds almost immediately to such heartfelt sincerity and singing talent.

Erin by now had certainly captured Pat's heart and before he realized it, he along with the audience, was clapping furiously after each of her songs. After her singing routine was finished, she had ten curtain calls. Pat leaned over the bar and he said to Mr. La Rocco, "Would it be alright, if I visited with Erin in her dressing room?" Mr. La Rocco laughed as he said,

"You see Pat, why Enrico is so in love with this Irish beauty?" He went on, "However, a word of caution before you get too involved with her, Mr. Capish has more or less chosen her to be with him, at many of his functions and so, I would be careful not to offend Mr. Capish, should he get wind of your attention to Erin, if you know what I mean." He winked at Pat, who was leaving his bar stool, heading straight for Erin's dressing room.

Pat rapped on Erin's dressing room door as she said, "Who is it?" Pat cleared his throat as for a moment, he was sort of tongue tied, but finally he said,

"I'm a friend of Enrico's and he told me that I should at least see and talk to you, as from what I understand, you will be working for us, as I'm a partner with Enrico, in our new business venture." For a couple of seconds there was no answer and then Erin said,

"One moment sir, while I put on my robe." Erin finally opened the door and they're standing in the doorway, was a very tall man with premature, salt and pepper, gray hair and a beautiful smile, on his reddish Irish face. Erin thought to herself, *'he must be at least six feet tall'*. Erin for some reason liked tall men. There was no question about it, Erin and Pat, immediately became attracted to one another. Pat then said,

"May I come in?" Erin wasn't used to anyone around the Kit Kat Club, or even Enrico, who ever asked her permission, about anything. They just took, and they came and went, as they damned pleased. Erin then said, as she was trying to get a grip on her flustering speech,

"Why yes sir, you may." As she pointed to a small side chair, which sat, along side her dressing table. Erin sort of gave her outstretched hand to Pat, as though he might shake it, but instead, Pat kissed it. They both sat, looking at each other, in a state of wondering, just what to say and who should say something first and what would he or she say, to begin the conversation. Finally, Pat who believe it or not at his age, was smitten with Erin, finally said,

"Well, I had told Enrico that I should at least see who it is, that we would be hiring to handle a certain end of our business affairs." Erin smiled as she regained her composure, and then she said,

"First aaaaa Mr.aaaaa, what did you say your name was?" Pat with his beautiful smile said,

"My name is Pat Monahan; and Enrico and I are boyhood friends, as we both grew up close to each other; Enrico in 'Little Italy' and myself, in Canaryville, however we met while we both attended St. Patrick's grammar school." Erin looked long and hard at this handsome Irishman, and as with most beautiful women, who are naturally attracted to the opposite sex, her feminine charms sort of naturally flowed from her, beginning with a flirtatious look and then with her sensual body language, which was very responsive to his own demeanor. Erin then said,

"Mr. Monahan, please call me Erin, as I would feel more comfortable if our association was more on a friendly basis, than a formal one." Pat then said,

"Fine Erin, but only if you call me Pat." Erin laughed, as she once again, extended her hand to Pat, who this time shook it. For the next hour, both Erin and Pat talked about their lives and the unusual twists and turns, where one's life, sometimes takes. Finally, Erin looked at her watch and then she said,

"Well Pat, It's getting late and I must be going home, as I'm exhausted." Pat without hesitation said,

"Would it be too forward of me, to ask to take you home, wherever that might be?" Erin studied Pat for a moment longer and then she said,

"Pat, I would be honored, but would you allow me to get dressed, as I don't think I would care to go home in my robe." Pat laughed, as he turned and walked out into the hall, outside Erin's dressing room. Erin once again thought to herself, *'Pat certainly is different from these Sicilian men, who wouldn't allow me any privacy whatsoever, as they undress me with their eyes.'* She smiled as she wondered, just how Enrico would take it, with Pat taking her home, would there be trouble? Erin and Pat walked to the Kit Kat Club's, parking lot and Pat helped her into his beautiful Stutz 'Bearcat', sport's car and they drove off down Michigan Avenue, toward the New Michigan Hotel. When they arrived, Pat had the doorman park his car, while he escorted Erin to her room.

Pat knew of the Michigan Hotel and it's reputation as nothing more than a fancy whorehouse and Al Capish's headquarters. As Pat walked Erin to her door, he could see the many prostitutes coming and going from their rooms, as they tended to the needs of their male clientele. They reached Erin's door, and Pat opened her door with her key and after kissing her on her cheek, and as he was about to leave, Erin asked him,

"Pat, I realize that it is quite late, but would you care to come in for a nightcap?" Pat thought about it for a moment and then he said,

"Erin, normally I would, but not tonight, as I have another commitment, which I am already late for, thanks to you, but, I would very much like to see you again and perhaps at that time, I could share a nightcap with you."

Erin seemed puzzled by Pat's turning down her invitation, as she knew that most men in Pat's situation, would have jumped at the chance to have a nightcap and then, they would have proceeded from there. With a slight pout on her pretty face, showing her disappointment, she gave Pat a kiss fully on his mouth, as he turned around and left.

Pat walked back down stairs as he headed for the parking lot. As he was about to get into his car, two men approached him, wearing wide brimmed, black felt fedoras and black overcoats and one man said,

"Look Mick, we have noticed you're liking that Mick whore and so, let us give you a few woids' of caution; she belongs to somebody else. So, if I was' you's, I wou'd' find some other broad to screw, or else we'll break both of your frigg'n' legs, put you's' legs in cement, and dump you's' in the Chicago River." He continued, "Do's' I make myself clear?"

Pat would normally have hit both of these mobster hoodlums, but tonight, he thought better of it, as he knew that both men were pack'n' heat and he was no match against armed hit men. Although, his Irish temper was difficult to control, as he had fought many such Sicilian punks, all of his young life, while growing up in Canaryville.

However, he also knew of their vendettas when they were crossed, as they never gave up until they restored, their so-called honor, the insult, being real or imagined, was either satisfied, through violent beatings, breaking both knee caps, leaving the victim usually crippled for life and or else, he was murdered

The genesis of this primitive 'get even' mentality, it has been debated, was probably found in its Arabic roots, as Barbarossa's mother, many historians agree, was probably born in Morocco, while his father, was born in Greece. Barbarossa, the Mediterranean Sea pirate captain, used Sicily as his base of operations, for the plundering of merchant ships, which traveled throughout the Mediterranean Sea and all of its ports of call. As a result, his pirates had sexual relations, with the native Italian population, of Sicily, producing these animalistic-psychotic persons of mixed blood.

Pat looked at both men momentarily, as though he was taking a mental picture of them, perhaps for future reference and then he said,

"Okay boys, I get the message." Pat got into his sport's car and sped away, wondering just how he would explain this situation to Erin, even though Mr. La Rocco warned him about Al Capish, he really didn't think that Mr. Capish was serious about Erin. Pat now had to try and figure out, how to get a message to Erin, without Al Capish's thugs, finding out about it. He mulled over in his mind, just what he could do to tell her of his problem with Al Capish and his affection for her.

Pat realized that Erin was not just your usual high class prostitute, but was the victim of a crime organization, which would stop at nothing to intimidate, bribe and murder if necessary, to get what they wanted; power and money. They corrupted everything and everyone that it touched.

CHAPTER 13

❀

Bordello Elaganté
-Dress Rehearsal-

Erin had moved from the Kit Kat Club and was now busy, interviewing and screening possible prostitutes for the Bombay Club's grand opening. While Erin was immersed in this selection process, she felt hurt, that Pat hadn't even bothered to call on her, after what she thought was an interesting evening, especially when he said that he would.

Erin liked Pat, fact is, she liked him much more than Enrico and she had developed strong emotional ties with Pat, just from a single meeting with him. Erin didn't like the organizational ties though, that bound Enrico to a higher authority than himself and that was the Mafia. He would always be a servant to the organization, even above his own family, and no one else. She knew that she would always be secondary in his life and that she felt, was not a position that she cared to be in.

As she became more and more involved in the Mafioso and its brutal activities, where it would either murder or destroy anyone or anything, which stood in its way, she became more and more frightened. In other words, she felt that she knew too much and of course, the Mafia knew what she was a witness to. She knew also, that both the Chicago police department and the mayor were nothing more than puppets, as 'Big' Al, paid off, bribed, or blackmailed, the police, the judges and the politicians. Al Capish technically, owned Chicago.

It became clear to her that someday, she would have to get away from this organization, which owned a person's soul and his or her loyalties, or become a slave to the organization and eventually, end up in some back alley, turning tricks or in the street, if she were lucky, if not dead.

She knew first hand, that Al Capish was nothing more that a psyopathic animal, whose appetite for sexual pleasures, was never ending. She knew also, that while he seemed rational most times when he was out in public, but she also knew the dark side of him, and his craving for narcotics, when he was alone with her, or with a raft of his personal prostitutes. His appetite for unusual sexual perversions with his prostitutes was devoid of any compassion or love. Women were just things to be used and nothing more.

After pondering her position relative to Al Capish, in that he possessed her, body and soul, she had to find a way of severing, his hold on her. Erin wanted a normal life, one that included marriage and kids, and not this world of demented sexual pleasure and drugs. Her Catholic upbringing had a strong hold on her values, in spite of her tyrannical father.

Meanwhile she had completed her screening of her harem of prostitutes.

All of these girls for the most part, were ex-showgirls, brought in from New York and Cleveland. All were beautiful, poised and sensual, in their approach to men. All were hooked on drugs, which made them very easy to manipulate, as their only source for drugs, was through the Mafia, as they dared not go anywhere else, for fear of the consequences. Girls who disobeyed this unwritten rule, either found themselves hideously disfigured by a razor, or else, had their throats slit and were dumped in the Chicago River.

No expense was spared, as Pat and Enrico had brought in some of the best designers in America, along with some superb craftsman and artists from Italy, to decorate the Bombay Club, into a palace of pleasure. Its main foyer's floors and walls were made from green Carrara, Italian marble, imported from Italy. Greco-Roman pillars, lined the walls with pictures of the Italian renaissance, hung between each white pillar. Lush silk drapes, were hung in every room, all in muted colors, nothing to indicate low class, but everything, to seduce the patrons, in their quest for sinful pleasures. No expense was sparred in offering the finest Bordello in the western world.

Hanging in the foyer of the Bombay Club, was said to be the largest Waterford Crystal Chandelier in the world. It literally glittered with its thousands of crystals, shimmering in its soft glow. Paintings of nude women were hung throughout the club, as sort of trophies, for the men to view and to stimulate their erotic nature.

Several small rooms were reserved for gambling, with semi-nude show girls, clad only in their lace panties and with peek-a-boo, sheer-peignoirs, covering their otherwise, naked breasts, and with just enough bare flesh showing, to excite the male patrons. They served free drinks and allowed the rich patrons, to fondle and caress the girl of his choosing, while being served his favorite drink.

Ominous signs of the unsettling economy, were starting to appear in the stock market, but inside, wealth and opulence, were seen everywhere, and people seemed totally oblivious to such warning signs.

CHAPTER 14

❀

The Island Queen
-On The Ohio-

Both Jimmy and Bill, walked up the boarding ramp on the paddle wheeler, the Island Queen. Captain, Jedadieha P. Hawkins, captained her. She was built a little different than some of her sister river boats, who traveled the major rivers in the United States, in that she was not a side paddle wheeler, but rather, she had one immense paddle wheel, located at her stern. This design, allowed her to get closer to shore and so she was much easier to load and off load, her cargo and passengers. As they came aboard, they were greeted by a huge black man, who asked, "Gents, waas', can a's be's' a do'n' fo' ya 'll?" Jimmy than said,

"We're looking for work, as the carnival we worked for, burned to the ground. The black man seemed puzzled by what Jimmy had said and then he said,

"Wells' su', aa's' don't rightly knows' of any jobs hereabouts, but I can take ya'll to see Mr. Wallace, who manages the ship's folk." They all walked to the rear of the giant boat and the black man knocked on the door, which had a sign nailed to it in gold letters, which read, 'Homer Q. Wallace'-Purser. A voice from inside said,

"Come in." Seated behind a large oak desk, was a small man with pince-nez glasses, which had slipped so far down his sweaty nose, that he looked like he might be seeing through his nostrils. Without looking up from a yellow ledger, he was posting figures to, he said,

"Sit yourselves down and I'll be with ye' in a minute." Jimmy thought to himself, this purser was from somewhere up in New England, probably from around Boston, as he spoke with a distinct New England accent, a kind of nasal lisp, coupled with old English sounding words, as well as his phraseology. Finally the man put down his quill pen and he said, "Well gents, what can I be a doin' fer ye'?" Jimmy then said,

"Well sir, we're in need of a job; we can do most anything, from manual labor, to most semi-skilled jobs, such as carpentry or some masonry." The little man studied Jimmy and his Indian friend, for the longest time, before he asked,

"Where'd' you work, before now?" Jimmy once again responded,

"Well sir, we were working in a carnival, which burned down several days ago, leaving us stranded more or less, without any work and we don't know the area at all." The purser studied them both, once again and then he said,

"I'm sorry gentlemen, but we're all full up with deck hands, roust-a-bouts, stevedores and all manner of help." The purser without waiting for Jimmy to reply said, "I'm sorry to ask ye' young man, but I'm curious, why is yer' face covered, on the left side, by your hat?" Jimmy was going to tell him that it was none of his damn business, but he decided that this little man might be genuinely interested in his face covering, not from a nosy standpoint, but rather, from a humanitarian standpoint. So, Jimmy responded,

"Well sir, I was wounded in the war and this particular wound is not very presentable shall we say, and so, I chose to cover it as it might be too repulsive, for some folks to look at." The little man then asked Jimmy,

"Would ye' mind if'n' I looked at it, as I've a personal reason for asking ye'?" Jimmy was somewhat hesitant to take off his cap, as he didn't like to witness the revulsion on the faces of persons, who were shocked when they saw his face and the hurt he felt, after they're reaction to his hideous face, but he said to himself'

'Oh what the hell.' Jimmy slowly took off his cap. As Mr. Wallace gazed intently at Jimmy's face, he had tears in his eyes. Finally, he saw the extent of Jimmy's disfigurement and he gasped. Jimmy had noticed Mr. Wallace's tears, as he was taking off his cap and he wondered why, he was crying. Mr. Wallace's shoulders shook, as he openly wept, leaving both Jimmy and Bill puzzled. Finally, Mr. Wallace said,

"Thank you young man, I'll now tell you of why I was so interested in your facial disfigurement and my sad story." He went on,

"My only son Ben, was just about your age, when he enlisted in the army, during World War 1. I tried to put some sense into him, by asking him to please finish college as a medical doctor, before he embarked on what he felt was his patriotic duty to serve his country." He continued,

"Ben would have made a fine doctor, for he had compassion and a certain deft with his hands, that few surgeons have. Well to make a long story short, Ben was wounded in the war and he was sent to an army veteran's hospital in up state, Massachusetts. Before I first visited him, after he got home, he told his army doctors, that he had no family and therefore when I visited him, his doctor told me of what Ben's wishes were; not to see or be seen by anyone." He went on,

"You see my boy Ben, had half of his lower jaw and mouth blown away, by a motor shell and the sight of him made me cry. When I finally convinced the doctor that I was Ben's father, and after they checked Ben's enlistment papers, he finally admitted that he had a father and a mother, who were alive and living in the state."

He continued, "Now after I saw Ben and he intently watched my face and eyes, to see how I was reacting to his injuries, he couldn't help but notice my human emotions, and I guess that my facial expression told him what he wanted to know; how would his family react to seeing his terrible wound. His mother, 'my wife', I had told her, that she best not go see Ben for awhile at least, not until, his wound healed somewhat, which I knew was a lie, as Ben's wound had no chance of healing whatsoever, as you just can't grow back a new jaw." He continued,

"The following week after my first visit, Ben was found by an orderly, hanging from a beam in his room. I couldn't tell my wife of this tragic news, as it would have killed her, but eventually when we received notice from the army of his death, she read the government's letter. She didn't comment at all, at least not at first, she seemed resigned to his death, and after his funeral, we came back home and I lay down on the couch, as I was emotionally exhausted. When I awoke, I hollered for my wife, Mae, Mae, I hollered repeatedly. I got up from the couch where I had been sleeping; I sort of panicked, when I looked around the house for her, as she was nowhere to be found, until I looked in the back yard. There to my horror, my wife was hanging from our old oak tree, swinging too and fro, in the same tree, that our son, swung on, when he was a little boy." He continued,

"Needless to say, I was devastated, having first lost our only son Ben, and then, losing my wife, all within a week. Therefore, after I sold our home and settled some accounts I had had, with some of the local businesses, I found this job, as a purser, on the Island Queen. My job now, is my life, as I don't have any other, anymore."

Both Jimmy and Bill, had tears streaming down their faces after listening to Mr. Wallace's tragic story. Both lads reached over his desk, and they hugged Mr. Wallace, and shook his hand. Finally Bill, who was very stoic, as he never said very much, as he let Jimmy do the talking for them both, said, "Sir, I know that Jimmy only inquired about menial jobs, but I would like you to know sir, that Jimmy is a lawyer and a damn good one. And so I just thought that if you might know of someone here in Cincinnati, or even in Kentucky, who might be needing some legal services, you might give Jimmy, some consideration."

"Hmm," said Mr. Wallace, "Perhaps I do?" He went on, "The Island Queen is the largest riverboat in our fleet and is also I might add, the largest river boat on either the Ohio or the Mississippi Rivers. She literally is the 'queen of the rivers'." He went on,

"We travel a full ten months of the year, from here to Pittsburgh, and then on to New Orleans, and we stop at all of the major cities in between. We are literally a floating palace, that is, we can accommodate up to two hundred passengers, some with luxurious suites, and we feature extravagant floorshows and gambling, twenty-four hours a day, seven days a week." He went on,

"But let me get back to my initial thought, because we're the flag ship of our fleet, the owners require that we have a person with some legal training on board, for many obvious reasons. The person we now have on board, has just a smattering of legal knowledge and really, he isn't fulfilling the contractual requirements of the owners. He's sort of a pompous ass, if you ask me and thinks of himself, as a sort of a ladies man. However, as he is the nephew of one of the owners, a wink was made on his behalf, and he was given this legal position." He continued,

"Much to the chagrin of the owners, he had an affair with one of the chorus girls and she is now in a family way and she is suing the company for six million dollars, claiming seduction and rape." He went on, "If we lost the lawsuit, it would bankrupt the company and we would cease to be in business. She has found a big shot Chicago lawyer, a big name back there. His name is Clarence Duncan and I guess, that he specializes in such lawsuits." Jimmy had a kind of quizzical expression on his face as he searched his memory for what he thought was a familiar name and then he said,

"Duncan, Duncan, sure, I know that name, I know it well. Mr. Clarence Duncan was a classmate of mine at the University of Chicago and we graduated together, class of 1916." Jimmy kind of smiled to himself, when he heard a familiar name from out of his past and certain college memories filled his mind for a moment. Mr. Wallace then said,

"I don't suppose that you would be interested in defending the Hayes, Pickering & Haffendorf Enterprises Ltd., which is the name under which, our company, is registered in the Commonwealth of Delaware." Jimmy thought for a minute and then he said, what about my friend here Bill John?" Mr. Wallace thought for a minute before he answered Jimmy and then finally he said,

"Well Jimmy, as I said before, I really don't have any opening's for a common laborer, or for even a semi-skilled craftsman, for that matter." Jimmy kind of frowned and so he said,

"Well Mr. Wallace, I couldn't accept your offer without my friend here, also being considered for a job, but I thank you very much just the same." Jimmy then turned on his heel after shaking Mr. Wallace's hand, as did Bill, and they began to walk out of Mr. Wallace's office. Mr. Wallace then said,

"Now hold on a minute Jimmy, if you won't accept my job offer to defend my company, without Bill also being considered for a job, well, I think that I can perhaps, bend the rules some and certainly find a job for your friend." Both Jimmy and Bill had smiles on their faces. Mr. Wallace then said,

"I'll need to go before the owners and explain to them, the terms and conditions, that you have proposed Jimmy, but let me ask you this, what are your salary requirements, as the owners would need to know, before they would approve of you're being hired?" Jimmy thought for a minute and then he said,

"Well seeing as how I don't have a job and I'm not quite sure what a top lawyer would get in defending your client, say in Chicago, so I'll settle for this; you pay me whatever your former legal person was being paid. Plus expenses and oh by the way, for this particular case, I would like Bill to accompany me, as my legal assistant, and he too would be paid a salary, plus expenses and finally, should I win this case, I would be paid, a flat fee of five thousand dollars. Also before I forget it, Bill and I would need to purchase a couple of suits, shirts, shoes, a top coat, etc., if we're expected to appear in court. After all, we can't appear as two bums, while representing your company, can we?"

Mr. Wallace sat for a minute mulling over in his mind, what Jimmy had just proposed, and then he said, "I can't give you an approval as yet, as I have to consult with the owners first and if they agree, I'll get back to you. Where are you staying?" Jimmy laughed,

"We're not staying anywhere for the moment, as your boat was the first place we came to, after the carnival burned to the ground." Mr. Wallace then said,

"I'll tell you what Jimmy, you and Bill can share a vacant room on the Island Queen for a few days, as we'll be in port here in Cincinnati for a few more days, making repairs. Our stern paddle wheel, became entangled with a tree trunk and it snapped, several of the paddle boards, which are bolted to the huge turning drum." Jimmy then said,

"If the owners agree to hire me to defend their company, I would like to interview the man who is responsible for this litigation to begin with. I'm sure that in intimate conversations with the lady, he may have been told, just where she worked as a chorus girl, before she came to the Island Queen, as who knows, she made have a history of this sort of extortion, or other secrets?

CHAPTER 15

❈

The Interview
-Custus Ambrose Perkins-

Three days had passed and there came a light rapping on the door, where Jimmy and Bill were staying. It was Mr. Wallace and he said after Jimmy opened the door,

"I've got good news, it's a deal, the owners have agreed to your terms and I have everything in writing. After you read it, please sign it and you can get started. In addition, I'll arranged to have Mr. Perkins talk to you this afternoon, in my office, if that is acceptable to you?"

"Fine," said Jimmy, "and we'll be needing some money in advance, should we both need to travel somewhere, in order to trace the movements of this chorus girl, who is the plaintiff in this case." Jimmy went on, "By the way, do you know the name of this girl?" "Mr. Wallace then said,

"All's' I know her by, is probably her professional name and that is Aurélie de Muier." He continued, "I'm sure that is not her real name though, but that is the name she gave me when I hired her."

After a light lunch, Jimmy and Bill went to Mr. Wallace's office to await Mr. Perkins. It was just about ten minutes later, when there was a knock on Mr. Wallace's cabin door and Mr. Wallace said,

"Come in." A short slim man entered the cabin. He was balding, with sandy hair and a small thin moustache. He was dressed somewhat stylish with spats and a high celluloid collar affixed to his lemon yellow shirt. He wore brown suspenders with button openings around his waist, which the suspenders were fastened too. Actually, his suspenders were a little too short, as they seemed to be pulled up so tight, that the man's crotch must have been bothering him some, as his cuff-less brown stripped trousers, were pulled up to his ankles. Because of this, he walked sort of bent over, as though he might have back trouble. Mr. Wallace introduced him, to both Jimmy and Bill. Mr. Wallace had a small conference table next to the wall and he motioned everyone to be seated at the table.

After everyone was seated, Jimmy told Bill to take notes, as the interview began. Jimmy started by asking if Mr. Perkins knew Miss de Muier's real name. Mr. Perkins got red in the face, as he answered, "No sir, I never questioned her about any other name she might have. I just assumed that her name was Aurélie de Muier, at least that's the name she told me to call her." Jimmy interrupted him by asking,

"Did you always called her by this name?" Mr. Perkins said,

"No sir, I mean, when we were together, she asked me to call her kitten, which I did." Jimmy went on with his questioning of Mr. Perkins when he asked him,

"When did you first meet Miss de Muier?" Mr. Perkins answered,

"Well sir, the closest I can recollect, oh lets see, I believe that it was just about two months ago, when I first noticed her or she noticed me."

"How was that, I mean, under what circumstances did you both meet one another?" Mr. Perkins's face was now becoming bright red, as he fumbled with his tie and tried to clear his throat, looking down at his shoes, as he answered Jimmy's question.

"If'n' I can remember correctly sir, I was standing off stage, watching the chorus girls, rehearse their number for the evening show, when I noticed a sort of cute chorus girl, smile at me. She gave me that kind of a flirtatious look, the kind of a look, that a young school boy might get, from a girl class mate, in the fifth grade." Jimmy smiled and then he continued to pursue his line of questioning,

"Mr. Perkins sir, do you know what you're being charged with, by Miss. Miss de Muier?"

"Well yes sir, I do, I guess she is accusing me of seducing her and raping her, and I'm not really sure of what the word seduce means."

"Did you", asked Jimmy? Mr. Perkins had a sort of puzzled look on his face as he answered,

"I guess I did, but I don't rightly know, as I can't remember." Jimmy then said.

"What do you mean, you can't remember?"

"Well sir, it was like this, she invited me to her cabin one evening after her show was over and I accepted, why I'll never know, but as you can see, I'm not what they might call a catch, or a good look'n' man. I guess I was somewhat, whatch'd' you calls it, taken with her and the special attention she 'done giv'd' to me." Jimmy looked at Bill for a moment and then he asked Mr. Perkins another question,

"Do you know why Miss de Muier got hold of a Chicago lawyer to handle her case?" Mr. Perkins answered,

"Well no sir, I didn't find out that her lawyer was from Chicago, until I was served with court papers, accusing me of what I just mentioned before." Jimmy then asked,

"Do you know if she had worked in Chicago previously, before coming to work on the Island Queen?" Mr. Perkins looked down at his shoes for a minute, as though he thought that Jimmy might be asking him a trick question and he wasn't prepared to answer right off, but then he said,

"Yes, she did say she had worked for a small show club in Chicago, but I don't know where it is located." Jimmy then asked him,

"Did she tell you the name of that show club?" Mr. Perkins thought for a minute or two and then he answered,

"Well sir, I plumb forgot for the moment, I believe that she mentioned it, but if'n' I can think of it later, I sure will be a tell'n' you." Jimmy had been looking at Mr. Perkins's left hand for a long time, and finally he asked,

"Mr. Perkins, are you married, as I see you wear a wedding ring?" Both Mr. Perkins and Mr. Wallace turned red, as I guess they both didn't want to reveal Mr. Perkins's marital status to anyone and Mr. Perkins had forgotten to remove his wedding ring. Mr. Perkins face was now becoming even redder in the face, than before and the perspiration was literally running off of his forehead and down his neck, as he said,

"Yes sir, I was, I mean I' am." Jimmy looked puzzled, as he now looked straight at Mr. Wallace and without saying anything, Mr. Wallace finally said,

"Well Mr. O'Brien, I mean we, er' myself and the company, did not want Mr. Perkins's name being read, in either the Cincinnati Bugle or the Covington Free Press, as a seducer and a raper of women. As Mr. Perkins's wife, Nellie Mae, is both a grammar school teacher, as well as a Sunday school teacher at the Northern Kentucky Baptist School and church, Missouri 'Synod', and her father is the Reverend Cyrus O. Wellington and Mr. and Mrs. Perkins have two sweet little girls; Ida Mae and her sister, Lucinda Rose." He went on,

"If word of this scandal ever got out, it would ruin the Reverend Mr. Wellington and his wife, Nellie Mae's mother, the former Mrs. Bertha Lovingsworth." He continued, "These folks are pillars of southern society right here in Cincinnati and throughout Northern Kentucky." Jimmy with a sort of surprised look on his face finally said,

"I will do everything that I possibly can, to keep this scandal out of the newspapers, although if the case should go to trial, I couldn't keep the press out of the court room. These proceedings are considered public, and you both must realize, that newspapers such as you mentioned, are always looking for some dirt or the smell of a scandal. They all seem to thrive on such tawdry news; it's the public's insatiable appetite for it, which dictates what these newspapers print, because it sells newspapers." He went on, "Up north, we call it, 'yellow journalism'." Jimmy stopped his questioning for a moment as he asked Bill,

"Have you been getting most of what we all have said?" Bill answered,

"Yes I have." All of a sudden, Mr. Perkins spoke up,

"I just thought of the name of that club, where Miss. de Muier said she worked at in Chicago, its name is the Kit Kat Club, yes that's it." Jimmy upon hearing the word Chicago, triggered his memory, as he seemed to be mentally traveling back to his days at the University of Chicago, when he and some of his classmates, had spent an unusual amount of time, whoring around on South Michigan Avenue. Jimmy knew that Al Capish owned the Kit Kat Club and he also knew of its shady reputation as a front, for drug dealing and prostitution. He could hardly keep from smiling, as his mind reached back into an era, where he had many pleasant and carefree memories, before the war.

Jimmy cleared his throat, as he brought his mental wanderings from a better time and place, back to now, as he asked Mr. Perkins,

"I'm now going to ask you some very unpleasant questions, but no matter how unpleasant you may think they are, remember, the prosecuting lawyer, will ask you in the most salacious detail imaginable, all of the most descriptive details of your alleged sordid affair. Now, you may perceive as insignificant, such as the graphic details of your sexual liaison with Miss de Muier. But Mr. Duncan, will go so far as to make the vocal utterances, before the court, of what most people feel, are the normal squeals, grunts, groans and even screams, one hears during the sex act itself, brought on at the height of orgasm and passion. He will not only try to embarrass you, but he will titillate the courtroom and the jury itself, with his court room theatrics, as its this kind of juicy detail, that the public clamors for and trial lawyers like Mr. Duncan, find so irresistible." Jimmy went on,

"Mr. Perkins, how many liaison's did you and Miss. de Muier have?" Mr. Perkins thought a minute and then he said, "I believe that it was only one." "Only one?" said the surprised councilor.

"Yes, only one, if I can remember correctly, fact is, I hardly remember that one meeting we had, at all."

"Why was that?" asked Jimmy. Mr. Perkins thought for a minute as if he was trying to remember exactly what happen that evening in Miss. de Muier's room and then he said,

"When I arrived at the door of Miss de Muier's room, Miss De Muier had nothing on, but her smile, I guess I almost fainted." He went on, "I never ever seen my own wife without any clothes on, in all the years we'd been married and we share the same bed. Anyhow, she began to kiss me all over and then she began to undress me. I felt somewhat embarrassed, but I will admit, that I was becoming more and more aroused; kind of like a hog at rutting time, I guess. Finally, she walked over to a small table, that sat next to her bed, where she had a bottle of Champagne, with two glasses."

He went on, "She bent over the small table and she poured two glasses of champagne, and that was the last thing I remembered. When I awoke, I was totally nude and so was she. I was so sick, that I vomited in her bathroom toilet. My head was splitting such, like I had a migraine headache." Jimmy then said,

"You know Mr. Perkins, it is quite possible that you didn't have sexual relations with Miss de Muier at all." Mr. Perkins then said,

"How can that be, I mean, she claimed that I raped her and as I said, we were both nude in the bed, although as I said, I can't remember anything about that night." Jimmy sort of smiled and then he said,

"Mr. Perkins, did you ever hear of knock-out pills?"

"No sir, I don't believe that I ever have."

"Well knock out drops or pills, are what some people use to cause another person, to become incapacitated and/or unconscious, and so, they don't remember anything." Mr. Perkins thought about what Jimmy said,

"But Mr. O'Brien sir, why would she want to cause me to become unconscious, as she seemed to like me?" Jimmy answered,

"Because, she had plans to frame you and then blackmail you, for you're allegedly having raped her, causing her to become pregnant." He went on, "She evidently knew that you were related to one of the owners of the company, and so she figured, that you would become the patsy, excuse my expression, in her little scheme of blackmail and extortion. I hate to say this to you Mr. Perkins, but she had no more feelings for you, than she would have had, for a fly." He continued, "If she could prove in a court of law, that you had raped her, she could not only ruin your career and marriage, but she might conceivably destroy this huge maritime company." He continued,

"She probably figured right, that no one in the company would want this sordid mess to become general knowledge. She wouldn't have to sue you and the company you work for in court, if she figured correctly, that you and her lawyer would reach a settlement out of court, for a considerable amount of money. Not six million dollars of course, as that sum is usually what the plaintiff's lawyer comes up with, in order to shock and scare the defendant, but the settlement would be something less than that, perhaps a million dollars or less." Jimmy then said,

"Mr. Wallace do you have the papers, that the court served Mr. Perkins?" Mr. Wallace answered,

"Why yes I do, there right here in my desk."

"May I see them?" Jimmy read the papers and then he found what he was looking for, the trial date, which was November 22, 1928. Jimmy then said, "Well, it looks like Bill and myself, will be making a trip to Chicago to see if we can find out, a bit more about Miss de Muier and her secret lover." Jimmy then said to Mr. Wallace,

"Mr. Wallace, Bill and I will need money for the round trip train fare to Chicago, hotel accommodations and our food, 'per diem' if you will. In addition, if I figure correctly, we'll be gone roughly two weeks, which should give me enough time hopefully, to wrap up this case in favor of Mr. Perkins and the Hayes, Pickering & Haffendorf Enterprises Ltd." Jimmy continued,

"Bill and I will pack our suitcases and head for the train station. We should be in Chicago the morning after, tomorrow morning, if we make our connections." He went on, "To keep you informed as to what progress we're making, I will telegraph you some information, every second day by telegraph; any questions?" Mr. Wallace looked at Mr. Perkins and then he said,

"I guess not and I wish you both, the best of luck."

CHAPTER 16

❦

The Rats Lair
-The New Michigan Hotel-

As the train steamed into the La Salle street station in downtown Chicago, arriving in the early afternoon, Jimmy and Bill, got off and after collecting their baggage, they hailed a cab. It had been drizzling for the past day and a half, and so the weather was somewhat typical, of what one might find, on any given day in Chicago; damp and chilly. Jimmy told the driver, "Kit Kat Club, driver."

The driver gave both of his passengers a sort of touristy look, figuring that these two gents, were salesmen, looking for a good time. They would be prime meat for some doll and her pimp boyfriend, to roll them.

'*How many salesman have I driven over to the tenderloin district for a good time*' he thought, '*only to pick these same salesmen up, a few days later, who were by now, either broke/beat-up, or both*'. He then drove off in a model 'T" Ford cab, which was painted yellow and had small black squares painted, every inch or so, as decorative trim, right below the windows, running from front to back.

As they pulled up in front of the Kit Kat Club, Jimmy told the driver to wait a few minutes, while he looked the club over from the outside, as he wanted to sort of get a feel for where the club was situated on South Michigan Avenue. After all, it had been quite a few years, since Jimmy had walked the streets in the Southside of Chicago, both as a child growing up in Canaryville and as a student at the University of Chicago.

He then told the driver, "New Michigan Hotel please."

Now the driver thought to himself, '*either these gents know where there going, or else, they are unsuspectingly, entering the headquarters of Al Capish, the Mafiosi gang leader for all of Chicago and the surrounding area.*' The driver shrugged his shoulders, but he didn't say anything. He knew better, as idle comments, have a way of finding themselves, traveling back to the source. He also knew the consequences of such idle gossip, as several of his cab driver buddies, have never been seen or heard from again, because of their blabbermouths. He shuddered, as his thoughts, brought back, some very unpleasant memories, which he wanted to forget.

Jimmy and Bill got out of their cab and Jimmy paid the driver. They both walked into the New Michigan Hotel and made their way up to the registration counter. A young man was behind the counter and he greeted them both, as he inquired, "Are you gents salesman?" Jimmy winked kind of knowingly, at the young counter clerk, who was now starring, at Jimmy's pulled down cap, which covered the left side of his face. A bellboy picked up their luggage and took them to their room on the second floor, right adjacent to the elevator after they had registered. The room had two double beds and after the bellboy put their clothing into a dresser, Jimmy tipped the young man, with a dollar bill. "Thank you sir, thank you very much." Jimmy smiled, as the young bellboy, closed the door behind him.

Jimmy then said to Bill, "Did you happen to notice the dozens of heavily made-up girls, who seem to be everywhere you turn?" Bill answered.

"Yes I did, it seems like this place is the headquarters for the prostitution industry here in Chicago." Jimmy then said,

"Well believe it or not, it is. I thought, what better place to be, then right here, in the headquarters of the number one gangster in America, and having the largest collection of prostitutes, and call girls in America."

Both Jimmy and Bill had a good night's sleep and got up early and they decided to have breakfast in the hotel's coffee shop. As they entered the coffee shop, the hostess, a heavily made-up blonde-floozy said, "Follow me," as she escorted them to a small table in the rear of the coffee shop. They both ordered ham and scrambled eggs, with buttered white toast. While they waited for their breakfast, both Jimmy and Bill, had a good opportunity to look around the coffee shop, just to see who was having breakfast.

It took them only a minute, to spot what to them looked like gangsters. All of these men wore wide brimmed fedoras and all wore stripped, dark brown or black, double-breasted suits. They all wore contrasting spats, with their black or brown, highly polished shoes. All had 'pinkie finger' rings, and all wore diamond stickpins, stuck to their ties. None smiled, but you could tell what their nationalities were, either Sicilian or Italian, as their faces were swarthy. Most spoke in their mother tongue, which was further dramatized, by their continual hand waving.

Jimmy could see where their guns were hidden under their suit coats, as they showed a tell tale bulge, which wasn't hard to miss. While Jimmy and Bill gave them the once over, Jimmy and Bill didn't go un-noticed by this group either; actually there were several groups of men just like the group, which they both had sized up, seated at several tables throughout the coffee chop. In addition, several, what to Jimmy looked like prostitutes, or showgirls, sat at separate tables eating breakfast. Jimmy noticed in the light of the coffee shop's glaring lights, how ghastly some of them looked, even with their overly made-up faces. Rouge, powder and lipstick, could not hide their sins, no matter how much they smeared on their once, pretty faces.

Their faces showed the dissipation brought about, by their lifestyle.

Drugs and booze, coupled with the wear and tear of serving many 'johns' each and every night, took its eventual toll. All of the make-up in the world couldn't hide the dark circles under their sad, lifeless eyes. Their life style in a way was similar to a professional baseball player, in that they both relied on their youth, to stay in the game at a certain level. As age and fast living, caught up with them, they both started their gradual decline. The hotel prostitute, eventually became a street walker, no longer attractive enough, to land the big fish, while the professional ball player, was either sent back down to the minors for a short stay, before he was released, or he left baseball for good, as he no longer could keep pace with the younger players.

After breakfast, Jimmy and Bill left the coffee shop and they decided to walk south on Michigan Avenue. Neither had realized it, but they now had an interested third party accompanying them. This third party was not walking with them however, but he was very evident, as he walked about a half-block behind them. One of the men who was seated at the table, where Jimmy and Bill first observed what looked to them like, Mafiosi gangsters, was now tailing them.

Bill first sensed that someone was following them, after about a block, as his Indian senses, kicked in. All Indians have a lifelong developed skill, of being able to sense anything that seems to them, to be out of the norm, in that this person was keeping pace with them, although at a measured distance. When they turned a corner, he soon turned that same corner. Bill then said to Jimmy,

"Don't look around, but we're being tailed. This man has been tailing us, ever since we left the coffee shop." Jimmy's mind was now racing to try and figure out what their next course of action would be. He said to Bill, "While I think we could handle this guy, if we wanted to, however I don't want to jeopardize our investigation of who is the man that got Aurélie pregnant. So I think what we will do, as we turn the next corner, and while we're out of his sight, we'll wait about ten seconds, and then we'll re-appear in front of him, as we walk back the way we came." He went on, "Upon seeing us walking toward him, he will be in a sort of quandary as to what he should do. I'm sure his boss told him only to follow us, to see where we were going and now, faced with a different scenario, he won't know what to do."

As Jimmy and Bill suddenly appeared in front of the mobster, both Jimmy and Bill, could see the shock of seeing the two lads, show on the mobster's face, as the lads walked toward him and the dilemma he now faced, what should he do? The mobster's face became a little reddened as he walked by the lads, and trying to act as though he wasn't paying any attention to them. It was at that precise moment that Jimmy said to the mobster; *"Buon giorno il signore, É un giorno piacevole no né"* 'Good morning Mr., it's a pleasant day' isn't it?' as he smiled. The mobster was thunder struck; to have a suspicious person, who he was tailing, now address him in Italian. Bill tipped his hat as he walked by.

Bill then asked Jimmy, "How in the hell do you know how to speak Italian?" Jimmy smiled as he said; "I took several language courses, while in college and one of them was Italian. I'm not fluent in it, but I can converse, when it is necessary." Bill laughed. They had walked another block when Jimmy turned slightly and sure enough, the mobster was back on their tail. They passed by the Kit Kat Club, which was closed, as it probably wouldn't open until around five p.m. They continued walking and returned to the hotel, where they were staying and went up to their room.

The first thing Jimmy noticed was, that someone had been in their room and had gone through their clothing and what ever papers they had, which was only their train tickets. *'Thank god',* thought Jimmy, that I didn't take the court papers with the pending law suit with me, as this might really have given these mobsters, the reason why we're here, or at least, made them much more inquisitive, to find out. Bill said to Jimmy,

"What do we do now?" Jimmy answered,

"Nothing, if we leave, that will draw further suspicion to us and these mobsters might try and question us, their way, so I think it is in our best interest, to sit tight and do our thing." Jimmy went on,

"We'll eat lunch downstairs in the Coffee shop, as that's where we ate our breakfast this morning. I want these gangsters to feel that we've got nothing to hide and the reason we're in Chicago is for a little fun and nothing more. I really don't want them to become anymore suspicious of us, than they already are." Jimmy continued, "Now it wouldn't surprise me, that we might be getting a knock on our door, from some little girl who wants to find out if we're lonely and would we like some company?"

After they had eaten their lunch in the coffee shop and had returned to their room, a soft knock was heard on their door. Jimmy said,

"Who is it?" A female voice answered,

"Gents', please open your door, as I would like to speak with you." Bill was looking at Jimmy, to see what the girl's reaction would be, when Jimmy answered the door, showing his face. Jimmy walked to the door and before he opened it, he took off his cap, revealing his ugly wound. After he opened the door, a young girl, who was probably no more than fifteen years old, stood there in her negligee, with nothing under it. She began her spiel and then she looked up and noticed Jimmy's ghastly wound, she without finishing her salacious speech, let out a scream, and ran back down the hall, to wherever, she had come from.

Jimmy laughed as he said, with a bit of self-deprecating and acerbic humor; "The dolls no longer find me attractive; perhaps it's my aftershave." Bill smiled, but he didn't laugh, as he knew, that Jimmy's heart had already been broken, as he could no longer lead a normal life.

CHAPTER 17

Erin's Deception

-Social Disease-

Because of her having become, unwillingly involved, with Al Capish, on an intimate basis and where she never knew when he would want some of her sexual favors, she soon realized that that she had no life of her own.

She now knew the reason why, Enrico had suddenly grown cold and indifferent toward her, as he feared Al Capish's wrath. To continue seeing Erin would be like someone signing his own death warrant. She didn't know though, why Pat hadn't contacted her since they're first meeting. She really liked Pat, as he seemed like everything, she'd always dreamed about in a relationship with a man. Pat was warm, he had a charming personality, he was polite, he had an infectious laugh, and he was handsome or cute, as some girls might call him.

Of course she couldn't know of the threat made on Pat's life, by Al Capish's henchmen, however, she knew that she had to sever if she could, her relationship with Mr. Capish, if she were to somehow, have at least a semi-normal life. Erin liked men; she apologized to no one for that. Fact is; she had always liked men, except her father of course, although she tended to find excuses for his tyrannical conduct. Men fascinated her, and at a very young age, she soon realized the spell she cast over men and the power she had, in dealing with men and what she could get from men, with her innate charms and her beauty. 'Men are such fools, when it comes to a beautiful woman', she thought, 'like little boys.'

However, she knew also, that she was now in a no-win situation with Al Capish, with his animalistic and sexual, psychopathic behavior. In controlling her, he would never allow her to see other men and she would have-spent her entire youth, before he would ever have allowed her, to lead a normal life.

Eventually, after having had his pleasures with her, and being tired of her, and after finding a younger-beautiful and a more naive girl, someone he could teach his perverted sexual needs to, he would probably set Erin up, in one of his many controlled brothels. Where she would either die before her time, or else, would end up in some insane asylum, like the one in Elgin, Illinois, dying of syphilis of the brain, or some other social disease, contracted through her many, many sexual contacts, with men of all walks of life. She by then would have preferred cocaine to food.

Erin had met a chorus girl in the Kit Kat Club, a Rosie McCauley, shortly after Erin, first began to sing her torch songs there. After becoming good friends, their conversations, always seemed to center around the subject of men, which was not too unusual, for any girl or young woman, to talk about and giggle. The need to have a girl friend, to confide in, and to be able to reveal her inner most thoughts to, her secrets and dreams, was so very necessary. Secrets that neither woman, would have told their own mothers, was what girl friends most often needed to share with one another, especially in the brutal world they both lived in, where women were treated like meat.

Rosie told Erin about a particular boyfriend she had had, who was both mean and who was controlling. He beat her regularly; he was what she referred to, as a psychopathic animal. This girl had given Erin a good, if not a desperate idea; of what she had to resort to, in order to, finally get rid of her boyfriend, who was dominating her life, and one whom she feared, might actually take her life, if she didn't obey him. He was so jealous of her he actually followed her around.

He didn't work, as he lived off of Rosie's earnings as a stripper and part time hooker; he was like a part-time pimp. They shared a cold-water flat over on West Madison Street, in the wino/bum district. Many girls and women, found themselves in situations with men, similar to what I described herein

Rosie's solution was unusual, to say the least and questionable, as it had unbelievable risks attached to it, but never the less, one which just might release Erin in her desperation, from her bondage with Al Capish, short of her committing suicide, as a last resort. However, suicide was out of the question, as her Catholic upbringing, put that thought out of her mind, as taking your own life according to the Catholic Church, is a mortal sin.

Erin was becoming frustrated in that she couldn't pick, chose, nor come, and go, as she pleased, without risking the vengeful nature of her psychopathic and maniacal-paramour, and where *'vendetta'* was a favorite code word in the Italian Mafia's vocabulary, and was used at the drop of a hat, for it meant redemption of honor. This psyopathic animal was stifling her free spirited ways and her natural carefree-Irish enthusiasm for life.

Erin's girl friend Rosie, showed Erin what *she* had to do, when all of the other chorus girls had already left for the evening or morning, as it was already early morning, after the Kit Kat Club had closed, to get rid of her abusive and controlling boyfriend. Both were taking off their makeup, seated at their respective dressing tables, when Rosie, looking both ways to make sure no one else was in the dressing room, she suddenly got up and being slightly embarrassed, she pulled down her panties, revealing to Erin, a series of red like marks around her genital area. Erin's friend stunned her, by such a revealing display, of a woman's, most private part of her anatomy. While Erin sort of gulped, Rosie then said,

"See Erin, doesn't it look like I might have some kind of a social disease of some sort?" Erin's face was now bright red and she almost didn't want look at what her girl friend was showing her. However, she was nevertheless, intrigued by what she saw. Rosie went on to tell Erin, that she had a woman tattoo artist, right here in South Chicago, add these red marks to her genital area with an indelible tattoo ink pen. The hope was, that after her vicious boyfriend saw these ugly looking red marks, he would drop her like a hot potato, by mistakenly thinking, that she had somehow, gotten herself infected with some social disease, by some 'john'.

Rosie then said, "I know it's an extreme measure to take, but I didn't know of any other way, of getting rid of my abusive boyfriend, short of murdering him." Erin after overcoming her initial shock, at seeing her girlfriend's, fake tattooed evidence of some disease, on her genital area, thought further, *'I wonder if I dare have this done, in order to rid myself of Al Capish?'* Erin then asked,

"Tell me Rosie, can those red marks be removed?" Rosie thought for a minute and then she said,

"I'm not really sure, as I asked the tattoo lady that same question and she said, she might try a watered down solution of some kind of mild acid. But she said, as she never tried it before, she wasn't sure if it would work, or not, and didn't know, if it would make the situation worse, plus the pain of having acid put on such a tender part of my body." Rosie went on, "Now in my situation, I couldn't stand what I had to endure, day in and day out, and so, I became so desperate to rid myself of this animal, that I guess, I would have tried anything short of suicide, as like you Erin, I too was raised a Catholic. She went on, "But it worked." Erin then said,

"How has your new boyfriends reacted, to what they surely have to see, whenever you engage in sexual relations?"

"Well, I realized that they were bound to see this rather questionable looking area, but I soon put their minds at rest with my explanation. I've only had one man, ever leave me for that reason."

Erin was thinking about whether or not, Al Capish would be turned off by what he saw, or would it matter to this moron, or would he in a fit of rage, cut her throat, figuring that somehow, she had betrayed him and could have also, given him this contagious disease."

After writing down the tattoo artist's name and address on a small piece of paper she had in her purse, she thanked Rosie, but she never told Rosie, whether she had planned on using this rather drastic measure, to rid her self of her similar problem; Al Capish. After all, Rosie and Erin, had just been talking casually, about Rosie's problem with a particular boyfriend and Erin never revealed, that she had a similar problem with Al Capish, only ten times worse. But she reasoned, *'desperate situations, sometimes require desperate measures.'*

The address of this lady tattoo artist was way out in the southeast part of Chicago, known as South Chicago. The artist's name was Mademoiselle Fife le Roach. The Mademoiselle was a former stripper, who had long ago; reached the age of when strippers were supposed to retire and hang up their 'G's- strings and pasties. The term Mademoiselle was a sort of a misnomer, as with her five former husbands, the name wasn't particularly appropriate. Generally, the crowds decided when you no longer had the many so called charms, that the rowdy supporters of the art of strip-tease, would tolerate, as they would often throw rotten tomatoes at you on stage. This traditional act was to hasten your retirement, if you did not see the handwriting on the wall, or the sag of your breasts, before then.

Erin pondered the dilemma she now found herself in; *'should she or shouldn't she, risk a certain disfigurement and embarrassment, in order to protect what ever life she might have, after ridding herself of these sexual ties, with Al Capish, if in fact, his eyes told his moronic brain, to resist her sexually'?*

After all, Erin knew that some men, considering her beauty and her beautiful body, would disregard such warning signs and proceed with their love making regardless. When testosterone is brewing, the head below takes over from the brain above and it absolutely, throws caution to the wind. That, I guess was nature's plan.

As, the reproductive purpose, was paramount, regardless of the consequences.'

Erin knew that this coming Wednesday, was a so called election holiday in Chicago, where by, all so called speakeasy-clubs, including the Kit Kat Club, would be closed. Even though, during prohibition, no liquor was supposed to be served, in any of these places, at anytime, but as the Chicago police department, under the control of Al Capish, winked, and with the politician's nod, they all served their rotgut booze anyway.

So this appearance of shutting their doors for one day, was merely a ruse, to appease the Federal government, and so, she thought that maybe she should visit this so called, lady tattoo artist, this coming Wednesday.

CHAPTER 18

❀

Interview

-Art 'Fingers' Washington-

Jimmy and Bill left the New Michigan hotel about four thirty in the afternoon, and they walked to the Kit Kat Club. When they arrive, Mr. La Rocco was just unlocking the front door and Jimmy and Bill were his first customers of the day. Mr. La Rocco greeted both lads, and as they followed him back to the bar, Mr. La Rocco said,
"What will it be gents". Jimmy said,
"I'll have a beer and so will my friend." Mr. La Rocco didn't remember ever having seen these two men in his club before and so he asked,
"Are you gents' salesman?" Jimmy had already told Bill that is what they were, as far as their Chicago trip was concerned, and they sold toilets. Jimmy answered,
"Why yes," answered Jimmy, "we are salesmen." Mr. La Rocco then asked,
"Where you from?" Jimmy gave Mr. La Rocco a kind of 'its none of your business look', but then he thought, with his none of your business, facial expression, that it would lead us to nowhere fast and so he said,
"We're from Cincinnati," with a smile. Mr. La Rocco pursued his line of questioning by asking,
"What do you gents' sell?" Jimmy answered him,
"We sell," and he paused for a minute, as he leaned across the bar, as though he didn't want anyone else sitting around the bar, to hear what he had to say, not withstanding, that there was no one else in the bar, except himself, Bill and

the bar tender. He whispered, "We sell toilets." Mr. La Rocco began to laugh; fact is he laughed so much, that he had a fit of coughing. Mr. La Rocco with tears in his eyes poured himself a shot of rotgut booze, to clear his throat. Finally, after wiping the tears from his eyes with a dirty bar towel, he reached across the bar and he shook Jimmy's hand.

"That's a good one," as he continued to laugh. Jimmy now felt that he in away, had gained the bartender's confidence and so he said,

"When does the stage show begin?" Mr. La Rocco said,

"It will start in just about a half-hour from now." He continued, "I've got a treat for you gents this evening. The torch singer I used to have, who sung here on a regular basis, has returned for this evening's performance." He went on, "Believe me gents, you ain't' heard anyone sing, until you've heard our lovely songbird sing and I might add, she's a knockout of a broad." Jimmy then asked,

"May I ask, what is your name sir?" Mr. Rocco answered,

"My name is Tony La Rocco, but you gents' can call me Tony." Jimmy then said,

"My name is Jimmy and my friend here is Bill." Tony now took a good look at Jimmy's hat and he asked,

"What's the matter with your head, if I may ask?" Jimmy thought about Tony's inquisitive question and then he thought, no sense getting on the wrong side of the bartender, as we've got more important work here and we might need the bartender's help, and so he said,

"It's a war injury and it's not too pleasant to look at, and so I keep it covered with this hat."

"That's too bad," said Tony, "What a lousy break." Jimmy kind of shrugged his shoulders and went on drinking his beer. Bill who rarely asks questions about anything, said,

"Tony, do you own the Kit Kat Club?" Tony answered,

"Yaa', I do." Tony continued, "Its a high class joint, as you will see, when you listen to and take a look at our singer." Jimmy then asked,

"Tony, you said *she* used to sing here, where does she sing now, if she does?" Tony looked at Jimmy for just a moment and then he said,

"Well, I really shouldn't say anything for awhile, but I don't see where it would hurt anything, if I told you gents." He went on, "My son Enrico and his friend Pat, are two partners in a gentlemen's club, called the Bombay Club. They expect to open it, in just about two weeks and Erin our singer, will be singing there and also, she will handle the broads, if'n' you know what I mean," as he winked at Jimmy. Tony had a smirk on his fat face, as his eyes seemed to wander a bit, like he was thinking of a piece of apple pie he had just eaten." Jimmy listening to Tony's statement about this new club and he figured that it was a high-class whorehouse.

Jimmy and Bill resumed drinking their beers, as Tony rinsed some bar glasses, wiping them with his dirty bar towel. The Kit Kat Club was now starting to fill with customers. The audience was mostly men, but there were some women in attendance, with their boy friends. It was just about six p.m., when some lights were lit over the stage, together with a spot light, that shined on the corner of the stage, where Jimmy felt it would be shinning on the singer, who would be making her entrance momentarily. Jimmy noticed that the band or orchestra consisted of six musicians, plus a 'nigger' piano player, who sat off to the far side of the stage. Fact is, Jimmy noticed, the band was mixed, that is, it had four 'niggers' and two whites playing their various instruments.

First, a drum roll was heard, as an introduction, for the singer to come out on stage. Her first song of the evening would be *'Some of these Days'*. As the spot light picked up a very young woman's shapely outline and then she came to the center of the stage. As she did, the audience erupted with applause, as the entire audience was on their feet, clapping and stomping there feet.

Both Jimmy and Bill, sort of gasped at the sight of this woman or girl. Jimmy thought that she was gorgeous, probably he thought, she was the most beautiful woman he had ever seen. She was attired in an emerald green gown, which reached to the floor and she had glitter sprinkled over her hair, and on her bare shoulders. As she bowed to acknowledge, the audience's accolades, her milky white breasts, revealed her deep cleavage. She was a full-grown mature woman, no doubt about that, thought Jimmy to himself. A kelly-green headband, which had a large, what to Jimmy, looked like a diamond broach, affixed to it's front, covered her forehead, and held her raven black hair, tight to her head.

She belted out her introductory number, *'Some of these days'* with emotion and just the right amount of sensuous body sway. That song brought her ten bows, as this was her so-called, trademark song. Her singing captivated both Jimmy and Bill; both lads were in love. These so-called torch song singers did not easily impress Jimmy, who had much more exposure to this type of nightclub life, as a young man in college. Most of these singers had no voice training what so ever and were overly made up and whose voices, were sort of raspy. However, in the honky-tonk environment that these ladies of the night sang in, the crowd wasn't too particular. To compete with the noisy audience, most of these singers had to almost shout their songs, in order to be heard above the din of the raucous crowd. Even the little band had to play their songs in a very fast and loud tempo. There seemed to be little synchronization, of just who was leading and who was following, between the band and the torch singer, as each, tried to out-do the other.

Erin continued with her body of work; some songs were the oldies, from an earlier time, the Victorian age, World War 1 and some, were more modern in the Ellington and Gershwin tradition, written mostly for the roaring twenties and that era, exclusively. Erin sang from her heart, she appeared like an angel with a magnificent voice, a voice that was trained in the classics, which it was. However, she understood and she liked these more modern songs, songs more of her age, with their sultry beat and even she, could belt out rag-time songs, which were difficult to sing, as they were primarily written for the piano in two-fourth time.

However, the crowd loved her.

It was almost four a.m. and Jimmy and Bill, were feeling no pain. Jimmy felt that they had better kind of go slow, as if they got drunk, they wouldn't accomplish their objective, to try and find out, who may have known, the former chorus girl; Aurélie de Muier.

Tony the bartender said, "Drink up gents', its the last call, as we'll be closing soon." Tony gave Jimmy and Bill, a beer on the house, which they really didn't want or need, but they couldn't refuse, without insulting Tony. Several of the band, came over to the bar, to have their one for the road, before heading home. Among the small group of musicians, was the Negro piano player, Art 'fingers', Washington. Jimmy said to Art, "May I buy you a drink, as I sure enjoyed your piano playing."

Now Art never got any kind of recognition from anyone, especially so, since Erin began to sing at the Kit Kat Club, so he was flattered, by Jimmy's kind words, about his piano playing. Art then said to Jimmy,

"I surely thanks y'all' sir, for your kind remarks, about my piano playing, as it's very rare, when anyone takes the time to comment favorably on my piano playing. If I hear anything, its usually how bad I play." Jimmy patted Art on the back and then he asked again;

"Art, could I buy you a drink?" Art responded,

"That would be most kind of you sir." Jimmy than said,

"This here is my good friend, Bill John." Both Jimmy and Bill shook Art's hand. After a few more drinks, Tony said,

"Okay gents, we're closed, so you'll have to move your asses, out of here." As Jimmy, Bill and Art, left the Kit Kat Club, Art then said,

"I don't know if'n' you gents' are interested or not, but I know of a night spot, not too far from here, that never closes its doors, but its' a black and tan club, that is, it allows the mixing of the races." "But", he went on, "Perhaps ya'll are too tired to visit this club with me, or don't want to for other reasons?" Jimmy sensed that Art was trying to get a sense of just how prejudiced, Jimmy and Bill might be, in either refusing his invitation to visit a black and tan club with him for racial reasons, or for some other reason. Jimmy of course knew of the plight of the Negro in the North, since Lincoln emancipated the Negro. His own personal experiences, while growing up in Canaryville, told him of the blatant bigotry of the w.a.s.p majority, who despised the Irish Catholic and all that he stood for. He knew that without his father's political clout, he wouldn't have been allowed to attend one of the most prestigious universities in America, The University of Chicago.

Therefore, he was involved in a never-ending struggle within his own conscience, to bring himself, to empathize with the plight of the Negro, as it was similar to his own Irish Catholic experience. Jimmy knew full well, just how the Irish Catholics as an ethnic group, hated the Negroes, as the Irish could see that the Negro, was becoming a threat to the Irishman's own job security, while the Irishman was at the bottom of the socio-economic ladder, relegated there, by the Protestant majority.

Of course, since the potato famine in Ireland, the Irish now literally controlled all of the major cities in the United States, but they were still not accepted as socially equal, to their Protestant counterparts, as they clawed their way, up the social ladder. Many wasp clubs, still excluded Irish Catholics and Jews, and forbid their membership in their social functions. The Masons were particular vehement, against the Irish Catholics.

The three men walked just about a mile over to south Wentworth Avenue and there on the southwest corner of Wentworth Avenue and Twenty-ninth Street, was a small black and tan club, called the Beehive. The three men entered the club and everyone there seemed to know Art. They all looked at his two white companions and a short fat Negro woman, who was as wide as she was tall, escorted the three men to a table in the rear of the club. A small band was playing Dixieland music, which Jimmy liked very much. It's toe-tapping melodies, were sort of contagious. It was music born in New Orleans and Memphis, with a twist of Chicago's own ragtime interpretation.

Jimmy could see a mixed crowd of both whites and blacks. Seated at the same tables and out on the dance floor, he saw white women dancing with black men. That was something he had never seen before.

While both he and Bill had had enough to drink, Jimmy felt that he would promote his friendship with Art, as long as he could. Jimmy said to Art, "Art, how long have you been playing piano at the Kit Kat Club, if you don't mind me asking?" Art thought for a minute and then he said,

"Wells I guess aa's' been playing piano at the Kit Kat Club, for almost five years, come this April." Jimmy continued with his line of questioning. "How long has that beautiful black haired singer been singing there?"

"Well," answered Art, "She's been singing there for just a little over a year now." He went on, as the rotgut booze was beginning to loosen his tongue. "Erin, I means, Mademoiselle de la Durequex, which is her stage name by the way, has a boyfriend, or did have, until Al Capish moved in on her and I believes', that Enrico La Rocco jr. is afraid of Al Capish, and so I believe, he's sort of cooling it, as they say." He continued, "Many a man's been trying to get into her pants, but they's' is afraid of big Al." Jimmy thought that perhaps now would be a good time to ask Art about the chorus girls and so he said,

"Art, you pretty well know all of the chorus girls I would think and perhaps, you may be personally acquainted with some?" Art then said,

"Why's' Jimmy, is you and Bill, interested in getting to know some of them, on a, shall we's' say, on a more personal basis?" Jimmy laughed as he said,

"Well Art, we might, but for the moment, we had heard of a particular chorus girl by the name of, oh what is her name, let me think a minute." Jimmy screwed his face up a little, to give Art the impression, that he was trying to remember the name of this particular chorus girl, he had momentarily forgotten. When he finally said, "Oh yes, now I remember, I believe her name is, Aurélie de Muier, or some French sounding name like that, but I don't know her real name, as I think that name might just be her stage name?"

The pained expression on Art's face, at the mention of the chorus girl's name was startling to see. Tears began to drip from Art's eyes, as he began to cry uncontrollably. Jimmy watched Art's face and Art's shoulders began to tremble. Jimmy knew that he had stumbled on to something, but he wasn't quite sure what it was. He waited a few more minutes, as he gave Art his handkerchief, to blow his nose in and then he said in a most soothing voice,

"I'm so sorry Art, I did not know that you were acquainted with this chorus girl." After Art got control over his emotions, he said,

"Jimmy, how in the hell, did you stumble on to her?" Jimmy had to think fast as he didn't want Art to think that he and Bill were looking for her, as though some salesman and told us, that if you want a good time, why contact Aurélie de Muier, as though she was a prostitute or something and so he said,

"No Art, the reason Bill and I are interested, is that her brother reported her as being missing and as we work for a private detective agency back in Cincinnati, Ohio, her brother has asked us, to try and find her. That is how we came upon her stage name." Bill's face went from shock to admiration, with a slight smile, as to just how quick, Jimmy's mind worked, to come up with this ruse, of them being private detectives.

Jimmy went on, "Her brother said that she is using a stage name and that she rarely uses her real name." Jimmy continued, "Neither Bill nor I, have any interest in her, other than to see if we can locate her for her brother." Jimmy continued, "In her letters to him, she indicated that she was working at a small Chicago show club by the name of the Kit Kat Club, and so we came to Chicago, hoping that someone might shed a little light, in helping us locate her." Art who seemed to buy Jimmy's explanation, of why he and Bill were asking him these questions said,

"I didn't know that Aurélie had a brother, as she never mentioned him to me before, of course Aurélie, was very closed mouthed about her background and her family for some reason." He went on; "I met Aurélie, shortly after she came to the Kit Kat Club as a chorus girl. She seemed to take a shine to me, as I did to her. She was not like the average chorus girls, in that she wasn't a whore, in the strict sense of what a whore is. He continued, "As you gents must know, that one of the reasons that a girl can get hired at the Kit Kat Club, is that they must be willing to put out, otherwise Mr. La Rocco wouldn't hire them." He went on,

"Now I'm not passing judgment on her, as I believe that she, like so many other girls, were desperate for a job, and so they would do almost anything for these Mafia guerrillas, especially after being seduced with cocaine, to weaken their resistance." He continued, "Now I'm not here to tell you that I haven't sinned, cause I have, but as a Negro, aa's' has to do many thing's, sometimes, that I really don't likes' to do, as I needs' my job." Art seemed to want to get something off of his chest, as he kept on talking; almost rambling at times. Art continued talking,

"Aurélie, who I called kitten, as that is the name she wished me to call her by, had a real name and it was Mary O'Donnell." Art's shoulders once again, began to shake, as he started to cry. Art then after getting control of his emotions, said, "Auréilie or Kitten, had no prejudices what-so-ever, and so, she became my girl friend. That is why I like it here in the Beehive, where no one asks any questions of you or your gal and so, Kitten and I guess, sort of fell in love." He continued,

"I won't lie to you, kitten and I, had many a hot time if'n' you know what I means', she was one hot broad and so, she became pregnant. While I was delighted, Kitten was not too happy with her situation, not being married and getting pregnant, by a poor 'nigger' piano player. Nevertheless, I did offer to marry her, but she never would give me an answer. We lived together for a while, in a small cold water flat, just about a block from here." Art once again began to sob, as he said,

"One morning early, it was shortly after we both got off from work, we stopped for breakfast and again, at the Beehive for a drink and some talk, with our friends, most of whom were fellow musicians and show people. Kitten said that she didn't feel well, as I guess her morning sickness was beginning and she said that she wanted to lie down. I shrugged my shoulders and I said to her, "Okay baby, you go ahead, and I will stop by the newspaper stand, to see if any of my numbers had won, in the Chicago Southside numbers racket." He went on,

"I usually do win sometimes, but not that morning. I walked by the neighborhood barbershop and hollered in the door to my old friend and barber, Tootsie Calvin. I figured that Kitten would be fast asleep, when I went upstairs to our room. When I opened the door, and looked in, Kitten was no where to be found, and so I sort of panicked. However, I then thought, well, perhaps she's in the toilet down the hall, as all of the tenants, shared a common toilet. I hurried down the hall, I knocked on the door, No answer, and so I said, Kitten, it's me, Art, and still no answer. So I forced my way into the toilet and they're lying in the bathtub, was kitten, with her wrists slashed. Her wrists weren't slashed very deep, but she still lost a lot of blood and so, I was able to wrap her wrists with a couple of towels, stopping her bleeding and then I ran downstairs and as luck would have it, a 'beat' cop was just walking by. I told the cop about Kitten and he ran to a call box, where he rang in the emergency call number. It was only about ten minutes later, when an ambulance came and took Kitten away to the Cook County hospital. Kitten didn't abort the baby, but after she recovered from her loss of blood, she was put in the Cook County's mental ward, for observation." Jimmy than asked Art,

"Did you visit with Kitten?" Art answered,

"Oh sure, I had to, not only because I was worried about her, but the Cook County hospital needed someone, who could be considered her next of kin, so to speak, so I had to sign some forms. Dr. Seymour Titlebaum, who is the Chief of Staff for the Cook county hospital's mental ward, asked me if I knew that she was pregnant and I said, I sure do, as she's carrying my baby." He went on, "So once again I had to sign some forms stating to the effect, that I knew that Mary O'Donnell was indeed pregnant and the doctor estimated that she was just about four to six weeks pregnant." Jimmy than asked Art,

"Well what happened after that?" Art thought about Jimmy's question and once again, he burst out in tears and then after composing himself, he said,

"I don't have a phone and so, I had given Tootsie Calvin's barber-shop's phone number, to the hospital, as he being the neighborhood barber had a telephone, whereas, none of us could afford one. Anyhow, it was just about a week later, when I passed by the barber shop and Tootsie hollered to me and he said,

"Ah's' just got a call from the hospital and they says', that Kitten, has run'd' away." I immediately took a streetcar to the hospital and when I got there and went upstairs, I met Dr. Titlebaum in the hall and he said, that your girl friend, left the hospital in the middle of the night and he wanted to know if I knew where she had gone. I told the doctor that no, I didn't know that she had run'd' away from the hospital, as she never came home to our flat." Art then said,

"And so gents, I don't know anymore than that, as kitten never came home that morning and that is the last I've seen of her." Jimmy looked at Bill and he shrugged his shoulders. Jimmy than said to Art,

"Art, you have been most helpful and we are most appreciative of your information concerning kitten. Also, both Bill and I can only say just how sorry we are, that you've lost kitten as we know, just how much you loved her." Bill then said to Jimmy,

"Jimmy, I think it best that we be getting back to our hotel room, as I'm beat. Also, we've got a lot of work to do, before we return to Cincinnati." Jimmy then said,

"You're so right Bill, and so Art, we'll be seeing you and oh, before I forget it, should we find kitten and she happens to be living in another state and city, would you be willing to go see her, if of course, she would like to see you, and if we can make the arrangements?" Art answered,

"I would be most appreciative and I would be indebted to you, if you do find kitten and yes, I would like to visit her, if I can get away from the Kit Kat Club for a few days." They all shook hands, as Jimmy and Bill left the Beehive Club and they returned to the New Michigan Hotel.

CHAPTER 19

※

The Bombay Club
-The Grand Opening-

With the wealthy clientele's limousines, pulling into the parking lot, one after another, the lot was filling rapidly. If they would continue to come in such numbers, many limousines would have to be parked along the street, fronting the Bombay Club.

Enrico, Pat and Erin, stood in the foyer, greeting the patrons, as they sauntered into the club. After the three, personally greeted each person, a beautiful young and vivacious girl, would then meet each patron, and would ask the patron of his pleasures and/or, offer to escort him around the interior of the club, for him to inspect at his leisure, the many facilities that the club offered. From private spas, to two large Olympic size swimming pools, plus steam rooms and adjoining massage facilities with naked lady masseurs. There also were three large gambling rooms and a dozen or more, smaller and private gambling rooms. In addition, two oversized cabaret style rooms, where the customers could dance or take in a Parisian style floorshow, were available, plus wire betting on horse races, a very large ballroom, and finally, private rooms where the patron could seek his sexual pleasures, with one of the beautiful female chaperones or hostesses, as they were sometimes referred to.

When Enrico had to see somebody in private, who came in personally to see him, he left Pat and Erin by themselves for a few minutes. It was at that time, that Erin asked Pat,

"Why haven't you bothered to see me or call me?" Pat apologized profusely, as he told Erin,

"I am so sorry, but I was threatened by two of Al Capish's big guerrillas, who followed me out of the New Michigan hotel, the night I escorted you to your hotel room. As I was walking to my parked car, they told me, not to try and see you again, or they would break my legs, if I did, and they would put me in a cement coffin, and dump me in the Chicago River, if I attempted to see you again. "He continued, "I really didn't know how to get in touch with you, figuring that they would monitor any phone calls made to your room by me, and would intercept any mail that was addressed to you, before you had a chance to read it"

Erin's Irish temper was rising as she knew, that she could no longer live the kind of life she was living and expect to have any kind of a normal life, not with Al Capish, watching her every move and demanding his many sexual pleasures from her. She thought about what Rosie McCauley had told her and what she did, to get rid of, her abusive and controlling boyfriend. She said to herself,

'I've got to take the risk, regardless of the consequences'

Erin sang two evenings a week in the Bombay Club and she was a sell out. Men from all over the world, through word of mouth came to the Bombay Club, to gaze upon and to listen to, Erin's most beautiful voice, as she sang her torch songs and other crowd favorites. Many came to partake in her hidden pleasures and her sensual allure.

It was just bout eleven p.m., when a murmur and an air of excitement arose, down in front of the Bombay Club. Word had been passed from the doorman to one of the bellboys, that Al Capish and the mayor, the Honorable, 'Big Jim' Thompson, were entering the club. Al Capish and their entourage came to the club in five black Lincoln limousines, along with his personal armed, bodyguards. These limos, all had false bottoms, fabricated under the floor of these huge black Lincoln's, in which to carry bootleg booze. Al Capish had twelve bodyguards and the mayor had four detectives with him. Erin quickly said to both Enrico and Pat,

"If Mr. Capish asks about me, tell him that I am escorting one of the wealthy guests around the club, as I don't wish to see him."

Erin quickly made a beeline to the rear of the club, where she encountered a young hostess, chaperoning a wealthy English Lord, around the club. Erin whispered something into the ear of the young chaperone, who then excused herself, as Erin took over her escorting duties.

The English lord was a bit miffed, but only for a moment, as his eyes feasted on Erin. The English Lord looked to be in his late sixties, or thereabouts. He wore a tuxedo and on his chest, he had three rows of ribbons, probably won, both in the Great War and for meritorious service in India.

As Erin and the English Lord, rounded a corner, Erin spotted Al Capish out of the corner of her eye. He saw her at about the same time. He was about to tell one of his bodyguards to tell Erin to get her ass over to where he was standing, but the mayor whispered something to him and after a minute of trying to digest what the mayor had told him, Al looked the other way. Erin of course, never knew what the mayor had told Mr. Capish, but it obviously had something to do with the English Lord. Mr. Capish through one of his many bribed senators and representatives, in Washington D.C., had been trying to negotiate with the British government, to have the British, ship their booze into Mexico, where the booze would then be smuggled across the Mexican border at the small sleepy Mexican town, of Matamoras and then into Texas. From there, it would be trucked north, to all of the major cities in the east and the mid-west.

Al Capish knew, that no Englishman would ever turn his back on making money, legally or illegally. A sort of chime could be heard through-out the club and an announcement was made, via the many bell boys, who ran through the club announcing, that the beautiful chanteuse, the lovely Mademoiselle de la Durequex, would begin this evening's performance, in the grand ballroom, named the Taj Mahal, in just about ten minutes. The grand ballroom was named for the most favorite wife, of an East Indian prince, by the name of Shah Jahan.

With the English lord as her escort, arm in arm, Erin and the English Lord, made their way through the gathering crowd, to the back stage of the grand ballroom. The English Lord was given a chair, just off of the stage, so that he had a perfect view of Erin.

As the drum roll began, a hush came over the crowd, as the world's most famous chanteuse, Mademoiselle de la Durequex, walked out on to the stage. She was wearing an ivory colored dress, which was extremely low cut, both front and back and across her forehead, she wore an emerald green and black, silk head dress. Attached to her headdress was what looked like, a ten carat diamond broach, which was surrounded by a dozen emeralds. Around her neck, she wore a double string of gorgeous cultured pearls, which hung almost to her waist. Several colorful feathers were affixed to her waist. As the spotlight shown on this lovely creature, the orchestra began the introduction to Erin's most famous torch song; *'Some of These Days'.* The crowd loved this most beautiful chanteuse.

After finishing her 'set', and receiving fifteen curtain calls, Erin returned to her dressing room with the English Lord, on her arm. Erin deliberately did not sing any Italian opera favorites, even though she new that Al Capish loved her to sing them. Erin who still was trying to avoid Al Capish, asked the English Lord, if he wished to proceed to one of the pleasure rooms, for him to sample, what Erin called, the sinful pleasures of life. The English Lord was more than willing and then he asked what did she charge for such personal entertainment. Erin had been thinking about what she might charge anyone of these wealthy gentlemen and so she blurted out, one thousand dollars, for the first half hour.

The English Lord kind of stammered as he answered her, "All right my dear lets have a go." Erin and the Lord then took the elevator to the second floor and walked to a room with a gold letter 'E' over the door, which was Erin's private room. Erin who with her Irish sense of humor, had made, several dozen gold plated statues, of the Greek goddess of love, Diana, which she had intended to give, to any of her paramours, who paid her one thousand dollars for a half hour's worth of amorous entertainment.

The English Lord was her first customer in the Bombay Club and the first recipient of the gold statue. The English Lord having been severely wounded in World War 1, only asked Erin to walk around the room in various suggestive poises, so he could ogle her, as he was unable to have sex with her, because of his war injuries.

CHAPTER 20

❦

Mademoiselle Fife le Roach
-The Tattoo Artist-

Erin took a horse drawn streetcar, which ran on South Chicago Avenue, out to South Chicago and to the corner of Avenue 'O' and Sparks Street. She walked about a half a block, to what looked like a run-down tenement. The building had three stairwells with stairs, below ground level, that led to three doors. The address Erin was looking for was Number 1331, as that was the address, which Rosie Mc McCauley had given to her. She walked down several steps and to a door, in what was then called, a Bohemian basement apartment. She saw the sign **'Tattoos-by Mademoiselle Fife le Roach'**, (Tattoo Artist Extraordinaire). Erin knocked on the door and she heard a screeching voice say, one moment please, as I'm just fix'n' me' breakfast.

It was about a minute more, when the door opened and they're standing in the doorway, was a woman, who looked to be in her seventies. She was kind of short and fat. She had on a pair of dime-store reading glasses, with bent-up frames, which were so filthy; Erin wondered how she could see anything. She was wearing a dressing gown that was new, at the turn of the century. Covering the lower part of her old, patched and tattered dressing gown, she had on an apron.

She had one silk stocking with several runs in it, attached to a garter and the other silk stocking, was wrapped around her ankle, where it had fallen, after her garter evidently broke. Her white hair was streaked with red color or else, her red hair was turning white? She had make-up on her face, which to Erin, looked like it was put on with a putty knife, (*'Once a show girl, always a show girl'*, Erin thought). On her upper lip and chin, she had what could be determined, as a three-day growth of stubble, with a few wild hairs, each several inches long, growing from her neck. Standing in her stocking feet, she said to Erin,

"Well what can I be a do'in' for you, honey?" Erin answered,

"May I come in?"

"Oh certainly," answered the old lady, forgive my manners, but as I haven't had my morning tea, I'm not quite with it as yet." Erin walked into the tattoo ladies, small one room, basement apartment, which was located right behind the building's coal bin, as Erin could see coal dust on the walls of the old ladies room. Erin looked around the old ladies one room. On all of the walls in her single room, the old lady, had pictures and posters of someone, which resembled her, in her younger days, while performing in some of the better show clubs, in the United States and Europe.

Erin thought to herself, that Mademoiselle Fife had been, a very pretty woman when she was young and quite shapely. Erin sat on the edge of an old moth eaten, covered with cat hair, couch, which evidently had been the favorite spot of the old ladies, scruffy Calico cat, as the cat spat at Erin, when Erin sat down. So in disgust, it finally turned and climbed up on top of the ice box, where it could have a bird's eye view, of what was going on, down below.

The old lady gave Erin the once over and then she said, "What can I do for you, pretty lady and by the way, you can call me Maude, as that's my real name?" Erin shook her hand and then Erin began her story.

"A friend of mine, a chorus girl, had some very difficult problems, with a so called boy friend, who dominated her life. He beat her, acted as her pimp and had her under his thumb so to speak, controlling her every move, such, that she couldn't even go to the bathroom, without him watching her." She went on, "I believe that this went on for a couple of years and finally, she took what might be called, a desperation measure, to try and get rid of this animal, this leech, and that is where you come in, Maude. Maude interrupted Erin, as she said,

"How so?" Erin took a deep breath, as she was trying to tell Maude what she wanted to tell her, in a most delicate way, if she could. Erin then said,

"Well Maude, from what she told me, you tattooed a part of her body, 'her genital area', that you felt, would not only discourage this animal, but would scare him into disassociating himself from this chorus girl, and cause him to find for himself, another show girl, for him to abuse and control."

Maude looked at Erin for a couple of minutes, while she searched her memory, to see if she could recollect, if she could, what Erin said she did, and who she did it to? Many of the doors in the old ladies mind, were dusty, and shut tight, and others, she had to try and pry open, as best she could, by concentrating on a particular event. This mental ritual, usually took Maude a few minutes, before she could recollect just what the other person was talking about.

Then Maude's old eyes, sort of lit up, as she said, oh, now I remember, I did do a tattoo, for a pretty young girl by the name of Rosie I believe, yes, that was her name, it was Rosie McCauley, is that right?" Erin said,

"Yes, it was Rosie McCauley." Maude then said to Erin,

"I never did find out, if what I did for Rosie, actually worked or not, as she never came back, to tell me." Erin then said,

"According to Rosie, it worked." Maude then asked Erin,

"Would you like to 'Nosh', that's an old German/Yiddish expression, which means, have a bite to eat 'und' coffee, or tea and a biscuit with me?" She went on, "I don't get much company or even business for that matter anymore, and so, I get kind of lonely for company, for someone to share a story, or a memory, or two, with me. Especially so, since you and I are really kind of sisters under the skin so to speak, seeing as how we both were/are in show business." Erin said,

"I would very much like to visit with you Maude and I would certainly like to hear about your life, especially your career as a chorus girl, or what ever it was that you did, performing in those many cabaret and stage shows."

It so happens, that Maude was in the Ziegfeld Follies, after the turn of the century, both as a featured singer and later as a chorus girl. Maude had taken ballet lessons as a young child and her mother was the world famous, ballerina, Le Meré, (Mae O'Malley), who had danced with the great French Ballet Company,' De Francois le Begeré' in Paris, before the Great War. After Maude's recollections of her career, a sort of placid smile came over her face, and with tears in her eyes, she asked Erin.

"And now darling, won't you please tell me a bit about yourself, as I would very much like to know, all about you, if you don't mind." Therefore, Erin who was utterly captivated with Maude's life and career, her five marriages and the fact, that she had no children, because of a beating given to her, by her first husband, who was an Irish drunkard, began her story.

Her early childhood, her accidental landing a job at the Kit Kat Club, her various short lived romances, her classical voice training under the tutelage, of

Sister Angela Clare and on and on. Finally, after several hours of gossip and giggles with Maude, Erin said,

"Maude, I think that we should begin the procedure, as I should be getting back to my room. Erin was somewhat worried whether or not, Maude could see out of her glasses to perform her tattooing on Erin's body. But she said to her self, *'I'll leave it up to God, to decide my fate."*

Erin stripped down, so that Maude could begin her tattooing. Erin was a little embarrassed at first, but as Maude was tattooing her, Maude kept up a constant barrage of small talk, leaving Erin not the least bit frightened, nor embarrassed. It took Maude just about an hour to tattoo Erin's genital area and when she was done, she handed a small mirror to Erin. Erin was almost afraid to look, but she finally mustered up the courage to look. At first, she was shocked by what she saw, as the area around her genitals, was so ugly to look at, it almost made her sick.

Dozens of small red marks, covered this very personal area, but finally, after a few minutes of studying herself, she said to Maude,

"Maude, if this don't turn some guy off, then I don't know what would." Maude looked at Erin with tears in her eyes, as she said,

"Erin my dear, I really hated to do this to you, as a last resort, but I understand from what you've told me, that you couldn't go on living like you've had to, with this animal, whoever he is."

Erin then thanked Maude, for what she did and of her telling about her life and her wonderful career. After paying Maude and giving her a most generous tip, Erin kissed Maude on her cheek and then she left.

Erin's streetcar ride back to the New Michigan hotel was fraught with worry, as to how Al Capish would re-act to what he would see. *'Would he cut her throat, beat her, or would it be some other fiendish torture'?*

Erin kept from crossing her legs, as the pain in her genital area from the tattooing, was quite intense.

CHAPTER 21

❀

The Plaintiff's Lawyer
-Barrister Clarence Duncan-

Jimmy and Bill arose about five a.m. the following morning and they went downstairs to the coffee shop for breakfast. The same bunch of gorillas and their molls, were sitting at several tables, having coffee and breakfast. Bill asked Jimmy,

"Jimmy, what's our plan of action today?"

"Well," said Jimmy, "We'll pay a visit to my old school mate, Clarence Duncan, as I want to see if after hearing the evidence that we were able to find, he will drop the lawsuit against our client and his employer." He went on, "Now I know that it would have been pointless, for me to try and force the doctor who attended Aurélie de Muier, to provide me with her medical file as evidence, without a court order. The file would reveal her pregnancy and her mental condition, but should it become necessary for us to do so, I will get a court order and force him to provide me with her medical records."

Jimmy had found Clarence Duncan's address and phone number in the Chicago telephone book. Mr. Duncan had his offices over on South Dearborn Street, just a few blocks west of the loop. It was just about a quarter to nine and so Jimmy flagged a cab. As they both got into the Model 'T' Ford-yellow cab, the driver said, "Where to?" Jimmy said,

"906 South Dearborn." The trip took just about ten minutes with some construction delays and slight congestion, as they had to get by an accident between a horse drawn garbage truck and a taxicab. As they got out of the cab, it started to rain. Both Jimmy and Bill, dashed into the lobby of the building, to get out of the rain. Jimmy walked over to the tenant index, on the lobby wall and found what he was looking for, the listing for Clarence A. Duncan-and Attorney at Law.

The building elevator they rode in, was one of those that looked like a metal birdcage. Mr. Duncan had his office on the sixth floor. The elevator operator opened the door and Jimmy and Bill walked down the hall, to room 608. The elevator was gilded in a gold color, to give it the appearance of real gold. As they opened the office door and walked into the foyer of the office, a blonde girl who was the receptionist, was sitting at her desk said,

"May I help you?" Jimmy answered,

"Yes, is Mr. Duncan in?"

"Yes he is, do you have an appointment?" Jimmy answered,

"No Miss, we don't, but please tell Mr. Duncan, that an old friend is here to see him." The receptionist then said,

"May I tell Mr. Duncan your name?"

"Yes, my name is O'Brien, Jimmy O'Brien, class of '16'". The receptionist was gone for only a minute, when out came a very tall man, wearing spectacles. At first, he didn't recognize Jimmy, with Jimmy's hat, hiding the left side of his face, but finally he said, "Well I'll be a monkey's uncle and a son-of-a-bitch, if it isn't my old drinking buddy, Jimmy O'Brien." They shook hands and Mr. Duncan gave Jimmy a big hug. Jimmy then introduced his friend Bill,

"Clarence, this here is my good friend, Bill John." Clarence looked at Bill for a moment and then he shook his hand. Clarence then said,

"Come into my office for a few minutes, as I must be in court at ten sharp, as I'm defending a client." He went on, "Now I'll be gone most of the day, but perhaps we could get together for supper, say around six p.m., if that is okay with you guys?" Jimmy said,

"That would be just fine, as Bill and I, will do some shopping, while we kill some time, but which restaurant will we meet you at?" Mr. Duncan said, "We'll meet in a small German restaurant over on Randolph and State Street, called 'Old Heidelberg'". He went on, "I'd love to hear about you and your friend Jimmy, but I'm strapped for time and we can reminisce, this evening at the restaurant."

"Fine," said Jimmy. Jimmy and Bill spent the remaining part of the afternoon, walking through the huge department stores, which were situated along State Street. Marshall Fields, Carson Pierre-Scott, the Boston Store, Mandel Bros., the Fair Store, Maurice L. Rothschild's and finally Goldblatts Department Store. It was five thirty in the afternoon and so Jimmy and Bill, walked over to Randolph and State Street, to the restaurant.

They told the Maitre d', that they wanted a table for three, somewhere in a more secluded place, within the restaurant. The Maitre d' looked at Jimmy's hat, pulled down and covering the left side of his face, and he I guess, understood Jimmy's request. He sat them at a table, off of the kitchen, by itself.

CHAPTER 22

❦

A Small World

-Antagonists-

Clarence Duncan arrived at the restaurant at the time he said he would, and the Maitre d' escorted him back to the table, where Jimmy and Bill were sitting. They all shook hands and after an hour or so of small talk; kind of catching up on both Jimmy's and Clarence's lives, Mr. Duncan said,

"Well Jimmy, I know there is a reason for you coming to Chicago to see me and I'm sure it's not to reminisce about old times." Jimmy laughed as he said,

"You're so right Clarence, our finding you, was not by chance or perhaps, even serendipity, but for the reason; that you and your client, are suing a client of mine, and we're here to see what we can do, to persuade her and you, to change your minds, and to drop the law suit." Clarence then said,

"What's the name of my client?" Jimmy then said,

"She goes by the name of Aurélie de Muier, but her real name is Mary O'Donnell." Clarence seemed surprised at Jimmy's mentioning of Miss de Muier's real name, Mary O'Donnell. Clarence then said,

"Well Jimmy, how is it that you're involved in this litigation?" Jimmy proceeded to tell Clarence how he came to be involved in this lawsuit. Clarence kind of smiled at what Jimmy was telling him. Now, Clarence knew that Jimmy could be a very effective advocate, as in their law school mock trails, Jimmy was unbeatable, both in prosecuting and in defending his client. Clarence once again asked Jimmy, what information he had, that would cause Miss de Muier, to want to drop her lawsuit, against the defendant.

Without revealing to Clarence, any of his planned defense strategy, he said,

"Well Clarence, I can prove that Miss de Muier was pregnant, when she left Chicago for Cincinnati, Ohio and that she tried to commit suicide, to avoid giving birth to a baby, she did not want. Further, I know who the father is and if necessary, I can produce him, as a defense witness. I can also prove, that my client did not have sexual relations with your client." Of course, Jimmy didn't know how he could prove his latter statement, but no pompous lawyer worth his salt, is above bluffing, as much of the court room theatrics, is bluffing. Clarence's facial expression went from what might be perceived as confident, to a facial expression of someone, who now had some concern, as to the future outcome, of this pending lawsuit.

Clarence scratched his chin, as he asked Jimmy,

"You say you can prove that my client was pregnant, before she left Chicago for Cincinnati!" Clarence went on, "How much was she pregnant, I mean, how many weeks or months was she pregnant, according to what you have found out?" Jimmy before he answered, thought about Clarence's question, and *wondered if he should reveal those facts or not, at this time*? However, after mulling around in his head, the pros and cons, he said

"Well for now, lets just say for the sake of an argument, that she was at least a month pregnant and perhaps, even more than that?" Clarence thought about what Jimmy had said, and then he said,

"Now even if we drop the assault and rape charges against your client, I know that the defendant's uncle, who is Mr. Josiah Pickering and who owns at least a third interest in this shipping company, would not want the appearance of a scandal, to be read in the local newspapers. And perhaps, even in the national news papers and so, I believe, that he would want to settle this case out of court and avoid any unpleasant, publicity." He went on, "Therefore, it is my feeling, that Mr. Pickering, would be willing to pay my client a sum of money, to avoid any publicity what so ever, at any cost". Jimmy of course was listening to Clarence's argument, regarding his client, then said,

"You maybe correct in what you say, but I want to at least advise you, that should the seduction and rape portion of this case be dropped and in essence, the case not be brought to trial at all, then with your admitted intention, to notify the newspapers, in order to sensationalize and to smear Mr. Pickering and his consortium, I will make it my duty, to sue both you and your client for extortion and perhaps even blackmail, whenever your client's baby is born." Jimmy went on, "I will Clarence, bankrupt you and see to it, that you never again, be allowed to practice law, anywhere in the United States." Clarence suddenly became red in the face, as he pondered Jimmy's threat, of recourse litigation and it's possible consequences to him. Jimmy said further,

"I know Clarence, that you always play hard ball, and I'm aware of your methods in winning your cases. "Now, I'm not suggesting, that they are illegal, but I will say that they are unethical, to say the least." He went on, "As you know Clarence, I too can play hardball, even though it's been awhile since I've defended anyone in court. So I suggest to you, that you think long and hard, about trying to extort monies from Mr. Pickering, before you threaten, to make this case a public spectacle and thereby, besmirch the company of which, Mr. Pickering, is the senior partner." Jimmy went on,

"Clarence, its lawyers like you, that give the law and us lawyers, a bad name, in the public's eye." Clarence didn't like to be accused of what Jimmy was accusing him of, even though he knew that Jimmy was right and so he said,

"Careful old friend, of what you're saying, as I don't take such comments about my legal ethics, too kindly." Jimmy then said,

"I agree, that we shouldn't get into personal attacks about each other and therefore, let me leave you with this thought; think about what I have said, and I'll give you my address, where you can contact me and I hope to hear from you, within the next week or so." Mr. Duncan then said,

"Okay, where are you and Bill staying, and how long will you be in town, should I need to get in touch with you, before you leave?" Jimmy answered,

"We're staying at the New Michigan Hotel and I expect, that we'll be in town, for just a couple of more days, as we have some more investigative work to be completed, back in Cincinnati."

"Boy," said Clarence, "You do realize that the New Michigan Hotel is Al Capish's headquarters."

"We didn't, but we do now." Jimmy didn't want to tell Clarence, that they deliberately stayed at the New Michigan hotel, for a reason and of course, the reason was, Miss de Muier's boyfriend, Art Washington.

CHAPTER 23

❦

'Scarface's' Anger
-A Day of Retribution-

Erin had left the New Michigan hotel and had moved into an elegant suite, at the Bombay Club. These rooms of course, were reserved for the Madam of the Bombay Club and were decorated as such; all were very elegant and plush. All of the furniture in her setting room was French provincial, and was covered in mauve colored, 'plush' velour, with royal-red trim. Her bed was made into a heart shaped design. In the style of the day, cupid dolls, were painted on some of the walls and most of her pictures in her bedroom, were of naked ladies; all tastefully painted and therefore, were considered art and not, pornographic.

Aside from these nude pictures, Erin had chosen pictures of flowers, to sort of compliment these nude pictures, as she loved flowers. After greeting guests and performing her songs in one of the cabarets, Erin was tired. Dealing with her girls on a daily basis, was a chore by itself, as she more or less, had to use kid gloves, covering an iron fist, in dealing with some of their petty problems.

Jealousy was the most serious problem, as after all, most of these girls, were not your common street walking hookers, but many had college degrees, and most were considered beautiful. They knew that the business world couldn't compete with this high-class Bordello, when it came to making money. Many of these girls were making money in the six figures, depending on their male cliental and their willingness, to make their gentlemen friends happy.

College degrees for women in those days were primarily in the education field and not in the business world, where men, dominated. Erin had just walked back to her suite, when she heard a knock on her door. She went to the door and she said, "Who is it?" A man answered,

"Who' Ju'd' think it was doll, its me Al, open da' door." Erin's jaw dropped, as she wasn't prepared mentally, to face Al Capish, at least not tonight. She tried to change her facial demeanor, so as not to let Al know, of her concern about her tattoo, and whether or not, he would find out that her supposed contagious disease, was just a ruse to fool him.

Nevertheless, she gathered herself together and she opened the door. There standing next to Al Capish, was one of his favorite whores, a girl by the name of Lucrezia Costallini Pizza, who was a sort of high class Sicilian prostitute, who Al brought to America from Sicily, when he made a trip there last year. Lucrezia wasn't beautiful, but she certainly was pretty with her jet-black hair, olive skin and her pouting mouth, and she had a gorgeous body.

Al gave Erin a kiss and he patted her on the ass, as he said, "Okay dolls, lets have some fun." Lucrezia was the first to take off her clothes and Erin gulped, as she marveled at the size of Lucrezia's breasts. To Erin, they looked like watermelons. Lucrezia was au naturel, in that she didn't shave any of the normal places on her body, which had hair, in the European tradition. She had almost, as much hair on her body, as Al did.

Lucrezia hopped into bed, with her legs spread, as Erin was undressing. Erin after she took off her panties, turned to face Lucrezia, who was lying on the bed naked. Lucrezia was giving Erin the once over, as any other female would do, as she knew that Erin was Al Capish's favorite whore.

Al had taken off most of his clothes, except his hat, as Al was sensitive about his balding head. He took off, his stockings, his garters and his shoes, as well as his boxer shorts, and of course, his ever-present cigar he kept in his mouth, when Lucrezia let out a scream and her use of curse words in Italian and broken English, couldn't be duplicated by anyone. She said,

"Goddamn a', figlio di uno, ciò che il 'n inferno, ha noi ha preso qui, questo, ha preso syphilis o lo strisciando!" "Goddamn a, son of a bitch, what the frigg'n hell, have a' we got here, wid'a' this a' bitch Al?" *Lei è preso il o lo strisciando."* 'She's got the syphilis or the creeping crud!'

Al then grabbed Erin by her arm and turned her around, so that she was facing him. He then looked down at her genital area, as he said in Italian, *"Che' un lei ha preso, lei la femmina, un frigg' n' la malattia, chi lei è stato banging, dietro il mio dorso?"* 'Wat' a' you got, you bitch, a' frigg'n' disease, who a' you been a' banging, behind a' my back haah'?'

Al's face went from its normal swarthy complexion, to a face that was almost black, as his temper was beginning to rise. He bit down on his cigar, until half of it, fell smoldering, on the floor.

Erin just stood there, waiting for Al to either beat her with his fists, or slit her throat, when Lucrezia piped up, "Come on Al, lets a' not a' bother with this a' 'Mick' whore, lets a' you and a' me, do our thing a'."

Al had thoughts of murdering Erin, right then and there, with his twisted brain, but he also was aware, that The Bombay Club's financial success, was primarily because of Erin, as she was the drawing card, for the entire operation. Al was no dummy, as his business moxie, somehow calmed his need to get revenge, on this Irish whore. He thought to himself, *'I'll deal with this broad later, after I've cooled down and I can think better.'*

Then without waiting around for Al, to think about what he should do with her, Erin walked out, and made her way, through his entourage of body guards, who were ogling her and making sexual gestures with their hands and bodies, while expressing their animalistic sexual thoughts, verbally. After either giving one or more of Al's body guards a bit of her Irish temper, with a few choice swear words of her own, and then shoving a couple of this guerrillas aside, who were blocking her way, she continued down the hall to one of the hostess's rooms, where she locked the door and laid across the bed.

She was now perspiring profusely, as her adrenalin was now starting to leave her body; although she was still shaking and sobbing, uncontrollably, as this trauma was almost more than she could endure, as she continued to anticipate the worst from this mad moronic gangster, Al 'Scarface' Capish.

Erin thought to herself, *'I sure expected more than a tongue lashing, much more, I really expected to be murdered by this animal, or at least, have my face battered and broken by his fists. But, just maybe, God was looking out for me this evening, and Al won't have any desire to touch me again, and he will eventually, forget about me.'* Erin made the sign of the cross.

Erin fell fast asleep and in the morning, she returned to her suite, to shower and to get dressed, selecting a suitable dress from her now vast wardrobe, for the coming day.

Both Enrico and Pat had adjoining offices in the Bombay Club. It was from these offices that they conducted their day-to-day business, although Enrico spent most of his time, managing the affairs of the club, while Pat on the other hand, had his investment brokerage business to run, on North Michigan Avenue, and so, he usually came into the Bombay Club, only in the evenings.

Erin was walking by Enrico's office, when she heard him holler, Erin, can I speak with you for a moment. Erin thought to her self, *'my, how polite Enrico is, normally he would holler, hey Erin, get your ass in here.'*

Erin went into Enrico's office and they're sitting in a chair, next to his desk, was a voluptuous blonde that Erin had never seen before. The blonde's natural endowments, were almost hanging, out of her revealing low cut dress and with her crossed legs, her skimpy dress, was up around her waist, and the overpowering smell, from the cheap perfume she wore, was sickening. Enrico had a slight smile on his face as he said,

"Erin, I'd like you to meet Kitty; Kitty, this is Erin, our current Madam and singer." Enrico stammered for a minute, as he cleared his throat, before he said,

"Erin, Kitty is your replacement, she will take over your duties as the Madam for the Bombay Club and you, if you would still like to, you can remain with us, as our featured singer." Erin knew right then, that Al Capish had a hand in this personnel move. She figured that with my supposed disease, he wouldn't want it to become known, that Erin O'Hara, a.k.a., Mademoiselle de la Durequex, had somehow become infected by one of her 'johns,' and therefore, she could no longer represent the Bombay Club, at least not in a sexual way, with her contagious disease.

Erin was both hurt and relieved in away, as she loved to sing for her adoring audiences, but she hated the life that brought her to the Bombay Club, and what she had to do in a very demeaning way, to satisfy her clientele, who craved her body in a most licentious way. Erin realized long ago, that this was not the way; she had always envisioned her life on the stage. Erin then said to Enrico,

"I'll think about what you have just told me and I will decide whether or not, I will stay on, as a singer with the Bombay Club." Erin's response to his change in madams was not at all, what Enrico had expected. Enricos's face, became ashen white, his hands began to tremble, as he bit off the end of his cigarette, without realizing it. He knew, that without Erin as the main attraction, as the Bombay Club's most famous chanteuse, the Bombay Club for all intents and purposes, might as well go out of business, as there were other, almost as fancy, so called Gentlemen's clubs in Chicago, and all of the other major cities in the United States. Enrico tried hard to mask his inner feelings, but he could not, as much as he tried. He never had figured on the notion, that Erin might leave, but he knew her Irish temper very well.

Enrico figured that if Erin did quit, Al Capish would blame Enrico for her leaving, and he would pay the price, no matter that it was Al himself, who had sent word to Enrico, to dump the Irish 'Mick,' as madam of the now world famous Bombay Club. Erin then went back to her suite and pondered whether or not, to stay on as a singer or to leave. However, if she left, where would she go? Finally after an hour or so, of mental deliberations of this shocking news, Erin decided to leave the Bombay Club and seek work elsewhere. Erin felt that she would try and salvage, what little personal respect she had left for herself, but, she also believed that as a human being, she had every right to try and pursue her singing career elsewhere, where it might be more appreciated and not require her to prostitute herself, to these lecherous animals, that frequented such places.

Life she thought, isn't always fair; as Sister Angela Clare, had more than once told her, but she also told her, to believe in God, and herself, and that life's great struggles, would eventually be overcome. Erin opened her door, and motioned to the bellboy, who stood at the end of the hall to come, and she told him to flag a cab and to help her with her suitcases

Erin only took what clothing she had bought for herself, with her own money and left all of the dozens of garments, bought for her, by Enrico, as part of her wardrobe, although she did take her specially built shoes. She had penned a note and left it on her nightstand, which read,

༄

Mr. La Rocco:

After careful consideration, I have decided to leave my position as the chanteuse, with the Bombay Club.

Erin

Erin got into the waiting cab as she said to the driver, "La Salle Hotel driver."

CHAPTER 24

❦

Mr. Pickering
-Final Report & Threat-

Jimmy and Bill had arrived back in Cincinnati on the early morning train from Chicago. They took a cab down to the river front and they walked up the gangplank to the office of Mr. Wallace. Jimmy knocked on the door and a voice from within said, "Come in." As both Jimmy and Bill entered Mr. Wallace's office, and upon seeing them, Mr. Wallace immediately arose and shook both of their hands. He then said,

"Gentlemen, please sit down." He went on, "I received your last telegram Jimmy and what you and Bill had found out, concerning Miss Aurélie de Muier, alias Mary O'Donnell, and her obvious lies and her attempt to extort money from Mr. Perkins's uncle, by blackmailing Mr. Pickering. In addition, I've read your missive to her lawyer, Clarence Duncan, where Mr. Duncan is supposed to consider your findings and drop the lawsuit, against Mr. Perkins." He continued, "But what really has me concerned Jimmy, is your statement about her lawyer, who if he drops the case, he will still try and extort money from Mr. Pickering, Mr. Perkins's uncle, and in doing so, his threat to smear Mr. Pickering and the Hayes, Pickering & Haffendorf Enterprises Ltd, of an unknown sum of money. "Jimmy then said, after listening to Mr. Wallace's concerns,

"Well Mr. Wallace, I had advised Mr. Duncan, not to proceed with his obvious threat to blackmail, if you will, to try and extort some unspecified sum of money, from Messer's. Perkins and his uncle, Mr. Pickering and the company itself." He continued, "I of course, don't know if Mr. Duncan was merely bluffing, or whether or not, he was serious; time will tell." Mr. Wallace then said,

"If what you say is true, then what should we do in the meantime?" Jimmy after much thought said,

"When and if, we get a telegram from Mr. Duncan, that he and his client, Miss de Muier, stipulate that they are dropping their lawsuit against Mr. Perkins, and we also hear from the Ohio, 15th. Circuit Court, in writing, verifying the actual dropping of the lawsuit itself; then I think, we will have to wait and see, if either Mr. Perkins or Mr. Pinkerton receives from lawyer Duncan, a note suggesting a sum of money to be paid to him, or else, he will notify the press of this whole sordid situation." Mr. Wallace than asked without waiting to hear what Jimmy had to say further,

"What action should we take, I mean, if and when, we do get a note from lawyer Duncan, suggesting a certain amount of hush money be paid to him, to keep this story out of the newspapers?" Jimmy thought for a minute and then he said,

"Well, what I propose really depends on Mr. Pickering and the company." He went on, "Mr. Wallace sir, as you may know, there are persons like Mr. Duncan, who will try and get money, by trying to besmirch, if you will, the good name of your company. The very name of this esteemed company, which is known far and wide, as a very respectable company and it's name as such, is so valued by the owners, that they would probably pay any price, to ensure that they are not dragged through the mud, by some of these sleazy newspapers. Newspapers, who count their readership, on the amount of dirt, they can report on, no matter if the dirt is the truth, or is just made up so to speak. It's called, 'yellow journalism.'"

"But," he went on, "Once the lie is printed, it then becomes a never ending snow ball, which becomes larger and larger, as it sort of feeds off itself."

"I know", Mr. Wallace answered,

"But what do you propose that Mr. Pickering and the company do?" Jimmy scratched his chin as he said,

"What I propose, is going to take quite a lot of nerve, but in my opinion, it is the only way to stop dead in it's tracks, what I think, will become a never ending blackmail scheme, to extort more and more money from the company." Mr. Wallace who was becoming more and more irritated by Jimmy's sort of lengthy diatribe on the merits of this case, finally said,

"For Christ sake Jimmy, what is your plan?" Jimmy then said,

"Well Mr. Wallace, my advice to the company, is to involve the federal authorities in this case, with marked bills, which the feds. can track down, finding who ever got what money, and when, and therefore, who might be involved in this blackmail scheme, which as you may or may not know, blackmail is a federal offense." Jimmy went on, "It is my understanding that the feds, in their desire to find such persons, would not use you companies' name in any pending criminal law suit, and Mr. Pickering would most likely be referred to as a John Doe." Jimmy continued,

"My advice to the owners of this company and Mr. Pickering in particular, is to wait on receiving a note of blackmail from lawyer Duncan and then we can proceed from there." Mr. Wallace had a look of concern on his face, as he mulled over in his mind, what Jimmy had just told him and finally he said,

"Jimmy, the owners of our company have been very much impressed by your work on the current case and it would be my guess, that they would like you, to prepare a written paper on your strategy; should Mr. Pickering and the company, receive a blackmail note from lawyer Duncan. Finally, if they do, I would think, that they would still like to retain your services, if you are willing?"

CHAPTER 25

Black Friday
-October 1929-

Erin was awakened early in the morning, by loud shouting. At first, she thought perhaps, that Al Capish's mobsters were trying to break into her room, but as she listened longer, she discerned, that the shouts and the clamor were coming from the street. She got up and looked out of her fifth floor window, which faced La Salle Street. To her, it looked like hundreds of people were shouting something, while clutching newspapers in their hands, which was not clearly audible to her. She thought, *'I wonder if there could be a fire in the hotel'?*

She quickly wrapped her silk kimono around herself and she ran down the hall to the elevator. Standing, facing the elevator was an older couple. Erin asked them, "Do you know what all of the commotion is out in the street." The older man looked at Erin with a sort of sad look in his eyes, as he said,

"Young lady, we're in a depression, as the stock market has just collapsed and all of the banks are closed." He went on, "Many of those people you see running about in the street, are probably aware, that all of their life savings, have just been wiped out."

Erin was still not sure of the significance of what this older gentlemen said, as she had no stocks, nor any money in any bank, as all of her life savings, little as they were, were located in a money belt, she had tied around her waist. Erin had managed to save some fifteen hundred dollars over the past two years, from singing at the Kit Kat Club and the Bombay Club. It wasn't much though, for the personal abuse, she had to suffer, to earn it. As for singing, she would have sung for nothing, as it gave her, the audience's adulation and for her audience, she gave to them, nothing but pleasure, but the other money, was what she called her blood money, money earned by laying on her back and allowing some creep to find his sexual gratification, in her. She was ashamed of what she had become and so she vowed that she would never again sell her body, for either cocaine or for another's pleasure, unless of course, it was her fiancé or her husband.

Erin had tried on several occasions, to try and kick her cocaine habit, but each time, she succumbed to the euphoric and addictive hold, it had on her; a hold so strong, that she would do most anything, to satisfy her insatiable craving for this most pleasurable and sweet innocent looking, powdery white substance. To imbibe in this mind-numbing narcotic, with its ability, to wash away the pain, that she had to endure, was like a never-ending search for utopia; her promised land.

Erin however, was a very strong willed woman and she knew, that she had to beat this devil, or it would cause her total degradation and her death.

In discussing her problem with some of the chorus girls at the Kit Kat Club, who tried and failed to kick their habit and others, who were successful, she found a method that some said, had worked for them. Those girls who finally kicked their habit said, it was to shut themselves up in a room alone, and when they had the urge to snort this evil white powder, they said that they would use, pure powder sugar, as a sort of surrogate substance. While the sugar didn't satisfy their cravings for cocaine, it did however, act like a placebo, in that one's own mind was kind of tricked into believing, that this innocent white powdery sugar, was really cocaine. They told Erin, we know it's hard to believe, but it worked for us.

Therefore, after things quieted down around the hotel, she had left word with the floor maid, that she didn't wish to be disturbed for any reason, by anyone, for a few days. Her excuse was, that she was a writer and she needed to be left alone, while she worked. Erin had brought in some groceries, canned food, that didn't require ice to keep them fresh and candy, lots of candy. The first few days of her forced abstinence, from her sort of security blanket 'cocaine', she would throw up, almost continuously. She actually sat on the floor in the bathroom, with her head hanging over the toilet bowl. She would perspire profusely and she had uncontrollable shakes.

Her hands would tremble and her face would twitch, as though she were having a fit. Her beautiful emerald green eyes were glazed over, highlighted by the dark circles underneath them, almost like she was in a stupor. She continually mumbled to herself and she would sing at the top of her lungs, various operatic pieces, as her singing would tend to detract her mind, from her constant focus, which was on cocaine. However, gradually after about three days, she found that she no longer had this terrible craving, for this beautiful white powder, this sexual paramour, which held her in its arms, ever so tightly.

She knew that she was winning her personal battle, over what kept her and so many other pretty young women, under the control of such animals, like Al Capish and Enrico, who treated them like they were nothing but, meat.

By the end of the week, Erin's spirits had returned and she was looking forward to finding herself a job, not realizing of course, just how bad the economy was. In talking to several of her friends at the Bombay Club, before she had quite her job, they had told her of a night spot in Niles, Illinois, a sort of far northwestern suburb of Chicago, owned by another mobster, but who was Irish, not Italian. The name of this club or roadhouse was the Shamrock Club. The owner's name they said was Byrne 'Mugs' Rooney. Mr. Rooney was in direct competition with Al Capish and he controlled much of the vice on the far north side and the northwest suburbs of Chicago, while Al Capish controlled all of the south side and its suburbs, plus small towns like Chicago Heights, Illinois. Niles, Illinois at that time was not incorporated into any township or city, as it was in a very rural section of the northwest part of Chicago and not under any type of law enforcement, other than the state police, who rarely visited the area. It was comprised mainly, of truck farms, where vegetables were grown for the Chicago market. German immigrants owned most of these truck farms.

But the Shamrock Club, had its own following of primarily, Irish Catholic immigrants, who chose to live in a more rural area of Chicago, after they were able to afford to leave the Irish ghettos, like Caneryville on the south side of Chicago and the Little Hell neighborhood, on the north side of Chicago.

There had been several gangster murders, over the past several years, blamed on both Al Capish and on Byrne 'Mugs' Rooney, as each gang, tried to destroy the other. The Chicago police department usually looked the other way, as most of the brass was on the payrolls of both mobster leaders.

Byrne 'Mugs' Rooney had grown up in the Little Hell neighborhood in the north side of Chicago and he attended St. Julian's Catholic grammar school.

Erin had no idea just where, Niles, Illinois was, and so she flagged a cab and she asked the driver, "Sir, do you know where Niles, Illinois is?" The driver thought for a minute and then he said,

"Well miss, I believe that it is quite a ways, northwest of here." Erin then said,

"Can you take me there?" The driver laughed and then he said,

"Look miss, I could probably take you there, but it would cost you an arm and a leg, as it is so far out in the sticks." He went on, "However, I believe that there is a railroad line that commutes to the northwest suburbs and that is called the Northwestern commuter line, and it comes into the Union station, which is just about a half a mile from here." Erin thought for a minute and then she said,

"Then take me to the Union station, please."

CHAPTER 26

-The Demise of the Bombay Club-

-The Blame Game-

It was less than six months after Erin had left the Bombay Club and the stock market crash, that they, both together, caused the Bombay Club to finally have to close its doors. While Erin's leaving, had a definite negative impact on the attendance itself at the club, but the prostitution and the gambling, was at least giving the club, a more or less break-even financial status. In addition, Al Capish, was literally, pouring thousands of dollars into the club each month, to help it stay afloat and to weather the storm, at least temporarily, as Al didn't know just how devastating this so-called 'Great Depression' would be, nor how long would it last.

But the straw that finally broke the camel's back so to speak, was the stock market crash itself, as most all of the high rollers, had dropped their memberships in the Bombay Club, in order to assess their individual financial situations, and to lick their financial wounds, as best they could and spend their money, on less frivolous items.

Many of the club members were totally bankrupt and some committed suicide, rather than face their creditors and their own families. Others dropped out of society and never returned to their former luxurious ways of life they once knew, abandoning their families and adopting new identities.

Al Capish had installed small cameras in most of the small rooms, to take pictures of the unsuspecting customers, who were engaging in sex in all of its perverted forms, thus violating the Bombay Club's, absolute privacy rule. His thinking was, that he would eventually blackmail these wealthy customers, who would pay any price, to keep their names out of the newspapers and from their families, in order to avoid a ruinous scandal. Al Capish didn't have any scruples when it came to making money and of course, blackmail and extortion, were two of his favorite ways to make money, always preying on the moral weaknesses, of his wealthy customers.

Al Capish had called a meeting with all of his Dons, his Capos and some of his Consigularies, at the New Michigan Hotel, to discuss the 'Great Depression' and the effect it was having on his empire. He also, particularly invited several underlings, including Tony La Rocco and his son Enrico. All of these chieftains, Dons, Capos and Consigularies, all gave Al, the 'Godfather', the traditional kiss on both of his cheeks and then they all knelt down, and kissed his Mafiosi ring.

Al was still smarting over that Irish bitch, who had the nerve to leave the Bombay Club, just because some other broad replaced her as the madam. However, he smiled to himself as he thought about the pleasure she gave him in bed, as she was one hot broad. This thinking to himself, further infuriated his warped mind, as he said out loud, to no one in particular,

"*Nessuno cessa Al Capisch, a meno che dico cosí*". 'No one quits Al Capisch, unless I say so, see'!

He looked directly at Enrico, who was now showing visible signs of nervousness, he was starting to fidget in his chair, as beads of perspiration were showing on his forehead and starting to run down the neck of his shirt. He kept his eyes looking down at the floor, as he didn't wish to make eye contact with Al Capish.

Al then said to Enrico, "*Non l'Enrico, lei il rotten sporco, no-buono, il figlio-di-un-la femmina, che la questione, lei potrebbe il controllo quel whore di Mick?*" He went on, "*Io il wimps di bisogno di nella mia organizzazione, l'ama.*" 'Enrico, you dirty rotten, no-good, son-of-a-bitch, what's the matter, you couldn't control that 'Mick' whore?" He went on, "I don't need wimps in my organization, like you." With that last remark, Al got out of his chair and he walked over to where Enrico was sitting. Behind Al Capish's back, he had hidden a baseball bat. Enrico was now sobbing, as was his father. He raised the bat over his head as he screamed, "*Il bastardo*," 'Bastard'.

With that, swear word uttered from his fat red lips, he swung the bat, hitting Enrico in the head, and crushing his skull, like an eggshell. Enrico slumped unconscious, in his chair, with blood starting to ooze from his mouth and head. Al with spittle leaving the corners of his mouth, and with the look of a crazed man on his contorted face, with his black eyes flashing, he continued to bash Enrico's face, over and over, all the while swearing in Italian, until Enrico's face, was no longer recognizable. Enrico's face now looked like it was made out of mush, with no recognizable sign, that it at one time bore the resemblance of a human face. His teeth were now hanging outside, of what was left of his jaw. The smell of death, now seemed to permeate the room, like a death shroud, trying to cover up that violent scene, which just took place there.

Al threw the broken and bloody bat, over in the corner, as a grime reminder to 'any and all', who would either stand up to, or cross, Al 'Scarface' Capish, the Godfather.

Tony La Rocco, Enrico's father, just sat there like he was frozen to his chair, however, he couldn't stop either his bladder, nor his bowels from re-acting, to what his eyes had seen; they both moved, involuntarily. All of the other members of Al Capish's Mafia organization never uttered a word, as most were kind of transfixed at what they had just witnessed. Some began to laugh and others, even giggled nervously, in a sort of an involuntary bravado reflex, a spontaneous reaction, to what they had just viewed, and also, not to be perceived, as not approving of Al Capish's, violent action

After Enrico had fallen from his chair, Al Capish then told Enrico's father and two of his bodyguards, *"Portare questo son-of-a-bitch'n il grumo di crap, e la discarica lui nel Fiume di Chicago."* 'Take this son-of-a-bitch'n', lump of crap, and dump him in the Chicago River'.

Mr. La Rocco, with tears streaming down his face, picked up his son and with the help of these two guerillas, they carried Enrico out the back door of the New Michigan Hotel and put him in the trunk, of a black limousine. All of Al Capish's limousines had black oilcloth, placed on the bottom of their trunks, for just such a purpose; so as not to stain their cloth covered trunks, with their victim's blood. Other gang enemies evidently, had also traveled that way, when they too, met the same fate as Enrico La Rocco, for crossing the Godfather, Al Capish.

Then all three men got in, and one of the gangsters drove over to South Water Street and the Chicago River, right next to the Illinois Central Railroad's, loading docks. There they dumped Enrico's body, into the Chicago River. Enrico's body disappeared for a few minutes under the black murky surface of the river, before it resurfaced and started to move away from Lake Michigan, and then the body moved west of downtown Chicago, with the slowly moving current, moving it east to west.

CHAPTER 27

❀

The Interview

-Byrne 'Mugs' Rooney-

Erin got off the train at the Niles station. She looked around for any signs of the Shamrock Club, but she couldn't see any, nor could she see any other establishment, which looked like a club of some sort. The town consisted of one small grocery store and to her, something that looked like a combination blacksmith shop and gas station. She then looked to see if she could spot a taxi. She thought that most cabbies would know where the Shamrock Club was. After about ten minutes of sort of stomping her heels, and pacing back and forth on the train platform, in kind of a nervous gait, she spotted a young boy, standing at the opposite end of the platform.

"Well," she thought, *'I'll walk down the platform and maybe that young boy, can tell me where the Shamrock Club is'*? As she walked closer to the young boy, he evidently had been watching her, since she got off of the train. As she approached him she said, "Young man, do you know if there are any taxi cabs here in town." The young man answered,

"No mum', there aren't any cabs hereabouts." Erin had a kind of disgusted look on her face, as she pondered what she should do next." Finally, the young boy asked, "Is there any thing that I can do for ye', mum'?" Erin then said,

"Yes there is, can you tell me the whereabouts of a club, called the Shamrock Club?" The young boy looked at Erin for a minute or two and then he said,

"Yes I can." Erin who was becoming more and more irritated with Niles, Illinois, and this question and vague answer routine, with this young boy said,

"Is it far from here?" The young boy who was chewing bubble gum and who continued to blow huge bubbles, which when they broke, flattened on his nose and forehead, and then he licked them off, as he put the flattened gum, back into his mouth said,

"Its about two kilometers from here, I reckon." Erin then said,

"Tell me that in miles if you please, as I don't understand kilometers. Also, can you tell me how I might be able to get there; is there some other form of transportation here in Niles, that I can use, as you said, that there are no cabs?" The young boy studied Erin some more and then he said,

"Well lady, if I can figure it right in miles, it's just a wee bit over one mile and I can take ye' there, but it will cost ye'." Erin who by now was just about ready to give up, on her trying to get transportation to the Shamrock Club said,

"And how will you take me there, do you have a car, or a horse-and-buggy, and how much do you charge?"

"No ma'am, I don't have either, but I do have me' bicycle, as you can see, but it will cost ye' a nickel." Erin had to laugh to herself, as she looked at the little boy's bicycle. Erin could see that it was a boy's bike, as it had a bar running from the seat to the fork, where the handlebars were connected. Erin then laughingly said,

"Well son, just how do you expect to take me to the Shamrock Club, when you're bike only has one seat?" The little boy looked puzzled by Erin's stupid comment, at least to him her comment seemed stupid, and so he said,

"Well mum', out here, we put the passenger on the bar." Erin looked kind of surprised and again she laughed, as she said,

"How far is it again?"

"Well mum', as I said earlier, its jest' about a shade over one mile, as the crow flies, maybe a little more." Erin kind of muffled her laughter, as she thought to her self, *'they should see me now, down at the Bombay Club, Mademoiselle Adrienne de la Durequex and her fancy taxi'.*

Erin gave the boy a nickel, picked up her skirt and she sat down on the bar. Holding on to the handlebars with her left hand and her hat with the other, they started their trip, down a slippery rutted clay road, where the rain of the previous evening, left the road very treacherous."

The little boy was very strong, as he was able to peddle his bike, over this rough road, and maintain his balance, with a passenger seated on the bar. Every now and then, as they bicycled over some rough part of the road, the bike would sort of dip and wobble, as though it might fall, and then the young boy, would take his one hand off of the handlebar grip, and place it on Erin's waist to keep her from falling off. Erin smiled to herself; as she knew darn well, that this young boy was getting a cheap feel.

For Erin, this bicycle ride, besides being a rather unique way of getting somewhere for a mature woman, it brought back some very pleasant memories of a little boy, back in Canaryville, who she had a crush on and who used to ride her the same way, on his rusty old bike. His name was Michael 'Red' McGrath. She had a small tear in her eye, as she thought about such innocent times, in another world, a world of childish innocence and delight. *'The thrill of sneaking a ride on the back of a horse drawn ice wagon, as it meandered down a dirt alley, while sucking on small cold pieces and shavings of ice, on a very hot day, which resulted from the iceman's pick. All this, while trying not to get wooden splinters in your mouth, along with the ice; splinters that came from the wooden planks, on the bed of the ice wagon, nipped off, by the iceman's pick. The iceman used his pick, to pry apart, the twenty-five, fifty and one hundred pound blocks of ice, which he would then heave up on his huge, leather protected shoulder, with his ice tongs. He then had to walk up, one, two, three and sometimes even four floors, on rickety old wooden stairs, which led to the iceboxes, that either sat out on the back porches, or else were crammed into a very small kitchen, in these Irish-ghetto tenements, on a hot summer's day'.*

And oh yes, *'the picking of hot tar from the street, which had been recently poured into some cracks in the street to seal them, was always a pleasant treat and a time for relaxing, while you talked with your little friends, about who knew what, while chewing on your pieces of hot tar'.*

You could chew on this hot tar for hours, as no one could afford regular gum, when she was a little girl. It sort of tasted like licorice, but she thought, it was difficult to get out of your teeth, as it was sort of gummy and chewy, as it stuck to your teeth.

As the little boy's bike jostled her, from the bumps he rode over and around, and the deep ruts in the clay road, it seem to jar her memory even more, back to a better time, even though for a little girl, growing up in such a dysfunctional family, it didn't seem so good at the time

Her mind raced back to the games that she and her little friends played. Let's see she thought; there was *'Kick the Can', 'Run Sheep Run', 'Relevio', 'Olié Olié, Ocean free', 'Stick Ball'* and even baseball, which the boys sometimes would let her play, if they were short a player or two, or when they played, *'Piggy Move-Up'.*

Although she could never figure out why the boys argued so much, when they were playing baseball, as she figured that no matter how long the game was, the arguments consumed, at least seventy percent of the time. Sometimes these arguments led to fist fights. She liked to be asked to play baseball, with the boys, as she was very much attracted to them, and she always watched them, when they played.

These little boys, with their knickers, buckled at the knee, and with their socks with many holes, falling down around their ankles and ending up disappearing in their shoes, which caused them to limp some. Some of their shoes had sharkskin tips on them, which made them ideal for kicking stones and cans. Such shoes, made all the difference in kicking a stone further than those kids, who didn't have sharkskin shoes and that was a fact.

Their little suit coats, remnants from a five-dollar suit, purchased at Goldblatt Bros. Department Store, on south State Street, whose pants were long since worn out, or sweaters, all with their elbows worn through. And, oh yes, their peaked wool caps, pulled down on one side of their heads, to give them a sort of rakish look, a look, that little girls, found so cute and which made them giggle so. Most had dirty faces and to her, it just seemed like boys, didn't care much for soap and water and they all smoked cigarettes, as she guessed, that smoking to them, was a sign of manhood or something?

Erin thought she heard someone say; 'here it is ma'am, the Shamrock Club." Erin was kind of rudely awakened from her mental sojourn, as she traveled down her nostalgic-memory lane and she kind of resented the interruption. Erin looked at the place; and she thought to her self, *'this is nothing but a glorified roadhouse, should I or shouldn't I, bother to inquire about a job here'. After all, she thought, after performing at the Bombay Club, this place looks like something; you might expect to see, on West Madison Street, a high class flop house, where most of the bums resided, in Chicago'.*—Well she thought,' *I'm here and I do need a job badly, so what have I got to lose by inquiring'.*

Erin hopped off of the bicycle and after straightening her skirt and her hat, she said to the young boy, "What's your name young man?" The young boy answered,

"Me' name is Matt, Matthew Dugan, mum'." Erin said,

"Matt, will you wait for me, as I might not be very long in here and as I have no way of getting back to the train station, I'd be obliged to you, if you would wait for me, and for your trouble, here's another nickel." Matt had a big smile on his face as he said,

"Yes mum?." Erin who had a curious look on her face, as she asked Matt, "Matt does your parents live here in Niles and are you from Ireland, as I detected that, in the manner by which you speak?" Matt answered,

"Well mum', me' mither' lives here with me' self, as me' father died on the crossing, he had some kind of a fever and he was buried at sea." Erin then said,

"I'm so sorry to hear that, do you go to school, Matt?" Matt looked at Erin with sort of a suspicious eye as he said,

"No mum', I don't go to school, as I try and help me' mither', who has to take in washing and she does ironing also, to help her pay for the small flat we live in, she and I, that is." Erin had a tear in her eye, as she could envision from her days growing up in Canaryville, with her drunken father, just how Matt, and his mother must be getting along. 'Tis' sad', she said to her self, 'oh so sad'.

Erin walked over to what looked like the front door and she opened it and walked into a smoke filled bar, with what appeared like a small dance floor, adjoining the barroom itself. Seated on several bar stools, were what she supposed, were the regulars, men who couldn't find work and who lived more or less, doing odd jobs and who were on the dole. Most were probably living with their mothers, as no one would hire them. Erin knew full well the shameful bigotry of the w.a.s.p.'s, which had controlled many of the jobs in the city of Chicago, although she knew, that situation was rapidly changing, with the large amount of Irish immigrants moving in both from the East coast and from Ireland itself. However, there were still certain neighborhoods in Chicago, where these small-minded bigoted men, were still in power.

As Erin's eyes adjusted to the smoke and the semi-darkness of the interior, she spotted a man behind the bar, and so she walked over to the bar, and before she could ask him, if he might know where Byrne 'Mugs' Rooney was, the bartender said to her,

"What's your pleasure young lady?" Erin said.

"I'd like a beer sir." The bartender, who was probably in his late fifties, had gray hair, which was parted in the middle, in the style of the day and he had on a bright yellow-stripped shirt with fancy green garters, adorned with green shamrocks, on both of his upper arms. He had a large gray, handle bar moustache, which had what looked to Erin, like food stains on it. The bartender then said,

"We don't usually get single ladies in the bar area in the afternoon and so my dear, what brings you to the Shamrock Club?" Erin answered,

"I'm looking for a gentlemen by the name of Byrne 'Mugs' Rooney, and would you know where he might be?" The bartender gave Erin the once over and then he said, "And what would a pretty young thing like yer' self', be a wanting to see Mr. Rooney for?" Erin though to herself, *'I wonder what this guy's story is and why is he so nosy, she immediately thought of Enrico, although this guy was much older'?* So Erin said,

"I don't like to be rude sir, but what business is it of yours, as to why I'm looking for Mr. Rooney?" The bartender was somewhat taken aback by this young ladies brashness, as he said with a smile on his face,

"I'm 'Mugs' Rooney young lady and what can I be a do'n' for ye'?" Erin got red in the face as she said,

"I'm sorry sir, but I came here to inquire about a singing job as a friend of mine, thought that you might have an opening for a singer." 'Mugs' looked Erin over with a careful eye and as such, Erin was becoming a little bit nervous, as she thought, *'oh boy, what have we here, another Kit Kat Club'.* Mugs' then said,

"Well young lady, I really don't have an opening now, as I've got a singer and as ye' probably know, business is down, pretty much all over, with the depression and sech'." Erin had a look of disappointment on her face, as she said,

"Well sir, I thank you for giving me the time to talk with you anyhow." Erin was just about to leave when 'Mugs' said,

"Er', young lady, as long as you're here, why don't ye' sing a song fer' me, just in case, I might have an opening for a singer, at some later time." Erin looked around the room and then she asked, do you have a piano and a piano player, as she couldn't see any piano?" 'Mugs 'then hollered, hey 'Murph', the young lady would like to sing a song and she needs a piano player."

Out of the shadows and sitting at a corner table alone, was a man, who Erin figured, to be in his late sixties or early seventies. He was playing solitaire. He had a derby hat on, cocked to one side and he too, had fancy green garters wrapped around his upper arms, adorned with green shamrocks. He was sporting a polka dotted green and white, bow tie, plus he wore wire-rimmed spectacles and he had on, candy-stripped white suspenders. He was smoking a cigarette, whose ash was just about to fall on the floor, when he said to Erin,

"Follow me doll, as he led Erin up on to a raised platform, and in front of, what to Erin, looked like a small dance floor. Sitting in the corner, was a small black ebony, upright piano. 'Murph' turned on an overhead light, and then he said,

"What's your pleasure doll." Erin looked at the man and she said,

"What do you mean, what's my pleasure?" the piano player then said,

"What song do you want to sing doll?"

"Oh", said Erin, "do you know, '*Some of these Days*'?" The piano player said, "I sure do." Erin then asked him,

"Don't you use sheet music to play from?" The piano player who was missing his two front teeth, said,

"Naw', sheet music only gets in my way. If you can hum it, I can play it." As he started to laugh hysterically, as Erin said,

"I'm ready when you are." The piano player amazed Erin, as his fingers, seemed to glide so effortlessly across the keyboard, as he began playing the introduction. Erin started her now famous torch song, and as she sang, the regulars seated at the bar, all awakened from their individual thoughts and drunken stupors, as her vocal embellishments with her stylized singing, became the focus of their attention. Even 'Mugs' was taken with her, as Erin without thinking, moved her sensuous body in time with the music. Fact is, 'Mugs' had never in his entire life, ever heard such a beautiful rendition of this famous torch song. When Erin finished, the small crowd in the bar clapped their hands and stomped their feet.

Erin with a sly smile on her face and a twinkle in her eye, made a slight bow to the small bar crowd. She thanked the piano player and was about to leave the small stage, when 'Mugs' walked over to where she was standing and he said, "Young lady, before ye' go, do ye' know any Irish songs or ballads, as the crowd that drinks in here, is primarily Irish?" Erin thought for a second and with a large smile on her face, she said,

"And why wouldn't Erin O'Hara, know a few Irish tunes, that she could be a singing?" With that, she whispered something to the piano player and he with a big smile on his face, began playing, 'I'll Take You Home Again Kathleen.' Well, the crowd went bananas, as Erin brought the roof down. In addition, if that wasn't enough; she was asked to sing four more, beautiful Irish ballads; two love songs and two laments. Even 'Mugs" with tears in his eyes, couldn't restrain himself, as he said to Erin,

"Where'd' ye' come from' darl'n', from some dream, why I've never heard sech' singing in me' entire life.?" Erin of course was beaming; she loved the attention that her club crowds gave her, I suppose in away, it satisfied her yearning, for some recognition, which she never got from her drunken father and that is the one thing, that most girls crave from their fathers', aside from of course, a father's love. "Mugs' then said to Erin, "Would ye' be a hav'n' sometime, to let me hear a bit more about yer' self?" Erin looked at her watch and then she said,

"I would, but I've got my chauffeur waiting for me outside and I should tell him that I'll be a bit longer, so that he doesn't leave." 'Mugs' looked kind of shocked, when Erin said that she had a chauffeur waiting outside for her. He then said,

"What do ye' mean by a chauffeur, darl'n'?" Erin said,

"Perhaps you know him Mr. Rooney, his name is Matt and he drives a bicycle." 'Mugs' almost split a gut laughing, when she mentioned little Matt Dugan to him. Erin got up, and she walked to the door, Matt was still standing outside the door, and she said to him,

"Matt, here's another nickel, would you mind waiting a little longer as I've got some more business to attend to with Mr. Rooney." Matt said.

"No mum' it's fine with me, take your time, as I've got nothing else to do."

CHAPTER 28

❁

Clarence Duncan
-Extortion & Blackmail-

Sure enough, Jimmy received his anticipated telegram stating that Miss de Muier and the Clarence Duncan law firm, was dropping their law suit, due to some extenuating circumstances.

However, it was sometime later in the week, when Mr. Perkins received a certified letter addressed to him from Mr. Duncan, who was acting as the intermediary, although it was really meant for Mr. Pickering. The letter advised Mr. Pickering, that if Mr. Pickering didn't put fifty thousand dollars in small bills, in a cardboard shoebox, and send the box to a P.O. Box address, on South La Salle Street in Chicago. Mr. Duncan would have no choice, but to leak certain unpleasant and very tawdry information to the press, concerning Mr. Pickering's nephew, Mr. Perkins. The extortion letter from Mr. Duncan, put a deadline of one week from receipt of the certified letter, that he must have the money in his hands, or he would leak this information to the press.

Jimmy had taken the telegram he had gotten from Mr. Duncan, to Mr. Wallace's office. After Mr. Wallace had received the certified letter and they both of course, had already read the telegram and now the letter, Mr. Wallace then said,

"I'll call Mr. Pickering, to find out if he can see us right away." Mr. Wallace telephoned Mr. Pickering and he was told to come right over. The trio walked over to the Sunshine building, where the offices of, Hayes, Pickering & Haffendorf Enterprises Ltd. were located.

It took the trio just about twenty minutes to reach the building, where Mr. Pickering had his office, along with the offices of his other two partners.

Mr. Wallace opened the outer door to Mr. Pickering's office and a young blonde receptionist said, "May I help you?" Mr. Wallace then said,

"We have an appointment with Mr. Pickering and he is expecting us." The receptionist using her inter-com. said,

"Mr. Pickering sir, Mr. Wallace is here to see you, with two other gentlemen." They all heard Mr. Pickering's voice, on the inter-com.

"Send them in." Mr. Wallace was the first to enter. He shook Mr. Pickering's hand, and he then introduced Jimmy and Bill to Mr. Pickering. Mr. Pickering then said, after shaking their hands,

"Please have a chair, gentlemen." Before Mr. Wallace could say anything, Mr. Pickering said,

Mr. O'Brien, I would like to thank you on behalf of my company, for your fine investigative detective work, in finding out the facts concerning my nephew in our and his favor. You have no idea what this has meant to myself personally, to Mr. Perkins, and to the other owners of our company."

Jimmy said, "It was all in a day's work sir, if you don't mind that trite statement." Mr. Pickering then said,

"Never the less Mr. O'Brien, your work for our company has not gone unnoticed by my partners and myself, and we feel, that if you would find it to be in your best interests, we would like to retain you so to speak, as our corporate legal representative." Jimmy was kind of taken back by Mr. Pickering's offer and he just sat there for a full minute, trying to digest what he just heard. Finally, Jimmy said,

"Mr. Pickering sir, I believe that we could come to some mutual and acceptable agreement, after I sort of catch my breath." Mr. Pickering smiled. Mr. Wallace then spoke,"

"As you know Mr. Pickering, it was Mr. O'Brien's feeling, in the summation paper he wrote for the company, that even if we won so to speak, the case regarding Mr. Perkins, we might get a blackmail letter from Mr. Duncan. Well, I've just received such a letter, advising us, that if we didn't pay him his hush money, Mr. Duncan would leak some tawdry and damaging information about Mr. Perkins, which would surely have an unfavorable impact on the corporation, even though its not true." Mr. Pickering had a sort of a scowl on his face when he said,

"But, didn't we win this case?" He went on, "Do you mean to tell me that now, we must pay an undisclosed amount of money to this greedy lawyer, or be subjected to an extortion and a blackmail threat, in order to keep Mr. Perkins's unproven affair and the pregnancy resulting from his alleged affair, from the newspapers?" Mr. Wallace then said,

"I'm afraid I do, Mr. Pickering, sir." "But," He continued, "Mr. O'Brien besides alerting us to this possibility, is advising you and the company, not to give in to this blackmailer and he further advises you, to seek help from the F.B.I." Mr. Pickering looked worried as he said,

"Why not pay him what he wants, and rid ourselves of him and the threat of blackmail?" Mr. Wallace then said,

Mr. O'Brien, I think that it is time for you to speak to Mr. Pickering, about what will take place, if and when, Mr. Pickering accedes to this blackmailer and sends him hush money." Jimmy cleared his throat as he said,

"I understand your not wanting to involve the F.B.I. in this matter, but believe me, once you send Mr. Duncan this so called hush money, that will only be the down payment, as he will continually hit you and the company up, for thousands, and thousands of dollars on a never ending basis." Mr. Pickering slumped in his chair with a look of pessimism on his face. Jimmy continued,

"As I told Mr. Wallace, with the government involved, they will trace the money you send, in marked bills to Mr. Duncan, and to where ever it leads them, and they will not reveal your name, Mr. Perkins's name, or the companies name. Further, what Mr. Duncan has already done by sending you that certified letter, is to violate the federal law, in using the mails for, threats, intimation and blackmail. That is considered as I said, by the government, as a violation of federal law and of course, is punishable with a fine and imprisonment." He went on, "One thing that is bothering me though, about this whole sordid mess, is that I'm sure, that Mr. Duncan being a lawyer and a very good one, surely must realize this and so, why is he acting this way?"

Finally, Mr. Pickering, with trepidations, said to Jimmy, "Mr. O'Brien, will you ask the F.B.I. to visit us tomorrow?"

CHAPTER 29

Cards on the Table
-Erin & 'Mugs'-

Matt sat on the stoop, while he threw pebbles, into the many mud puddles, surrounding the Shamrock Club, and dreamed of being a baseball player in the big leagues and hopefully, with the Chicago Cubs, while he waited for Erin. "Mugs' escorted Erin to his office which was behind the bar. He offered Erin a chair, while he began his little speech.

"Erin, er' may I call you Erin?"

Erin said, "Why sure, as that's my name." Mugs' seemed to stop what was going to be a well-rehearsed speech, as he realized that he was looking at a possible gold mine, and he was a little bit nervous, but first he thought, he had best find out some more, about this Irish beauty and so he said,

"Erin, you had mentioned to me about your childhood, growing up in Canaryville, etc., but I would like you to give me some more details, about your professional career." Erin was undecided as to where she would begin, so she hesitated for a moment, and then she said,

"Well sir, it all began when I ran away from St. Agnes orphanage, out in Lemont, Illinois. I hitched a ride into Chicago and the driver left me off on South Michigan Avenue. I happened to walk by a club, called the Kit Kat Club, and it had a sign in the window advertising for a singer." Mugs then interrupted Erin when he said,

"Erin, please call me 'Mugs'." Erin said,

"Yes sir, Mr. 'Mugs.'" 'Mugs' laughed at Erin's use of 'Mr.' in front of his name, but he didn't say anything more about it. Erin continued,

"Well, I auditioned for a Mr. Tony La Rocco, who owns the club, and after I sang that torch song, *'Some of These Days'*, he evidently liked my singing, as he hired me. I had no idea at the time, what I was getting into, or perhaps a better term would be 'involved', with the Kit Kat Club." She went on, "Mr. La Rocco had a son Enrico who evidently was attracted to me, and I must confess, the feeling was mutual, so I guess you could call us, more than just friends, as we ended up lovers."

Erin felt little embarrassment in telling 'Mugs' about her sordid life, though by now, she had become sort of numb to it. Her life in her own mind was certainly not over, but she felt, that she had lived several lives for what she had been through. For a rather naive young girl, she certainly had gained some street smarts, but Erin would be the first to admit, that once she fell in love, her street smarts went out the window, as when you heart takes over, your mind, sort of shuts down. She continued,

"Being totally naive when it comes to drugs of any kind, Enrico introduced me to cocaine at several parties he had held. It was talked of, as a sort of party drug, harmless they said. Then he would leave some on my nightstand, as sort of a pacifier and seducer, in case my craving became so over powering, that I had to have a fix during the night. I would join Enrico when he snorted cocaine in the early morning hours, after I finished my gig at the Kit Kat Club. Enrico would eventually withhold this rapturous drug from me, thus forcing me to do anything he wanted, until I could get my fix. At the time, I had no idea what these Italian/Sicilian gangsters, were like. I became hooked on this drug and I then became his whore and paramour. He would lend me out so to speak, to any of his favorite gangster associates, for their animalistic pleasures." She went on, "Now I'm not saying for one minute, that all people of Italian and Sicilian decent, are animals or gangsters, I am not, as some of my closest friends that I grew up with, are Italian and Sicilian." She continued,

"Finally one evening, the mayor, 'Big' Bill Thompson and Al Capish showed up at the club and I sang an Italian love song, and I more or less innocently, dedicated it to Al Capish. Well, the next thing I knew, I had unwittingly, become his mistress or whore, if you want to get down and dirty, without offering me any say so in the matter."

Erin was telling 'Mugs' her most private an intimate happenings, that she normally wouldn't have told anyone, not even her own mother, had her mother, been alive. However, perhaps in her own mind, in a psychological way,

'Mugs' somehow represented the parish priest and deep down, she felt she had to sort of confess to someone, even though she knew that 'Mugs' certainly was not a priest and she hadn't made her confession to a Catholic Priest, since she was eleven years old. She was sort of cleansing her soul as it were. She went on,

"Al Capish without a doubt, is the most barbaric sadistic and sexual animal, that I have ever known, or ever have had the misfortune to know. After many, many sexual trysts with Al Capish and some of his Capos, from other large cities and his cadre of whores and perverts; I knew right then and there, that if I were ever to have, at least a semi-normal life, I would somehow, have to break both my drug habit, and the invisible chains, that were binding me to Al Capish. He treated me and his other whores, as nothing more than pieces of meat.

I also knew, that no one walks away from Al Capish, unless they're willing to risk being tortured, murdered, or forcibly, injected with heroin, until you wouldn't know if you were alive or dead, and probably could care less." She continued,

"Such animalistic perversions, you wouldn't believe. Well anyhow, I found out how I might be able to try and sever my relations with Al Capish and it worked, or at least, I believed that it I did." 'Mugs' interrupted Erin's confession of sorts, as he said to Erin,

"How in the hell did you ever sever relations with Al Capish?" Erin looked at 'Mugs' with a sort of a passive expression, on her pretty face as she said,

"Mugs' that is my secret, and I'll take it to my grave." Erin went on, "Anyhow, Al Capish threw me out of his bedroom and I went home to my hotel room." Erin then said, "Oh, I'm getting ahead of myself, Enrico and his Irish friend Pat, Pat Monahan, were making plans to open up the most beautiful gentlemen's club in America. I'm sure you've heard of it, the Bombay Club." Mugs' nodded in the affirmative. She continued,

"I was not only the featured singer at the Bombay Club, but I also served as the Madam of the club. I'll have to tell you, it was probably the most beautiful building I have ever seen in my life, if you can call a glorified whorehouse such; it looked a lot like a museum. Its yearly membership fee was ten thousand dollars and it catered only, to the wealthiest of gentlemen, throughout the United States and the world; from United States Senators, Congressman, European royalty, extremely wealthy American industrialists, politicians of both stripes, wealthy playboys and yes, even wealthy Lesbian women. They had special rooms for them." She continued,

"For any gentlemen who wished to visit with me, shall we say, he would have to pay me personally, one thousand dollars for one-half hour's worth of pleasure." Mug's' mind was starting to wander, as he could visualized what Erin looked like in bed, nude. Even at "Mugs' age, he still could get excited about such an adorable creature. He was getting turned on, just thinking about her, but he soon realized that he would have to put such thoughts out of his mind, at least he felt, for the immediate future. He thought further; *God must have been a magnificent designer, when he created woman'*. Erin continued,

"My job at the Bombay Club was short lived, as I guess, that Al Capish who was the silent partner in this business venture, got word to Enrico, to dump me as the Madam, thinking I guess, that this dumb Irish 'Mick', would still stay on as the featured singer; it was kind of a Sicilian vendetta. Well, was he ever wrong, I gave my letter of resignation to Enrico, when he broke the news to me, that he was replacing me, with some voluptuous blonde and I walked out the door. So 'Mugs', that is just about the jest of my story." "Mugs" who was listening to Erin's strange story in rapt silence, with a tear in his eye, said,

"How did you kick your cocaine habit, I mean, few people that I know of, can?" Erin thought about 'Mugs' question for a few moments, and then she said,

"With powdered sugar!" 'Mugs' facial expression went from sympathy, to incredulity. "Let me explain 'Mugs; both Cocaine and powdered sugar are sweet, but powdered sugar's more so than cocaine, as cocaine has more of a bittersweet taste to it. And so, I was fortunate enough to have run into a chorus girl, who had kicked the habit herself and so she passed on to me, some of her ways, to trick the mind into believing that what I was snorting, was cocaine, not powdered sugar. Besides, the powdered sugar acts if you will, like a placebo, as the mind must try and convince itself, or fool itself, into believing, that the powdered sugar, is cocaine." She went on,

"I know what I've just told you is hard to believe and I would agree with you, that it is, but believe me, it worked, at least for myself. Now I would have to be honest and tell you that ninety eight percent of those who try this seemingly foolish trick fail. That is, either their craving for the drug is so intense, that they won't let go of it; as its kind of like one lover, who refuses to give up on her or his lover, and won't admit that their lover has left them." She continued, "The soothing caress of these drugs is so reassuring, so warm and comforting, that it's like a child with his or her security blanket." Erin continued,

"However, the real test comes when a person tries to quit and then the withdrawal symptoms take over. The shakes, the drooling, the vomiting and the hallucinating, the deep dark mysterious, and scary dreams, which seem to take, hold of you. Believe me 'Mugs', it is at this point that most druggies, go back to their friend, their security blanket, their drugs, their paramour." She went on,

"Of course will power is really the key to success in this battle of mind over matter." Erin's mind then seemed to drift off for a few moments, while old 'Mugs', was trying to digest what Erin had just told him, he thought; *'this beautiful creature, this creation of God, so adored and yet so abused by man'.*

"You know Erin, I'm a bit concerned for your safety, because of your dangerous encounter with Al Capish, as I happen to know just how Al operates first hand." He went on, "Even though you believe that he was behind the decision, to remove you as the Madam of the Bombay Club, and I believe that he was, I don't believe that he is through, trying to make you pay, for you're leaving the Bombay Club." He went on,

"I don't know if you know it or not, but since you left the Bombay Club, the customer base has dropped off considerably. While its true, that you're leaving, coupled with the stock market crash, has had a disastrous effect on the club itself and so, I don't know who had the greater effect on the club's business down turn, you, or the stock market, but it really doesn't matter. Al can't do anything about the stock market crash, but he never forgives nor forgets, people who he believes in some way, crossed him and as you said, vendetta is the choice Sicilian word." He went on,

"Al believes in total control of everyone who comes under his purview, his web of corruption; he is power and money hungry. He corrupts, he seduces and above all, he seeks revenge on any and all, who would cross him or try to leave his *'la famiglia'* or family." 'Mug's thought for a minute and then he asked Erin,

"Where are you staying?" Erin answered,

"I'm staying at the La Salle Hotel, in downtown Chicago, as I thought that if I couldn't get a singing job with you, I wouldn't be too far, from other opportunities, in and around the Chicago 'loop'." 'Mugs' had a look of concern on his face and then he said,

"There is something I haven't told you yet and that is this; the Shamrock Club is a roadhouse, but not just any roadhouse, by that I mean, its main purpose is, well, its a Bordello, if you know what I mean. Meaning that we have a large number of prostitutes working here, from five p.m. to the wee hours of the morning." He continued,

"There is another larger building, attached to the bar and dance area, which is where the prostitutes conduct their business. The Madam who runs this part of the Shamrock Club's, sexual entertainment, is an old broad by the name of

Molly, Molly O'Shaunessy. Molly is a real character with a heart of gold. She at one time, back in the early twenties, was a featured headliner at New York's most famous supper club, the Trocadero." He went on,

"She danced under the name of, Mademoiselle Louise and from what I understand, she was Maurice Chevalier's lover." and a few other Hollywood and New York society big shots, including the mayor." He went on, "If I were you, I would vacate the La Salle Hotel a.s.a.p." and take your personal belongings out here to Niles, and find a room at one of the local tourist homes, as there are no hotels out here in Niles." Erin then said,

"But 'Mugs', why would I do that, I don't have a job out here in the Shamrock Club, as you said, you already have a singer?" "Mugs looked at Erin, as he said,

"Are you kidd'n', after listening to you sing, I'm quite sure that my boss would agree, that you are just what the Shamrock Club needs, not some over the hill fat mama-torch singer, whose drunk most of the time." Mugs' then said, "When can you start?" Erin thought for minute and then she said,

"But 'Mugs', we've not discussed salary and benefits yet." 'Mugs' then said,

"Well I don't think that I could pay you what you were probably making at the Bombay Club, but I can come pretty damn close. And I'll tell you something else, based on the up swing in customers coming out to see (should there be), and to hear you sing, over and above a certain amount, I'll give you a percentage of what ever we take in." Erin thought over 'Mug's offer and then she said,

"You know 'Mugs', you spoke about having a boss, but don't you own the Shamrock Club. 'Mugs' thought for a minute, about how best to answer Erin's question, and then he finally said,

"Well I do, but I have a sort of partner or partners actually, and they head-up an organization, that might be called the Mafia, not the Sicilian Mafia mind you, but the Irish Mafia." He went on, "This organization offers me protection from the likes of Al Capish, who would have taken over my business years ago, but for the Irish Mafia."

He went on, "The Irish Mafia is run by two gentlemen, a Jew and an Irishman. The Jew's name is Myron 'Lips' Bernstein and the Irishman is, Cornelius 'Mick' McGrath. Myron is the 'brains' behind the operation and Cornelius is the muscle. Together, they have been able to hold off Al Capish and his mobsters, in their attempt to move in and take over the rackets, on the north side of Chicago and its northern suburbs." He continued,

"I grew up with Con McGrath—we both graduated from St. Vincent's grammar school, in that part of the North side, called 'Hell's Point', an Irish ghetto, much like the one you grew up in, on the Southside of Chicago, called Canaryville." Erin then said,

"Okay 'Mugs', you got yourself a deal, when do I start?" 'Mugs' thought a minute and then he said.

"How about tomorrow?" He went on, "Go back to the LaSalle Hotel and gather your personal things, and then leave the La Salle Hotel that same day and catch a train back to Niles, and I'll have a car waiting for you at the train station, here's my phone number for you to call me, when you're leaving." Erin then said.

"Fine 'Mugs'," as she shook his hand and, "Oh", said Erin, "and one more thing, I've no interest what so ever, in any connection with your Bordello, I've put that part of my past, behind me for good." She thought some more and then she said, "Someday, I hope to find a boy friend and who knows, maybe I'll even find myself a husband." Erin had a sort of a whimsical smile on her face, when she said, the word, husband. "Mugs' smiled at her, but he didn't comment.

CHAPTER 30

❀

The F.B.I.

-Agent Moore-

Jimmy, had phoned the F.B.I and after telling them what the problem was, citing blackmail and extortion, the F.B.I., assigned an agent to this case, a Francis Moore. Agent Moore walked over to the Sunshine building, the following morning. The Sunshine building, was only a half block walk, from the Cincinnati's offices, of the F.B.I. and he went directly to Mr. Pickering's office, where Mr. Wallace, Jimmy O'Brien, Bill John and Mr. Pickering, were waiting to hold their first meeting with agent Moore.

After reading the blackmail letter demanding fifty thousand dollars and the telegram, which notified Mr. Wallace of lawyer Duncan's, dropping the case against Mr. Perkins, agent Moore said,

"Gentlemen, what we've got here, as you already know, is a classic case of blackmail." He outlined for the group, exactly what would take place and how the money would be handled. He instructed Mr. Pickering to make out a check for fifty thousand dollars and he would then take the check to the United States Treasury Department, after clearing this action with his immediate supervisor. The U. S. Treasury would then issue fifty thousand dollars in small *'used'* bills, in tens and twenties, and all with secret markings on them, so that the government could more easily trace this money, to find out who is spending it, who was getting it, and for what reason. Mr. Moore then said,

"Mr. Pickering, I would like Mr. O'Brien and his partner, Mr. Bill John, to travel to Chicago and to await my instructions, as to what I would like them to do." He continued,

"I too, will travel to Chicago, after I contact the F.B.I.'s Chicago office and have some of their personnel assigned to this case, as probably, most of the action regarding the money, will take place in Chicago. Further, I want both Mr. O'Brien and Mr. Bill John, to make reservations at the La Salle hotel in downtown Chicago, as this is the hotel, where most of the time, the bureau's agents, stay at." He went on, "The fifth floor, is generally reserved for the entire year, by the United States government, although we don't use all of the rooms on the fifth floor and so, several of the remaining rooms are used by the traveling public." He went on,

"Now normally, I wouldn't reveal this information, that I'm about to tell you because of certain security reasons, but I feel that because I believe, that we are going to run up against one of the most formidable group of lawyers and who have, almost unlimited resources to fight us in court, I want you all to be prepared. I also, don't want what I say to you today, to leave this office; it is to be treated as top secret, is that clear?" They all nodded in the affirmative. He went on,

"A Lawyer by the name of Clarence Duncan, who sent you the blackmail letter, heads up a very large cadre of lawyers in Chicago, who represent Al Capish and which he retains them, on a yearly basis, for his many nefarious business dealings." He continued,

"So Mr. O'Brien, your former class mate and friend, at the University of Chicago, is up to his ass in Al Capish's rackets. His involvement in vice; prostitution, gambling and other such illegal ventures, certainly makes' him an accessory and that is why I believe that he had no choice in the matter of sending by U.S. mail, that blackmail letter, even though as you said, he should know better. I'm sure that Al Capish was ordering Mr. Duncan, to do, what he wanted him to do, and Mr. Duncan couldn't refuse, but regardless, Mr. Duncan is up to his ass, in legal trouble." He continued,

"We have been watching Mr. Duncan for the past several years and we're just waiting for the right moment, to arrest him and bring him before the United States Courts, for his many illegal activities, involving Al Capish and of course, his own personal culpability." Mr. Pickering then said,

"Now Mr. Moore, I'd like to remind you, that you gave your word in front of these gentlemen, that in no way, will I, or Mr. Perkins, nor our company, regarding this blackmail scheme, will become public knowledge, as none of us, could possible afford such notoriety or publicity, as such publicity could ruin the company." Mr. Moore than said,

"You have my word sir, and what will happen, is the government will seek an indictment of Mr. Duncan and his legal staff, before what is called a Petit Jury. If the jury finds sufficient evidence to support such an indictment, then the case will go to trial." Mr. Pickering then said,

What about Al Capish, won't he also, have to face charges?" Mr. Moore looked down at his shoes and then he said,

"I'm sorry to say, that he won't, as there is no proof that Al Capish had anything to do with you and your company being blackmailed. While I personally believe that Al Capish is guilty as sin, and is behind this blackmail scheme, but the government has no way of proving what I think."

CHAPTER 31

❀

The La Salle Hotel
-La Vendetta-

Jimmy and Bill John arrived at the La Salle Street train station, at just about six a.m. After having a donut and a cup of coffee, they hailed a cab and the cab driver asked, "Where to gents" Jimmy answered.

"The La Salle Hotel, driver." As their cab drove up to the front of the hotel and the doorman opened the door of their cab, they both got out, and there standing next to a newsstand in front of the hotel, was a beautiful young woman, a woman who looked very familiar to both Jimmy and Bill. She was sobbing and when she saw Jimmy and Bill, she tried to cover up her face with her hankie, blowing her nose and then she started to walk back into the hotel. She clutched a newspaper in her hand.

Both Jimmy and Bill, ran to the front door of the hotel, so they could open the door for her. Meanwhile both Jimmy and Bill were also, trying to rack their brains, as to where it was, they both saw this beautiful woman. Jimmy finally remembered where he and Bill saw her; it was at the Kit Kat Club over on South Michigan Avenue. Jimmy because of his appearance, didn't want to necessarily engage the young lady in unnecessary conversation, but when the lady paused, and looked like she might faint, as her face went from one that was peaches and cream, to one that was now turning white, he pulled a chair up, for her to sit in.

He took the newspaper she had tightly clutched in her hand from her, as he tried to fan her with it. It was obvious to Jimmy, that what ever she saw in the newspaper, caused her to cry, as her shoulders were still shaking and tears were running from her pretty eyes. Jimmy said to Erin,

"I'm sorry Miss, for whatever you saw in the newspaper that made you cry, but is there anything that my friend and I can do, to help ease your sorrow." He went on, "May we help you to your room?" Erin then said,

"You both are so kind, to offer to help me and I'm sorry for my feminine display of my emotions, but I just read an article about a body that someone found, washed up along the Desplaines River and the bodies face, was unrecognizable, as evidently, the face had been beaten so savagely, that it was no longer recognizable." Jimmy then asked,

"If it was so unrecognizable, how could you identify it from that newspaper article?" Erin who was just now bringing her emotions under control said,

"Well, sir, the article said that the body had a tattoo on its right shoulder, which read *'Mama Mia'* and under that expression, it had one word *Rosa*. My former boyfriend or lover had such a tattoo on his right shoulder and he was a Consigliere for Al Capish. His mother's name was Rosa, his father owns the Kit Kat Club, and the father's name is Tony La Rocco. Jimmy looked at Bill and sort of nodded his head. Jimmy then asked the young lady,

"Shouldn't you perhaps, tell the police of your being acquainted with this man and identify him?" Erin studied Jimmy for a moment and then she said,

"I don't know how to tell you this, but I cannot become involved in this murder. If I did go to the police, Al Capish would soon find out about it, and then he would send a couple of his guerrillas and I would be murdered, after first being tortured and worse, perhaps I might be brought to his office for his own brand of *La Vendetta*. *'Revenge'.*" She went on, "No thanks, I know Mr. Capish only too well." Jimmy who was holding her hand and trying to comfort her said,

"My friend and I awhile back, visited the Kit Kat Club and we saw you perform and let me say this to you Miss, we've never seen or listened to, such a performance in all of our lives; you were, oh what would I call your performance—er, you were simply magnificent."

Erin was smiling with her shy smile, as her beautiful face, was now returning to its normal color. Up close, her natural beauty stunned both Jimmy and Bill. Erin then said, "My name is Erin O'Hara and I would like to ask a favor of you two gallant gentlemen." Jimmy then asked,

"And what would that be Miss?"

"Would you both accompany me to my room, as I've suddenly become frightened by this news and for another reason, which I'll tell you about later on." Jimmy and Bill looked at one another and together they said,

"No problem miss, it would be our pleasure." In helping Erin to her feet, Erin had inadvertently, brushed Jimmy's hat, and it fell off the side of his face, revealing his hideous and grotesque facial disfigurement. Erin looked slightly stunned, as she took notice of Jimmy's face, but she neither said anything, nor did her facial expression change that much, which Jimmy sort of took note of. Erin smiled at Jimmy, as she squeezed his hand. Jimmy had quickly placed his hat back on his head, with it being pulled down, so it would cover the left side of his face.

In discussing this blackmail situation with agent Moore, it was agent Moore's idea for Jimmy, to buy himself a small handgun. Agent Moore knew from experience, that once it was known, that Jimmy O'Brien was the lawyer who was assisting the government, in its attempt to prosecute Clarence Duncan and his law firm, that his life could be in jeopardy. Therefore, both Jimmy and Bill, had purchased small, six shot colt, revolvers, before leaving Cincinnati. They also had purchased underarm holsters, which were small enough and positioned such, that they wouldn't be noticed, as there was no telltale bulge, underneath their suit coats.

Jimmy, Bill and Erin, walked to the first floor elevator and then Jimmy asked Erin, "What's your floor Miss?" Erin said,

"Why its five." On they're way up in the elevator, the elevator operator, a young lad, who couldn't be any older than sixteen, if he was that, seemed a little nervous and Jimmy first noticed his body language, as did Bill. Finally, as the elevator slowly reached the fifth floor and before the young lad opened the hand operated, door opening mechanism, he turned to Jimmy and he said,

"Are you gents government agents?" Jimmy laughed as he said,

"Why no we're not, why, did you think that we were?" The young boy thought for a minute as to how he would best answer Jimmy's question and finally, before he opened the elevator door, he said,

"Well sir, there are many government agents who stay at the La Salle Hotel, who rent rooms on the fifth floor. You two gents, reminded me some, of agents, however, the reason I mentioned it at all, is a short while ago, I took two rather gangster looking types, to the fifth floor. I thought that this was most unusual and when they got out of the elevator, they walked down the hall and they evidently had a key to room 508, which I know, is the room that this young lady is staying in and they entered." He continued,

"They both looked toward me, before they went into room 508, but I had momentarily stepped back into the elevator, so that they couldn't see me. However, with the mirrors we have attached to both sides of the door, to enable us to see if there could be hotel guests, who might be coming down the hall, to ride down in the elevator, I was able to see what they were doing without me being seen." Jimmy looked worried, as did Bill, whereas Erin was visibly shaken. They all got out of the elevator as Jimmy turned, and he shook the young elevator operator's hand as he said,

"Young man, what is your name?" The young man answered.

"Me' name is Tommy, Tommy Kearns sir." Jimmy laughed, as he could tell that this was another Irish lad, full of hope and promise, trying to make a living and chances are, he was supporting his mither', while his father, if he had one, was in some neighborhood saloon, drunk. Jimmy then said,

"We are truly grateful for your very sharp observations and your concern, which may save all of our lives, Tommy." Jimmy than said, "Oh, and before you go back down, do you know if anyone is staying in the adjoining room, which I guess is room 512?" The young boy thought for a minute and then he said,

"No sir, no one is in room 512, at least not yet, perhaps later on in the day though, someone might rent it." Jimmy then said,

"While my friend and myself, are not government agents per se, but we are connected with the government and so, would you ask the desk clerk for a key to room 512, as it is a matter of life and death. We'll wait here on the fifth floor in the broom closet, until you return." The young man whose eyes were now wide open said,

"Yes sir." As the young man sped down to the lobby, passing floors who had guests, impatiently waiting for his elevator, he stopped at the first floor and he raced over to the guest registration desk, where he whispered to his friend, Tony Newsome, "Tony, I need the key to room 512 pronto." Tony who was busy with a guest and so rather than question the elevator operator, as he normally would have, he handed the key to him and the elevator boy raced back to the elevator and he returned to the fifth floor.

The broom closet was rather small for three persons, and so, Erin, Jimmy and Bill, were kind of cramped. They all kind of faced each other, and Jimmy whom of course, already had, strong feelings toward Erin, smiled at her, as her perfume, seemed to overpower his senses. Just the smell from her freshly washed hair, was enough to tie his stomach in knots.

Erin studied Jimmy's face, that part of his face that she could see in the dimly lit broom closet, and she remarked to herself, *'What a pity for such a handsome young man, to have to endure this disfigurement, all of his life. Perhaps he was wounded in the war, she thought?'* Erin still held Jimmy's hand, as tightly as she could and didn't seem to want to let go of his hand. Jimmy of course, didn't mind, as just the touch of her, was enough to make him slightly giddy. He was falling in love and he didn't know it.

Bill John also took note of Erin's presence, even though with the rather stoic expression on his face, no one could tell just what he was thinking, as he never showed any emotion, what so ever. He thought to himself, *'No wonder a white man's brain, turns to mush, when in the presence of such a beautiful woman'.*

His mind raced back, to when he was quite young, back on the reservation, when he too, was in love with an Indian maiden; the chief's daughter. Her name was 'White Flower' and she too, had long jet-black hair, which she wore braided. His would be romance soon ended however, when the chief announced that his only daughter, would be betrothed to another brave from a neighboring tribe and so, with a sigh and with a broken heart, Bill John, felt that he should leave the reservation and enlist in the army, which he did.

He never forgot her though, as she was always in his heart and she always would be. After getting the key to room 512 from the elevator operator, Jimmy said,

"Here's my plan; I will enter room 512 and I will start pounding on either the wall separating the two rooms, or if there happens to be a connecting door, I'll pound on it." He went on, "My purpose in doing this, is to cause one of the gangsters, to leave room 508 and to walk next door to room 512, where he will pound on the door and while swearing, he'll tell me in no uncertain terms, to open the door. Just a soon as I do, he'll step into the room and I of course will have my gun trained on him. Meanwhile, you Bill, will open the door to room 508, which will be unlocked, but you won't make your move, until you see the one gangster enter room 512, so that he can't see you." He continued,

"After the action in room 512 has taken place, the gangster in room 508, thinking that his buddy is returning, won't pay that much attention to you and so you will have the drop on him with your gun drawn." Bill then asked,

"Okay Jimmy, we've now got both of these gangsters with their hands up, so what do we do with them?" He went on, "As you know, it will be something much like having a tiger by the tail. If we let them go, they'll turn on us, so, I suspect that your next move, will be to kill them." Jimmy smiled as he said to Erin,

"Erin, do you have any objections to Bill and myself, killing these two gangsters?" Erin said, as she continued to shudder,

"These are just two pieces of crap, that neither us, nor the world needs." She went on, "I'm quite sure that if you don't kill them, then they of course, will eventually murder the three of us, as Bill said." She went on, "No," she said, "These two, are nothing but psychopathic animals. I'm sure, that had you two, not crossed my path, and you might say, Devine Providence had been looking out for me; I might by now, either be dead, or, had been taken to Al Capish, for his sadistic methods of torture, which are always sex related, when it comes to his female conquests."

"Finally," Jimmy said, "Now my hope is, that they will try something stupid, like trying to pull their guns on us, as I would prefer that they do this, as it gives me less concern, in killing them, then if I have to kill them, in cold blood; execution style, so to speak. Also, Erin, I want you to remain in the broom closet out of sight and out of harms way, is that clear."

Jimmy's eyes seemed to pierce Erin's soul, as she responded to the commanding tone, of his strong words. Jimmy without thinking, leaned over and gave Erin a kiss on her dimpled cheek, as both he and Bill left the cramped broom closet. Erin had a slight smile on her face, as she thought about Jimmy's kiss, the nerve she thought, but she was only kidding, as she loved the attention that men gave her.

She now for the moment, seemed to drift off, as she thought about Jimmy. *'What was he really like; someone who had to suffer the ignorant stares of the public, who possibly had to hide from society, so as to avoid the constant stares and the pity'? 'Did he have a girl friend before his hideous injury and perhaps, still does?' 'Where did he grow up, what was he really like as a friend, or even as a lover, was he kind'?* She thought further, *'did he have a family, and did he have brothers or sisters?'* and then she thought; *'why am I so interested in this poor handicapped man?'* There was no question about it; Erin was interested in Jimmy, in spite of his hideous injury. Perhaps, it was Erin's own brutal childhood, that had taught her empathy and compassion, for the afflicted and the hurt they had to constantly suffer, and the forgiveness, as taught to her by the Sisters, or was it something else? She put her ear to the door of the broom closet to hear if she could, the sounds of gunfire and what they would mean for her safety.

CHAPTER 32

❀

Tit for Tat

-20's Justice-

Jimmy opened the door to room 512 very carefully, so as not to make any sound. He searched the room with his eyes, checking the bathroom and the closets. He saw that there was a connecting door to room 508, but it was locked. Therefore, he waited a few seconds more and then he began to pound on the connecting door with the butt of his revolver. Jimmy after a few minutes of pounding, placed a hand towel around the barrel of his pistol, just in case he had to fire his gun, the towel would muffle the noise of the shot. Jimmy nervously waited for one of the gangsters to begin knocking on room 512. A minute went by and finally, Jimmy heard a banging on his door and someone shouting at him in Italian, through the door,

"*Che è l'inferno tutta la racchetta, Goddamn esso, apre questa porta prima che lo calcio in e batte i suoi cervelli in, lei son-of-a-bitch.*" 'What the hell is all the racket, Goddamn it, open this door before I kick it in and beat your brains in, you son-of-a-bitch." Jimmy slowly opened the door to room 512 and as he did so, the gangster started to enter the room. Without saying another word, Jimmy fired his pistol at the man's head, with the bullet entering his forehead and exiting, the rear of his head. The gangster was dead before he hit the floor.

Jimmy quickly dragged the gangster into the bathroom, so that his head wound wouldn't bleed all over the rug. He then ran to the door and looking across the hall, he found splattered up against the wall, the back of the gangster's head. He quickly wiped up the surrounding blood and brains, and he walked back into his room and he flushed the piece of scalp down the toilet.

Meanwhile, Bill had heard Jimmy begin his pounding, as he waited for one of the gangsters, to leave room 508 and begin to pound on room 512. Before he left the broom closet and opened the door to room 508. Bill thought he heard a muffled shot coming from room 512, but with his own adrenalin pumping through his veins, he wasn't sure. Bill walked over to room 508 and he slowly opened the door.

"*Chi pesta l'inferno, perché lei non ha tagliato secondo la lunghezza la sua gola di goddamn Sal?*" 'Who the hell is pounding, why didn't you slit his Goddamn throat, Sal?' Because his partner Sal didn't answer, Luigi slowly turned and as he did, he was shocked by what he saw, as a man with a gun, was standing in the doorway looking at him. The man had a long braided ponytail and his dark face was filled with rage. Luigi, in sort of a foolish bravado move, reached for his gun, which was underneath his suit coat. As he did, Bill fired one shot, hitting Luigi right in the center of his forehead, killing him instantly. He dropped where he stood. Bill immediately dragged him into the bathroom, so that his head wound, wouldn't bleed on the room's carpet.

Erin, who heard the two muffled shots, couldn't stand not knowing what was going on, and so she carefully opened the door to the broom closet and she peeked out. Not seeing anyone at first, she didn't know whether or not, to look in both rooms, '*supposing she thought, that the gangsters had killed both Jimmy and Bill?*' She then quietly closed the door to her hideaway, remembering the stern warning from Jimmy, about not leaving the broom closet and so, she would have to await her fate so to speak. Her shaking had returned and she was weeping, as she was now totally traumatized, by the series of events, leading up to today's encounter with two of Al Capish's guerillas and her recent escape from Al's filthy clutches. All of this seemed to her, like a bad dream.

She thought she heard a strange noise, like someone was prying open a door, and the noise sounded close by. Then she could hear what sounded like something being dragged across the hall and then the dragging noises stopped. Jimmy and Bill had waited until the elevator in the elevator shaft, had gone on up, past the fifth floor, before they disposed of the two bodies, dumping them rather unceremoniously, down the elevator shaft, where their thuds, echoed up the elevator shaft.

Erin then saw the handle of the broom closet-door jiggle and then it opened and standing there with a smile on his face, was Jimmy. She sort of swooned, as she fell into Jimmy's outstretched arms, weeping. Jimmy held her tight in his arms, as she tried to pull herself together, as her nerves were frazzled and her adrenalin, which had been surging through her veins, was starting to subside. Jimmy could feel her rapid heart beat, as he held her ever so tight, in his arms. Her soft body, which Jimmy felt underneath her dress, was turning him on. Erin then said,

"Oh Jimmy, am I ever glad to see you and you too Bill." Bill's face also had a slight smile on it, as he stepped into full view. They both smelled of gunpowder. Erin then said,

"Tell me what happened, where are the two gangsters?" Jimmy then said,

"Well Erin, our two friends, lets say, had a hard fall." Erin wasn't satisfied with Jimmy's answer, so she looked at Bill, for further comment. Finally, Jimmy said,

"Well if you must know, we threw the bodies of the two gangster, down the elevator shaft and they probably won't be found, until a certain smell is detected by one or more of the hotel guests." Erin shuddered thinking about the fate of these two gangsters, who were here to kidnap her, to torture her, and to eventually murder her, after they satisfied Al Capish's sexual, La Vendetta.

Erin then said, "Let me gather up my clothes and personal items, and put them in my suitcase, as I had planned on checking out today anyway."

Jimmy and Bill made a through search of Erin's room, to make sure that none of her items were left, as Erin may have over looked some, and also, to check to see, if either of the two gangsters had left any of their personal items lying around the room.

They waited for the elevator, which was operated by Tommy Kearns. Finally, it seemed like five minutes, before Tommy's elevator finally reached the fifth floor, Tommy opened the door, and he greeted them with a big smile. Jimmy gave him back, the key to room 512 and he said to Tommy,

"Thanks so much Tommy, as you probably saved our lives" Tommy looked down at his shoes, as he slyly smiled and then he said,

"No problem sir, I felt that you folks needed the key to room 512 for a good reason and I was just glad that I could oblige." Jimmy then said,

"Tommy I would appreciate it very much if you didn't remember anything that happened here this morning, is that okay with you, as Jimmy slipped a five dollar bill in Tommy's hand?" Tommy said,

"I don't know a thing sir." Jimmy then asked Erin,

"Erin you said that you were checking-out today, do you mind me asking, where you're going?" Erin thought for a minute and then she said,

"I've been offered a singing job in another night club, up in Niles, Illinois and before I get on the train to go to Niles, I'm supposed to call the owner of the club, and he will have a car waiting to pick me up at the train station in Niles." She went on, "There are no taxi's running in Niles and no other means of transportation either, other than a little boy with his bike."

Jimmy looked somewhat hurt and a little embarrassed, as he didn't know how to tell Erin, that he would like very much, to get to know her better and so he kind of stammered, as he said, "Neither Bill nor myself have made reservations at the La Salle Hotel as yet. And we were wondering, if because of todays'events and from what you've told us, there seems to be a long standing problem with Al Capish and you, is that correct?" Erin answered,

"That is correct."

"So perhaps you wouldn't mind if we traveled with you to Niles and made sure, that you get settled properly at some tourist home, as I would imagine, that those are the only kind of lodgings, one would find in these small towns outside of Chicago?" He continued, "Now we don't want to appear foreword, nor do we wish to intrude on you private life, but we think, that you might feel safer with us along?"

Bill kind of smiled to himself, as he took notice of Jimmy's referring to us, rather then himself, as Bill knew from Jimmy's comments and with his facial expression that he was acting like a lovesick schoolboy. Although Bill felt that there could be nothing better, then if Jimmy, could find someone to share his life, someone he could love and who would love him unconditionally, in return. Bill admired Jimmy and they had formed a close bond, ever since the war.

Erin didn't quite know what to say to Jimmy. She was pleased that he had offered to accompany her to Niles, Illinois, especially since the events of today and those of the past, still seemed to haunt her. Finally, Erin said,

"Well Jimmy and Bill, I actually have been trying to think of a way, that I might ask you both, for your protection and I thought that I might be asking too much of you, I mean, after all, you probably saved my life today, and to have to drag you all the way up to Niles. Illinois, I just thought, that would be asking a little too much." Jimmy had a smile across his face and finally he said,

"Erin, it would be our privilege, to accompany you to Niles, Illinois." Erin squeezed Jimmy's hand, as they hailed a cab. After they got into the cab, all three, sat next to one another and once again, Jimmy felt the warmth of Erin's beautiful and sensual body, next to his. They're did seem to be a sort of chemistry, between Erin and Jimmy, although Jimmy, because of his facial disfigurement, felt that perhaps, Erin was just being compassionate towards him and he was miss-reading, her feminine signals, of what she felt towards him, or else he was just wishful thinking.

After all, he thought, why would a most beautiful woman, fact is, the most beautiful woman, I ever saw in my life, have any feelings toward me romantically, other than pity of course? He tried to divert his mind to other thoughts, so that he could protect his own mental state, from self-pity, as he knew, that once he entered that dark mental state of hurt once again, his emotions would take over, and then feeling sorry for himself, would soon take over.

Jimmy had an intellectual mind and he was a very smart lawyer, and he understood, how the mind processes its self-pity and where it would lead. One of the strengths he felt, that this wound of his, gave him, was the ability to rationalize his physical disability and to learn from it. He also knew, that self-pity, leads to self-destruction, a road he wanted to stay off of, at all costs.

Jimmy was not a very religious person, but he believed in God and he also felt, that there was such a thing as Devine Providence, and as such, that God works in mysterious ways. He felt that while he was dealt a devastating blow from a physical standpoint, that God would offer him another way, to cope with his problem. After sitting in the cab for a couple of minutes, the cab driver finally said,

"If it isn't too much to ask, would someone tell me, where you want to go, or would you rather sit in my cab and play footsies, with the young lady?" Erin laughed, as she said,

"The La Salle Street station driver." All three looked at one another and they all broke out in a fit of laughter.

CHAPTER 33

❀

Settling In

-Erin's Security-

After the newly made friends got off the train, a car was waiting to take them to the Shamrock Club. Before the driver started to drive them to the club, Erin said to the driver, "Driver, before we go to the club, would you mind if I got myself a room, in one of the local tourist homes, as I would like to get settled and put my suitcase somewhere?" The driver replied,

"No miss, I don't mind at all, where would you like to go." Erin replied,

"Well sir, as I don't know where there are any tourist homes here in Niles, as I'm new here, so I thought that you might be able to pick one out for me." The driver thought for a minute and then he said,

"My mother has a tourist home, just about two blocks from the club and she also fixes meals, should you like to eat in." Erin said,

"Sounds fine with me, driver, lets go see your mother's place." The driver then drove over to his mother's tourist home. The vacancy sign planted in the front lawn read;-'**Mrs. Mary O'Sullivan's, Comfortable Rooms; rented by the day, the week, or the month and meals can be included, at a nominal cost**'-. When they arrived out front of Mrs. O'Sullivan's tourist home, all three got out of her son's car and they walked up to the front porch, where a woman stood, with her hands on her hips. Erin was the first to speak as she said,

"Good morning ma'am, I'm looking for a room to rent and I'd like to rent it by the month, if you have a vacancy?" Mary O'Sullivan gave all three persons the once over as she said,

"What about these two gents?" Erin was about to answer her question, when Jimmy then spoke up,

"Do you have another vacancy?" Erin looked at Jimmy with a surprised look,

"Why yes I do, but they're not adjoining." Jimmy then said,

"Fine, we'll also take that other room too, if it's okay with you?" Mrs. O'Sullivan looked kind of curious, not shocked, as nothing shocked her anymore, having been an ex-chorus girl, most of her young life. Erin then asked,

"I don't understand Jimmy, why the extra room?" Jimmy then explained his reason, for wanting to rent an extra room.

"Erin, because of what seems like an on going problem with some of your past acquaintances, I feel kind of obligated to have Bill stay in that room at least and until, I feel that your safety is not being threatened by anyone." Bill re-acted as shocked as Erin did. Jimmy went on, "As a lawyer, I've got some business to attend to with the federal government and I have been asked, to help the government's lawyer, for the next few months." He went on, "I should be able to come up to see you on the weekends and Bill and I, can share this room, if Mrs. O'Sullivan has a small cot, I can sleep on, at that time." Jimmy looked at Bill and then he said,

"Any problem Bill?" Bill who at first seemed uncomfortable with Jimmy's announcement, who now, kind of seemed resigned to his new position and also, he kind of liked the idea of being close to Erin; Indian or not, Bill was a man first. Erin then said,

"Jimmy, I had no idea that you were a lawyer, as I was led to believe, that you did other kinds of work." Jimmy answered her,

"What you say is true Erin; I've not gotten back to the practice of law on a full time basis, as with my facial disfigurement, it is difficult and so, Bill and I worked for various carnivals and circuses, in order to make a living and speaking for myself, to kind of avoid the stares and the pity of the public."

Erin understood Jimmy's plight. While he tried to avoid public scrutiny, harsh as it was, she craved it, as a way of overcoming her feelings of self worth. Her father had kind of browbeat his children, telling them of how worthless they were and that they wouldn't amount to anything, when they were little, in order to raise his own feelings, of low self esteem. Many parents tend to browbeat their offspring, in order to try and make themselves feel superior.

CHAPTER 34

❀

Erin Steals the Show
-The Jew and the Irishman-

They all climbed back into Mrs. O'Sulllivan's son's car and he drove them back to the Shamrock Club. Erin introduced Jimmy and Bill, to 'Mugs' as her friends, who have come to see her opening night performance at the Shamrock Club. "Mugs,' had kind of a worried look on his face as he told Erin,

"Erin my darl'n', I hope for both our sakes, that you do good tonight." Erin then asked 'Mugs', the reason for his concern." 'Mugs' seemed at a loss for words, as he kind of hemmed and hawed, trying to find the right words to tell Erin, of why he was so worried, finally he said,

"As I believe I told you, Myron 'Lips' Bernstein and Cornelius 'Mick' McGrath, along with myself, are the owners of the Shamrock Club, right." Erin nodded her head in the affirmative. He went on, "Mr. Bernstein and Mr. McGrath are silent partners." He continued.

"Well, when I hired you after I heard you sing, I felt that you could be a tremendous asset to the Shamrock Club. The club has sort of fallen on hard times, with the Depression and Prohibition, well it seems that our former singer, is a niece to Mr. McGrath, and because I replaced her with you, Mr. McGrath is not too happy with me, fact is, he's threatened to fire me." He went on, "Secondly, because I offered you the salary I did, plus a percentage of the profits over and above a certain fixed amount, he was furious, as was Mr. Bernstein, the club's brain trust." He continued, "So Erin, I'm in deep shit as they say, and so, I hope you can sing, like you've never sung before and convince

Mr. Bernstein and Mr. McGrath, that what I did, by hiring you, was not a mistake."

"Now I've taken the liberty to have put, a small notice in the local paper, saying that a new singing sensation, 'Miss Erin'-The Irish Nightingale, would be our new feature headliner and singer." Erin sort of smiled, when 'Mug's gave her a new and different billing, instead of these more glamorous French, but pretentious sounding, exotic names for her. 'Mugs' underlined his concern, by saying,

"Erin, sing your repertoire of familiar songs, and sing your heart out, but I would like you to finish your act, by singing many of the Irish's favorite ballads and laments, as I had told you, we have a very large Irish customer base; okay?" Erin answered,

"Fine 'Mug's, I'll do my very best." Erin wasn't scheduled to go on, until nine p.m. and already, the bar area was overflowing with customers. The crowd became so large, that 'Mugs' had to get a couple of dozen folding chairs and he placed them in an area, normally reserved for the dance floor. However, he had placed reserved signs on fourteen of them.

Jimmy and Bill sat at the bar, close to the stage. It was just about fifteen minutes after 'Mugs' put out the folding chairs, when in walked Myron 'Lips' Bernstein, followed by, Cornelius 'Mick' McGrath, and a dozen or so, Irish body guards.

Mr. Bernstein, who had a slight build, was dressed in a gray cashmere topcoat. He had on a black, silver striped suit. He wore light gray spats, over his black, patent leather, high-button shoes. He had on a gray Homburg and when he removed it revealing his hair, which was turning gray, and was parted down the middle, in the style of the day. On his upper lip, he wore a pencil thin moustache. He also wore what looked like, eyebrow pencil, an affectation of either a dandy, or a pimp. He wore a diamond stickpin in his lapel, next to a posy boutonniere. On his little finger, he had a ring, set with a diamond, which must have been ten carats, if it were one. His silk shirt, with its white celluloid collar was a pale blue and on his shirt pocket, he had his initials monogrammed in gold, which read, M.L.B. He dressed much like a gambler. His thin gray suspenders, were decorated with yellow flowers, and he sported a silver tipped, ebony cane, which could hold a shot or two, of Bombay gin, in it's handle, his favorite drink.

In stark contrast to Mr. Bernstein was Mr. McGrath, who had a stocky build, and a beer belly and who was dressed like a Chicago Ward Alderman. He wore a gray suit, which he could no longer button, as his huge belly, occupied the space where the lower button would normally have been buttoned. He wore a black shirt and a green tie. He wore red suspenders, which were set too high, which gave the appearance, that perhaps his pants were too short. Over his high-buttoned black shoes, he wore red spats. He also sported a diamond stickpin in his lapel, which was shaped like a horseshoe. He had a green carnation in his lapel and on his little finger, he wore a ring with a small two-carat diamond, set in a horseshoe design of smaller diamonds. Under his great bulbous red nose, he had a walrus moustache, which showed, part of his recently finished supper. He wore a gray bowler, with a small Shamrock pin, stuck in its hatband; he certainly was dressed to make a statement, but it certainly wasn't a fashion statement, as it was a bit garish, but his dress fit his lifestyle; brash.

The rowdy crowd, was getting restless, as they soon began to chant, *'Erin, Erin, Erin',* while stomping on the floor with their shoes. Erin could hear the noise from the raucous crowd, back in her dressing room, which she shared with the Shamrock Club's, chorus girls. "Mug's hurried back to Erin's dressing room an he knocked on the door once and then he entered, not waiting for anyone to say,

"Whose' there, or come in." The chorus girls were all in different phases of dressing. Some had nothing on; totally nude and others just had their panties and brassieres on, while others were fully dressed in their skimpy and glittering costumes. Mugs took no notice of this feminine array of nudity, as he 'Mugs', was in a state of nervous panic, with his two partners sitting impatiently, while waiting for Miss Erin, to make her appearance, as he said to Erin,

"Are you about ready honey, as the crowd is acting crazy." Erin who was not the least bit nervous or afraid, said to 'Mugs',

"I'll be right there, I'm almost finished, putting on my make-up."

Once again, Erin wore her favorite emerald green gown, with its many sequins. She sprinkled on some silver glitter, on her hair and on her bare shoulders, which was her usual stage costume and her face, just glowed. It looked like since she had kicked her cocaine habit, her complexion now had returned to its former radiance, whereas with her snorting cocaine, it had become somewhat paler and she had to compensate for that look, with additional make-up and rouge. Just before she was about to leave her dressing room, 'Mugs' had rushed to the small stage to introduce Erin to the noisy audience. He said,

"Ladies and Gentlemen, it is the Shamrock Club's pleasure, to introduce to you tonight, our star performer, 'Miss Erin-The Irish Nightingale.' Erin, who was standing just behind 'Mugs', but off stage behind the curtains, waited for her entry music and the spot light. Erin was stunning, in her emerald green gown with the silver glitter, sprinkled on her raven black hair, which was held in place, by a small silver and black turban, with an emerald broach fastened to it. Her curly hair, showed above her forehead, and with her low cut gown, revealing the deep cleavage, between her ample, milky-white breasts.

Erin was stunning, with the spotlight, reflecting off of the silver glitter, on her hair and her shoulders, giving her stage presence, an almost ethereal aura. The small orchestra began to play her introductory number, *'Some of These Days'*. Erin then walked to the center of the stage, amidst wild applause and with her beautiful Irish smile, showing her perfectly white teeth, she began to sing.

The enthusiasm of any audience has a direct and proportional effect, on the entertainer, as the entertainer, always responds in kind, to a receptive audience. Erin was no exception, as the crowds, listened in rapt silence, as she sang her heart wrenching introductory song. Her first song brought the house down. Her stage presence, her beauty, her sensual body movements, and her beautiful voice, thrilled the crowd.

The mostly Irish crowd was totally in love with the Irish beauty. Erin continued singing and when she finished her prepared repertoire of songs, she then began to sing the many beautiful Irish love songs, laments, and finally, she sang *'My Yiddish-a-Mama'*, a favorite Jewish song, of the Jewish vaudeville circuit. Myron Bernstein had tears in his eyes, as he listened to Erin's most captivating rendition, of one of his most favorite Jewish songs.

There was no question about it, Erin had not only captivated the crowd, with her spellbinding voice, she had both Messer's', Bernstein and Mc Grath, in tears. The crowd stood clapping and stamping their feet, as Erin received eighteen curtain calls. "Mug's was delighted, as he watched the faces of his two partners and their response to the Irish beauty.

Jimmy had ordered a bouquet of red roses that he had sent to Erin in her dressing room, before she went on stage. Don't think for a moment, that a bouquet of roses doesn't make a possible suitor's point, as Erin was quite taken with the flowers, that Jimmy had sent to her, along with his note, declaring his love for her. He wrote,

My Dearest Erin:

'I hope that you like my bouquet of roses, as they convey, my undying love for you, cause as you know, red roses are the flowers of true love.'

With much love and affection;

Jimmy

Both Mr. Bernstein and Mr. McGrath hurried back to Erin's dressing room, to congratulate her, on her stellar performance. After knocking on her door, and hearing Erin's reply to come in, they entered Erin's, dressing room. Mr. Bernstein kissed Erin's outstretched hand, as did Mr. McGrath. They both told her how marvelous her performance was, and they hoped that she would have a long and productive career, singing at the Shamrock Club. Erin smiled as she thanked them both for their kind remarks. 'Mugs' stood to one side beaming, as he too heard Mr. Bernstein's remarks about Erin. 'Mugs' knew right then, that he had made the right choice in hiring Erin.

Both Mr. Bernstein and Mr. McGrath invited Erin for a cocktail, to celebrate her opening at the Shamrock Club. Erin was tired and she really didn't want a drink, but she thought that one drink wouldn't matter, in order to be polite to Mr. Bernstein and Mr. McGrath. After Erin had drank her cocktail, she was about to get up, when Mr. Bernstein said,

"What's your hurry doll, the evening is young." Obviously, Mr. Bernstein had other thoughts in his mind concerning Erin. Erin then said,

"Thanks Mr. Bernstein, but no thanks, as I'm really tired and I best be getting home now." Mr. Bernstein started to grab Erin's arm, when he felt something sharp in his back, like the feel of a gun, pressed against his backbone. He turned and there standing with a gun in his back was Jimmy O'Brien. Jimmy then said,

"Mr. Bernstein, please, with all deference to you, the young lady is tired and I would like to see that she gets home safely." Mr. Bernstein was shocked, to see that somebody was able to penetrate his score of bodyguards and was able to put a gun in his back. Mr. Bernstein's face was bright red and it was all he could do, to control his hot temper as he said,

"Young man, it seems that you got the drop on me and therefore, I suggest that you escort the young lady safely home, but I'm sure that we'll meet again, under, lets say, different circumstances." Jimmy smiled as he, Erin and Bill, walked to the exit door of the club and waiting for them outside in the parking lot, were Mrs. O'Sullivan's son's car and her son, waiting to take them home.

They all got into the car and headed for Mrs. O'Sullivan's tourist home.

Erin put her head on Jimmy's shoulder, as she sort of nodded off; she was exhausted from this evening's performance. Jimmy of course, was delighted that Erin would want to snuggle against him. He had a smile on his face. Erin showed no hesitation in treating Jimmy, as though he was just another of her many beau's and Jimmy was delighted.

CHAPTER 35

Marked Money
-Clarence & Jimmy-

Jimmy caught the train the very next morning, returning to Chicago and he rented a room at the La Salle Hotel.

The marked money was beginning to turn up, in the strangest places. With cab drivers, grocery stores, whorehouses, speakeasies, and buses, just to name a few. As each bill was recorded with its brief history, if it could be ascertained, by questioning those people who received the marked money, when and where, and who they got it from. Some person's memories were faulty and others drew a blank, when it came to naming a source for the marked bills. Still others, knew exactly who gave them the marked money and when, and for what. It was an exhausting task, to say the least.

However, gradually and over time, all roads so to speak, led the F.B.I. to Clarence Duncan and some of the prostitutes, that Al Capish had working, in his many speakeasies, and roadhouses, through out Chicago and Cook County. Some of the marked money, showed up at the many race tracks that Chicago had, such as Washington Park, Olympia Fields, Hawthorn, Sportsman's Park, and Arlington Park, plus a few more. Race tracks and whore houses, seemed to get the most marked money and it seemed that Clarence Duncan was the primary spender of this marked money.

The government was slowly building its case against Clarence Duncan, dollar by dollar. It took only a month, and Mr. Pickering received a second blackmail letter, demanding the payment of seventy-five thousand dollars.

Jimmy O'Brien was notified by the F.B.I in Chicago, of this second blackmail letter.

Erin had now been singing nightly at the Shamrock Club for over a month, when she had a visitor in her dressing room. The visitor was none other than Mr. Bernstein. Mr. Bernstein was now about to apply some persuasive muscle and what he thought was his irresistible charm, in trying to seduce Erin. He told Erin outright, that she was his property and told her in no uncertain words, that whoever was her current boyfriend, like that guy with the covered face, she was to tell him to get lost or else.

Now the Shamrock Club's nightly business, had quadrupled since Erin began to sing there, Erin felt that regardless, no one tells her what to do and whom she should choose, as her boyfriend. Moreover, it certainly wasn't this Jewish matzo ball, Mr. Myron Bernstein. He reeked from cheap cologne, but it couldn't hide his almost intolerable, body odor. Someone I guess had forgotten to tell Mr. Bernstein, that he should take a bath first, before using cologne. Erin was somewhat frightened of Mr. Bernstein, as she remembered only too well, her captive association with Al Capish and his drugs.

Myron Bernstein thought of himself, as a gift to the ladies and he felt that he was therefore, quite a ladies man, at least in his mind. He had a super ego and Myron Bernstein, was another gangland psychopath. Erin mustered up her natural Irish courage and she told Mr. Bernstein to his face,

"Look Mr. Bernstein, I'm not interested in you period, and as I had told 'Mugs', my only interest in the Shamrock Club, is as a singer and nothing more. Now if for some reason, my job duties also involve becoming your paramour, then I quit, right here and now, as you can take this job and shove it."

With that statement, Erin began to put her clothes into a shopping bag, as her suitcase was at home. Mr. Bernstein was now in a rage, to think that some two bit Irish whore, would dare tell him to his face, that she was quitting; *'no one tells Myron Bernstein that she is quitting'*. Mr. Bernstein grabbed Erin by her left wrist and with her free fist; Erin swung it and hit Mr. Bernstein in the mouth, knocking him to the floor. He staggered to his feet, with blood now seeping from the corner of his mouth, but meanwhile, Erin ran out of her dressing room and into the parking lot, where she spotted Mrs. O'Sullivan's son's car. She ran to the car and she jumped in, telling the driver to drive back to the tourist home. Mr. Bernstein by then had followed Erin out and into the parking lot, where he saw her get into a car as it sped-off.

CHAPTER 36

Subpoena

-The United States vs. Clarence Duncan-

Agent Moore acting on behalf of the United States government now had enough evidence to request that the United States Court of Northern Illinois, issue subpoenas for Clarence Duncan and his associates.

It was early on a crisp fall morning, when a United States Marshal arrived at the offices of Clarence Duncan and Associates, with a dozen subpoenas. The blonde secretary in the front office, signed for the dozen subpoenas and the marshal smiled, tipped his hat and went about delivering his other subpoenas.

The blonde secretary opened the subpoenas, one by one, and placed them in her 'in' basket, so when Mr. Duncan came in, she could give them to him. It was just about fifteen minutes later, when Mr. Duncan came into the office, smiling at his voluptuous blonde secretary and he cracked a somewhat dirty joke, for which his blonde secretary giggled, in her child like voice.

She had a tendency to lean forward, whenever Mr. Duncan came into the office, so that her large breasts would deepen her cleavage, as her milky white breasts, hovered above the papers on her desk, like two huge mounds, shielding her desk, from the gaslights, which flickered on the wall. The gaslights, lit the office ever so brightly, and she always lighted a fire, in her bosses' loins, whenever he came near her. The blonde secretary then gave the contents of her 'in' basket to Mr. Duncan, who didn't notice the dozen subpoenas, which lay, just underneath another piece of incoming mail. It was only about ten minutes later, when the blonde secretary heard a single pistol shot, coming from Mr. Duncan's office.

The blonde secretary ran to Mr. Duncan's office, where she found him slumped over his desk, with the back of his head blown off. Mr. Duncan had placed the barrel of his small 30 caliber pistol, in his mouth. Neither he nor any of his associates, would ever again, practice law in the state of Illinois or anywhere else, for that matter.

Mr. Duncan's associates were all sentenced to ten years each, as co-conspirators, in the United States Federal prison, in Leavenworth, Kansas, for blackmail and extortion.

CHAPTER 37

❁

A Surprise

-Myron, Erin and Bill-

Myron Bernstein when he saw Erin flee in a car, ran to the back of the Shamrock Club, where his orange and brown, Duesenberg SJ was parked. He hoped in and he sped out of the parking lot, throwing up, great clouds of gravel and dust. He knew where Erin was staying, as he had asked 'Mugs' the night before.

Erin thanked Mrs. O'Sullivan's son, as she got out of the car and ran into the tourist home, crying. Bill was having a cup of tea with Mrs. O'Sullivan, when Erin burst into the kitchen. Erin ran to Mrs. O'Sullivan crying, seeking comfort and protection. Bill John, then raced upstairs to get his pistol and by the time he returned to the kitchen, there stood Myron Bernstein, confronting both Erin and Mrs. O'Sullivan, who was standing her ground, with an iron frying pan in her hand.

Mr. Bernstein had a cruel smile on his face, as he sort of laughed to himself, at the old lady with the frying pan in her hand, held high above her head. I guess he made the mistake of thinking that Mrs. O'Sullivan wouldn't use the iron frying pan, as he circled the kitchen table, trying to reach Erin and as he got closer, Mrs. O'Sullivan brought the iron frying pan down on his head, knocking him to the floor. He lay on the kitchen floor, unconscious. By then, Bill had come back down the stairs, with his pistol in his hand. He took a quick glance of the scene and then he set about frisking Mr. Bernstein.

He found a holstered 38 Special revolver, a small stiletto tied to his leg and a Derringer, held in a small holster, underneath his belt. He told Erin to take the

Derringer and fasten it to her garter, as he felt that she would need some additional protection, when dealing with these psyopathic gangsters.

Evidently, both 'Mugs" and Mr. McGrath, heard the commotion with Mr. Bernstein's failed attempt, in trying to seduce Erin and they heard his car race away from the Shamrock Club. Both Mr. McGrath and 'Mugs', decided to follow Mr. Bernstein. Because Mr. Bernstein had asked 'Mugs' for Erin's address, he had a hunch that was where he was going. So both Mr. McGrath, "Mugs', and several of Mr. McGrath's body guards, all piled into Mr. McGrath's black Lincoln Phaeton and they too, raced out of the parking lot, headed for Mrs. O'Sullivan's tourist home. Racing down a couple of dirt roads, they saw Mr. Bernstein's orange and brown Duesenberg, parked out in front of Mrs. O'Sullivan's tourist home.

They all got out and climbed the porch, leading into Mrs. O'Sullivan's tourist home. They opened the door and went inside. Walking through the parlor, they saw the kitchen and they're lying on the floor, was Mr. Bernstein, who was just now, trying to get up. Erin was seated in one of the kitchen chairs and neither Mrs. O'Sullivan, nor Bill John, were visible. Mr. Bernstein's forehead was just now showing a red knob, where Mrs. O'Sullivan had hit him with her frying pan. The bodyguards and Mr. McGrath looked around, searching the kitchen with their eyes, trying to see if they could, anyone else who might be hiding in the kitchen. Mr. Bernstein was now writhing in pain, holding his head, and bristling with anger, he called Erin every swear word known to him, with his extensive repertory of curse words. Erin, who was now calm, just sat there, looking at a copy of the Saturday Evening Post.

Seeing his own bodyguards, which gave him courage, Mr. Bernstein once again tried to grab Erin by her arm. A woman's voice from the dining room, said, "Touch her and I'll blow you to kingdom come" and another voice said,

"And if she don't get you there, I sure as hell will." Both Mrs. O'Sullivan and Bill John stepped out of the shadows in the dining room. Mrs. O'Sullivan held a two-barreled shotgun in her arm, while Bill, held a revolver in his right hand. One of the bodyguards looked like he might try and reach for his gun, which he carried in his shoulder holster. Bill noticed his move and then he said, "Try that again Mr., and I'll blow a hole, clean through you." The bodyguard looked at the stranger, who held a gun on him.

What he saw, kind of frightened him, as Bill's soul piercing, black eyes, were glaring at him and he knew that this man, who ever he was, meant business, and so he put his arm back down by his side. This whole scene looked somewhat ridiculous; with two overly dressed men, a bartender who was still wearing his apron, and four bodyguards, dressed in their black topcoats, being held at bay, by an old lady toting a shotgun and an Indian with a pistol.

Finally, Mr. McGrath told Mr. Bernstein, to sit down and to apologize to the young lady. Mr. Bernstein who was both embarrassed and raging mad, by the turn of events, as he never expected Erin would reject his charms said,

"The hell I will, why should I apologize to this Irish whore." Erin who had maintained her composure was now getting hot under the collar so to speak, as she looked at 'Mugs' and she said,

"'Mugs' I'm so sorry that my singing engagement has come to this kind of an end, but I'm nobody's whore and I resent this greasy-smelly creep, calling me a whore, when he is nothing more than a cheap two-bit, gangster." She went on, "Now as for you 'Mugs' you have treated me with nothing but respect and I appreciate that very much." Mr. McGrath now spoke,

"Now as you know young lady, you did sign a contract with us as a singer and I feel that you cannot brake it." Erin who by now, had her Irish temper up, said,

"Look Mr. McGrath, while I did sign a contract as a singer, I did not however sign any contract, that says that I also am required, to submit to the lecherous advances of this greasy creep and therefore Mr. McGrath, it is your company, who broke our agreement and contract, not me." Mr. McGrath was at loss for words for a minute and then he said,

"Well Erin you got me there, but I would appreciate it, if you would reconsider, after you've had a few days to calm down. I will give you my assurance, that neither Mr. Bernstein, nor anyone else connected with the Shamrock Club, will ever again, bother you and also, I will double your salary, as it is obvious to me and my partners, that you have exceeded our wildest expectations in drawing the kind of crowds to the Shamrock Club nightly, that you have." Mr. Bernstein was incensed at Mr. McGrath's offer, and resented that he wasn't consulted about what he felt about the offer, as he was after all, the supposed brains' of the partnership.

Before Erin had a chance to reply, Bill said,

"Let me assure you gentlemen, that should this creep, or anyone else, ever lays a hand on Erin again, I will kill that person and take his scalp, regardless of how many bodyguards you have." This new turn of events, with a threat by someone, who was obviously an Indian, caused a chill to run up the back of Mr. Bernstein. Mr. Bernstein thought to himself,

'What the hell, are we living in the Wild West, I can't believe that I'm being threatened in such away, by a savage Indian?' Erin finally said,

"Mr. McGrath, I do enjoy singing at the Shamrock Club, with my many Irish fans, and because of that, I will take your new offer under advisement and let you know of what my plans are, in a couple of days."

Mr. McGrath and 'Mugs', had big smiles on their faces, while Mr. Bernstein, was still grumbling to himself. Evidently, there had been bad blood between Mr. McGrath and Mr. Bernstein, as the gossip had it, that Mr. Bernstein had tried to rape Mr. McGrath's youngest daughter, Deirdre, who was only thirteen. So their partnership in the North Side Irish Mafia, was precarious to say the least?

They all left one by one, until it was just Mrs. O'Sullivan, Erin and Bill, sitting at the kitchen table, discussing the traumatic events, which had just taken place. Mrs. O'Sullivan then asked Erin,

"Are you seriously considering returning to the Shamrock Club darl'n'?" Erin who needed more time to consider just what her options were with her near disastrous encounter with that Jewish weasel, Myron 'Lips' Bernstein and what he still might try to do to her said,

"I'm not sure Mrs. O'Sullivan just what I should do, I love singing at the Shamrock Club and I need to make a living somehow but, I don't have to lose my self respect and my body, to these psychotic gangster animals." She continued, "I really do like 'Mugs' and Mr. McGrath, as they both have treated me with respect and the offer they just made me, is almost too good to be true." Erin went on, "As you know Mrs. O'Sullivan, most girls like myself have great difficulty walking the straight and narrow in the so called, 'club' business, as most of these entertainment jobs, always seem to come with strings attached and with the Mafia, controlling the kinds of places, that we singers have to go to make a living, its difficult. However, I do believe that I will return to the Shamrock Club, with the assurances of both 'Mugs' and Mr. McGrath, that there will be no funny business, especially from that Jewish creep, Mr. Bernstein."

CHAPTER 38

Out of the Past

-Pat Monahan-

Erin had returned to the Shamrock Club after a few days of rest and reflection. Her singing and her mere presence, gave the Shamrock Club some international notoriety and customers were now, beginning to come to the Shamrock Club in droves, both from the entire continental United States and Europe itself. Of course, Erin, had a loyal following, from the Kit Kat Club and from the Bombay Club, even though the Bombay Club's existence was short lived, as it went bankrupt. Erin only sang, five nights a week, at the Shamrock Club, as she could almost dictate her working hours and her salary. She sang Wednesday evening, through Sunday evening.

Word had been received, that a body was found stuffed, in the small trunk of an orange and brown, Duesenberg SJ and the body was identified as that of Myron 'Lips' Bernstein, a notorious gangster and brains of the Irish Mafia, led by Cornelius McGrath. The killing was believed to be the work of the rival Southside Mafia, led by Al 'Scarface' Capish and so, the police didn't really want to investigate it, any further than they had to. Nevertheless, some wondered if in fact, it might have been the Irish Mafia itself, which did the killing?

When the Bombay Club went bankrupt, and Al Capish went on his rampage and his personal *La Vendetta* took place, Pat Monahan and his father, decided that it was in his son's best interest, health wise, to leave the country. Meanwhile, his father would try and mollify Al Capish, until he cooled down. Pat's investment brokerage business went belly-up, when the stock market crashed and so he now had no primary business, which could produce a stable and a livable income, other than his and his father's investments in some local Southside real estate.

Pat had relatives living in Dublin, Ireland, and so he was able to lay low, for the past year or so, with them.

It was on a late fall evening, and a Wednesday, in 1931, when Erin had just begun her singing routine at the Shamrock Club, and seated at the bar, was a very tall and good-looking Irishman, by the name of Patrick Monahan. Pat had gotten word from some of his old business associates that Erin O'Hara, was now singing at the Shamrock Club in Niles, Illinois. Pat had never forgotten Erin, after their brief encounter and his being warned by a couple of Al Capish's gangsters, to leave the Irish broad alone, or suffer the consequences.

Erin had never fully understood why Pat so abruptly dropped her, even though he said, that he couldn't get in touch with her, fearing that Al Capish's gangsters, were monitoring Erin's phone calls and were opening her mail. Pat took Al Capish's threats very seriously. Pat waited until Erin had finished her act and the curtain had fallen for it's final time, after she received fifteen curtain calls, before he went back to her dressing room and knocked on her door. Erin said,

"Who is it?"

"Its an old admirer." Erin thought for a minute to see if she could recognize his voice, but it didn't ring a bell with her. Erin then said,

"Who ever you are, you'll have to do better than that, as I have several old admirers." Pat laughed as he said,

"Tis' me, Pat Monahan." Erin carefully opened the door and after recognizing Pat, she gave him a big hug and a kiss. Pat then said,

"May I come in Erin?" Erin was in the process of taking off her gown, after having removed the small amount of make-up she wore. She stepped behind a small Chinese screen and finished taking off her gown and putting on her dress. Erin then said,

"What brings you here, to my neck of the woods Pat?" Pat said,

"Well to be truthful with you Erin, I'm not sure. I got into my car this evening, intent on attending a supper, for one of my friends, when before I knew it, my car was turning into the parking lot, here at the Shamrock Club."

Erin laughed as she said, "You're not Irish for nothing are you Pat, still with the blarney." Pat had a sort of a contrived hurt look on his face, as he said to Erin,

"Now Erin, would I be telling you a fib?" Pat went on to say,

"Erin, I'm starving, could I buy you breakfast; I know of a secluded restaurant, out on Milwaukee Avenue, just a little northwest of here?" Erin thought for a minute and then she said,

"Why sure Pat, I'd like that." Erin may not have truly realized it at the time, but her list of admirers was growing. When she hadn't returned from her singing gig, Bill was becoming very nervous, as he was now pacing his bedroom floor, in Mrs. O'Sullivan's tourist home. In the past year or so, Bill made it a sort of a ritual, to have a cup of coffee with Erin in the morning, after she finished her nightly performance. Bill didn't realize it at the time, nor did Erin, but Bill had fallen in love with her. It wasn't too difficult for any normal red-blooded male, Indian or otherwise, to have his brain turned to mush, after talking to and watching Erin, in her very provocative dressing gown and she with her flirtatious and seductive eyes, it was more than just a little disconcerting, when they had their morning coffee together, to say the least. Erin was a natural born flirt, no question about that, as she loved to tease men to see them get flustered. It was kind of cruel, but that's the way the game is played, and she certainly enjoyed playing it.

As an Indian though, Bill was taught as a little boy on the reservation, to shy away from white women, as they could lead him astray. Bill also never showed any emotions and so, it was very difficult to read his face.

Erin most times without realizing it, had a woman's natural ability to use all of her God given charms, which men went limp over; perhaps limp isn't the right word? Erin enjoyed her control over most men, excluding of coarse, the animalistic psychopaths, working for Al Capish and people like 'Lips' Bernstein, whose only interest in women, was to have sex with them and to degrade them as though they were nothing more, than pieces of meat, to be used and then discarded.

Mrs. O'Sullivan who could hear Bill pacing the floor over the kitchen, as she was making morning coffee and breakfast, finally rapped on the kitchen ceiling, with her broom handle, as she hollered,

"Bill, come down here, as I don't think Erin is coming home this morning." Bill put on his bathrobe and slippers, as he hurried down the two flights of stairs and into the kitchen. He asked Mrs. O'Sullivan,

"What do you mean, that Erin won't be coming home for breakfast, where is she?" Mrs. O'Sullivan had a slight smirk on her cherubic like, rosy-cheeked, Irish face as she said,

"Well, according to my son Mike, Erin went to breakfast with a gentlemen in a sports car of some sort." Bill then said,

"Did Mike say where they were going?" Mrs. O'Sullivan who could see right through Bill's stoic, Indian demeanor, as she said,

"No he didn't, but why do you ask, do you have a particular interest in Erin and therefore, are you concerned about her going out with the wrong kind of gentlemen?" Bill's face now had a reddish cast to his already dark features, as he said to Mrs. O'Sullivan,

"No I don't, but as she has had so much trouble with these rotten gangsters, that I have taken a sort of a protective view of her and her acquaintances." Mrs. O'Sullivan now laughed out loud, as she said in a kidding manner,

"You know Bill, you may fool most people with your stoicism, but I can read you like a book. You're in love with Erin and you don't like to admit it to yourself, or anyone else, that I might be right." Bill liked Mrs. O'Sullivan, as he could talk to her about anything, no matter what the subject was. She reminded him a lot; of his own mother, in her mannerisms and the way she talked, so plain, and yet so direct. Mrs. O'Sullivan was built a lot like his mother, short and stocky. He kind of stammered as he said to her,

"Mrs. O'Sullivan, for an old doll, you make a lot of sense. I hadn't realized that my feelings for Erin, were so obvious, at least to you". He went on, "You remind me a lot of my mother, who could see right through me, no matter how much I tried to steer her away from my most inner thoughts." Mrs. O'Sullivan said,

"Bill, God gives us mothers, a sort of a seventh sense, if you want to call it that, in our ability to see right through our children's fibs, otherwise we could never run a household full of little fibbers and actors." Bill laughed out loud a he said,

"I do believe that you have hit the nail on the head, yes, I am in love with Erin, although at first I thought that it might be just infatuation." Mrs. O'Sullivan now had a worried look on her pixie Irish face, as she thought to herself, how will Erin, ever let Bill down gently enough, without breaking his heart, as I know that she has no emotional feelings for Bill, other than her gratitude for his protection. Mrs. O'Sullivan also knew of Jimmy O'Brien's love for Erin, but she thought that because of his facial injury, Erin wouldn't probably allow herself to get serious with him. I guess that Mrs. O'Sullivan forgot, that love is sometimes, blind.

Jimmy came out most weekends to see both Erin and Bill, as he was still aiding the government in the prosecution of the several remaining federal cases. It had been a year since Clarence Dunkin, committed suicide, to avoid prosecution for blackmail and extortion.

Jimmy's courting of Erin, if you could call it that, was difficult, to say the least. His only two days off were, Saturday and Sunday, whereas those two days, were Erin's busiest and when she got home, so early in the morning, she was exhausted. Jimmy also was very much attuned to his friend Bill, and it soon became obvious to him, that Bill also, was in love with Erin. Perhaps thought Jimmy, *'I wouldn't stand a chance of having Erin favor me, especially with my facial disfigurement'.* Jimmy knew that Bill and Erin had their morning coffee together; each and every morning, and that alone thought Jimmy, might give Bill the edge.

Jimmy also knew that in spite of Bill's rather standoffish manner, most women found him interesting, as his *'Plain's'* Indian, facial features, and his ponytail, intrigued some women. Perhaps, Jimmy thought, *'I should not waste my time in trying to compete with Bill and I should see if I can find some employment in Chicago, as my service with the government, was winding down'.* Jimmy then telegraphed Mr. Wallace on the Island Queen, advising him of his desire to remain in Chicago, at least for a while.

Jimmy liked Chicago, after all, he grew up in Chicago and his roots were deeply planted in the soil of the Southside. Jimmy's rather unhappy moods lately, didn't go unnoticed by Mrs. O'Sullivan, who liked Jimmy very much and it pained her to see him trying to win Erin's heart, and knowing that he didn't stand a chance in seeking her love. After all, thought Mrs. O'Sullivan, most men would give their right arm, to put their shoes under Erin's bed.

She kind of laughed to herself, as her mind wandered back to her days in New York, when she was the toast of Broadway and was the most sought after woman on the 'Great White Way'. Mrs. O'Sullivan as of late took many nostalgic trips down memory lane, as it brought her much comfort, knowing what and who, she once was. The wealthy male gentlemen, who sought her love; these so-called Stage-door-Johnnie's, who would wait at her dressing room door each and every night, like puppy dogs, after her Broadway shows closed for the evening and of course, the New York social circuit, which she became the queen of. Niles, Illinois was a far cry from Broadway though, she thought, both in time and in distance. Sometimes, it seemed so long ago, she thought, but at least, I have my memories and no one can take them away from me.

They should see me now! She thought of her many marriages and as a young and beautiful woman, she became so fickle, thinking that it would never end. She soon realized only too quickly, that youth and beauty are but a fleeting moment in time and as she knew only too well, that youth is so wasted on the young. She sighed, as her mind came back to today's events.

CHAPTER 39

❦

A Business Proposal
-A Century of Progress-

Erin and Pat had breakfast in a small French cafe, out on Milwaukee Avenue. After they both reminisced about what had happened to each other, over the past two years or so, Pat said,
"Erin, have you heard about the World's Fair that is coming to Chicago in 1933?" Erin who had little time for reading the newspapers, especially with her evening singing engagement, said,
"No not really Pat, I guess I've just been too busy." Pat then said,
"Well myself and a group of business men, have put in our bid, in order for us to reserve so to speak, a certain amount of space, so that we can begin construction of the so called French Pavilion, with a French cafe, which will be featured in what will be called, the 'Toulouse-Lautrec Exhibit'. It is our feeling, that if we could sign you up for, lets say, a very lucrative two-year contract, as our featured chanteuse, we believe, that this French exhibit and its cafe, would bring world wide attention to The Chicago World's Fair's French Pavilion and yourself.
While you're on top of the world now, so to speak, in America Erin, I'm sure that this exposure could make you an international star. Erin thought about Pat's proposal, as she mulled around in her mind, Pat's intriguing offer. She realized that singing at the Shamrock Club as nice as it was, and so convenient from her room at the tourist home, was not her final theatrical act in life, at least she hoped that it wasn't. She wanted more and she felt that she was now at

the top of her singing career, however, she wanted international exposure, and perhaps Pat's idea, might be just what she was waiting for. Finally, she asked Pat,

"Pat, what about Al Capish, is he also a silent partner in this business enterprise, cause if he is, I don't want any part of it or of him?" Pat became serious for a moment, as he said to Erin,

"No Erin, he is not. It is my understanding that he is up to his neck in tax problems with the feds. They contend, that he is not paying his fair share of income taxes, based on his lifestyle and I believe that they might have the goods on him now." He went on, "Now I would agree, that in order to put Al Capish away for a long time, he will fight the feds at every turn and these court battles could take several years." He went on,

"Several prominent members of the United States Senate, are in his back pocket, and they owe him many favors, including his knowledge of their trysts, with some of his prostitutes, which he has filmed for blackmail purposes." He continued, "One of these senators is head of the United States Tax Sub-Committee, which oversees the Internal Revenue Service, and he is the Right Honorable Simpson T. Oliver 11. Al will now call-in, all of his 'IOU's." Erin said,

"Well Pat, let me think on it, okay?" Pat said,

"Fine, there is no hurry, as they have just begun construction on the fair and it will take just about a year or so, to complete it, but I would like to know if you're interested now, so that I can tell my associates, that you are inclined favorably towards it." Erin thought some more about Pat's proposal and then she said,

"Yes Pat, I am interested, but I won't commit myself as yet, as I would like to learn more about this project. Do you have any artist renderings of what your French place, will look like?" Pat then said,

"I don't have any sketches with me, but I can bring some for you to see, the very next time I see you." He went on, "How about this same time, tomorrow?" Erin said,

"That's fine with me Pat." They both got into Pat's vintage Stutz 'Bearcat' and they drove to Erin's tourist home. Erin leaned over and she gave Pat a kiss on his cheek, as she got out of the small red, bobtailed sport's car. Pat smile as he said,

"Until tomorrow." As Erin got out of Pat's car, Bill John had been watching her, as he stood in his bedroom window. Erin opened the front door as she gave Mrs., O'Sullivan a kiss on her cheek, and then she said,

"Boy, am I ever bushed." Mrs. O'Sullivan asked Erin,

"I hope you don't mind me asking Erin, but who was that fella', an old friend?" Erin was a little agitated with Mrs. O'Sullivan asking her about Pat and so she thought, *'its really none of Mrs. O'Sullivan's business, but she thought, I can't be mad at her, as she's been so good to me.'* Erin then said,

"Well Mrs. O'Sullivan; Pat and I go back a ways and I haven't seen him for the past two years, until he stopped by the club, as he heard that I was performing there." Bill John was listening to their conversation at the foot of the upstairs landing and he didn't like what he heard.

Jealousy most times, goes hand in hand with love, even though it's not its most desirable companion, although mostly, they're inseparable. Erin went upstairs, as she told Mrs. O'Sullivan that she was so tired, that she was going to lie across the bed. Mrs. O'Sullivan said,

"Okay me' darl'n', I'll' see you when you get up." Erin fell sound asleep and when she awoke, there standing in the doorway of her room, was Bill John. He kind of scared her, as she didn't expect to see a man standing in the doorway of her bedroom. Erin said to Bill,

"Bill you startled me, what do you want?" Bill was a little flustered having been caught by Erin, watching her sleep. He said, with his reddening face,

"Nothing Erin, I was just about to go downstairs and have some supper and I thought that you might oversleep and be late for work, and so I was about to wake you." Erin didn't like the fact that Bill had been watching her sleep, it was like he was invading her privacy and besides, she felt that she didn't need him or anyone else, to keep tabs on whether or not she got up on time for her job. She thought further, *'what does he think I am, some kind of a schoolgirl?* Bill could tell that Erin was miffed at him and he didn't know how to get out of his predicament. He knew that once a woman is mad at you, it usually takes a good long while, before she comes around, if ever. He thought further, *'even in the Indian culture, the same is true.'*

Erin freshened up and she went downstairs to have a bite to eat, before she had to get dressed for her evening's performance, at the Shamrock Club. There was little conversation, around the supper table and Mrs. O'Sullivan could tell that something was wrong between Erin and Bill. She thought further, *'you don't have to be Irish to figure that out.'*

Pat stopped by the tourist home the very next morning, with his set of sketches for the proposed French Pavilion at the Chicago World's Fair. Erin invited him in for morning coffee. Erin introduced Pat to Mrs. O'Sullivan and to Bill John. After a moment or two, Bill excused himself, saying that he had some business to attend to and he left the kitchen. Mrs. O'Sullivan looked at Erin with a look of *'well ain't' he the one?'*

Pat could sense a certain bit of tension in the air, but he didn't say anything, as he felt that it was none of his business. Erin cleared the kitchen table as soon as they had their coffee, and had eaten, two pieces of soda bread. Mrs. O'Sullivan baked her soda bread, twice a week. Pat laid out his sketches on the table, so that both Mrs. O'Sullivan and Erin could see them clearly. With Pat explaining the sketches to Erin and to Mrs. O'Sullivan, both women seemed entranced with such a beautiful project. When Pat was through explaining the sketches and putting his own take on the project, he asked Erin,

"Well Erin, what do you think of the project?" Erin was at a loss for words for a minute and then she said,

"Pat, I believe that you really have got something here, I've never seen such a beautiful project." She went on, "Is the French government involved in this project?" Pat then said,

"Oh but definitely, they are the primary party in this massive project, as they are financing almost all of it and any other part of this project, not financed by them, they are hands-on." He went on, "Without their participation, this project couldn't have gotten off the ground." Pat could tell that Erin was excited, and so was Mrs. O'Sullivan, but both for different reasons; Erin for what this project might do for her career and for Mrs. O'Sullivan, as it brought back so many pleasant memories of when she was in show business and when she was the toast of Broadway. Pat then asked Erin,

"Well Erin, are you still interested?" Erin with her beautiful smile, said,

"I sure am." Pat then said.

"Good, I'll inform my associates of your decision." He continued, "Oh Erin, before I forget it, we'll need, that is my associates and myself, will need you to sign a letter of intent, whereby you will have agreed to the terms and conditions of our contract, when we have formalized and finalized them, is that okay with you?" Erin thought for a minute and then she said,

"That seems fine with me Pat, but as you know, I will have to first see, just what my salary will be and certain other conditions. If I'm a hit singing at the French Pavilion, I would like a guarantee of at least a six month engagement, at the world famous Moulin Rouge in Paris, after the Chicago fair closes." Pat smiled as he said,

"Erin if you perform like you do every night at the Shamrock Club, I won't have to ask the French government on your behalf, they will make you a fantastic offer, which I'm sure, will certainly include the Moulin Rouge cafe, in your role as a chanteuse; the lovely and vivacious, Le Madam Adrienne de la Durequex." Erin was stunned for a moment, as she had almost forgotten her stage name, from her gig at the Bombay Club and for Pat to remember her name that was something else. Erin gave this handsome Irishman, Pat Monahan, a more serious look.

Erin smiled, as she now entered her little world of dreams, as her gorgeous eyes became glazed, as her dreams, the ones she held tight to her bosom, which were at the very core of her being, and as a child, learning how to sing under the tutelage of *'Sister Angela Clare at St. Teresa's Parochial grammar school'*. She thought, *'Sister would be so proud of what I've accomplished*. But then for a moment she frowned, as she thought,' *but what about the other part of my not so happy past, what would Sister think of that?'* Erin now returned from her mental sojourn, back to reality, as she looked at Pat and Mrs. O'Sullivan, who were studying her dreamy face.

Both Mrs. O'Sullivan and Pat could tell, that Erin was trying to remember something from her past, as she had both a smile, which turned into a frown, on her beautiful face.

CHAPTER 40

❀

South-Chicago Bridge & Iron Works

-Jimmy O'Brien-

Jimmy who had gradually curtailed his visits to Mrs. O'Sullivan's tourist home, as he felt that there was no place in Erin's heart for him and he couldn't help but notice, Bill's feelings toward Erin. Not that he could blame Bill, I mean, after all, he knew that Bill had certain emotions which he at most times, was able to hide, but not when it came to Erin. Jimmy also realized that their work schedules, just weren't compatible and so, he didn't have a lot of opportunity to court Erin, whereas Bill John, had coffee every morning with Erin and Mrs. O'Sullivan, and some courting certainly can be accomplished, just over a cup of Mrs. O'Sullivan's coffee. Besides, how would Erin cope with someone like myself, whose face has to be hidden from the public, could she be expected to have a normal life?

Anyhow, Jimmy thought, I've got to see if I can get some kind of a roustabout job here in Chicago. Jimmy had read in the 'Chicago Tribune' newspaper, that a huge world's fair; called 'A Century of Progress', celebrating Chicagos' one-hundredth anniversary, would be built on what was called Burnham park, on some re-claimed land. The city of Chicago was now, adding to the shoreline, by filling in Lake Michigan, just south of the Shedd Aquarium and was creating a piece of land called North Island.

He looked in the telephone book for the address of the South-Chicago Bridge & Iron Works', local union office. He found it and it was within walking distance from the La Salle hotel, over on Wabash Avenue. Jimmy knew that he would soon have to check out of the La Salle hotel, as it was a little too high for him to pay for a room, from his own pocket. While 'Uncle Sam' footed the bill for his room and board, he could afford to live in the lap of luxury, for at least a while longer.

He knew that many an Irish family living in Canaryville, let rooms and so he thought, after he got a job, he would see if he could rent a room in Canaryville. He smiled to himself, as he walked over to Wabash Avenue and the union headquarters, of the South-Chicago Bridge & Iron Works, thinking about the several gangsters, he had noticed from time to time, lurking around the La Salle hotel, looking for their hoodlum friends, who disappeared without a trace.

It had been reported a while back, that an unusual smell was detected in one of the elevator shafts, in the La Salle Hotel, like the smell of rotten meat, and upon investigating, the police found two bodies. The bodies were believed to be gangsters, as they both had guns in their holsters and were dressed like gangsters. Although their faces were no longer recognizable, as the length of time that they evidently lay in the bottom of the elevator shaft, in a foot of water, caused their faces to bloat to such an extent, that even the coroner couldn't tell who they were. However, with cases like this, the police figured that these were just two more gangland killings and so, they really didn't care.

Jimmy entered the union headquarters and a man was sitting at the desk when Jimmy asked,

"Sir, are you hiring for the World's Fair project as yet?" The man was reading the Daily Racing Form's, daily race results and for a minute, he didn't even acknowledge Jimmy. Finally, he said,

"Yes lad and what can I be a do'n' fer' ye'?" Jimmy repeated his earlier question. The man was studying Jimmy very carefully and finally he said,

"And what's yer' problem, I mean why are ye' hiding the left side of yer' face?" Jimmy once again became a little self-conscious of his facial injury, and he was slightly irritated that this big Irish galoot, would be asking him such a personal question anyway. Finally, after Jimmy's temper quieted down some, he answered,

"I was hurt in the war."

"Oh", said the man. The man then asked, "What's yer' skill, if ye' have any?" Jimmy thought about the man's question and then he answered him,

"I'm a roust-about, that is I do mostly manual labor jobs." The man then said,

"Fill out this application completely, especially where it asks what your nationality and your religion is." Jimmy was curious as to why these two questions were even on the application, but he didn't say anything. Jimmy then asked the man, "Can I borrow a pencil?" The man, angrily said,

"Here", as he gave Jimmy a well chewed, pencil stub. Jimmy proceeded to fill out the application. After he had finished, he got up from his chair and he handed the application to the man at the desk. The man finally put down the Daily Racing Form, 'the horse bettor's bible', as he angrily looked up at Jimmy, as evidently, the man felt that Jimmy was interrupting his horse picks of the day. The man glanced at Jimmy's application, and then he said,

"Jimmy O'Brien ah, and a Catholic, why didn't you say so, as we could have dispensed with the formalities of you filling out the application." Jimmy was puzzled by the man's comments as he asked him,

"I don't understand your comments, about me filling out the application." The man gave Jimmy that kind of a hard look, which means, what are you stupid, or something. The man then said, "What I mean's is this; if'n' I knew you were Irish and a Catholic, ye' wouldn't have to fill out the work application." The man could see by Jimmy's facial expression, on the uncovered side of his face, that Jimmy didn't understand what the man meant and so the man explained further,

"Look, the South-Chicago Bridge & Iron Company, only hires Irish-Catholics." Jimmy was taken aback, as he never had heard of such a thing. While he knew that the Protestants wouldn't hire Irish Catholics and he knew of their demeaning signs, with the acronym, N.I.N.A.; 'No Irish Need Apply'. The Protestants had used these signs, as a means of discouraging any Irish Catholic, who might try and obtain employment, long before the potato famine in Ireland, but he never figured that the reverse would happen.

Evidently Jimmy thought, it must be payback time, as the Irish Catholics now controlled all of Chicago's patronage jobs; they also controlled all of the wards, and they held all of the elected positions, from the mayor, on down. This was also true, in all of the large cities in America. As the Irish like to say, *'What goes around comes around'*.

The man got up from behind his desk and he extended his hand, as he said, "Jimmy me' boy, me' name is Mike Duggan and I'm the union steward. You can report for work on Monday at six a.m., out at the fair site and ask for the general foreman, a man by the name of Cornelius 'Turk' Hennessey." Jimmy shook Mike's hand as he said "Thanks," and he turned and walked out the door.

Jimmy now had second thoughts about renting a room in Canaryville, as he thought that it was too far from the fair site, and as they're was probably no public transportation to the site, as far as he knew, plus he thought, that perhaps he could find a room closer to the work site. Well in any case, *'I'll know more, after I begin my work shift'*, he thought.

Monday morning and Jimmy had walked from the La Salle hotel, over to Lake Michigan and the World's Fair site and he asked a young man, who was standing, leaning on a shovel, "Do you know a foreman, by the name of Con Hennessey?" The young man answered,

"Yes and I do, 'Turk', sits on his fat ass, over in that small shack, right along side that pile of steel girders." Jimmy said,

"Thanks," and he walked over to the shack. He opened the door and seated on a chair, which was probably old, when Lincoln was a boy, sat a fat red-faced Irishman. The man looked up at Jimmy as he said,

"And what can I be a do'n' fer' ye' lad?"

"I was sent by the union steward to see you about a laborer's job." The fat man said,

"Me' name is Con 'Turk' Hennessey, but the lads around here call me 'Turk'." 'Turk' gave Jimmy the once over and he kept looking at the side of Jimmy's face, which Jimmy had pulled his hat down over and he said, "Tell me' lad, what is wrong with the side of your face?"

Jimmy would still got peeved, when people made inquiries about his face, but once again he figured, I have no choice but to tell him, as I don't want to lose my job, before I even get it. "Well sir, I was hurt in the war and so I keep it covered, as I don't want to offend anyone." 'Turk' then said,

"If'n' ye' don't mind, I would like to see it." Jimmy kind of hesitated, but then he took off his cap. "Turk", then said, "God almighty. I'm so sorry lad, I didn't realize, that it was so bad."

"I can certainly understand yer' reluctance to show anyone your face, but as your boss, I feel that I needed to see it." He went on, "Tell me lad, does it handicap you in anyway, from doing any type of manual labor?" Jimmy answered,

"It's never bothered any of my work assignments before now, and so I don't believe that it would." 'Turk' had a sort of worried look on his fat face as he said,

"How about ye' gett'n' along with the other lads ye' come in close contact with?" Jimmy of course, prior to now, had really only one person who he came in close contact with, other than when he was in court, and that was Bill John, who could careless, about how Jimmy looked, as Bill John was his friend. 'Turk' studied Jimmy some more as he said,

"The only reason I'm ask'n' you is this; I don't care where you go, they'll always be someone, who is going to make comments about yer' face and these comments will be made, in the most degrading way." He continued, "And these people will not let up on you, until you stop them and in the construction and iron business, the only way to do that, is to fight. Are you up to fighting some of these punks?"

"Well", said Jimmy, "I grew up in Canaryville and had more than my share of street fights, and also while in school, I was on the boxing team." 'Turk' looked at Jimmy some more, with a smirk on his face, as he asked him,

"What are ye' meaning, by the school's boxing team?" Jimmy kind of smiled, as he realized that 'Turk' had no idea, that Jimmy was a college graduate and a lawyer as well. Jimmy then said,

"Well sir, its because of my face, that I have tried to avoid the general public as often as I can and so that is why myself and a friend, sought work in the various carnivals and circuses that travel around America. However, I am also, a graduate of the University of Chicago and I have a law degree. And it is with this school, that I was on their boxing team." 'Turk' sat there, with the most unusual look on his face, like this lad must be conning me, so why then, is he looking for a common laborers job?" 'Turk then said,

"I still don't understand why yer' look'n' for a laborer's job, when you could be a sitt'n', in some big shot law office in downtown Chicago." Jimmy got angry for a moment and then he said,

"Goddamn it 'Turk', do you know that no one will hire me in any of these law offices, for fear of me, upsetting their employees? People look on me, like I was Frankenstein's monster." He continued, "I'm sorry about getting so upset 'Turk', but it's difficult, when people ask me, and I have to explain to them, what it's like, to be a monster. He went on, "So I've had to kind of hide in the shadows so to speak. So, if you don't want to hire me, then say so, and I'll be moseying along."

'Turk' sat for a minute, like he was trying to think of something to say, to help ease the pain that this lad was going through, but he couldn't think of anything at the moment. Finally, he said,

"By the way young lad, I don't even know your name." Jimmy said,

"My name is Jimmy O'Brien." 'Turk' thrust out his hand, as he shook Jimmy's hand, and he said, "I'm pleased to be a meet'n' ye' Jimmy and yes, I do have a laborer's job opening on this construction site, however, it will only be temporary." Jimmy then said, "Temporary, Mr. Hennessey, why only temporary?"

'Turk' smiled, and then he explained why he felt that Jimmy's employment as a laborer, would be only temporary. 'Turk' said,

"The reason I figure that you would be working temporary as a laborer, is this; you told me that you have a law degree and I'm sure that either the union, or the South-Chicago Bridge & Iron Company, would have a place for ye', if'n ye' want it, as a lawyer." He went on, "Not that I couldn't use ye 'as a full time laborer. But I think you'd be wasting yer' time, as I believe that ye' have the promise of a fine future, providing we can get ye' situated in a position, where ye' might not have to be seated, right next to some woman, who might be frightened by yer' face." He continued,

"I'll make ye' no promises, but I will do my best, to see if I can get for ye', a job more suited to your education. It bothers me Jimmy, to see you having to hide from the public, but meanwhile, you're still going to have to face, some ignorant punks in the labor gang, you'll be assigned to, who will try and make your life difficult, if not miserable." Jimmy thanked 'Turk' for his kindness to him and for his promise to try and obtain a legal position for himself, working for either the union or the company. 'Turk' finally said,

"Jimmy, take this piece of paper to a foreman, by the name of Francis Murphy, who goes by the name of 'Murph'. He and his gang work, mixing cement, which is devilishly hard work. You'll probably be a wheel barrower, that is someone who wheels cement to and from, where ever it's needed." He went on, "At the present time, 'Murph' and his gang of twelve, are located jest 'about a half-mile from here, as you walk toward the lake" Then Jimmy asked,

"Mr. Hennessey, is there any kind of transportation for me to get from where I'm renting to here?" Mr. Hennessey then asked,

"Where's yer' room Jimmy?"

"Well, I had planned on living back in Canaryville, but it's too far of a walk to get here." Mr. Hennessey then said,

"Jimmy me lad, you're in luck, as there is a horse drawn streetcar, which leaves Canaryville every morning, at five a.m. and it arrives here at jest' about six-thirty and it leaves every night for Canaryville, at seven p.m. So if you want to live in Canaryville, we do have transportation set up for all of the Irish workers, who live in Canaryville."

Jimmy once again thanked Mr. Hennessey and he walked out the door of the foreman's shack, walking toward the work site where he would find, 'Murph'.

It took Jimmy about five minutes to reach a bunch of workers who he guessed might be the gang that 'Murph' was foreman of. He spotted who he thought might be 'Murph', as this person, was talking to two men and 'Murph' seemed to be giving them instructions. Jimmy waited until the person he thought might be 'Murph' was through talking and then he walked over to this man and he said, "Mr. Murphy sir, my name is Jimmy O'Brien and Mr. Hennessey said that you have an opening in your gang and so he sent me to see you."

'Murph' looked at Jimmy and then he said,

"Have ye' ever done cement work before?" Jimmy said,

"No sir, I have not, but I'm willing to learn." 'Murph' looked at Jimmy's hat pulled down, covering the left side of his face, but he didn't say anything, which Jimmy thought was unusual. 'Murph' told Jimmy, just what he expected of him and that if he kept his mouth shut and did what he was told, he would get along just fine within his gang. 'Murph' then called out to a very large man, who was carrying a shovel.

"Hey Mike, I got a new lad fer' ye' to break in and his name is Jimmy, Jimmy O'Brien." Mike looked over at Jimmy with a sort of a scowl on his face. To Jimmy, Mike looked like he had been drinking most of the night, as his eyes were blood shot and he sort of staggered, as he walked. Mike was a big man; Jimmy guessed him to be well over six feet tall and he was well built.

Mike said to Jimmy, "Go get yer' self' a wheelbarrow and then follow me." Jimmy spotted several wheelbarrows, sitting over by themselves. He walked over, and he picked out one.

CHAPTER 41

❀

Winners & Losers
-Erin, Pat & Bill-

Bill John became very moody after Pat Monahan started to monopolize, Erin's free time. Bill could gradually see, that Erin while being very polite and nice to him, wasn't really interested in him as a suitor, or as a lover. Finally, one evening after Erin had gone to work at the Shamrock Club, he and Mrs. O'Sullivan had a heart to heart talk concerning Erin.

Actually, Mrs. O'Sullivan wanted to talk to Bill about his feelings concerning Erin and Erin seeming to fall head-over-heels, for the tall Irishman, as she knew where such a love triangle such as this one, could certainly lead; and violence wasn't out of the question. Mrs. O'Sullivan had grown quite found of the tall Indian, who became sort of Jimmy O'Brien's sidekick, or shadow, since the war. Mrs. O'Sullivan could hear Bill pacing across the bedroom floor, back and forth, back and forth, which was directly over the kitchen, so she took her broom handle, and hit the kitchen ceiling with it a few times, and finally, Bill came down stairs. Bill said to Mrs. O'Sullivan,

"Why are you making such a racket old lady, with that damn broom handle?" Mrs. O'Sullivan with a very sad look on her face, said to Bill,

"Bill, sit down, as I want to talk to you about a subject that is bothering you and it certainly is bothering me also, although I'll admit, not in the same way and for a different reason." Mrs. O'Sullivan began with a sort of entree, starting out with a rather conciliatory tone in her remarks as she said,

"Look Bill, I think the world of you as does Erin, however, Erin does not love you and so I think that you should move on with your life." She continued, "I've noticed that Jimmy no longer comes up here to visit or court Erin, as I believe, he felt that it was you she favored, considering his hideous facial problem and being the gentlemen that he obviously is, he left the scene to you, rather than try to compete with you over Erin's affections. Now Bill, I'm not faulting you one least bit, for falling in love with Erin. God gave Erin, unbelievable beauty and brains and you are just a love smitten man." She went on,

"Beauty sometimes, can be a curse as well as a blessing. Take me for example; I was at one time, considered the toast of Broadway and had men literally falling at my feet, as I was considered one of the most beautiful women in the world. That's quite an honor to carry around and it doesn't make you the least bit humble. Moreover, don't think for one moment, that I didn't think, that I was somehow better than everyone else. Foolish as that may seem, but when a young girl, any young girl, who has men offering to buy you the world, humbleness goes out the window and narcissism sets in." She went on,

"Such adulation, can completely screw-up a beautiful young girl's mind, confusing her such, that she wouldn't know real love from infatuation and could care less. In addition, it can set her up for a bad fall. Look, I was married three times and each time I got married, reality never lived up to my expectations, of marriage. So I became disillusioned and thought that suicide might be the only way out." Of course, when it came to taking my own life, I was never serious, because of my strict religious upbringing, but it had crossed my mind never the less. Now look at me, most people wouldn't give me the time of day, I'm just an old fat broad, who most everybody affectionately, calls 'ma'." She continued,

"So why am I telling you all this, its because I care, both for you and for Erin, and I know where this can lead and it ain't pleasant for anyone," Bill after politely listening to Mrs. O'Sullivan's dissertation on love and the courting of a young girl said,

"With all respect to you and what you have just told me, I'm not sure why I should just walk away, as I've never walked away from a fight in my life." He went on, "I had thought that I might have a chance with Erin, until Pat showed up that is, and then the climate suddenly changed." He went on, "Now admittedly, I may be totally naive when it comes to women, but am I that wrong in my thinking, that I detected a sort of chemistry between Erin and myself?"

Mrs. O'Sullivan waited a few minutes before she was able to mentally formulate a reasonable answer for this lovesick Indian, who she hoped, would change his mind. Mrs. O'Sullivan then answered Bill,

"Look Bill, you had every reason to think that Erin might have strong personal feelings for you. However, as I said earlier, those feelings were not true love, but were gratefulness, for you're being there to protect her, after what she had been through, with these Mafia gangsters. These animals, had almost ruined her life and tried to deprive her of what every young girl and young woman fantasizes about, and that is; real and genuine love, kids, a home and a loving and caring husband." She continued,

"These are the things that young women dream about night and day, since they were little girls." She went on, "I don't blame you Bill for having fallen in love with Erin, as she is most desirable; she's sexy, flirtatious, vivacious, beautiful and she is having the time of her life right now. I certainly am slightly jealous of her myself, oh to be young again, but as I said, God only gives us so many years of youth and allows for the foolish mistakes, that all youth seem destined to make and so, I fully understand both of you're positions." She continued, "Now let me let you in on a little secret, and promise that you will not tell anyone else, especially Erin." Bill said.

"Okay, I promise."

"Well," said Mrs. O'Sullivan, "I've got news for you, as she looked from side to side, as though she didn't want anyone else to hear her little secret. And then she said, "Erin's romantic fling with Pat, is just that, nothing but a fling and further, its my predication, that they will soon break-up, even though she for the moment, is caught up in his Irish charm." Bill interrupted her for a moment, when he asked her,

"Well if it isn't Pat, then who in the hell, can it be?" Mrs. O'Sullivan then said,

"It probably is someone, who you might least expect her to be in love with and his name is Jimmy, Jimmy O'Brien. I didn't believe that she was at first, but there are certain signs that I have noted, concerning Erin and Jimmy, when they're together, that gave me this feeling. Please don't ask me how I know or why, or what are these signs, but most women are intuitive, when it comes to these things. We women are a very peculiar species, as you already know. However, I will tell you this much, Erin shares a certain compassion with Jimmy. Life in away, has been cruel to both of them. Erin craves attention and Jimmy because of his disfigurement, kind of shies away from the public. But, theirs of course is something deeper, much deeper, as I believe that they have become soul mates." She went on,

"As you know Bill, when Jimmy is around his small circle of friends, who pay no attention to his face and where he can let his hair down so to speak, he is very witty. He knows a million jokes and I've watched him tease Erin unmercifully and that of course as you know, teasing is a form of attention, and most women love to be teased. Its a precursor to love and affection." She continued,

"It stems from, I believe, when girls are little and come from a family of brothers, where teasing is constant and unrelenting. This is where most girls learn the inner most workings of a boy's mind." She went on, "The good lord knew exactly what he was doing when he put together the simple and rather uncomplicated minds of little boys and their sexual urges and the very complicated minds of little girls. Usually boys run on logic, except where their sexual desire takes hold and then their animal drives prevail, whereas girls run on their emotions and their natural attraction to the opposite sex, as nature intended." She continued,

"Young boys usually only have one thing on their minds and that is, *'how do I get into Molly's pants so to speak'*, whereas young girls might have similar feelings about boys, but they are more able to control their sexual urges and thus, proper courting usually takes place. This ritual, usually leads to marriage, which most always, leads to children, which is called propagation, in the Catholic faith. It's a never-ending cycle, as God intended that it should be. Its kind of hard to screw with Mother Nature, if you'll pardon my pun."

Bill laughed as he said,

"For an old Irish broad, you sure are a pretty damn good philosopher." Mrs. O'Sullivan laughed out loud. Bill then asked,

"Assuming you're right, in what you've just told me, then what should I do, leave?" Mrs. O'Sullivan answered Bill in this way, "If it were up to me, I would say yes, after I made some kind of an excuse to Erin, for you're having to return to Chicago to find a job, as your money is getting low, which I'm sure that it is. I believe that you are living on the five thousand dollars that Jimmy split with you, after he won that court case, am I correct?" Bill nodded his head in the affirmative.

CHAPTER 42

❀

Suspicious Guest
-Al's Long Arm-

It was just about three-thirty in the afternoon, when Mrs. O'Sullivan heard a knock on her front door. She wiped her hands on her apron, as she was in the process of baking bread, before she answered the door. She went to the door and there standing outside, was a swarthy faced man, with a big black cheroot in his mouth, wearing a black fedora, who to Mrs. O'Sullivan, seemed like he was seven foot tall, as he was that huge.

Mrs. O'Sullivan said to the man, "What can I be a do'n' for you sir, do you need directions?" The man came right to the point, when he answered her in a rather gruff voice, in which Mrs. O'Sullivan could detect a foreign accent.

"Naw', I would like to rent a room, and you're sign said vacancy." Mrs. O'Sullivan became a little nervous, as she didn't like the looks of this man, as there was something about him, that her intuition warned her about and then finally she said after hesitating in answering the stranger,

"Why yes I do, is there just you sir?" The man answered,

"Look lady, does there look like anyone else standing here wit' me?"

Mrs. O'Sullivan was now getting her Irish up, with this insolent speaking foreigner, as she said, "I've got a room upstairs in the rear, would you like to see it, I mean, to see if you want to rent it?" The man answered,

"Naw', dat' sounds just a' fine, as I'll only be staying a couple of days, as I should finish my business by then." The strange man then gave Mrs. O' Sullivan a kind of crazed look, as he had one eye, that didn't seem to focus very well, as it moved from one side of its eye socket, to the other?" Mrs. O'Sullivan then said, "For a one day's stay, it will be two dollars, with payment in advance." The stranger pulled out a wad of bills from his pocket and he peeled off a ten spot. Mrs. O'Sullivan then said,

"Don't you have anything smaller, as I don't have change for ten dollars." The man said,

"No matter doll, keep the change." Mrs. O'Sullivan then said to the big stranger,

"Follow me." She then turned and asked the stranger, "Don't you have any luggage?" The stranger said,

"Naw' doll, I only be here, for only a couple of days, if that, so who needs luggage?" as he began to laugh. When they reached the room where the stranger would be staying, he turned and he looked directly at Mrs. O'Sullivan and he said,

"Whose' else is stay'n' here?" Mrs. O'Sullivan now found herself in a dilemma, how should she answer this creep; should she lie, or should she tell him, just who is staying at her tourist home? Finally, after stuttering some, she said,

"At the moment, I have three guests, although one is in Chicago on business." He looked at her for a moment and then he said,

"Doll, you said on your sign, that you serve meals, is that right?" Mrs. O'Sullivan said,

"Why yes I do, unless you want to eat at the Shamrock Club; as they serve very lovely meals, and besides, they have entertainment; er' ladies, as she winked at him." The stranger looked at Mrs. O'Sullivan like he might be getting ready to murder her and then he said,

"Naw', I like to eats' with you and you're guests, its kind of like a family, as I would a' like to meet your guests, as I'm a friendly kind a guy." The stranger then broke out, in a fit of laughter; with spittle, starting to drip from the corner's of his mouth, which sent chills up Mrs. O'Sullivan's spine. Mrs. O'Sullivan then closed the door to the stranger's room and she walked downstairs. She heard him open up the door to his room as he hollered,

"Hey doll, when's supper?" Mrs. O'Sullivan said,

"I serve supper between six and seven." Mrs. O'Sullivan didn't like the looks of this creep, who she figured might be a gangster, perhaps one of Al Capish's hired hit men. She shuddered once more, as she was now feeling kind of scared with this creep in her house, who maybe was up to no good. Her son Mike and

Bill, the Indian, were out shopping for groceries and as far as Erin was concerned, she and Pat had gone for a picnic, after Erin got off work.

She expected her son and Bill, in just about fifteen minutes and with Erin, she wasn't sure, although she figured, that she would be home for her nap and for supper, before five o'clock. She heard what sounded like someone walking across the floor upstairs, as the sound was coming from Bill's room and now, that same sound, came from Erin's room. Evidently this stranger was searching both Bill's and Erin's rooms, looking for something. Perhaps he thought they might have a weapon stashed away in their rooms.

Mrs. O'Sullivan heard more footsteps, as the stranger evidently finished searching their rooms and he was now standing at the top of the stairs, listening. Mrs. O'Sullivan kept on with her kitchen chores and she was putting away some of her pots and pans, as she was finished, using the mixing bowls, she used for her bread making. She placed her bread pans in the oven and put the mixing bowls in the sink, for Mike to wash and put away, when he came home. Mrs. O'Sullivan was waiting for the stranger to come down stairs, but he didn't, as he returned to his room. She could hear his footsteps, as he walked to his room and she could hear him shut the door.

Mrs. O'Sullivan waited a good five minutes, before she walked into the dining room and from behind the China Cabinet, she found what she was looking for, her shotgun. She knew that she wouldn't have quick access to it, if she needed it in a hurry, located behind the China Cabinet, and so she thought, where can I hide it from his prying eyes, and yet, where I can have quick access to it, should I need it. Her eyes searched the dining room, they're standing between the dining room, and the parlor, was an umbrella stand, made from the foot and leg of an elephant. The umbrella stand had five or six umbrellas in the stand, of all sizes and colors. She put the shotgun down into the umbrella stand with the butt up and the barrel, touching the bottom of the stand. She then placed an old kitchen towel, over the top of the umbrellas and the butt of the shotgun, to hide it.

She could only hope, that if this creep meant to do them harm, she might be able to reach her shot gun, before he could act; if of course, the stranger meant to do them harm. Mrs. O'Sullivan knew that she would have to control her emotions, as with her very active imagination, she was beginning to become paranoid. After she finished hiding her shotgun, she was about to return to the kitchen, when she looked up and the stranger was standing in the hall, between her and the kitchen. She didn't hear him come down the stairs and she didn't know if he had seen, what she was doing with her shotgun.

She did hear his door close though, of course not realizing that the stranger could have closed his door and never went into his room, as he was only trying to make her think that he did, while he watched her hide her shotgun, in the umbrella stand. She rather boldly said to the stranger,

"Can I help you?" The stranger said,

"Naw', I just thought I would come downstairs and sit in the parlor and read, today's newspaper, if you don't mind, doll?" Mrs. O'Sullivan gave a sigh of relief, that the stranger evidently didn't see her hide her shotgun, or so she thought, as she said,

"No sir, I don't mind, please help yourself," She went on, "If you need something, why I will be in the kitchen, preparing supper." The stranger merely looked at her and sort of grunted. Mrs. O'Sullivan could hear a car pull up on the gravel parking space, in front of her home. She wondered whose car it was, Erin and Pat's, or her son Mike, and Bill? She wanted to go to the front door and warn them, but she new that if the stranger had come here, looking to kill someone, he wouldn't have allowed her to do so, and of course, she didn't want her stupid actions, to arouse any suspicions in the mind of this creepy stranger. Therefore, she just waited to see who came in the front door.

The door opened and in stepped Bill, but Mrs. O'Sullivan didn't see Mike, her son. Bill then said,

"I see we have guests." Mrs. O' Sullivan kind of rolled her eyes, so as to give Bill, some kind of a warning, but before he could make any sense out of her eye movement, the stranger had already followed Bill into the kitchen, where he said,

"I'm the new guest." Bill turned to look at the stranger and his heart fell to his stomach, as he could smell Mafia, aside from the strong garlic smell, which this stranger exuded from his mouth. Mrs. O'Sullivan wondered why Mike didn't come in, but she knew better than to ask Bill. Mrs. O'Sullivan than said,

"Bill, why don't you get washed up for supper, while I put away the groceries." The stranger almost said something, but he evidently thought better of it and so he returned to the parlor. Bill then answered, Mrs. O'Sullivan,

"Fine, I'll be down in a few minutes." It wasn't more than ten minutes, when the sound of another car, pulled up to the front of the tourist home. Mrs. O'Sullivan could hear Erin say goodbye to Pat, as Pat she guessed, wasn't going to stay for supper, although, sometimes he did. Erin walked up the front porch stairs and she walked a dozen or more steps from the front door to the kitchen, where she greeted Mrs. O'Sullivan, with her usual kiss. Erin then said,

"Do we have new guests?" Mrs. O'Sullivan answered her, with a rather frightened look on her face,

"Why yes we do, a gentlemen guest." Before Mrs. O'Sullivan could say anything more about the new guest, the strange guest came into the kitchen where Mrs. O'Sullivan and Erin were talking and he said,

"Yes doll, I'm the new guest and my name is Sal, short for Salvatore." Sal was giving Erin the once over with his cruel eyes, as he mentally undressed her. Erin could read his moronic mind, like he had a newspaper stuck to his forehead and the one word headline said, 'Sex'. Erin then said,

"Its nice to meet you Sal, my name is Erin." Bill then came down stairs and Mrs. O'Sullivan noticed, a sort of worried look on his face.

"Well" said Mrs. O'Sullivan, shall we sit down for supper?" Erin said,

"Give me a minute, to go upstairs to my room and wash my hands." Mrs. O'Sullivan then said,

"Fine Erin, we'll wait for you before we start eating." The stranger than said to the group, while they all waited for Erin,

"This old doll tells me, that you also have another guest, who she said was downtown on business, is that right?" Bill looked at Mrs. O'Sullivan and then he said,

"I'm not sure, as he had told me that he may be looking for a job somewhere in Chicago, and so he may not be coming back to Mrs. O'Sullivan's tourist home." He went on, "Perhaps he has found another job." At that moment, Erin came back down stairs, as she said to Mrs. O'Sullivan,

"Mary I'm starved, what's for supper"? Sal evidently didn't like the evasive answers; he seemed to be getting from Mrs. O'Sullivan and the Indian, so he said,

"Now look, you guys seem to be giving me da' run around and I would like a straight answer now; where is this missing guest, and I want a straight answer?" Bill than asked,

"Mr. Salvatore, what business do you have with this guest, as you don't even know his name?" Mr. Salvatore was getting more and more angry and so he told Bill,

"Listen you frigg'n' half breed Indian, I'll ask the questions, not you and his name is of little importance to me, all's I know is that he has something wrong with his face, as he wears his cap pulled down over one side of his face."

Erin, Mrs. O'Sullivan and Bill, all looked at one another, as each was thinking, why would this gangster be looking for Jimmy? Erin was somewhat relieved, as she initially thought that perhaps Al was trying to find her, to finish his *La Vendetta* against her. Although, she was also worried for Jimmy's sake, as she couldn't yet figure out, what Jimmy had done to have this creep, come looking for him? And then it dawned on her, as Jimmy had told her that he was working on an extortion and blackmail case for the U.S. Government, which involved Al Capish in some way. Jimmy also had told her of a former class mate of his, in law school, who evidently ran a law office, whose only client was, Al Capish and who ended up, committing suicide as he was about to be indicted.

The gangster now spoke, "Look, I want some answers and so to start with, I'll ask this half-breed one more time, where is this guy?" Bill, whose stoic demeanor didn't reveal the rage, that was now going on in his brain, said,

"I told you, I don't know if or when he'll be back, if he found a job, he won't be, if he didn't, he might." With that answer, the gangster reached across the table and hit Bill flush on the jaw, knocking him off of his chair and he lay, crumpled up on the floor, unconscious. Both Erin and Mrs. O'Sullivan were scared of this violent man, who came into their home and who was now threatening them, if they didn't tell him what he wanted to hear.

Now neither Erin nor Mrs. O'Sullivan, knew when or even if, Jimmy would be coming back to the tourist home, as Mrs. O'Sullivan had told Bill, that because of what Jimmy perceived, as the beginning of a romance between Erin and himself, he decided to leave her tourist home and return to Chicago, looking for employment. Sal the Mafia gangster then said,

"I want you two broads to help me carry this Indian upstairs, to one of the rooms, where I want you to tie his hands to the bed, so that he can't move." He went on, "Then we'll see who will give me a straight answer to my question, as to where the guy with the screwed up face is or, I will kill somebody and maybe it will be the old broad first." Mrs. O'Sullivan looked at Erin, as she was now starting to shake. Erin put her arms around Mrs. O'Sullivan, as she tried to comfort her, when the gangster hit the old lady across the mouth knocking her down.

Seeing Mrs. O'Sullivan lying on the floor, with blood streaming from her mouth, Erin rushed at the gangster screaming and calling him every swear word, she knew, who quickly side stepped her attack and hit her in the jaw with his fist, knocking her to the floor. Erin though stunned, staggered to her feet, as Bill was just now starting to come around. Bill couldn't move, as his hands were tied to the bedpost, with drapery cord, which the gangster had instructed them to use, to tie Bill's hands.

Erin's mind was racing to see if she could find away of killing this animal, before he killed all of them. Erin, suddenly smiled to herself, as she had completely forgotten, that she had 'Lips' Bernstein's, Derringer pistol, in its small holster, fastened to her garter, on her right leg. She now had to change her demeanor completely, from one of fear and loathing, to one of a seductress, to see if she could lure this ape, into trying to make love to her, as she was sure that he had plans of raping her anyway.

So, Erin, who had had, much experience in this kind of sexual seduction in dealing with these Mafioso gangsters, although these Mafiosi gangsters didn't really make love in the normal way, as they generally raped their victims, in the most brutal way; said to this animal.

"Al, I'm sorry about the way myself and the rest of us, have been treating you, when all that you really want to know, is where is the man with the pulled down hat and nothing more?" Erin was now slowly opening her blouse, to reveal her white breasts. She then slowly unfastened her skirt and let it fall to the floor. She hesitated in going any further, until she felt sure, that Al was taking the bait. She however, kept her right leg turned away from his view, so that he couldn't see the small pistol and holster, she had hidden underneath her flowered garter.

The gangster was just now starting to become aroused; as Erin could see, his eyes first narrow and then they opened, to reveal the contrast between the whites of his eyes and his black pupils. She could tell that he was becoming further excited, as she could hear his breathing, beginning to increase, as his nostrils began to flare, much like an animal in heat. Spittle stared to appear at the corners of his mouth, as he started to drool, in anticipation of what he was about to enjoy. He set his gun down on the dresser within his reach, and then he began to take off his suit coat and his pants. He kept his shoes on for whatever reason and he now was in the process of taking off his striped shorts. Erin noticed just how hairy his body was, as he resembled a gorilla.

Erin slowly and deliberately, walked to him, as she kissed him full on the mouth, while gagging on the taste, of whatever he had eaten for lunch and the 'Dago' cheroots he smoked, which had been soaked in 'Dago' red wine. He stunk both from perspiration and from the garlic he had eaten. Even his cheap cologne, couldn't mask his earthy smell, nothing could. He put his arms around Erin as, his hands slid down her backside, as he grabbed Erins' ass with his greasy fingers, Erin could feel his manhood, as he was preparing to move his hands and fingers, to Erins' most private parts.

All of a sudden, a look of surprise and pain came across his ugly face, as though someone had stabbed him with a very sharp object. The 'Dago' cheroot he was chewing on, fell from his gasping mouth to the floor. Two muffled bangs could be heard, like firecrackers going off, where you see the explosion first and then a short time later, you hear the bang. He actually was hanging on to Erin, to keep from falling, as Erin had pressed the Derringer's nozzle, up against his stomach, as she fired both barrels, into his gut. A small trickle of blood could be seen, exiting his mouth, as though his lower lip was bleeding. His legs became unstable, like they were no longer capable of holding up, his great weight.

Erin then backed away from him, letting him fall to the floor, as he said, *"Lei la femmina di miserabile;"* 'You rotten bitch'. The gangster was staring with his eyes wide open, at the ceiling fan, which was turning around, ever so slowly. It was doubtful that this creep, made it to *'Il paradiso',* unless he had a good Mafia lawyer, who would plead insanity.

Mrs. O'Sullivan was attempting to get to her feet, as Erin was assisting her. Mrs. O'Sullivan's right eye was starting to close and it was becoming discolored; she would soon have a shiner. Erin then went over to Bill and she untied his hands from the drapery cord, which held his hands fast. Bill was still groggy from Al's right cross. Bill sat on the edge of the bed while holding his jaw in his hands and Erin gave him a kiss on his cheek.

As Erin began to put her clothes back on, there was a noise downstairs, like someone had come in, and a voice said, "Ma, Ma, where the heck are ye'?" Erin hollered back.

"Is that you Mike, we're up stairs darl'n'." Erin could tell by the many footsteps, that there was more than one person coming up the stairs and so she looked at Bill and Mrs. O'Sullivan, as if to say, *"Oh no, are they're more of these creeps'?* Michael entered the room first, followed by five bodyguards, the guards that usually protect Mr. McGrath and Mr. Bernstein. Bill was sitting on the bed, holding his jaw. Erin was standing next to Mrs. O'Sullivan. Erin had just finished fastening the hook on her skirt, and she was holding on to Mrs. O'Sullivan, to keep her from falling, as her legs were still wobbly. Michael then said,

"What happened, ma?" Mrs. O'Sullivan who was frightened out of her wits' said, as she was trying to make a joke out of this very bad situation,

"Ah Michael me' lad, I've had a cranky tenant, who refused to pay his rent and so, I had to get rid of him, as this is not the charity ward of the Cook County Hospital, or is it?" Mrs. O'Sullivan then said, "Praise be to God Michael, how is it, that ye' brought these body guards with ye, are ye' clairvoyant?" Michael who had to laugh at his mother's terrible joke said,

"No ma, Bill here, told me when I let him off a while ago, to go back to the Shamrock Club, to see if any of Mr. McGrath's body guards were around, as he didn't like the looks of that strange black Lincoln limousine, parked out side the house. He had a hunch that it might be the mob, from the Southside and he wanted me to get some help, if I could." Bill said to the five bodyguards,

"Can you guys, dispose of the body and drive his car into Lake Michigan, in order to get rid of the evidence, but before you do, this guy evidently filched my pistol and so I want it back, before you dispose of him?" Bill reached into the gangster's inside suit coat pocket and found his colt revolver. 'Curly' Morrissey who was completely bald, then said,

"We'll wait until it gets a bit darker, and I know of a place, where we can ditch this punk and his car." The five bodyguards after re-dressing the gangster, they proceeded to carry the gangster down the stairs and put him, into his car, seating him in the front passenger seat. "Curly' then placed the gangster's black fedora, back on the his head. One of the five bodyguards would drive the gangster's car, to wherever they planned on dumping it, into the lake, while the other bodyguards would follow in their car.

'Curly' knew of a high, cement-loading dock, which dropped off, directly into Lake Michigan and into, about thirty-five feet of water along the waterfront, in the suburb of Evanston, Illinois, in an abandoned water pumping station. As this place had been used for such purposes, many times before, the Irish Mafia knew it as 'Curly's', underwater parking lot.

CHAPTER 43

Adversaries

-Jimmy's Fight-

Jimmy had been working for only a couple of days moving wet cement in a wheelbarrow, which was backbreaking work and his back, was breaking, figuratively speaking of course. Wet cement is much like liquid lead, in that its heavy and it sloshes back and forth, as you walk. Even in the carnivals and circuses, in which he did hard manual labor erecting tent poles and such, he never had to work so hard, in order to make a living. It was without question, the hardest work he had ever done in his life. Jimmy was paired with two others, a Pat Kearney and another man by the name of Mike Mullins. Pat never said much, as I guess he was afraid of Mike Mullins, who not only towered over him, but he also had a mean streak, which made him the classic bully.

Mike made it a point to criticize Jimmy for one thing or other and finally one day, he called Jimmy a monster, the faceless wonder and a gutless son-of-a-bitch. Jimmy soon knew, that he would be expected to fight Mike, as this of course, was the traditional way, the Irish immigrant, settled his scores with his tormentors and baiters. Otherwise, Jimmy's hideous facial problem would attract more and more attention from this gang of rough and tough Irishmen, who respected only toughness and had no empathy for Jimmy's condition, regardless of his having received his injury, fighting for the United States, in Europe.

Jimmy knew that Mike ate a very large lunch everyday, and he washed it down with two quarts of beer. The gang's 'gopher', a young boy, went for beer everyday, from one of the local saloons. It happened, shortly after lunch and before Mike had his afternoon nap, which was against company policy. However, who was man enough to stand up to this bully and report him, so nothing was ever said about Mike's taking a nap, after lunch each day? Finally, Jimmy had had enough of Mike and his mindless torment of him, with his insensitive remarks and Jimmy then said to Mike,

"Look Mike, you've have been calling me disparaging names everyday since I've been here, in front of the men and finally, you have reached the last straw, when you called me a son-of-a-bitch. No one calls me such a name, as it's disrespectful to my mother, God rest her soul."

With that last remark, Jimmy hauled off and he hit Mike in the nose, knocking him down and breaking his nose. Mike was not only stunned by Jimmy's fist, he was amazed that Jimmy would stand up to him, as he had figured Jimmy for a wimp.

Mike staggered to his feet and tried to wipe the flow of blood, around his mouth, which was now entering his mouth from his broken nose, gagging him. Before Mike could return to that classic pose of a street fighter, with his fists and arms raised high, so as to protect his face and body, Jimmy hit him once again in his nose and gave him two left hooks to his kidneys and a hard right to his gut. Mike folded up like a big rag doll, as he lay in a fetal position on the ground, screaming from pain, while Jimmy stood over him, egging him, to get up and fight. Mike began to vomit up his recently eaten lunch and the two quarts of beer; he had washed his sandwiches down with. His pants were soaking wet, from urine, as they reacted involuntarily, to Jimmy's two powerful blows to his kidneys.

Jimmy was fuming, as he began to call Mike, every foul name he could think of, including the name that he and most men respond to, in the most offensive way, which is, 'son-of-a-bitch'. Jimmy taunted Mike unmercifully and called him a yellow coward and that he was all bluff and he had no balls. Mike who was both physically hurt and angry, made one last vain attempt to tackle Jimmy, while he lay on the ground, trying to knock Jimmy off of his feet. Jimmy, who was expecting such an attack, kicked Mike, squarely in the head, knocking him unconscious. Jimmy knew, having had to fight the many street punks, while growing up in Canaryville, that fights such as this one, were not fought, using the 'Marquess of Queensbury' rules, as it was a dog eat dog world, and it was the survival of the fittest.

The workers who had gathered around the two men, were stunned by the ferocity of Jimmy's onslaught and his unrelenting attack on Mike, who had stood towering over Jimmy, like Jimmy was a little boy, at the beginning of the fight. Finally, when Mike finally came too, Jimmy said to him,

"If you make one more derogatory remark, about me or my face, I will kill you and I do not make idle threats, believe me." Mike mumbled something that amounted to an apology of sorts, as his few friends helped him to his feet. There would be no more work for Mike that day, as he had to seek medical attention. The remaining gang members, all congratulated Jimmy and they all patted him on the back. Jimmy had earned his place of respect, amongst the Irish laborers in his work gang.

Jimmy returned to his job duties, although the adrenalin was still surging through his veins. Nothing more was said to him about the fight, although early the following morning, the foreman of the project, 'Murph', stopped Jimmy as he was walking by the foreman's shack. He hollered out,

"Hey Jimmy, I'd like to talk to ye' about yesterday's fight with Mike Mullins." Jimmy walked over to the foreman's shack and he followed Mr. Murphy into the shack. Mr. Murphy pointed to a chair as he said to Jimmy,

"Have a seat Jimmy." He looked at Jimmy for a minute, as he was trying to see if Jimmy suffered any physical damage from having fought the toughest man in his gang. Finally, he said,

"Jimmy I'm proud of ye', to haven beaten that big bully, Mike Mullins. I honestly didn't think that anyone could beat that big bastard. My hat is off to you, and I believe that you certainly have earned the respect of all your co-workers." He went on, "I'm truly sorry that I didn't get to see the fight, but I have heard from several of the men who witnessed your savage attack on Mike. And they said, that it was probably, the most swift, and brutal attack on anyone, they had ever seen."

Jimmy seemed at a loss for words, as he didn't want any notoriety connected with his fight with Mike Mullins, as it would only bring him, more unwanted attention and he was trying to avoid such attention. Jimmy thanked him for his kind words, as he returned to his work site.

CHAPTER 44

❁

Unrequited Love
-Erin and Bill-

Mrs. O'Sullivan, who was suffering with a black eye, from the punch that the Mafia mobster hit her, was stirring her morning coffee. Neither Erin nor Bill had said one word to her, nor to each other. Mrs. O'Sullivan didn't like the chilly atmosphere in her home, especially around her kitchen table, as she liked both Erin and Bill and so she figured, that it was up to her, to step in and have Erin put her cards on the table so to speak. *'Was she or wasn't she interested in Bill from a romantic standpoint'?* Bill, who also was nursing a bruised jaw, was just staring at his coffee mug, and Erin herself, who had been hit by that Mafia mobster, was rubbing her swollen jaw. As it was Tuesday, Erin wasn't expected to sing at the Shamrock Club that evening, which would give her a little more time to recover from her bruised and swollen jaw.

Finally, Mrs. O'Sullivan said,

"Jesus, Mary and Joseph; look you two, I'm getting sick and tired of this silence. You're both acting like little children." She went on, "Erin, do you have any romantic interest in Bill what so ever, as he obviously is in love with you." Erin was startled by Mrs. O'Sullivan's rather blunt inquiry, as she thought about her question and she thought too, that it was really none of her business and then she said,

"Look, I love Bill, but I'm not in love with him, does that make any sense?" She went on, "I owe Bill and Jimmy my life and I'll be forever grateful to them for my life. They both have literally put their own lives in jeopardy, in order to protect me." She continued, "I'm at a stage in my life where I perhaps, had better make some choices about my life, or do I want to end up, a bitter old maid?" She thought for a minute more and then she went on.

"At the present time I'm seeing a wonderful man, Pat Monahan. While I like Pat very much, I'm not in love with him. I enjoy his company and his laughter, but to be truthful with you both, I believe that I'm in love with Jimmy O'Brien. Don't ask me why, as I couldn't tell you, but there's something about him, that I am attracted to." She went on,

"Perhaps it's his innate charm, his wit, his warmth, or perhaps, I have so much compassion for his hideous injury, in which he has tried to hide it and himself, from the ignorant public. Or maybe, its for some other reason, some deeper reason, that neither of us, understand, at least not myself." She continued, "While we both grew up in Canaryville, in an all Irish ghetto, where I had a much worse life as a little girl, than did Jimmy. However, fate played a cruel hand with Jimmy, by giving him that grotesque wound during the war, where as myself, I have been able to make something of my life. Although, my road to fame has had it's many pitfalls also, in that I've had to become a cheap whore, selling my body, in order to satisfy my dreams, while pleasuring others." She went on with her own, sort of public confession.

"Now I know that Jimmy loves me, as he said so, but I at the time, I didn't really give Jimmy, a second look, other than perhaps, to be appreciative of his protection. I suspect that Jimmy found it necessary to leave your tourist home Mrs. O'Sullivan, because he knew that Bill, was also in love with me, or at least he thought he was. So Jimmy, the perfect gentlemen, stepped aside to allow Bill to pursue me, without his interference." She stared at the old kitchen stove, as she mulled around in her mind, her many deep thoughts, as to how to make any sense out of what she was thinking and how best to explain it if she could, her situation regarding Bill, Jimmy and Pat. She then said,

"Love and infatuation, are like twin sisters, they both look alike on the surface and they act very similarly, but one is real and the other, is only a pretext, a disingenuous facade really. Now how can anyone know, which one is the real sister? Many of us end up marrying the wrong sister—'infatuation', and we regret it for the rest of our lives. We're always wondering; did we act too hastily, should we have waited a little longer, before we committed ourselves to another person? No matter how attractive that other person was and what is usually the case with youth, youth has no patience; it wants what it wants, right now. In the case of most young girls and women, they all want to get married to some prince charming, and so they allow many times, the twin sister, infatuation, to dictate who they think they're in love with. They all want to believe what they want to believe and no one can talk them out of it." She continued,

"Many young girls want to get away from home, as life at home can be brutal sometimes, as with an abusive-drunken father, who may at one time or another, have forced sexual relations on his daughter/s. In addition, her mother, who unwittingly, becomes an accomplice to such an act, as her only means of support, is from her abusive and drunken husband and therefore, rather than prevent such a hideous act, from taking place, she passively stands by and allows it to happen. The young girl/s, is totally unprepared for such a heinous act, resulting in life long scars and in many cases, suicide can be her only way out, or a life of drugs and prostitution, in some Mafia run, whorehouse."

"Life can be very confusing and I guess for some reason, God wanted it that way. How many persons do we know, who ended up in a wrong marriage?" She went on, "I'm sure Mary O'Sullivan had made several wrong choices, when she was a young and a beautiful woman, with men literally throwing themselves at her feet, by entering into several doomed marriages? I know from what Mary has told me, that she went through a cycle in her life, where she though that she could, just about have anything her heart desired, but one has to pay the fiddler, for our many indiscretions, so to speak."

Mary seemed to gaze off, toward the kitchen window, like she was looking into the future, while her past, kept blurring her vision. Both Mrs. O'Sullivan and Bill were amazed at the maturity of Erin's mental grasp of her life and life in particular. Neither spoke for at least ten minutes; while they all sat around the kitchen table, all reliving they're own lives, in a kind of quiet reflection, and each taking a sort of mental sojourn, of both the good and the bad in their lives. Finally Bill spoke,

"While I can't say truthfully, that I'm not hurt, but I certainly respect you're honesty and I'm glad that you were able to convince me, that I was being very foolish, in trying to make you love me. Life as you so eloquently stated, can be very hurtful, as what we think we want, is sometimes not the best for us at all." Bill looked at Erin and Mrs. O'Sullivan for a moment and then he continued,

"Well I guess its time for me to get my things together and to see if I can find Jimmy, as it looks like he may have found himself a job." Erin looked at Bill as she said,

"I'm so sorry Bill, that things didn't work out for you, but as I said, perhaps I've saved both of us, from a bundle of hurt, however, I will as I've said before, be forever grateful to both you and Jimmy, for what you have done for me."

She went on, "I hope Bill, that you can find Jimmy and perhaps you might convey my true feelings to him, as I hope that I haven't seen the last of either of you." She continued,

"Will you promise to keep in touch, and oh by the way, before I forget it, what I'm going to tell you now, is a kind of a secret? Pat Monahan and a group of investors are going to open an exhibit in the World's Fair, when ever it opens and they have offered me a job as a Chanteuse, singing in the French Pavilion, in a French styled cabaret, called the Toulouse Lautrec." She went on,

"The fair is expected to open next year, in 1933 and I believe they are planning on running it for two years; 1933-34. Most likely, if I'm a success, Pat has told me that the French government in addition, will probably; offer me a contract to sing in Paris, France, at the beautiful and world famous Moulin Rouge. You know the one, with the scandalous dancing girls!" Bill then said,

"That's great news Erin and I wish you nothing but the very best, as you certainly deserve it and yes, if and when I see Jimmy, I will tell him what you told me, to tell him."

CHAPTER 45

❦

Finding Jimmy
-Reverse Discrimination-

Bill gave both Mrs. O'Sullivan and Erin a kiss, as Mrs. O'Sullivan's son Michael, drove Bill to the train station. Bill's rather stoic and dark face, showed evidence of a tearstain, the origin of which, crept out of his right eye, when he said goodbye to both Mrs. O'Sullivan and Erin. It would take Bill quite a while to forget Erin, if ever.

Bill had been given a clew, as to where Bill might begin looking for Jimmy, when Erin mentioned, that she thought that Jimmy might try and find work at the Chicago World's Fair construction site. She happened to overhear him mention it, when he was talking to someone, seeking directions, who had stopped by the tourist home, while Jimmy was standing out on the porch.

Bill got off of the train at the La Salle Street Station and he began to walk toward the lake. Bill was a fast walker, and he covered the five miles to the fair construction site, in little over an hour. As he entered the construction site, he had to be careful of the many chain driven Mack trucks, and the other assorted makes, as well has horse drawn wagons, which were carrying dirt and debris from the site. Construction on the site was a twenty-four hour, seven day per week operation. He saw what to him, looked like a foreman's shack and so he thought that he would inquire about a job. Bill opened the door to the shack and he waited, while several workers were getting some instructions from what looked to Bill like, a foreman.

After the men left, Bill said to the man he thought might be the foreman.

"Sir, I'm inquiring about employment and I'm wondering if you might have any job openings?" Bill without realizing it was talking to the same foreman, who was Jimmy O'Brien's boss, Francis Murphy. Mr. Murphy gave Bill the once over with his eyes as he said,

"Young man I don't do the hiring, you'll have to go to the union hall over on south Wabash Avenue and ask for Mr. Mike Duggan." Bill then asked,

"Would you know the address of the union hall?" Mr. Murphy then said,

"Yes, the union hall is located at 1017 South Wabash Avenue." Bill thanked Mr. Murphy, as he left the construction shack and headed toward South Wabash Avenue. It took Bill a little over a half hour to reach the union headquarters on South Wabash Avenue, considering the hustle and bustle of the noonday traffic in the Chicago Loop.

Bill opened the door to the union office and seated at the front desk, was a man, who to Bill looked like a ruddy-faced Irishman. Bill approached the desk as he said, "Sir, I'm looking for a job and I was told that I would have to see you." The man then said,

"Who did you say sent you?" Bill thought for a minute trying to remember the man's name, which had told him to go to the union hall for employment and finally he said,

"His name was Mr. Murphy." Mike Duggan looked at the facial features of this young lad, thinking to himself, that this lad with his pony tail hair-do, couldn't be Irish, but anyhow he said to Bill,

"There are no openings as yet, but here, fill out this application and I'll keep it on file, should we have an opening." Bill wasn't fooled by this obvious subterfuge, of this red-faced, fat Irishman, to avoid telling Bill, that he wouldn't be hired for ethnic reasons. Perhaps Bill thought, *'is the fact that I'm an Indian, the reason'?* Before Bill left and after he filled out the application, he asked Mr. Duggan,

"Sir, I'm looking for a friend of mine, who I believe is working here at the fair construction site. I've kind of lost tract of him and I'm wondering if you might know his name.

Mr. Duggan spat a large wad of tobacco juice, into the large brass spittoon, which sat on the floor, next to his desk and then he asked,

"What's his name?" Bill said,

"His name is Jimmy O'Brien." Mike Duggan scratched his balding head, as he tried to position a couple of long hairs, back across the top of his head, where he had dislodged them, when he scratched his head, and then he said,

"That name doesn't ring a bell with me young man, how long ago did you say, he applied for a job?" Bill answered,

"I didn't, as I'm not quite sure, although it would have to have been, in the last week or so." Mike Duggan thought some more and then he asked,

"Can you describe this Jimmy, what's his last name?" Bill answered,

"O'Brien." Mike Duggan scratched the stubble on his chin as he said,

"No, the name still doesn't ring a bell. Perhaps you can describe him to me, is he tall, or is he short?" Bill thought for a minute and then he said,

"Well, Jimmy is fairly tall, over six feet I would say, and oh yes, he wears a cap, pulled down over the left side of his face, to cover a wound he received in France, during the war." Mr. Duggan's eyes lit up as he said,

"Oh sure, I know the lad, he's working with a cement group, working under a foreman by the name of 'Murph' Murphy." Bill then said,

"Thanks so much Mr. Duggan, I sure do appreciate your remembering Jimmy, I sure do."

Bill then turned around and he once again walked back to the construction site, where he first talked to Mr. Murphy. He reached the foreman's shack and he entered. Mr. Murphy was looking through some papers he had piled on his desk and when he looked up, after hearing the door open, he was surprised once again, to see this Indian lad, who he had talked to, only an hour or so ago.

Mr. Murphy said, "What brings you back young man, couldn't you find the union hall?" Bill answered,

"No sir, I found the union hall alright, but in talking to the union steward, I inquired about a friend of mine and he said that he works for you. I would very much like to see him, as we served together during the war." Mr. Murphy then said to Bill,

"What's his name and what does he look like?" Bill said,

"His name is Jimmy O'Brien and he keeps his cap pulled down over the left side of his face, as he was wounded in the war." Mr. Murphy answered,

"Oh sure, I know the lad, he's in a cement gang and what might be you're interest in him, if I may ask?" Bill said,

"As I said, he and I served together, during the war and he is my best friend." Mr. Murphy thought about what Bill had just told him and then he said,

"I don't want you to bother him while he is working, however, seeing as how you two lads are the best of friends, why don't you walk over to where he's working and say hello for a minute or two, and tell him, you'll meet him back in my office, at the close of his shift." Bill then said,

"Thanks Mr. Murphy, but where can I find Jimmy?" Mr. Murphy said,

"Walk out the door and turn to your left, like you would be walking toward the lake. He's no more than three or four blocks from here." Bill started walking toward the work site, where Jimmy was working. As he approached the work site, he could see several men wheeling wheelbarrows and he spotted Jimmy right away, with his hat covering the left side of his face." Bill hollered out,

"Hey Jimmy, it's me, Bill." Jimmy looked to his left to see who was calling his name and then he recognized his old friend, as he said,

"Bill, how in the hell did you ever find me?" Bill answered,

"You know how good we Native American's are in tracking, especially someone who smells as bad as you do" Jimmy laughed, as he gave Bill a hug and shook his hand. Bill then said,

"I won't keep you, but I'll be waiting for you in the foreman's shack, after you get off work, as I've got so much news to tell you." Jimmy said,

"Fine Bill, you can fill me in, on what's going on, up in Niles." Bill then turned and he walked back to Mr. Murphy's office.

CHAPTER 46

❀

A Broken Heart
-Erin and Pat-

Pat had been pursuing Erin like a bull in heat, since Jimmy and Bill left Mrs. O'Sullivan's tourist home and returned to Chicago. While Erin enjoyed Pat's company and as a young woman, she was flattered that he spent so much time courting her and showering her with expensive gifts. Finally, when Erin realized that Pat was head over heels in love with her and while she liked Pat very much, she was not in love with him, so she thought that she would have to tell him so. Erin had long ago, sized Pat up as a sort of Irish gigolo, a love em' and leave em', kind of a guy.

Erin knew that Pat could get most any girl he set out to seduce, as Pat was no different than any other red-blooded Irish-American young man, or any other young man, for that matter. He was good looking, charming and he had money, or at least his father had money.

She knew that she would have to break off her relationship with Pat, or he would suffer a broken heart. It happened one evening, when they both had attended a dinner party for one of his Fraternity brothers, from his college days. As they were driving home, Pat pulled his roadster over in a quite, secluded lover's lane, in one of the many forest preserves that Chicago, and it's surrounding area are noted for. They both had been drinking quite heavily and Erin was becoming slightly inebriated.

Pat made his move, after kissing Erin very passionately; he started to remove her blouse, in an attempt to arouse her passions, in order to seduce her. Erin had thought about just such a situation as this, with Pat, several times before, as she knew that sooner or later, he would try to seduce her. Finally Erin who had great difficulty in discouraging Pat at the moment, as she too, was in a very amorous mood, which the drinking, had added fuel to her sexual excitement and of course, with this forest preserve rendezvous, in a lover's lane, this romantic setting, had its obvious conclusion. Such a scene, with the risk of getting caught by a police officer, always added a sense of excitement, to this lovemaking scene and caused their passions to reach a fever pitch. With all of her self-control that she could muster up, Erin finally said,

"Look Pat, I like you very much, but I don't love you." She went on, "I have reached a point in my life, where such romantic flings are of little interest to me anymore, perhaps when I was younger and hadn't the experience in dealing with just such a situation, I might have been tempted, regardless of my feelings toward you, but not any more." She went on,

"I'm sorry Pat, perhaps its my fault for innocently leading you on, and for allowing you to get this far with me, without me telling you of my feelings for you, and if I did, I'm sorry, as I hadn't meant to hurt your feelings and I never would, as I think too much of you as a friend." She continued,

"Now if what I have said and my reluctance to have sex with you, would be the cause for you, not wanting anything more to do with me, well, so be it, as I certainly can understand your feelings. Also, if the later is true, then perhaps, you would see fit, not to have me work for your consortium at the Worlds Fair?" Pat, who was just now starting to realize that his amorous intentions toward Erin had just now, been dashed with cold water, was somewhat stunned, as this had never happened to him before.

Pat initially was hurt and mad, but he loved Erin too much, to try and hurt her. If nothing more, Pat was still a gentleman. Finally, Pat was able to bring his lust, under control and to straighten up his clothing, as he said to Erin,

"No Erin, a deal is a deal and I would never welsh on any deal, especially when it comes to you. I think too much of you and I regret very much, that I haven't been able to win your love, and thus, we might have considered marriage. But I do appreciate your candor, as much as it hurts me, and that you have a enough sense and self control, for both of us, to dampen my ardor for you." Erin started to laugh and then, as she had a fit of giggling, both from a thought that just came to her mind and to sort of end this evening's date, on a high note, as she said,

"You know Pat, we'd have never made love in this cracker box of a car, as I'm certainly not a contortionist and I know that you're not either." Both Erin and Pat had a good belly laugh, and then Pat, took Erin home.

CHAPTER 47

❀

A Bombshell
-Bill and Jimmy-

After Jimmy got off work, Bill was waiting for him in the foreman's shack. With more back slapping, they began their walk to the Canaryville streetcar.

Jimmy then asked Bill, all about Erin, Mrs. O'Sullivan and on and on. He was so anxious to hear what they all had been doing, since he left, especially Erin. Bill smiled to himself, as he knew of Jimmy's love for the Irish beauty.

Bill told Jimmy of the sudden appearance of one of Al Capish's mobster hit man, who was looking for you and how Erin handled the situation with Mr. Bernstein's Derringer. They talked about 'Lips' Bernstein, and his execution, gangland style and many other things. Finally, the conversation got around to Erin.

Jimmy asked Bill, "How are you and Erin doing, are you making any progress with her, in the love making department?" Bill, whose stoic demeanor rarely gave off any signs of his inner feelings, which the average person might read, had a pained look on his face, as he said to Jimmy,

"Its over." Jimmy then said,

"What do you mean its over?" Bill seemed to be having great difficulty, formulating an answer to Jimmy's question, finally said,

"What I mean is this, Erin told me in no uncertain terms, that she was not in love with me and although she said she loved me, but then she said, that she wasn't 'in' love with me. Does that make any sense?" Jimmy studied Bill's hurt face for a moment, as he probably more than anyone else, with the exception of Bill's own mother, knew Bill very well and of course, he could read Bill's face fairly well. Jimmy then said,

"Yes it does Bill, Erin is a good person and she is very honest. I believe that once she realized your feelings toward her, she knew that she would have to tell you the bad news, or break your heart." Jimmy then said, "Is Erin in love with that Pat Monahan fellow?" Bill looked at Jimmy with his piercing black eyes, as he said,

"No, she told Mrs. O'Sullivan that she was not in love with him either, although she valued his friendship. I mean, after all, he offered her a singing position in the new French Pavilion at the World's Fair and he said that she might have the possibility, of even going to Paris, France, to sing at the world famous Moulin Rouge, under the sponsorship, of the French government."

Jimmy ignored Bill's sort of evasive tactic, of telling Jimmy about Erin's career and not of her personal romances, for which, Jimmy was mostly interested in, until Jimmy finally said,

"For Christ sake, Bill, who then is she in love with, please tell me, as I've got a right to know. I mean, after all, I had already professed my love to her and I deliberately left Niles, so that you might have a chance to court her, if that is what you wanted, as I knew that you were in love with her also." He continued, "With my hideous face, I certainly didn't think that she would give me a second look." Finally, Bill said, after he looked both ways, and as he leaned over, as though he didn't want anyone else, to hear what he was about to say, whispered,

"Well, Erin told Mrs. O'Sullivan and myself, that she would tell us who she was in love with, if we promised not to tell anyone. Therefore, we both gave her our word that we wouldn't tell anyone of her secret. After all Jimmy, I'm a man of my word and as an Indian, my word is my bond."

"Bull shit." said Jimmy. At that moment the streetcar conductor said,

"Canaryville; all ye' dumb Irish asses, get off 'n' yer' ars'es', as its the end of the line. The conductor's name was Michael Flynn and a recent immigrant to America and Chicago. His comments always brought a lot of good-natured bantering, between himself and the Irish workers, who lived in the squalor of Canaryville. One Irish lad answered him by saying,

"Oh Mike, me' darl'n', so ye' couldn't hold a job in Dublin as a street sweeper, following horses and so now, we've got the miss-fortune, of seeing yer' ugly face here in Chicago, as a streetcar driver, and still following a horse's arse'. It's sad, oh so sad, it tis'." He went on, "I've got a good mind, to report ye', to the authorities, about ye', and yer' awful, bigoted jokes, about us poor dumb Irish, I have."

Ruckus laughter could be heard throughout the long file of Irish workers, who got off of the horse drawn streetcar, at Canaryville.

Jimmy then said to Bill, "Well, I'm waiting, who is this mystery person, who Erin claims she's in love with?" Bill while trying to keep a straight face, said to Jimmy,

"I've just told you that I cannot divulge who this mystery man is, cause if I did, I would be breaking my word, and my solemn oath to Erin, that under no circumstances, would I reveal the name of this person."

Jimmy was becoming a little agitated with Bill, as he knew that Bill was having some fun with him, but because Jimmy was so love sick over Erin, he couldn't stand not knowing who this mystery man was. Finally, Jimmy said,

"Look Bill, I know that you saved my life in France during the war and I'll be forever grateful to you, but once again, you're trifling with my feelings. I don't think its fair, after all, I've kind of put Erin out of my mind as best I could, considering my love for her, as I didn't want to stand in your way, if you wanted to pursue Erin." Bill had a sort of concerned look on his face as though he was caught between a rock and a hard place, concerning Erin, Bill and himself, but finally he said,

"I've given considerable thought about our friendship and Erin's swearing me to secrecy concerning who this mystery man is, who she claims she's in love with and so, I've decided to divulge his name to you, with the promise, that you not tell Erin, that I told you who this person is, otherwise I won't tell you."

Jimmy looked at Bill, trying to figure out if Bill was just having more fun at his expense, or what. Jimmy was getting a little exasperated over Bill's endless and cruel teasing, but finally Jimmy said, "Okay, I promise not to tell Erin, that it was you, who told me the name of this mystery man" Finally, Bill said,

"The mystery man is you." Jimmy looked stunned, as he didn't know whether to believe Bill or not, as Bill was prone to play jokes on Jimmy from time to time. Jimmy stammered for a minute or two, trying to believe Bill, but realizing, what Bill was saying, would be the cruelest joke ever played on him and one so hurtful, that it could destroy their friendship forever, if not true. Jimmy then said to Bill,

"Now once again, tell me that you're not joking and what you just told me is true, on your word of honor, if you have any." Bill tried to look hurt, as best he could, but he couldn't continue to toy with his friend's feelings, as that would be too cruel. Bill then said,

"I give you my word on my mother's life, that what I have just told you, is the gospel truth."

Jimmy continued to look at Bill, trying to figure out if Bill was lying, or this news, was just too good to be true. Jimmy started to cry, as in his emotional state; he could no longer keep his feelings, bottled up. Bill patted Jimmy on the back and he gave him a hug, the hug of a true friend.

Jimmy now had a huge grin on his face, from ear to ear, as he told Bill, this calls for a celebration and on the way to my room, we'll stop off at Mother Keenan's Co-op and Speakeasy, for a little libation and it's on me."

CHAPTER 48

✿

Hallucinating
-The Ghosts of War-

Jimmy rented one room from Mrs. Bridget Carberry a widow, whose husband a fireman, was killed in a fire on the southwest side of Chicago, several years ago. He worked for the City of Chicago fire department for close to twenty-five years, and they had raised ten children. The kids had all moved out but one, and that was Chauncey, who was a little retarded.

Chauncey did odd jobs around the three-story tenement, which at one time, was a six flat. Mrs. Carberry had the six flat, converted to a twelve flat, to increase her monthly income. Jimmy had to share the bathroom with six other tenants on his floor. Mrs. Carberry had worked out a schedule for the use of the one bathtub and as such, she had Chauncey rig up, a sort of curtain, hiding the toilet from anyone's view, taking a bath.

Whenever any females had to take a bath of course, no men were allowed to use the toilet facilities, until the lady had finished her bath. Sometimes this led to trouble, depending on which female was bathing, as some of the more inebriated lads, would try to invade the bathroom while excusing themselves, as though they didn't know, that a woman was presently bathing. In this way, they either got a free peek, or if the young lady were sort of free and easy and was looking to make a fast buck, this could lead to a sort of, short-lived romance; as short lived it had to be, as there was always someone pounding on the door, wanting to use the facilities. Many a young lad would leave the bathroom, dripping wet, while claiming that he had fallen in the tub. This always brought a laugh.

Bill had to sleep on the floor, as Jimmy had only, a single cot to sleep on.

Jimmy and Bill spent most of the night drinking, in celebration of Erin's confession of who her one true love was. They reminisced about their service in the Great War, their adventures in the various and many circuses that they both worked in, around the country and their work, aiding the government in having indictments issued, for Clarence Duncan and his associates and their association with Al Capish's gangsters.

However as their drinking became more intense, they both were becoming more and more inebriated, and they both unwittingly, opened up wounds, that their own mental escape mechanisms, had pushed deep into the dark recesses of their minds, by discussing the war and forgetting momentarily, what they both had seen and had been through. While the mind can tuck such memories, into the sub-conscious parts of it, in order to protect its mental fragility, but it doesn't take much, to trigger the conscious mind, to re-live those horrific scenes, they both had witnessed and were apart of, during the Great War. The mind can never rid itself of its memories; they're always there, even though they're not always easily remembered. Especially so, when a traumatic event happens, such as Jimmy being told by Bill, that Erin only loved him and on one else, coupled with the effect that alcohol was having, in weakening his own mental defenses.

Jimmy now began to shake, as his frayed nerves, were no longer under his control, as they now seemed to take over his whole body. Jimmy was now perspiring profusely. He started to mumble to himself incoherently, as Bill watched on Jimmy's contorted face, the horrors of the war, which Jimmy was now viewing for the first time, since he left re-habilitation with the Army medics.

He began to drool, his eyes glazed over. Bill reached over, putting his arms around Jimmy, as he tried to comfort him. While Bill experienced the same horrific scenes that Jimmy had, Bill seemed to be better able to control his own mental state of mind, than did Jimmy. Perhaps, it was the permanent reminder of the war for Jimmy, his grotesque face, which he could never run away from, as it looked back at him, each and every morning, when he shaved, looking in the mirror.

Jimmy gave out with a shrill scream, as he now envisioned, hands, hands that no longer were attached to the arms that once controlled their movement. Hands, that the German machine gunners, had severed from the wrists, of the

American Infantry soldiers, as they sprayed the American soldiers with deadly machine gun fire, severing their hands from their wrists, as the American's had been trying to attack the German machine gun nests. These hands had been attached to the many arms, that tried to penetrate the barbed wire barriers, and were now stuck to the barbed wire itself; pierced by the barbs on the wire, some with fingers, still twitching involuntary, controlled by their severed nerves.

The fingers of these hands were still twitching, more or less, in a reflex movement, as though their nerves, could reattach themselves, to the wrists and arms, which they used to belong to. The German's had strung miles of barbed wire, across no-man's land, in an effort to stem the allied counter attacks.

Jimmy could still see in his mind's eye, these hands and the blood that was now flowing from their severed wrists, where these hands had just moments before, been attached to. The soldiers who were writhing in agony, tried to reach up with their severed and handless stumps, as though they thought that they could reattach their hands, somehow. The mud and muck, was now covered with a bright crimson color, as the blood seeped into the ground and some, floated on the many pools of water, surrounding this macabre scene, like oil on water.

This scene in Jimmy's mind in away, reminded him of the many slaughtering pens, at the Union Stock Yards, where cattle and hogs were butchered, with the blood, running knee deep and reaching almost to the tops of the men's boots, who did the killing. Jimmy lay in the midst of this man made horror; lying on his back, with his bullet riddle leg, in this river of blood, seeping into the slimy muck, on this battle field. He couldn't get up, but these lasting scenes of carnage, would be forever engraved in his mind and then he saw no more, as an enemy shell, landed so close to Jimmy, it knocked him unconscious and blew half of his face away.

Finally, as though Jimmy's mind could no longer tolerate such visual carnage, or go mad, it shut down and Jimmy fell into a deep sleep. Bill spent the rest of the night, watching Jimmy sleep. Five a.m. came around all too quickly, as Bill shook Jimmy, in order to awaken him, as Jimmy had to catch the Canaryville street car, which left Canaryville at six a.m. sharp. Jimmy finally awakened, as Bill kept on shaking him, as Jimmy in his groggy mental state, wanted to go back to sleep. Bill knew that who ever didn't show up for work each day, was replaced by another union man and that person who had missed getting to work, was dropped to the bottom, of the so called, seniority list. This might mean, that the person dropped, might not get back to work for a month or more, if ever.

Jimmy finally got up and the first thing he asked Bill was, "Was I dreaming, or did you tell me that Erin said that she was in love with me?" Bill realized that Jimmy had evidently, had completely forgotten about, his mental relapse or breakdown, after visualizing the horrors that he had faced, in the Great War said,

"No you weren't dreaming Jimmy, Erin did tell me that." Jimmy had a big smile on his face, even though his head ached from a terrific hangover. Jimmy then told Bill,

"Bill, we'll talk more, when I get home tonight from work, about a strategy, to get you a job at the World's Fair site." He went on, "But for now, I've got to catch the Canaryville streetcar before it leaves." Bill shook Jimmy's hand and Jimmy went out the door.

CHAPTER 49

❈

The Plan
-The Half-breed-

Bill had spent the day killing time, by walking the streets of Canaryville and thinking to himself, about these poor Irish, who lived in similar circumstances to his own people, on the Indian Reservations throughout the country and his own reservation, back in Montana. However, he also realized that the Irish were now a force to be reckoned with. As just through the shear numbers of Irish coming to the big cities, and their need to survive, they now could exercise their political muscle, as they controlled most of the unions, the mayors and the alderman, and would eventually control the large city's unions in America, and make them, so called, 'closed shops'. That is, if you didn't join the company union within thirty days after you were hired, you wouldn't be allowed to work for the company that just hired you.

While the Irish could come and go as they pleased, except of course, where socio-economic circumstances, relegated them to living in certain poor neighborhoods. Where as the Indians, were pretty much forced to remain on the reservations set aside for them, by the United States government, for their own good, as the Bureau of Indian Affairs, more or less dictated such, and because of their extreme cultural differences from the white man.

The Indian couldn't or wouldn't, assimilate into white society, as he wouldn't adapt to the white man's customs. However, due to socio-economic circumstances, plus the prejudices of the Protestant majority, the Irish had been forced to live in the squalor of Canaryville, although for the most part, they had overcome the resistance and petty bigotry, of the Protestant majority, by literally controlling the city of Chicago itself. With the 'Great Depression' now in full force, however, jobs weren't that plentiful, other than a few patronage jobs, as no city construction work projects, was in the works, or being planned for, in the near future. The Irish made up roughly, ninety-five percent of the police force and the fire department, in most of the large cities, including Chicago.

He thought further, of the rather ironic circumstance, as both races, easily succumbed to the mind numbing benefits of rotgut whiskey and wine, as a way of trying to escape their cruel fate. While the Irish were now in positions of power, there were still plenty of Irish, who couldn't find work of any kind and the Protestant business leaders, still hated the Irish Catholic, which didn't help. Added to this of course, were the effects of the Great Depression on most workers, no matter their religious denominations.

Bill returned to Jimmy's room and awaited his return from work. It soon was seven o'clock and Bill heard Jimmy walk up the stairs. After discussing the day's events, Jimmy said to Bill, let's get a sandwich and a beer, down at McGillicutty's! Jimmy washed his hands and they walked just about a block, to a small neighborhood saloon and speakeasy, owned by Jake McGillicutty and his two brothers, Sean and Tom.

"What will it be lads, asked Tom McGillicutty?"

"Two drafts", said Jimmy. Both Jimmy and Bill, then moved to a small table in the corner of the saloon, after making a couple of corned beef sandwiches and taking several hardboiled eggs, together with, some green onions. A lunch or supper like this, could be had for just a ten-cent draft beer, as the food was free. After they had eaten, Jimmy said to Bill,

"I found out, that the South-Chicago Bridge and Iron Works, would hire only Irish Catholics."

"How do you know that, asked Bill?"

"Well," said Jimmy, "Mike Duggan told me that, over at the union hall."

Bill had an angry look on his face, hearing what Jimmy had just told him. Bill then said, "Goddamn it Jimmy, I thought only the Protestants, were prejudiced." Jimmy thought for a minute and then he said,

"And so did I, but it just goes to show you, that any group which has wrested the power away from the former controlling faction, reverses the tables and it now becomes the dictator of the terms and it exercises its own form of bigotry." He continued, "As the Irish like to say, *'what goes around, comes around.'*

Bill didn't like Jimmy's explanation or rationalization at all, of why the Irish did what they did and now they have become, the most hated group in Chicago, amongst other ethnic groups of immigrants, all vying for a piece of the economic pie, and he told him so. Jimmy than said,

"Look Bill, I don't make the rules and until they make me king, I just try, and get along." Bill said,

"King my ass!" After a few beers and the lads had eaten their supper, Bill said to Jimmy,

"All right Jimmy, what is your plan to help get me a job at the World's Fair construction site?" Jimmy looked at Bill for a minute or two before Bill asked again, "Well, I'm waiting." Jimmy answered Bill by saying.

"Here's my plan; when you go back to the union hall, tell Mike Duggan, the union steward, that your mother was Irish, and your father was an Indian. That is why you look like you do. If he should ask you what your mother's maiden name was, why tell him it was O'Malley, Maggie O'Malley and she was from County Cork." Jimmy went on, "Should he question you further, as to where your parents met, why tell him that your father was a scout for the Union Pacific Railroad and your mother cooked for that same railroad."

Bill gave Jimmy a dirty look, as he sat and thought about what Jimmy has just told him. Jimmy then added,

"Bill, I've been told that on most of the tall buildings being built back east; that the construction companies, prefer to hire Indians for work on the steel girders, as the Indian, not only can walk these steel girders with ease, they don't seem to be bothered by a fear of heights." He went on, "Their accident rate is one tenth that, of the white man." Bill kind of smiled as he thought some more about Jimmy's comments and then he said,

"I don't like to make up stories in order to get a job, as it burns my ass to have to lie, but I guess if that is the only way, I might get a job with the South-Chicago Bridge and Iron Works, then I guess, I've got no choice." Jimmy shook his hand.

CHAPTER 50

❦

Suspicious-Ruse
-Bill John vs. Mike Duggan-

Both Jimmy and Bill, left for work in the morning, however Bill got off the Canaryville Streetcar at Twelfth Street, before it made its turn, to go directly to the lake front and the construction site, while Jimmy continued on to his work site. Bill walked to the union hall and entered. Once again sitting at the front desk was Mike Duggan. He looked up from the Daily Racing Form he was studying, and he recognized the Indian, who had come to see him about a job, several days before. Before Bill could say anything, Mike Duggan said,

"I'm sorry young man, but I still don't have any openings." Bill was almost tempted to tell Mike Duggan to shove the job up his Irish ass, but then he thought better of it, as he said,

"Mr. Duggan sir, it might not make any difference, but I thought that I would at least tell you, that I'm half Irish on my mother's side. Her name was O'Malley; should that make any difference, on my being hired." Mike Duggan was kind of taken back by Bill's revelation, about his mother's Irish heritage.

Bill then went on to tell Mike about his father and mother, working for the Union Pacific Railroad and how they met. Mike was stroking his chin and wondering whether or not, if Bill was telling the truth. Bill was watching the expression on Mike's face, and he knew exactly what Mike was thinking, and so he said,

"Mr. Duggan sir, I'm not sure if you know it or not, but many construction companies back east, hire American-Indians to do their girder work, as the

Indian has almost perfect balance and he is not the least bit afraid of great heights." Mr. Duggan was now kind of interested in what Bill had just told him about Indians and their ability to work on steel girders at great heights. The reason for Mr. Duggan's sudden interest in Bill, was the Worlds Fair authorities, were constructing out on North Island, an amusement ride, called the 'Sky-ride'. The ride would consist of several gondola cars, attached to one another, which were enclosed, and they would travel on suspended cables and be able to take the tourists, over and around the entire World's Fair site.

Each of the cars was named for the characters, on the most popular radio show in America at the time, 'The Amos and Andy Show'. One car would be named the 'Kingfish', another with the name 'Amos' and another with the name of 'Andy', and another with the name of A.J. Calhoun, plus a few more character's names, taken from the radio show itself. To stress just how popular was the Amos & Andy radio show at that time in America was, that on Sunday nights in the movie theaters across America, the motion pictures would be turned off, and the theatre lights would go on, while the audience would listen to Amos & Andy over the theaters loudspeakers. Otherwise, none of the public would go to the movie theaters on Sunday night.

These cars and their steel carrying cables would be strung from giant piers or pylons, whose foundations were sunk deep into bedrock. The pylons consisted of huge steel girders, which were wrapped, in metal casings, to give them the appearance of airplane pylons, like the kind used in the Cleveland Air Races, which were so popular at that time, with the public.

The real reason for Mike Duggan's interest in Bill was that there had been a series of unfortunate accidents, which claimed the lives of eight, so called, girder 'monkeys'. Men whose jobs, consisted of climbing about these huge girders and putting huge bolts into them and then screwing large nuts on to the bolts, in order to secure them to one another. Because of these accidents, there had been a strike by the workers, who were now afraid to go back up and begin to anchor these girders to each other and to the giant pylons, as they considered the work site, now jinxed. With the superstitious Irish ironworkers, once someone mentioned a sort of evil spirit, or devil, none of the Irish would climb these steel girders.

Mike felt that if he could send Bill up to work on these girders, then the pride of the Irish worker, might in fact, overcome their silly superstitions, and they all then hopefully, would decide to return to work. Mike knew it was a gamble, but he was willing to try anything, as the project was now two weeks behind schedule. Mike then said to Bill,

Okay young man, you've got yourself a job. It's a tough one though, where you will be facing, not only a most difficult job, high above the ground, but you will also be facing certain Irish workers, who for one reason or another, may not like the looks of you, do you catch my drift?" Bill answered,

"I understand sir." Mike went on,

"The crew chief's name is Egan, Chauncey Egan and he is a real tough cookie. One of the incentives for working on these girder jobs, is that depending on how many girders you and your crew bolt together in one day, there are bonuses paid to the crew, who are able to attach the most girders together." He continued, "There are at the present time, three crews consisting of five girder monkeys each." He went on, "The job site is roughly two blocks from where the foreman's shack of 'Turk' Murphy is located, as you walk toward the lake. You can't miss it, as a couple of the pylons, are already standing." Bill thanked Mr. Duggan, as he left the union hall.

Bill walked back to where Mr. Murphy's shack sat and without bothering to stop and see Mr. Murphy, Bill walked a couple of blocks further, until he came upon more than a dozen men, standing around and talking to one another. As he approached the men, they all gave him the once over and then a tall rugged looking man said, "Can I help ye' lad?" Bill answered,

"I'm looking for Mr. Egan, as Mike Duggan has sent me to see him." Chauncey Egan gave Bill the once over and then he said,

"I'm Chauncey Egan, and what can I be a do'n' fer' ye'?" Bill then said, "I'm supposed to report to you, as I'm the new worker, assigned to replace one of your crew members, who was killed." The entire girder 'monkeys', had angry looks on their faces, as if to say, *no one works here unless we say so.* Mr. Egan then shook Bill's hand, as he said to all of the crews working under him,

"Look lads, we've got a job to do. We're roughly two weeks behind schedule and I agree, that it's most unfortunate, that we've lost eight men, but we've still got to get this 'Sky-ride' built, regardless of our superstitions." He continued, "I'm going to send this new lad up to begin attaching these girders together, if they're are no objections." There came a loud murmur of disapproval, from the crews gathered around Bill, as if to tell Bill, I wouldn't be going up to begin attaching girders together, if I were you. The men however, were all afraid of Chauncey Egan though, as he was the Irish heavyweight-boxing champ, of the fourth Ward.

Mr. Egan gave Bill a leather pouch with various size wrenches in it, so that he could begin fastening the girders together. The crews all looked on, as Bill put a safety sling around his waist and Mr. Egan signaled the crane operator to lift Bill up and onto, a small wooden platform, high above the ground. It was obvious to the men, that Bill paid little attention to their mutterings and their verbal threats. Bill arrived up on the platform, where he unclipped his safety belt from the crane's hook. Bill found what looked like blueprints, nailed to the wooden platform and studying one, he proceeded to signal the crane operator to lift up a girder and bring it up to a position, just about twenty feet from the platform.

Bill walked out on one of the attached girders, until he reached the end of the girder he was standing on. With hand motions to the crane operator, Bill managed to position the unattached girder in a position, where he could place four large bolts, through the girder holes of both large girders and then he screwed on the holding nuts by hand, until they were snug, tightening each one, with the appropriate wrench. He then walked onto an adjoining girder until he reached its end and then he signaled the crane operator, to lift up another girder, to meet the girder, he just fastened the other end to.

While he waited for the crane operator to lift the next girder, he thought about what Jimmy had told him, concerning the Indians, being so fearless and so sure footed, on these high girders and he smiled to himself. He hadn't noticed in himself, any fear of the heights whatsoever, as he was standing alone, balanced on the narrow girder. Looking east, Bill could see one of the Chicago water pumping stations, called the 'Navy Pier Crib', it was located, just about a mile from shore.

Meanwhile the crews which had refused to return to their jobs, after eight of their fellow workers were killed and with the superstitious nature of the Irish, being what it is, which had more or less united them, in what they believed to be a common cause; were now in a state of nervousness and confusion. They watched this stranger, climb about the girders, as though he was born for this perilous calling. They all had sworn, that they would not return to their jobs, until they could get a Catholic priest, to come out to the work site and say some prayers and sprinkle holy water. This, in the hopes of sort of exorcising, whatever demon or demons, were hiding high up in those girders, which caused the deaths of their fellow union workers.

Now they all began to have second thoughts, as this new man, didn't seem to be bothered at all, by any of these demons. They now commented to one another about this strange looking person, who claimed to be Irish, although he looked more Indian than Irish, with his pony tail, if indeed, he had any Irish blood in his veins at ta'll'. Meanwhile, Mr. Egan was watching Bill work, as he jumped from one girder to another, placing bolts in their proper holes and tightening the nuts, that securely fastened them, to the other girders, while all the time, watching his Irish crews out of the corner of his eye. He was waiting for one of the Irish crew, to swallow his superstitious fear, put on his safety harness, and return to his job, high in the structure, which he thought would act as a catalyst, for all the others, to follow suit.

It had only been about ten minutes, when a very tall young man by the name of 'Scooter' Fitzgerald, put his safety harness on and hollered to the crane operator, to lift him up to the highest girder, the one that Bill stood on. Mr. Egan thought that 'Scooter' was the first 'monkey' to return to work, after watching this new man, who seemed to adapt so well, to this dangerous job. But he was wrong, 'Scooter's' intention, by having the crane operator lift him up to the girder that Bill stood on, was to force Bill, to return to the ground, as these superstitious Irishmen, needed total support for their superstitious sort of strike. Mr. Egan was watching 'Scooter' as he walked toward Bill. He could tell that he was talking to Bill, but he couldn't hear what he was saying. Although, he did see Bill shake is head from side to side, meaning no.

He then saw 'Scooter' reach into his back pocket and pull out a large monkey wrench. He raised it over his head, as though he was about to hit Bill. Bill obviously expected such an attack, although he had hoped that his climbing up into the mass of girders, now over ten stories from the ground, to handle his work assignment, wouldn't lead to violence. As 'Scooter' brought down his monkey wrench, directly at Bill's head, Bill sidestepped his attack, and in an instant, Bill was now behind 'Scooter' and he held him in a choking grip. Scooter struggled to pry loose, Bill's vise like grip, and he dropped the wrench, he had tried to hit Bill with, in an effort to break Bill's choke hold, using both of his hands.

Both lads were now struggling to maintain their balance, especially Bill, who now had this mad Irish lad, who tried to kill him a moment before, while Bill now tried to save both himself and 'Scooter', from certain death, if they both fell off of the girder, they both were standing on.

Normally, Bill could have easily thrown 'Scooter off of the girder to his death, but he chose not to do so. Bill knew full well, that he would have probably been charged with murder if he did, in a union rigged, kangaroo style court, and he thought that perhaps by saving this hot headed Irish lad from death, he and his friends might be grateful, grateful enough to let bygones be bygones.

Bill shouted to the crane operator to raise his hook, so that he and 'Scooter' could be lowered safely to the ground. With 'Scooter' totally in Bill's power, Bill hooked his safety belt to the crane's hook and he then signaled the crane operator, to lower them both to the ground. Mr. Egan swore at the young Irish lad, who had attempted to kill his new hire, Bill John, as he said,

"Well 'Scooter', what in the hell were ye'trying to do, kill this new man?" "Scooter', who was frightened to death, by Bill's ability to force him to drop his wrench and to place him in a strangle hold such, that he could have easily have thrown him off of the girder, they both were standing on, said,

"Well I was only do'n' what I thought the lads would have wanted me to do, seeing as how this new feller', was about to take over our jobs." Mr. Egan grabbed 'Scooter 'by his lapels and he shook him as he said,

"Look you ass, I've no time to be a worrying about what ye' and yer' friends want, I've got a job to do and we're just about two weeks behind schedule. Now, either, ye' all, get back to work, or I'll replace the lot of ye." He continued,

"I've got no time, for such superstitious nonsense and I mean no disrespect to anyone. So, make up yer' minds; what we'll it be, go back to work, or punch out and turn in your badges, as you all will be fired, for failure to live up to yer' work agreement, with the South-Chicago Bridge & Iron Works?" They all looked at one another and grumbling, they all slowly began to return to their work positions, high above the ground. Mr. Egan said to Bill,

"Hold on a minute Bill, as I would like to talk to ye', before you return to work." Mr. Egan had a worried look on his face as he said to Bill; "I don't know how to tell ye' this, but ye've' probably have signed yer' death warrant with these superstitious and radical Irish workers." He went on, "I can only do so much from the ground, but when you and they are so high above the ground, why anything can happen." He went on, "From jest' in the few minutes ye've' been up on those girders, ye've' proven to me' self, at least, that ye'are probably the finest girder 'monkey', that I have ever seen, in me' entire life." He continued,

"Now if ye'would like, I perhaps can put in a good word for ye', with one of the other construction crews and perhaps they might be able to use ye'. It would be fer' yer' own good lad." Bill smiled at Mr. Egan as he said,

"I do appreciate you're kind words Mr. Egan about my working ability and your concern about my well being, but I couldn't leave now and find a safer job, as these guys would think to themselves that they had won." Bill continued, "As you must realize, being what is called a half-breed, by the white society, it makes it even more difficult for me to find work in this bigoted society, but it's for that reason alone, that I wouldn't back away from these punks and that's what they are, at least to me, punks." He went on,

"I realize only too well, that I am but one man, amongst fifteen or so others, who probably already have devised a plan to kill me. But, I'll take my chances, such as they are." He continued, "But, Mr. Egan, should anything happen to me, I would appreciate, that you contact a very good friend of mine, Jimmy O'Brien, who is presently working in a cement gang under his foreman, Mr. Murphy. Jimmy and I go a ways back, from the Great War."

Mr. Egan shook Bill's hand as he said, "I will." Bill then said,

"I know that handling girders, is a two man job at least, and so I don't know, if I'll get any cooperation from any of these punks. And if not, then maybe, I'll have to leave, not from any threat to my life mind you, but just the mere fact, that without a partner, it would be very difficult to work by myself, in trying to handle these heavy girders and really, next to impossible."

Finally Bill said, "I've never walked away from a fight in my life and as I've come to know a few Irishmen over the years, I have found that in most cases, if I've shown them my grit, then most will accept a half-breed into their clans, as a sort of a rite of passage."

Mr. Egan smiled as he shook Bill's hand once again. Bill directed the crane operator, to lift him up to, the same girder that 'Scooter' was working on, as Bill felt that if he could win over 'Scooter', and then the others might be swayed to accept him.

Bill spent the remainder of the day in sort of silent communications with 'Scooter', that is, they communicated with one another, but only by hand movement and neither one, said one word to the other. Yet, they're working relationship was almost flawless, like two dancers, in time with the music, as they went about, moving and anchoring these huge girders. Fact is; Bill and 'Scooter' broke the previous record for the number of girders bolted to one another, over a five-hour period.

CHAPTER 51

The Thaw

-Irish Psyche-

It happened on a Thursday morning, just before the morning work break. A rainstorm had arrived from the east, off of Lake Michigan and the working conditions up on the girders, became very dangerous. The girders were becoming slick, from the wet and oily surfaces and that, along with the winds, which accompanied the rain, were becoming strong enough, to blow the men, off of the girders, they were all now setting down on. They all had wrapped their legs around the girders they sat on, to keep from being blown off.

Mr. Egan, standing on the ground below, decided that it was too risky, to keep the men working under these dangerous conditions, so he lit a red flare, which was the only way he could signal the men, to come down, as his voice couldn't be heard above the howling winds and rain. Meanwhile, the crane operator was already raising his hook, to reach the men and to carry them all, safely down to the ground. He had made five lifts and had gotten all of the men safely on the ground, or so he thought. However, one of the men standing talking to the others, about the storm, said,

"Where the hell is Mick, I thought I seen him come down? Wasn't he with you Sean?" Sean answered,

"No, he wasn't with me, I thought he came down with ye' Michael." Michael Sullivan was Mick's father. They all then began to search the highest girders with their eyes, looking for Mick. Finally, one of the men said,

"I think I can see him, at least it looks like someone, clutching to one of the top girders. It looks like he may have become frozen, in that he has become so frightened, he has lost his nerve, and is unable to walk the slippery girders with this terrific wind, in order to reach the crane hook and be lowered to safety."

Such fear is not uncommon, with some of these workers. Where the heights they are working at, suddenly become so frightening, that the worker becomes terrified, and is paralyzed with fear such that he can no longer move. He then clings to a girder, usually crying hysterically. Many a monkey, who lost his nerve, usually ends up; falling off the girder, he was on, plunging to his death.

The storm was becoming worse by the minute. The wind coming off of Lake Michigan, had now reached speeds, of almost fifty miles an hour in gusts and that was driving the rain almost horizontal, into the faces of the Irish crews. The rain was becoming mixed with sleet and was stinging the men's faces. The temperature had dropped some twenty degrees in fifteen minutes.

To climb back up into the girders and to try and rig some kind of a harness around Mick, in order to safely bring him down, would be considered suicide. All of the men looked at one another and at Mr. Egan, who was trying in his mind, to figure out, how they could rescue Mick.

Finally, after seeing that no one had the nerve to try and save Mick, who at the most, could only hang on to the girder he was clinging to, for no more than ten minutes, Bill looked at Mr. Egan, searching his face and thinking that he might have an idea, in how to get Mick down. However, Mr. Egan just stood there with his fists clinched, in a helpless gesture. Mick's hands were becoming numb, from the wet/cold, and when he finally lost the feeling in his hands, he would most likely let go, and fall ten stories to his death. Bill then said,

"Quick, someone rig me some kind of a leather jacket-like harness of some sort, that I can fit around Mick, in order for me to bring him down safely. I know under situations like this, that I may have to resort to knocking Mick out, as he will probably try and fight me, which then could cause us both to fall off of the girder, that Mick is clinging to."

Michael, Mick's father, immediately did as Bill had asked. He took two safety vests, cutting one down the back and with some rope, he was able to sort of jury rig, a makeshift harness, one that hopefully, Bill might be able to wrap around Mick. None of the men made any offer to assist Bill in climbing back up to the top of these girders. They all knew, that climbing back up and trying to wrestle with Mick, in order to put the vest on him, that their own lives would be in jeopardy, if they did, as most likely, they and Mick, would fall off of the girder and plunge to their deaths in a failed suicide mission.

Bill ran over to the crane operator who had trouble-seeing and hearing Bill, as the sleet was so intense. Bill had to climb up onto the cranes steel tracks, to the crane operator's cab, in order to tell the crane operator, what he wanted him to do. Bill took off his work shoes, as he felt that the shoes would be a hindrance, as they could more easily slip on the slippery girder surfaces. Whereas, with his bare feet, even though the steel girders were icy cold, Bill still felt that he had a better chance of walking on the girders. Bill knew from experience, that his feet, would be more sensitive to the surface conditions of the steel girders, especially so, when trying to handle Mick.

Mick most likely, wouldn't be very cooperative, given his frightened state of mind and could very easily; cause them both to fall off of the girder. Bill hooked his safety harness onto the crane's hook and the crane operator lifted Bill up, to where he thought the wooden platform was, as he could no longer see the platform, from the ground. He came within, a foot of the platform and Bill, realizing that the crane operator couldn't see him or the platform, figured that he might just as well, try and reach for, a metal hook that had been screwed down into the wooden platform, as a temporary anchoring hook, for attaching cables to.

Bill leaning over, moving his gloved hand, back and forth across the surface of the wooden platform, as he couldn't see anything in this blinding sleet and windstorm, until he felt the steel-anchoring hook. He grabbed on to the hook and he pulled himself over and onto the platform. Bill was now sweating profusely, as even his own nerves, were starting to become frayed. He sat there for a moment resting, while trying to devise a plan in his mind, as to how he would, safely bring down, the young Irish boy, and himself.

Bill wrapped a rope around the girder he was on, fastening it to his harness belt, so that if he should slip off of the girder, the rope might be able to prevent him, from falling ten stories to his death. He would unfasten it, when he and Mick reached the wooden platform, just before he would hook his harness onto the crane's hook. Bill slowly crawled on his hands and knees, moving along the length of the girder that Mick was now clinging to. He reached Mick and Mick couldn't even turn to face Bill, as he was so scared of falling.

Bill now knew, that he would have to try and knock Mick out, as he knew that he couldn't remove Mick's frozen hold, he had on the girder, not even with super human strength, could he have moved Mick. Bill's first order of business was to secure a rope around Mick, to keep him from falling, after he hit him. Bill managed to wrap a safety rope around Mick's body, which he then tied to the girder, which Mick was clinging to. After he did this, Bill moved Mick's head a little to his left, so it kind of faced him and after that, he also had placed a safety rope around the girder, for himself, to which Mick was clinging too, Bill then hauled off, and he hit Mick in the jaw, knocking him senseless.

Mick now slumped against the girder he had been clinging to, being held securely by the safety rope, Bill had wrapped around him. Bill now frantically tried to secure the safety harness that Mick's father had devised, around his body. After he finished tying Mick's body into the homemade safety harness, He unfastened the single rope, which he had put around Mick initially, in order to keep him from falling after he hit him. He then laid Mick on his back, having placed a safety rope around Mick's body and around the girder, to keep him from falling off of the girder. He now began to pull Mick toward him, while seated on the slick and icy cold girder, as he had wrapped his legs around the girder, while sitting on the girder, moving inch by inch backwards, hoping to reach the wooden platform.

The sky was now jet black, as more and more storm clouds came in from the lake. The wind was howling and the rain mixed with sleet, was causing Bill's face to bleed. Bill kept pulling Mick toward him, as he slowly inched his way to the wooden platform. Finally, Bill's rear end, hit the platform and he stopped. Mick was just now starting to come around and so Bill knew, that he would somehow have to prevent Mick, from trying to get loose from his safety harness and perhaps, fall off of the girder, or the platform itself. Bill's position, relative to Mick's jaw wasn't such, that he could hit him again, so he took out a spare length of rope he had tied to his belt and he tied Mick's hands together.

Mick was facing away from Bill and so he didn't know who was behind him, holding on to him. Finally, Bill managed to get Mick onto the wooden platform. Bill was now, physically exhausted. Mick was starting to move, after he sat on the wooden platform. When Bill looked into Mick's wild eyes, he could see the stark terror, which lay behind them. Without thinking twice about it, Bill once again, hit Mick in the jaw, knocking him cold.

Bill knew that Mick, in his present mental state, that he could loose control over Mick, and if that happened, Mick would do something stupid and possibly cause both of them, to fall off of the wooden platform. He didn't like to hit the young boy again, but his primary concern, was to get them both, safely on the ground. Bill looked around for the crane hook and he saw that it was still, just about a foot short of the platform, moving back and forth in the violent wind. He knew that he couldn't reach the hook, with Mick now attached to himself, so he had thought earlier about what Mr. Egan did in order to alert his crews by using a red flare. This use of a red flare, was to signal the workers to come down from the girders, they all were standing on, to avoid the storm and so, he had taken several red flares, just in case.

Bill pulled the activating tape on a red flare, with the hope that the crane operator could see it, and by motioning the flare, toward the lake that he would understand, that Bill needed the crane hook, to be brought a little closer to the platform. Meanwhile, Mr. Egan had climbed into the cab of the crane operator, so he could tell him, if he could see, what Bill was trying to communicate, via the red flare, as two sets of eyes, are better than one.

The crane operator couldn't see out of the front window of his crane cab, as the rain and sleet had covered his window completely, whereas Mr. Egan, who was standing on one of the crane's tracks, and looking up at the girders, could barely see Bill's red flare, as it was faintly visible from the ground. Bill was frantically trying, to get the crane operator's attention, by moving the red flare toward the lake, hoping that the crane operator might understand, what his moving of the red flare in the direction of the lake meant. Mr. Egan thought that he understood, by Bill's motioning of the red flare, that he was trying to tell the crane operator to move the arm of the crane, toward the lake. Mr. Egan told the crane operator, to move the crane's hook, a little higher and to move it, foreword a foot or two.

Finally, the crane's hook was right over both Mick and Bill. Bill reached up and with all of his remaining strength; he managed to hook his two-man harness to the crane's hook. Bill who was now totally exhausted, lay back on the wooden platform for a minute, with Mick attached to himself, letting the red flare, fall to the ground. Mr. Egan saw the red flare fall and he hoped that it was a signal, to lower the crane's hook. He hollered into the crane man's ear, "Lower the crane." Slowly, the crane's arm lifted Bill and Mick, in order to clear the wooden platform and then he began to slowly lower it, from its raised position. As it reached the ground, the men all rushed over to what looked like, two bodies tied together. Mick was still out cold and Bill had fainted from exhaustion and dehydration.

The men placed both Mick and Bill into wheelbarrows and rushed them to the foreman's shack. Mr. Murphy always kept a bottle of brandy for *medicinal* purposes, stashed in his desk. Both lads were given a large drink of brandy and they both were then wrapped in some old blankets that Mr. Murphy kept in his foreman's shack. Bill came too first and then Mick awakened. Mick's jaw was swollen such, that his right eye was closed. Mick's father wrapped his arms around his son, as he thanked Bill, repeatedly. He said in a shameful tone of voice,

"Mr., me' self' and all of the lads, owe you an apology for acting the way we did, as without ye, me' son would no longer be amongst the living." All of the men came up to Bill and thanked him for what he did. Mr. Egan shook Bill's hand and he also thanked him for what he did. He then said,

"Bill, besides your obvious guts and skill, in walking those girders in your bare feet in this raging storm, there is no one that I personally know of, that could have done what you did. To bring down from that highest girder, this young man, who had obviously become so terrified of the position he found himself in, that he literally, froze." Mr. Egan then said to the men, "Lads, I believe that ye' all should go home now, and get a good day's rest, as were going to have to make up, for today's lost work, tomorrow." Bill then said,

"Thanks Mr. Egan for the high praise, I certainly do appreciate it, as it means a lot to me."

CHAPTER 52

Frustrated Passion

-Erin and Jimmy-

With Jimmy working six days a week, and with Sunday, his only day off, and with Erin, who was off on Monday and Tuesday, it became most difficult for Jimmy and Erin, to bring their ardor to fruition. Nevertheless, love somehow, will always find a way. Therefore, Jimmy took the late night train on Saturday evenings to Niles. He had worked it out with Erin, that the Shamrock Club's chauffer, would pick Jimmy up from the train station and drive him to the Shamrock Club, where Jimmy would watch Erin perform. After she finished her 'set' for the evening, the chauffer would drive them back to Mrs. O'Sullivan's tourist home, where they both shared Erin's room.

Mrs. O'Sullivan was not bothered by this arrangement at all, as she too, as a young girl, succumbed to the passions of love and wasn't bothered by the morals of the day, even though she knew it was wrong.

It wasn't too long before Jimmy discovered Erin's terrible secret and at first, he was somewhat shocked, but after Erin explained to him, the reason for her having it done and that they're was no way for Jimmy to catch this tattooed disease, Jimmy was both understanding and supportive. Fact is, both Jimmy and her, had many a good laugh over Erin's rather deceptive facade, in order for her, to discourage Al Capish, from his never ending desire, for her to satisfy his lubricious-sexual appetite, with several women at a time, in his bed. His perverted mind, knew no limits, to the depravity, he made his whores succumb to, with his animalistic rituals.

Al 'Scarface' Capish would someday, suffer the consequences of that most dreaded disease, syphilis, as it attacked his brain, driving him insane; a fitting end to a monster, in every sense of that rotten word.

CHAPTER 53

❀

A Century of Progress
-The Chicago World's Fair-

1933 was here before Erin knew it. However, Erin O'Hara was now the featured chanteuse, at the world famous Café, Toulouse-Lautrec, as part of the huge French Pavilion, brought over piece by piece, from Paris, France.

The Fair opened in the spring of that year and attendance, in spite of the 'Great Depression', was phenomenal. People came from all over the world plus, the forty-eight states, to see the wonders of 'A Century of Progress'.

Erin's contract with the Shamrock Club and Mr. McGrath had ended amiably, just about a month before the World's Fair opened. She was physically exhausted and so she did nothing for the entire month, but visit Jimmy, who had rented a suite of rooms at the La Salle Hotel in Chicago, for them both, so that Jimmy wouldn't have to travel so far, to visit her up in Niles, Illinois.

Jimmy by now, had become a lawyer for the South-Chicago Bridge & Iron Company and of course, Jimmy no longer, had any reason, to travel to Niles, Illinois to see Erin, nor did she, as both of their jobs, were now in Chicago.

As the construction part of the World's Fair had ended, Bill John, found himself without a job. Therefore, he applied for a job as a laborer and roust-a-bout, working for the World's Fair maintenance company, itself. Both Jimmy and Erin would on occasion, run into Bill, as his work took him to all parts of the Fair and he made it a point, as many times as he could, to see Erin perform. He still was in love with her. The worlds of both Erin and Jimmy, differed so greatly from Bill's, that they found that they no longer had much in common. Therefore, they slowly drifted apart.

France threw huge parties for Erin and the various foreign dignitaries, from many European and Asian countries, which came to see and hear, the Irish beauty perform. Without question, Erin was the rage of both North America and Europe. Never before, had the world's stage, ever seen such a beautiful woman, who could sing like the angels.

Night after night, Erin had to make a dozen or more curtain calls, She sang encore after encore of songs, which were native to the country, which, the visiting dignitary was from; always as a sort of a grand gesture to that person's country. Erin took it upon herself, to learn the favorite songs of certain countries, whose dignitaries were coming to America and to the Chicago World's Fair itself, to hear her sing and to see her radiant beauty up close. She tried to learn their favorite songs, in their native languages, if she could. She became the number one feature attraction, of the supper club set, of the world. Several Fashion magazines, all wanted her, to model clothes for some of the most famous designers from Paris, New York and Milan.

While Erin sang mostly the so called torch songs of the day, which made her internationally famous, she also on occasion, would sing songs from the many operettas, which were so popular at the time. In addition, she sang many of the songs from the numerous Broadway shows, from composers such as, Herbert, Porter, Romberg, Gershwin, Lehar, Strauss and even George M. Cohan, the great Irish composer and stage impresario and so many others, including songs from the Ziegfeld Follies. She included in her repertoire also, songs from Tin Pan Alley and she reached back, to the favorite songs of the gay nineties. Her voice control and her range were superb. Moreover, her ability to move her sensuous hips and her whole body, in time with the song she was singing, captivated the crowds, who literally adored her. Erin had now reached a high point, in her career.

She also was having trouble, turning down the offers of marriage from some of the wealthiest men in the world. Erin was attracted to men and she knew, that they knew she was. She was a man's woman! Erin seemed to emit an animal magnetism, an earthy attraction to men, besides her sensuous beauty, which drove men crazy. I'm sure that without her knowing it, Erin became in many men's minds at the time, someone to dream about and to have sexual fantasies with.

While Erin had to attend many social and official parties thrown by the French government and others, she at most times, attended these functions, alone, that is, the exception being, unless she had a male escort, provided by the French government, which was usually, a very handsome French officer.

That alone, started to put a strain on her relationship with Jimmy O'Brien, as he wouldn't attend these functions with her, considering the fact that he had to wear a cap, pulled down over the side of his face, to cover his hideous war wound. While Jimmy would have been considered quite handsome, had he not been so brutally disfigured in the war, and certainly would have been sought after by many girls, but he felt that he had to hide, from societies, never ending stares and their ignorant inquires, about his injury.

Finally, after almost a year of this unusual courtship or relationship with Erin, Jimmy finally said to Erin one morning, while eating breakfast in their suite, "Erin my dearest darling, I don't believe that it is fair to you and for your career, to have me as a sort of anchor around your neck. I cannot attend any of your many social functions as such; so I feel that for the good of our friendship, that we should call a sort of hiatus to our peculiar relationship."

Erin was sort of stunned by Jimmy's candor. While she had to admit to herself, that he was right, but she didn't feel that she could break his heart, by her telling him, what he had just said to her, first. She didn't think however, that he would have ever told her, what he just told her, as she knew just how much he loved her. Nevertheless, Jimmy was, as she knew, a perfect gentleman.

His comments, certainly gave her an easy way out, but now she had to question her love for him. Was it real, was it infatuation, or was it just her empathy, because of his war wound? Perhaps she wasn't in love with him, the same way he was with her, body and soul? She loved Bill John, but she wasn't 'in' love with him. She now began to have second thoughts about her feelings for Jimmy. Life was becoming very complicated and so finally, after mulling over in her mind, Jimmy's proposal, Erin said,

"You know Jimmy, that I love you, however, is my love beyond all reason, or is it related to my feelings about your war injury." If it's the later, then perhaps you are correct in telling me, that maybe we should both take a timeout or hiatus. In addition, should I continue with my career, wherever it leads me and perhaps at the end of it, which I don't imagine will be too much longer; as I've been singing now, for almost five years, which is when, most singers have already peaked at my age? There have been exceptions to what I just said of course, such as Sophie Tucker; *'the last of the red-hot mamas'*, but she has found her niche and as long as she remains in that niche, she has nothing to worry about. Whereas, I've chosen to do both, torch songs and semi-classical, but only because my voice has been trained in the classics, by Sister Angela

Clare. Added to this, is the strain of the nightlife, I'm forced to live and my very rigorous schedules, both as an entertainer and my many social commitments." She continued,

"I know Jimmy, that it would be unfair to you in away, if I suddenly gave up my career at its height and you and I were to marry. Then the realization might set in for me, that I gave up my career for my marriage to you and that I then might suffer the pangs of remorse and regret, that I should have, pursued my dreams, to their conclusion. Thus blaming you, for you're not allowing me, to reach that illusive goal, at the pinnacle of my career and that could of course, wreck our marriage." Erin continued,

"Perhaps you're right Jimmy, if after it's all over and my understanding fully, that I have finally reached the fulfillment of my dreams, whenever that might be, and knowing that I can go no further; then if we had the same feelings for one another, that of course would prove to me, that we were meant for one another." Jimmy with a pained look on his face said,

"So be it Erin, no matter how it ends, I will always love you." Jimmy then asked Erin, "Do you wish to remain in our suite of rooms in the La Salle Hotel, or do you wish to move someplace else" Erin answered,

"I've thought about taking a suite of rooms at the Drake Hotel, so why don't I move out and you can stay in this suite if you like." Jimmy then said,

"I really don't need a suite of rooms for just myself. The South-Chicago Bridge & Iron Company had offered me accommodations, at the Illinois Athletic Club on South Michigan Avenue, where they are lifetime members and they have several bachelor rooms, for their executive staff, should I want to stay there. I believe that I will take them up on their offer." So after some kisses and hugs, both Erin and Jimmy moved out of the La Salle Hotel, the very next day.

CHAPTER 54

❁

Montmarte, France
-36 Rue de Alliané-

The French government after the closing of the Chicago World's Fair and a 'Century of Progress' in 1934, offered Erin, an initial six month contract to sing at the world famous Moulin Rouge, in Paris, France. This of course, was Erin's most fervent dream, to appear at this world famous cabaret. She had always felt, that if she could sing at this famous cabaret, it would be the fulfillment of a little girl's dream; a dream, which she had often entertained in her mind, while she was washing floors at the Chicago Union Stockyards, so many years ago.

Erin chose to live in a famous or infamous suburb of Paris, a haven for off beat writers, famous French painters, play rights, left wing journalists, self professed-revolutionaries and other social outcasts. Erin when she was a little girl had passed herself off, as the sister of a pupil at St. Patrick's; an all boys, Catholic parochial grammar school and had wrangled a ride to the Chicago Art Institute on a family field trip, where she fell in love with the art of the French Neoimpressionists. Painters like Paul Cézanne, Georges Seurat, Paul Ganguin, Henri Matisse and Vincent Van Gogh and other lesser-known artists.

Now was the time she felt, which would probably be her last opportunity, to experience and to become a part of the life, of these vibrant, colorful Avant-Garde painters, who painted, hung out, argued politics, drank and made love to their many models, which for the most part, were prostitutes; these gifted creators, which society held in such disdain. Erin could empathize with the lives of these girls and women, who society had abandoned, for one reason or another and who had to fend for themselves, as an act of survival.

Erin was accepted into this closed knit society, almost immediately, as she was recognized as a fellow artist and one who didn't come to Montmarte to stare or to criticize. Erin's beauty however, would become a curse, as she attracted so much attention by the local artists, who were vying to paint her, in the nude of course. Erin liked this adulation, by these so called starving artists, as they somehow, satisfied her need, to be wanted and loved.

Erin shared a second story garret, with a chorus girl, who danced in the famous Moulin Rouge chorus line, a Mademoiselle Dominique de Flueré. Dominique was quick to attach herself so to speak to Erin, who she figured, knew nothing about Paris or Parisians, but one, who shared with Erin, the many hurts of life, and they both formed a sort of a feminine bond. Dominique was a Lesbian. They soon became the best of friends, as Erin was both vivacious and beautiful, as was Dominique, although Erin was attracted to men and Dominique was not, a rather odd, but never the less, a loving relationship.

Erin became the highest paid chanteuse in the world at that time. Once again, the world paid homage to this magnificent creature of God. Erin broke every attendance record at the Moulin Rouge. However, with her two day's off each week, Dominique and Erin spent the afternoon's, shopping and the evenings, drinking in the many small cabarets, which were so prevalent in Montmarte.

Dominique had a 'male' friend who was an artist of some note, who had received his art training, at the famous French art school, 'École des Beaux-Arts'. It wouldn't be too long before Dominique's 'male' friend, invited Erin to pose for him. Erin was not about to let just any artist paint her, but Dominique had shown her, many of his paintings of herself in the nude and she was intrigued by what she saw. In addition, Dominique's other lover, was a famous Lesbian painter, who she also poised for, who painted under the pseudonym or nom de plume of, Alexandrie de Donat. Her real name was, Adéle St. John. Dominique found sexual pleasure in both straight men and Lesbian lovers, as did Erin. In Erin's situation however, Al Capish had introduced her to this so-called forbidden love, while under the influence of Cocaine, several years ago.

She thought, that Dominique's male artist friend was excellent in figure drawing, in that he seemed to capture, the raw sensuousness of his women subjects, as shown by their voluptuousness, in his drawings, as though he was very intimate with his models, which he was. Once again, Erin's need to find a male friend, who she could talk with, while she was in Paris, was an almost overwhelming necessity. So she agreed. After all, Erin was no stranger to having men see her in the nude, as she was, not too long ago, a prostitute. There is something paradoxical within a woman's psyche, that while she professes modesty and virtue, she however, has a certain voyeuristic desire, to display herself, for others to see her, as God intended, au natural.

The artist's full name was Alain Maison. Alain's father, Messier Edgard Maison, was *Financer le ministre dans le gouvernement français*. 'Finance Minster in the French government'.

The painting sessions began on the first Monday of January 1935 and continued each and every Monday for six weeks. Well, it wasn't too long, before Erin had moved out of her shared apartment with Dominique and into Alain's apartment, which was a very modest garret. Dominique wasn't very happy with Erin, or with her former boyfriend for that matter, and she told both of them, what she thought of them and of course, this caused a rift between Erin and Dominique. But in France, love is expected to have it's many twists and turns and for the most part, such betrayals in France, are more easily accepted, than any where else in the world and as the French say, "*Tout juste dans amour et guerre*"; 'All's fair in love and war'.

After all, Dominique had pushed out, Alain's former mistress and model, several months before and didn't think anything of it. Montmarte was known for such indiscretions. It really was a way of life, for persons who refused to be governed by the mores of society and as the French say, "*Faire face à la vie, avec l'aban Don imprudent*". 'Face life, with reckless abandon.'

Erin was fascinated with Alain and his artistic ability, and he proved himself a handsome and worthy lover. Erin didn't think that she was in love with Alain, but she was infatuated with him, and that was for sure. Erin enjoyed his company and the company of many other French artists and sculptors. Alain was very tall for a Frenchman at that time. He stood well over six feet and was quite handsome, with his black moustache, his long black, shoulder length wavy hair and his olive complexion. He had many commissions, painting the wealthy women and their children of Paris.

His primary vocation was, as a portrait painter. However, one other attribute he had, which of course Erin didn't know about, was his services as a lover, to the many women patrons, whose husbands had taken a mistress or mistresses, depending on their wealth and their physical stamina. Alian had quite a reputation around Montmarte, as a *Clou* or 'stud'. Both Alian and Dominique, had long ago, fallen under the spell of drugs, which Erin so far had resisted, as she knew that it would only take a moment, before she drifted back into that evil world, of euphoric bliss and once again, be a slave to its irresistible lure and craving.

Erin had taken to the French language quite well. After only a few months living in France, she could carry on a reasonable conversation with her many French friends. Erin liked the French, even with their rather critical and snobbish attitudes, toward other nationalities, especially the Americans. However, because politics was something Erin wasn't particularly interested in, she never got into a political argument, with any of her French friends.

CHAPTER 55

※

Edgar Degas 11
-Papier-Mâché-

Erin had been introduced to many famous and not so famous, painters and sculptors, while she and her companions, frequented the many small cabarets and studios, in Montmarte. One sculptor in particular, intrigued her and he was the grandson of one of the most famous French painters and sculptors, of the nineteenth century; Edgar Degas.

Now Edgar Degas11 was not as talented as his famous grandfather, but the one artistic skill that was unique to his grandson, was his work in the medium, of papier-mâché. Erin happened to be at a gallery in Paris on a very rainy Monday morning, where Mr. Degas grandson, had a showing of his papier-mâché busts. That is, the French government commissioned Edgar, to create life like papier-mâché busts of famous French people, for a new modern French museum, that would open soon. He made life like busts, of the most famous French kings, generals and of Napoleon and Josephine, and other French notables, such as France's, most famous painters, composers, and authors.

Erin was fascinated with these papier-mâché busts and in particular, their heads, as they were so lifelike. She had an idea and she wanted to talk to Mr. Degas about, whenever he was free. Finally, after waiting for over two hours to talk with him, she waded through the guests and she said, *"Me parDonner Degas de mitre, est-ce que vous dînerez demain le soir à votre restaurant préféré, Le Clare de Suix dans Montmarte?"* 'Pardon me Monsieur Degas, will you be dining tomorrow evening, at your favorite restaurant, Le Clare de Suix in Montmarte?"

"*Oui, mais pourquoi est-ce que vous demandez?*" 'Yes, but why do you ask, Mademoiselle'? Erin then said,

"*Bien, jést-ce que demander étais si je pourrais discute une commission avec vous*"? 'Well, I was wondering, if I might discuss a commission with you?' Mr. Degas then said,

"*Oui, certainment Mademoiselle; et est-ce vous étes.*" 'Yes, certainly', Mademoiselle, and you are?' Erin answered,

"*Mon nom est Mademoiselle Adreinne de la Durequex et j'exécute au Rougue de Moulin de teh.*" Mr. Degas then said,

"*Mais de courase, me parDonner mon est cher, j'aurais dú vous reconnaitre asn je vous ai vu perform plusiers fois.*" 'But of course, please forgive me '*mon est che'r*, I should have recognized you, as I've seen you perform many times.' Mr. Degas then said,

"Perhaps we should speak English, as I think that I have a better command of English, than you do of French." Erin laughed as she said,

"Thank you Mr. Degas, I guess you're so right." Mr. Degas then kissed Erin's hand as he said,

"*Mon est cher,*" 'Until tomorrow evening.'

CHAPTER 56

❀

The Commission
-Mr. Degas & Erin-

It had been raining for the past two days and Erin was soaked to the skin as her umbrella had been blown inside out and she wasn't wearing any rain protection, other than her now broken umbrella, which was no longer functional. She only had a short walk, to reach the French cabaret where Messier Degas was to meet her. Her dress was soaking wet, and her dress, just clung to her body, revealing her most beautiful and sensuous shape.

Showgirls at that time and Erin was no exception, didn't wear bras, especially the Parisian women and so a thousand male eyes, would follow them, wherever they went. As I said, the walk from the garret of Alain Maison wasn't very far, to the small cabaret, where Messier Degas liked to have his supper. He along with many of his friends and other starving artists and writers, who made Montmarte their home, hung out. In earlier days, prominent writers and artists, such as the Irish author, Oscar Wilde and the Spanish artist Picasso, also enjoyed the give and take of their many intellectual discussions, while drinking wine or Absinthe, which is an aphrodisiac.

These avant-garde intellectuals discussed their art, their writing and the politics of France, over many bottles of wine and Absinthe. They always had spirited discussions and friendly arguments, over the merits of this or that, and of course, their mistresses.

Erin stood for a moment in the small doorway, leading into the restaurant, as she checked her make-up in a small mirror, she had in her purse and then, she combed her hair. She entered the dimly lit restaurant and the *Maitred d'* asked her, "*La Mademoiselle, est-ce que je peux vous aider?*" 'Mademoiselle, may I help you?' Erin answered,

"*Je cherche la table de Monsieur Edgar Degas.*" 'I'm looking for the table of Monsieur Edgar Degas. "*Oui Mademoiselle.*" 'Yes Mademoiselle', said the Maitre d'.

The Maitre d' escorted Erin, to a table in the rear of the cabaret, which had several persons seated around it. Mr. Degas got up upon seeing Erin and he pulled a chair from an adjoining table, for her to sit on. He then introduced Erin to the group, seated at the table. The group consisted of five men and three women. Erin didn't think that the women seated around the table, could be called intellectuals or artists, by any stretch of the imagination, as they all were overly dressed, with cheap feathered boa's and skirts, whose bottoms ended, where most girls wore their garters, but were underdressed, when it came to revealing, the more feminine parts of their anatomy. Their make-up, looked like it was put on, with a paintbrush. 'Bras' certainly weren't part of their feminine attire and neither were bloomers or panties. They were all prostitutes, but they preferred the term, models.

Mr. Degas began the conversation by asking Erin, what did she want him to do for her, in the way of a commission. Erin began her story this way,

"Mr. Degas, my ex-boy friend or lover if you will, was severely wounded during the war. The scar tissue on the left side of his face looks like ground up hamburger and his left ear is missing. He is a professionally trained lawyer and he would have been considered handsome, but for that injury. Anyway, to make a long story short, he has had to live in the shadows so to speak, since the war. He keeps the left side of his face covered by a cap, that he pulls down, to hide his hideous war wound.

He works at odd jobs as a laborer, as he feels that society wouldn't allow a grotesque face such as his, to appear in any kind of a decent job, especially so, where women might be offended. Mr. Degas than said,

"Well Erin, what has this gentlemen got to do with me?" Erin answered,

"I have loved the paintings of your grandfather. As a little girl, I many times, had the opportunity to view them, at the Chicago Art Institute. Yesterday, after seeing your brilliant exhibit of your papier-mâché busts, I became fascinated by your artistic skill, in replicating the faces of so many French notables. So, I thought that perhaps, you might be able to make a papier-mâché mask, so realistic, that no one could tell, if the mask was a mask, or if it were real, for my boy friend or lover." Erin continued,

"Now I realize that I don't know the first thing about papier-mâché. I don't know if it can be made durable enough, to be worn in all kinds of weather or how long, will it last, under the stresses of everyday wear and tear."

Edgar Degas scratched his head and then he sort of smiled at Erin, Finally after taking a moment or two, to think about Erin's rather unusual request he said,

"Erin, your commission kind of fascinates me and I am intrigued by it. I know this much about papier-mâché; it has been used by many peoples and various tribes, for thousands of years in the making of ceremonial masks, both for the living and for the dead." He went on, "We have ceremonial masks right here in one of the Paris museums, whose origins, date back some six thousand years and the colors on these masks, are as vibrant, as if they were painted just today." He continued, "What would be the kind of mask that you have envisioned, look like?" Erin said,

"Well Mr. Degas, it would be my sense, that if you could make such a mask, it would have to wrap slightly around the back of the head, about an inch I would guess. And then it would have to reach just about two inches above where the ear would normally have been and it would have to reach, just about a half inch, past where his sideburns would normally have been, toward his left eye." Mr. Degas then asked Erin,

"Could you perhaps draw a rough sketch of just where this gentlemen's wound is located, in reference to the side of his head?"

Erin was briefly taken back, by Mr. Degas' request for her, to draw the side of Jimmy's head, but she gathered herself together and she took Mr. Degas's pencil and she proceeded to draw the left side of Monsieur Degas's head, on a piece of butcher paper, which Mr. Degas had asked the waiter for. In her own mind, she kind of superimposed, Jimmy's injury against Mr. Degas's head. What Erin had drawn when she finished, was a large area that almost covered, the side of Mr. Degas's head.

Her recollection of Jimmy's hideous injury, showed a space, running from Mr. Degas's temple, up to his hairline on the left side of his face, to just below, where his ear should have been and then with a slight curve around the back of his head. Mr. Degas then said,

"You know Erin, if I decide to take on this commission, for your friend, what is his name?" Erin said,

"His name is Jimmy, Jimmy O'Brien." Mr. Degas went on,

"Well Jimmy would have to come to Montmarte, to my studio, where I could look at his war wound, measure his head and his wound. I would then need to take samples of his hair and mix my paints such, that I could exactly duplicate his facial complexion, etc." Erin asked,

"'What about his missing hair? Mr. Degas answered,

"I would use human hair and I would glue it to the mask, so that it would blend in perfectly, with his own hair." Erin then said,

"Mr. Degas, should you decide to take on this commission, then I would write to Jimmy and ask him come to Montmarte and we would go to your studio, for you to evaluate, whether or not such a mask could be made." She went on, "Tell me Mr. Degas, what is papier-mâché made from?" Mr. Degas thought for a minute and then he said,

"Papier-mâché is made from highly absorbent paper, water and glue. After the mask is made and I color it, I would then brush several coats of varnish over it, allowing each coat to dry in a sort of oven or kiln, I have constructed." He continued, "Now there are major difference in my masks and those which were made, several thousand years ago and the biggest difference is; the other ingredients, that I add to the mix of water and glue. I have perfected a secret formula, which increases the strength of the mask almost ten fold." He continued,

"I believe that my masks, can last far longer than any of the masks, the ancients made, because of the fact that I have access to stronger paper, better glues, paints and other modern chemicals, which I use to strengthen the mask's surface." He went on, "I believe that with reasonable care, your friend could conceivably wear his mask, for as long as he lives." Erin then asked,

"Mr. Degas, how would you fasten the mask to Jimmy's face and head?" Mr. Degas said,

"Well, my initial thought is, that I would find a high strength thread, a thread used by the Persians, in the making of their oriental rugs. The thread they use is super strong and can be made almost invisible, by painting it the color of Jimmy's complexion. I would attach it by each end and the top of the mask and run the thread through Jimmy's hair, so that it couldn't' be seen by anyone." He continued,

"I believe what I will do first Erin, is to make a sort of sample of what I think my mask will look like, based on what you've told me about Jimmy's complexion, his approximate head size and other personal observations, made by you, over the time, you and he were lovers. Also Erin, the bottom side of the mask, would not fit too tight to Jimmy's head, so as to allow for a certain amount of air, to circulate around the inside of the mask, to reduce sweating and the possible bleeding of the colors." He went on, "Tell me Erin, where was Jimmy wounded in the war?" Erin thought for a minute as she tried to recall, Jimmy's conversations with her, regarding the Great War.

"Well Mr. Degas, Jimmy was wounded in the battle for the Marne, in France." Jimmy thought about what Erin just told him and then he said,

"Erin, because your friend Jimmy, suffered such a hideous wound, in the American effort, to save France from the German Huns, it would be my distinct pleasure, for me to create his mask, pro-bono, that is, for free." Erin had tears in her eyes as she said to Mr. Degas,

"*Vous remercier, vous remercier.*" 'Thank you, thank you.' Erin continued, "Mr. Degas, I will write Jimmy to find out if he would be willing to come to France and have you make a mask for him? Oh and before I forget it, how long do you think that it will take, for you to make a mask for Jimmy?" Mr. Degas thought for a few minutes, as he thought about Erin's question and then he said,

"I would estimate that with several sittings and fittings, I believe that I could make Jimmy a mask, in approximately two weeks, three at the most. Also Erin, please call me Edgar, as I believe that Mr. Degas is far to formal for me, but might have been proper for my grandfather?"

Erin finished the evening talking to the various 'models', that found no harm, in making love to their men friends, in front of Erin. Erin was neither embarrassed nor surprised, as she did the same with Al Capish's gangster animals, while she was under the influence of cocaine

CHAPTER 57

❀

Erin's Letter
-Jimmy's Reaction-

Erin left the small cabaret, after saying goodnight to Edgar and his guests and kissing Edgar on both cheeks, which is the French custom. It had stopped raining and so she had no difficulty getting back to her flat, at 36 Rue de Alliané. Erin turned her key in the door and she opened the door to Alian's garret. She thought she heard giggling coming from the bedroom and when she walked into the bedroom, there lying in bed was Alian and a naked blonde. Both Alian and the blonde were under the influence of cocaine, as Erin could see the white powder residue on the nightstand, next to Alian's bed and the glazed look in both of their eyes.

Alian had heard Erin come in and when Erin walked into the bedroom, he said, "Come in Erin, hop in bed and join our little party." Erin was somewhat taken back by what she saw, but of course, she had realized that with the lifestyle of these French artists, what she was looking at, was common place. So really, Erin should not have been surprised by what she saw.

So Erin without saying a word to either of them, walked to her clothes closet and she put the few clothes she had hanging there, in her suitcase and she left without saying a word to either Alain or his whore. Erin only kept a few clothes in the garret, as she kept most of her clothes at the Moulin Rouge. She hailed a taxi and had the driver drive her to a local Hotel, The Parisian de Montmarte. Erin rented a room overlooking the main street and as she was so tired, she went to bed.

The first thing the next morning, she had her breakfast brought to her room, as she didn't sleep much the previous evening, mulling over and over, in her mind, her conversation with Edgar Degas and the project that she hoped, Jimmy would be receptive to. Finally she finished her breakfast, got out of bed and went to the window and watched the passing crowd, going too and fro, here and there, doing what ever, each of them does, most mornings in Montmarte. Montmarte was a village, which never sleeps. It was just one continuous, round the clock, series of activities.

Prostitutes coming home from their street corner trysts, together with the local drunks, many who had to face the wrath of their wives and the many artist and writers, who finally gave up the night, for the day, so that they could return to their garrets or sleeping rooms; to catch a few hours of shut-eye. To once again, begin this sort of artistic and intellectual ritual, that never seemed to stop, all over again: broken hearts, lover's quarrels, life's laments and it's tragedies. It had been going on like this in Montmarte, for a couple of hundred years or so. Life's candles were always burned at both ends, here in Montmarte, where youth seemed to want a swift rendezvous with death, not wanting to face old age, with its many infirmities and its need for the reckoning of one's sins, on life's, score card.

However, out of such human failures, and suffering, came some of the greatest art and letters, the world has ever known. Erin knew instinctively, that she too, was apart of the passing scene in Montmarte, if only for a moment, for she had certainly, left her mark.

Erin sat down at the small writing desk and she began to write a letter to Jimmy.

April 12, 1936

My Dearest Jimmy:

I hope my letter finds you well. I wanted to write to you to keep in touch and to tell you a little bit about my stay here in Paris. Paris is a beautiful city, the City of Lights; they call it, and the city of lovers. It is a beautiful city, especially so in the spring, with the Crocus, the Apple Blossoms and the Cherry Blossoms, all blooming along the Champs Élysées Boulevard, with the magnificent Arc de Triomphe at one end, which Napoleon began, during his reign as Emperor of France.

I live in a small suburb or village of Paris, called Montmarte. It is a haven for artists, writers, poets; the far 'left' of France. I think you might like it here, as every night, the intellectuals gather for discussions on art, politics and women, subjects that I'm sure, you would have a point of view on? I just love it here and evidently, the French love me, as I have broken all previous records for attendance at the Moulin Rouge.

Jimmy, while my career couldn't be any better, I find that it is not really, what I wanted after all. I miss you so, and the life that we had planned. But as you said, If I hadn't tried to reach the satisfaction of knowing, just how far I could go with my singing career, I might have never known, if I didn't take the opportunity that was given to me by God and the French government, to at least try and see just how far I could go.

You're so right, in that, it may have always prayed on my mind, if I hadn't tried, I might have blamed you, for not allowing me to at least see, if I might have reached those heights and that could have caused a rift in our marriage.

Now, let me get down to the real reason I'm writing to you. I've come across an artist whose grandfather was Edgar Degas, a French Neoimpressionist. I had always admired his work (the grandfather's), as a little girl, looking at his paintings in the Art Institute of Chicago. Anyway, his grand son who is also named Edgar Degas works in a medium called, papier-mâché. Papier-mâché is a thin kind of material, made from absorbent paper, glue and water, plus a few other chemicals. The artist, after he makes a sort of mask out of this material, then paints it so life like, that I couldn't tell it from a real face. Therefore, what I'm getting at is this. He said that he could fit you with a mask such; that no one could tell that your face had that injury from the war and that you wouldn't ever again, have to pull your cap down over your war wound, in an attempt to shield it from the ignorant public.

However, he would need you, to come here for several settings and a fitting, and it would take him between two and three weeks to finish it. I write you this letter, not knowing about your job with the South-Chicago Bridge & Iron Co. Do you like your new job? Is it what you wanted or expected?

Oh, before I forget it, Edgar Degas said that the mask would last as long as you live; it is that strong.

This Jimmy, could change your life, 'our' life, forever for the better and allow you to finally live a normal life. I do hope that you take what I've said in my letter to you, very seriously.

Perhaps your employer won't give you the time off to travel to Paris, France? However, there are other jobs Jimmy, so please for my sake, don't let this opportunity to change 'our' life, slip by. I await your reply and I can be reached at the Hotel, Parisian de Montmarte, 121 Rue de St. James, Montmarte, France.

P.S. If I don't hear from you in two weeks, then I will know, that you're not interested and won't be coming.

With all of my love, x x x x

Your dearest sweetheart, Erin

It had been just about two weeks, since Erin sent her letter to Jimmy, asking him to come to Montmarte, to at least sit and talk with Edgar Degas, about the idea of a papier-mâché mask, to cover his war wound. She waited for a letter every day from Jimmy, which never came. Erin was saddened in that she had not heard from Jimmy, since she wrote him and she now felt she had to tell Mr. Degas, that evidently, Jimmy was not interested in discussing the idea of a mask.

Erin had arrived back at the hotel at just about six a.m. after performing her act at the Moulin Rouge. The lobby of the hotel at that time of the morning was virtually empty. Four gas lamps lit the small lobby, casting their shadows on the wall paintings of nude women, which various artists painted, at one time or another; painting them, for room and board. Only the night clerk and the elevator operator, plus the bellboy, were on duty and all three were napping. She wanted to go to her room, as she was dog tired, and so she had to awaken the elevator operator, who was an old retired railroad man, by the name of Louis Dreyfus. She was just about to shake him, so that he would take her up to her room, when she thought that she sensed someone else nearby.

She turned and they're standing looking at her, was Jimmy, with a big smile on his face. She almost fainted, as she let out a scream, which awakened the three napping hotel employees. She literally, melted in Jimmy's outstretched arms and burst into tears.

They both sat on Erin's bed; as Erin asked, Jimmy a hundred questions about his job, Bill John and on and on. Jimmy answered each of her questions and he said, that Al Capish's gangsters, had staged a meeting (a trap), with Mr. McGrath's Irish Mafia and his mobsters, had machine-gunned them, killing them all. Al Capish had taken over all of the former business holdings of Mr. McGrath and the Irish Mafia, for the north side and the northern suburbs, of Chicago, including the Shamrock Club. Al Capish now controlled all of the prostitution, drugs, numbers, racetrack betting, and bootleg liquor, throughout Chicago and its suburbs.

After a short interruption for them to make love, Erin fell fast asleep in Jimmy's arms. While Jimmy sort of cat-napped, he spent most of his time in bed with Erin, watching her breath and telling himself, that he was the luckiest man alive, for God to have given him this Irish beauty, which many men would literally have killed for, she was that beautiful. Jimmy could now see certain tell tale signs of crow's-feet, that were starting to show around Erin's beautiful and smoky, Emerald-green eyes, a sign not only of age, but of the fast life Erin had to live, in that fickle world of show business. Her milky white skin on her body was flawless and her breasts were peaks of loveliness, and still firm.

He thought, what artist wouldn't give his right arm, to paint Erin, one of God's most beautiful creatures.

CHAPTER 58

❀

The Fitting

-Edgar & Jimmy-

Mr. Degas's garret studio was two streets over from the hotel, where Erin was staying and just about a block further north. His studio was quite large, with a huge window facing the morning sun. Erin knocked on Mr. Degas's door and heard some feet moving about. Mr. Degas finally came to the door. Evidently, he was painting and entertaining a model, which he slept with. She probably was his mistress. Mr. Degas opened the door and he greeted Erin,

"*Bon Erin de matin*", 'Good morning Erin'. Erin introduced Jimmy to Mr. Degas who shook Jimmy's hand. Erin could hear the sound of someone in the small kitchen attached to the studio and she could smell the aroma of *cafe Françoise,* 'French coffee'. Mr. Degas invited Erin and Jimmy to sit with him and his mistress, at a small table in his studio. He introduced his mistress as Mademoiselle Désirée de Deville. Erin sized Désirée up from head to tow very quickly, as one woman, always does to another and she had to admit to herself, that Désirée was a very beautiful woman. She had on, a Japanese silk kimono, with nothing underneath and one of her breasts was peaking out from under her silk wrap.

Jimmy sort of gulped, as he couldn't help but notice, this very beautiful woman also, whose one breast, was obviously waiting for her bosomy companion, to make it's appearance also. The top of her kimono was slowly opening, little by little, as she sat there listening to Edgar and Jimmy talk. Her smoky brown, flirtatious eyes were sort of glazed, while looking at Jimmy. She had seduction on her mind, as though Jimmy might be her next sexual conquest, regardless of her current paramour, Edgar Degas.

Erin knew that Désirée was deliberately moving her shoulders ever so slightly, in order for her kimono, to open further, so as to reveal her other breast to Jimmy. Désirée was a flirt and Erin knew that she was, as she certainly was trying to flirt with Jimmy and she made no effort to hide it.

Erin thought to herself, 'Well, *if Jimmy is interested in this, 'marche' or tramp, this whore, then fine, he can have her'*. Erin's Irish was beginning to surface, as she was conjuring up, in her own mind, what she thought, were answers to Jimmy's own thoughts, even though Jimmy hadn't professed any, at least not out loud, to her or to anyone else. Erin's imagination and her own jealousy, was getting the better of her. After about a half hour of questions by Jimmy and answers by Edgar, they both turned to Erin and Jimmy asked,

"Well Erin, did I cover most everything, that I should have, or do you have any other questions of Mr. Degas?" Jimmy had to repeat his question of Erin twice, as Erin's mind was now on an entirely different subject and she didn't hear a single word that either Mr. Degas or Jimmy had said. Désirée's bosomy companion, with its perky large nipple, had just now peaked out from under her kimono and completed it's own separate journey, joining her twin. Jimmy gulped, as he couldn't help, but notice the appearance of Désirée's other breast. Finally, Erin who seemed like she was in another world, said,

"No sweetheart, I believe that you have covered everything." Jimmy gave Erin a sort of curious look, as did Mr. Degas.

"Well," said Mr. Degas, if there are no further questions, then perhaps we can get started."

"Jimmy," said Mr. Degas, "Please sit over here by the window, as it gives me the light I need, for my preliminary pencil sketches of you and your wound." Jimmy got up and he walked over to the chair that Mr. Degas wanted him to sit in. Jimmy had not taken off his cap until now. When he did, both Mr. Degas and Désirée gasped, as they were not expecting such a grotesque wound, which they now looked at. Désirée almost fainted, as she had to turn away, putting her hand over her mouth, as if to forestall, the possibility of her vomiting. Even Mr. Degas was stunned by what he saw. He had no idea of just how grotesque, Jimmy's war wound actually was, from Erin's brief description of it, as a picture is certainly worth, a thousand words!

Désirée's ardor for Jimmy suddenly evaporated. Erin kind of laughed to herself, as she was watching Désirée's face, when she saw Jimmy's war wound. Désirée got up from the table and excused herself and she went back into the kitchen and never came out again, during the entire sketching and measuring, session. After Mr. Degas had finished what he called preliminary sketches and taking measurements of Jimmy's head with a rather large calipers, he said,

"So Erin and Jimmy, can we set up a schedule for Jimmy to come to my studio for more definitive sketches and some final measurements? I also will need a sample of Jimmy's hair, so that I can match it perfectly, or as near perfectly as I can." He went on,

"Oh Jimmy, I hadn't thought of it until now, but I would imagine that if we're both alive in lets say, twenty years from now, you will need a new mask. Not because the old one will be worn out, but a new mask will take into consideration, your aging process. That is, as the left side of your head will remain as of, lets say, April 1936, whereas the right side of your head will have aged some twenty years, as of April 1956. In other words, the left side of your face will remain; as it was, the day I gave your new mask to you. Do you agree?" Jimmy thought for a minute and then he said,

"God almighty, I never thought of that". He began to laugh. Mr. Degas went on,

"Your hair, if you have any by then, might be snow white, as you're becoming prematurely gray now. I know the Irish become gray at a very early age, I guess it's in their heritage, from having to fight the bloody English." He laughed and so did Jimmy. Erin didn't say anything, as she was still thinking about Désirée, as a possible seductress of Jimmy. Erin then said,

"As far as Jimmy and myself are concerned, we can come as often as you like, as I sing in the evenings at the Moulin Rouge, although I usually go to bed after I get home, or after I sort of unwind." Mr. Degas then said,

"Well, why don't we schedule Jimmy's appointment, oh lets say, roughly at one p.m., right after lunch, five days per week, unless Erin, you don't wish to accompany Jimmy to my studio and then we could make an earlier appointment." Erin then said,

"No Mr. Degas, I would like to accompany Jimmy each and every time he has an appointment, so that I can see the progress you're making." Erin was thinking about Mademoiselle Désirée, when she said what she said, about accompanying Jimmy. She thought to herself, '*I sure as heck, don't trust that whore, not after what I saw her do, to try and entice Jimmy.*" Mr. Degas than said to both Erin and Jimmy,

"Please call me Edgar, as I feel that calling me Mr. Degas, is too formal and I'm not that much older than either of you." He shook Jimmy's hand and he kissed Erin's hand, after kissing her on both cheeks. Erin and Jimmy left Mr.

Degas's studio and they walked back to the hotel. As they passed one of the many cafes or cabarets, Erin said,

"Lets have a drink Jimmy, to celebrate what I hope to be, will be a new life for you and for us." Jimmy answered,

"Its okay with me." The cabaret's name was, *'La Grenoville Affectueuse',* 'The Affectionate Frog'. Jimmy laughed when Erin translated the cabaret's name for him. As they entered, the Maitre d' approached, them and he said,

"Mademoiselle et le monsieur, je pouvoir le siège vous?" 'Miss and Mister, may I seat you?' Erin answered him in French and both Jimmy and Erin were seated at a small and rather secluded table, next to a fireplace. Erin noted the table's seclusion and she thanked the Maitre d' with a wink. A concertina player was playing French folk music. A waiter then asked,

"Quel est votre plaisir"? 'What is your pleasure'? Erin still couldn't get that whore, Désirée, out of her mind and it wasn't that she didn't trust Jimmy, but she knew just how weak, most men were, when it came to a beautiful woman, they're just like little boys, discovering girls for the first time. Jimmy could see the waiter's impatience with Erin's sort of 'day-dreamy' look and he then repeated his question, *"Quel est votre plaisir?"* 'What is your pleasure?' Finally, Erin realized that someone was asking her a question so she blurted out,

"Deux abienthe s'il vous plaît" Two Absinthe's please". Jimmy looked at her for a minute and then he said,

"What's bothering you Erin, as you don't seem to be here; like you're some-place else?" Erin then realized that she had been thinking too much about that whore, Désirée and so she said,

"Oh Jimmy, I guess I was thinking about Mr. Degas and hoping that he can make you a realistic mask." They were served their drinks and ordered two more. Absinthe is a very powerful aphrodisiac and as such, is a very potent drink. Erin knew exactly what she was doing, although she herself had never tasted or experienced the after effects of drinking absinthe. She only knew, from what her French women friends, told her, about the powerful effects it has, on the love making abilities of a man and a woman. Erin didn't know that if too much absinthe is consumed, it could cause paralysis and death. But she wanted to get Jimmy's mind off of that whore, Désirée, and so she thought that she would show Jimmy, that she was every bit as good in bed as Désieée was, in her mind anyway, if not better, at any and all costs.

Both Erin and Jimmy were getting woozy and Erin then decided that they should return to the hotel. They both by now were quite drunk and they staggered down Rue de Palm Avenue, trying to find Erin's hotel. Finally, after a long search, Erin remembered the little flower shop that was directly across the street from her hotel, the Parisian de Montmarte, and where they both were now standing, in front of. Erin began to giggle as she said to Jimmy,

"Boy, what stupid asses we are, when we can't even find our hotel." They both then staggered across the street and went up to Erin's room. Erin's plan didn't seem to work out, as they both fell fast asleep on the bed, awaking, about four hours later. Erin was puzzled and disappointed by what she had hoped would be a sexual orgy with Jimmy.

She heard a noise coming from the bathroom and she said to herself, Jimmy must be throwing up. The door then opened and out stepped Jimmy without a stitch of clothes on, wearing one of Erin' s hats. He had love in his heart, a silly grin on his face and sex on his mind, as Erin could see that Jimmy's was now quite aroused. Jimmy jumped into bed and he tore off every stitch of Erin's clothes. For the next two hours or so, their lovemaking went on almost continuously. The noises coming from their hotel room, brought smiles to the old bellboy, Louié Cheriac, as he thought about his dearly departed wife, Adéle and their little love nest. He wiped away a tear from his eye and he went about his duties.

Erin knew that it wouldn't be too long, before she had to get ready for her evening's performance at the Moulin Rouge and she could hardly stand up. She looked over at Jimmy who was now; sound asleep with a smile on his face. Erin also smiled, as she too was very pleased with Jimmy's passionate performance.

CHAPTER 59

❀

A Gift from God
-Edgar and Jimmy-

Two weeks had passed and Mr. Degas was now ready to fit his papier-mâché mask, to Jimmy's head. Neither Erin, nor Jimmy had seen the mask after it was finished, before it was placed in the kiln, or before Mr. Degas had painted it, with such painstaking realism. Mr. Degas had baked it with the first layer of colors and he now was giving it, the final curing of the many coats of varnish he had brushed onto it.

Erin and Jimmy sat in Mr. Degas's studio sort of fidgeting, as they both were very apprehensive as to what the mask, would feel and look like, on Jimmy's head. Mr. Degas greeted them both, as they entered his studio. He had them sit facing the large studio window, so that they could see what Mr. Degas had created for Jimmy.

Mr. Degas offered them both a cup of; cafe Françoise, but they both declined, as they couldn't wait to see Mr. Degas's creation. Mr. Degas went into his back room and when he returned, he held in his hands, what looked like a part of Jimmy's head, it was so realistic looking, that Erin began to cry, as she couldn't hold her emotions in, any longer. Jimmy just sat there kind of stunned, as he too, looked very carefully at the mask, almost feeling as though, he were back on the battlefield at Marne, France, some two seconds before he lost the left side of his head.

Mr. Degas now brought the mask over to Jimmy and he told Jimmy to hold it in his hands and to place it on the left side of his head. He fastened it with

Persian threads and then he tightened them slightly. Mr. Degas stood back a ways from Jimmy, so that he could gain a bit more of a perspective for his creation. He walked around Jimmy and Erin several times, looking at the mask and Jimmy's head, until finally he said, Jimmy and Erin, please go over to that full length mirror in the hall and take a look. Both Erin and Jimmy carefully walked over to the hall mirror. They didn't want to walk too fast and then be disappointed, but they also didn't want to walk too slow and not find out, what Jimmy now looked like. At first glance, Jimmy almost fainted, as he didn't recognize himself without his cap, pulled down over the left side of his face. Erin also, got weak in the knees, as she was so apprehensive at first, but now she let out a shout of glee, as she said,

"*Remercie vous, remercie vous, Monsieur, c'est seulement et si, vous sont un génie et un vrai artiste dans chaque sens du mot*" 'Thank you, thank you, Mr. Degas, it is just beautiful and so realistic; you are a genius and a true artist in every sense of the word.'

Jimmy too was speechless, as tears began to well up in his eyes, as he never expected what he saw. It was like some body had given him back, the left side of his head and the ear, which was attached to it, which the howitzer shell and taken from him, and really, his life. He couldn't even remember anymore, how he looked before he was wounded in France, during the Great War. Jimmy turned to Mr. Degas and he gave him a bear hug, as he said,

"Mr. Degas, I am speechless, how can I ever thank you for what you've done, it is nothing short of a miracle." Mr. Degas beamed like a proud father, as Erin and Jimmy sang their praises to him, about his extraordinary artistic skill. He too, had a tear in his eye, as he acknowledged the gratitude on both Erin's and Jimmy's faces. That was payment enough, for what he had created.

Then they all sat down at the little kitchen table and shared a bottle of wine to celebrate.

CHAPTER 60

❦

The Moulin Rouge
-Erin's Announcement-

At Erin's performance that evening, Jimmy sat in the front row in the V.I.P. section, along with several dignitaries and their mistresses. Jimmy surmised that they were mistresses, considering the ages of their consorts.

Erin made her grand entrance as usual, amidst thunderous applause. Her performance that evening was especially poignant, as she sang her heart out for Jimmy, who sat there beaming, as he was so proud of her. After her twelve or more curtain calls, Erin once again came back on stage for an announcement. As the spot light shown on her, dressed in her favorite emerald green dress, with the glitter sprinkled on her raven black hair, and with a slight blush on her cheeks, she placed the palm of her left hand over her heart, as she said,

"*J'aimerait remercier vous tout, de le de mon, pour le la plupart des et la plupart des, vous a Donné me, pendant mon ici à le célèbre Moulin. Je n'ai jamais dans ma vie entière, mon feutre si accueilli dans n'importe quel pays, comme j'ai en france et par les gens français. J'aime votre pays et c'est des gens. Viva la France.*" 'I would like to thank you all, from the bottom of my heart, for the most friendly and most gracious welcome, you have given me, during my performances here at the world famous Moulin Rouge. I have never in my entire life, ever felt so welcomed in any country, as I have in France and by the French people. I love your country and it's people. Viva la France.' She went on,

"However, I've got an announcement to make to you this evening and it concerns a certain young man, seated in the front row. His name is Jimmy O'Brien and while he hasn't officially told me that he wants to marry me, at least I can't remember if he did or not, but for tonight, I would like to tell Jimmy in front of all of you, that yes, Jimmy, I will marry you."

The French audience went wild with Erin's' public announcement of her forthcoming marriage to her sweetheart. The audience then began to shout, Jimmý, Jimmý, as they stamped their feet in unison. A second spot light came on and it shown right on Jimmy. Jimmy's face became bright red, as he arose and bowed to the crowd, acknowledging their acclaim. Jimmy had forgotten something that before yesterday, he would never have done, and that was, to get up in public to display his cap covered face, which of course, he no longer had to wear a cap, to hide his hideous facial wound. Jimmy was so taken with the moment that he completely forgot about his face.

Then he realized, that no one could see any difference in his face whatsoever, as both sides of his head were the same, at least they looked that way to the crowd. The crowd wouldn't stop, they wanted Jimmy to go up on stage and kiss Erin. Finally, with a little coaxing from those persons seated in the V.I.P. seats and with Erin motioning for him, to come up on stage, he walked to the stairs leading up to the stage. Finally holding Erin in his arms, he gave her a long and passionate kiss, to the applause of the adoring audience. Even the chorus girls and the Moulin Rouge orchestra, all joined in the clapping for Erin and Jimmy. Some even had tears in their eyes.

Finally, Erin motioned to the crowd to sit down, as she holding Jimmy's hand, walked back behind the curtain and to her dressing room. It was a night to remember.

When they arrived at Erin's dressing room, they opened the door and there standing in Erin's dressing room were two Moulin Rouge executives, Marcel Demuiré and Émile de Hugo, Both gentlemen had big smiles on their faces as they greeted Erin and Jimmy, offering them both, their congratulations, on their forthcoming marriage. Erin was surprised at the sight of these two gentlemen, as she really hadn't talked to either of them, since the Chicago's Worlds Fair, some two years ago.

Monsieur Demuiré held a piece of paper in his hand, as he handed it to Erin and then he said to Erin, Mademoiselle O'Hara, on behalf of the Moulin Rouge management, we would like to extend your contract for at least two more years, if that is agreeable with you. As you will see when you read the new contract, it doubles your salary and also, it offers you two months of paid vacation during the slow summer months, which of course, is when most of Europe shuts down anyway.

Erin was astounded by this good news, but she hesitated for a moment and then she said, "Monsieur's, I am flattered by you're most generous offer. But rather than give you a yes or no answer now, I would like to discuss it with my future husband, Jimmy O'Brien, after all, he is now my new manager, agent and spokesperson for Erin O'Hara." Both French gentlemen looked at on another and they said,

"But of course, Mademoiselle Erin, we understand perfectly and now, we will leave you two alone and we hope that you will find our offer and terms, most generous and of course, they are justly deserved by you. You're performances at the Moulin Rouge, have all been sellouts, which I might add, has never happened before, in the history of the Moulin Rouge."

CHAPTER 61

The Celebration
-Gai et les Lesbiennes-

Erin and Jimmy celebrated Erin's success and Jimmy's new face, with a wild party given by Erin, at the small Montmarte cabaret named Désirée le Désirée. This cabaret is a hangout for mostly gay and lesbian artists, actors and musicians. However, because Montmarte was such a cosmopolitan village, most persons living there, paid little, or no attention, to the clientele or societies labels for them.

Erin who enjoyed the Bohemian lifestyle of Montmarte, accepted such gay men and lesbian women and she never questioned their lifestyle. However having said that, Erin didn't particularly like mixed race couples, where either a black man would hook up with a white woman, or vice a verse. The French however, seemed to accept such people, and didn't look down on such liaisons, at all.

She felt that it was wrong and was against God's edict. Perhaps deep down though, Erin would often re-live the time, that she was brutally raped by a black vagrant as a little girl, and was beaten so badly by him, that her broken leg had been miss-'set' by a doctor, causing one leg to be a half inch shorter than the other.

Most of the men, who danced in the choruses of the many cabarets around Paris, were openly gay and a good many of the girls, who danced in these same choruses, were lesbians. Some though, became lesbians, not because of nature's predisposition so to speak, but the result of men who had beat them unmercifully, or would 'pimp' them, in order to make money for their wine and drug addictions. In addition, other men; lovers, husbands' and/or boyfriends, had abused them to the point, where they sought solace and protection, in the arms of another woman, who usually was a lesbian, and rightly so, as a woman, could more tenderly, empathize with another woman's plight, than could a man.

Life on the street was unusually tough for any young girl or woman, who tried to make it on her own, in these large cities, as circumstance most of the time, ensnared these women and generally forced them into a life of prostitution and drugs, in order for them to survive.

Erin had made many long lasting friendships, while she lived in Montmarte. Erin's closest girlfriend in Montmarte was a Lesbian, but that fact didn't mean that Erin was a Lesbian, as she still preferred men.

However, Jimmy was very uncomfortable being in this rather bizarre environment. Jimmy being attracted to women couldn't understand how gay men could be attracted to other men. As for lesbians, well he just couldn't understand them at all. While some of these lesbian women, were called butches or dykes, as they tried to play the male role in their association with other women. But he did see, many beautiful feminine women, who for whatever reason, were attracted to these dykes or butches, who dressed and tried to talk and act, like men. However, Jimmy loved Erin and so, he just went along with her and he realized, that God created such people, but he didn't understand why? He said to himself, *'its all I can do sometimes, to try and figure out what is going on in Erin's mind, let alone, try and understand what makes these other people, the way they are'.*

Erin attracted to her, many persons, both men and women, who were down and out, because she condemned no one and looked down on no one. Erin understood their individual hurts; their loneliness and she always demonstrated compassion for such people. Erin had lived enough of life, to understand that she should judge no one and she really accepted each and everyone, on their goodness alone. She realized that for whatever reason, in a philosophical way that fate dealt such people, a bum hand in life and they just had to play those cards that were dealt to them, to the best of their abilities.

Erin's success at the Moulin Rouge, certainly gave some of these people jobs, as she would make sure that someone at the Moulin Rouge, would interview them and judge their talents. Without Erin, most would never have gained access, to the Moulin Rouge and a possible stage career

In addition, Erin never turned down anyone who needed money, as she had a soft spot for those poor unfortunates, who were down and out.

After a wild night of drinking dancing and singing, Erin and Jimmy, somehow made their way back to their hotel, where they slept the early morning hours away, both fully dressed.

CHAPTER 62

❀

The Decision

-Why Not-

Erin and Jimmy finally awakened and they undressed, taking off their party clothes after a night of revelry and then, changed back, into their street clothes. They both were famished and both were nursing hangovers. They walked to a small French bakery and coffee shop on the corner, named, 'Le Petit Gâteau', 'The Biscuit'. They ordered, 'Doux bouilli oeufs et lard', soft boiled eggs and bacon with Café François, French coffee. Jimmy then said to Erin,

"God, what a night, I can't remember most of it. However, I do remember this, that you were the most beautiful woman at that party." Erin squeezed Jimmy's hand as they sat there, looking into each other's blood shot eyes. Erin after saying nothing to Jimmy for a full ten minutes said,

"You know Jimmy, it had been my intention all along, to leave the Moulin Rouge after my six months engagement and return to the states with the hopes of marrying you. But now, since you're here and have proposed to me, or did I propose to you? I can't remember?" She laughed as she went on, "No matter, I've been thinking that we should get married here in France and as long as were both together and with you becoming my agent and manager, perhaps we should stay another year, what do you think." Jimmy thought about what Erin had proposed, as he had been thinking along those same lines, ever since the executives at the Moulin Rouge gave Erin her new offer. He thought, that she could hardly turn them down, as obviously, her career was still going strong and so he finally said,

"Erin sweetheart, I don't know how to say this to you, but I've been thinking."—. Erin was trying to read Jimmy's rather pensive face, as well as to listen to, what seemed to her, like his reasons for him not wanting her to accept the new contract. Then he changed his facial expression completely and he said, "Erin my love, I think that you would be foolish, not to accept such a contract, as we'll be together and yes, we'll get married in France." Erin's face went from one of sad anticipation, to one, which was now bright and cheerful, as she said to Jimmy,

"Why you little devil, you're nothing but a tease and you delight in seeing me squirm in the wind, I've a good mind to cut you off, for as long as it takes us, to return to our hotel." Jimmy busted out laughing. Jimmy then said,

"You know Erin, in the back of my mind, I had sort of figured, that when we did return to the states, that perhaps you could get a job on one of those Ohio or Mississippi river boats, as a singer and I could handle the legal affairs for the owners." He went on, "I do believe that we would both enjoy that adventure very much, at least for a couple of years, until you decided to quit your career and then perhaps, we might think about a family." Jimmy had Erin's mind in a tizzy now, and that is all she thought about, was starting a family with Jimmy. Jimmy went on, "And further, you might not want to stay in Europe, working at the Moulin Rouge for the entire contract; or you might want to lets say, agree to work, only half the time, your contract specifies?" Erin thought about Jimmy's suggestion and she kind of liked it, as her singing gig at the Moulin Rouge, was taking its toll on her

Erin knew that she wasn't getting any younger and she thought, *'I've,—, I mean we've got plenty of money, so if money isn't the object, what is?'* Erin knew the answer to her own question. It was the adulation of the patrons, who clamored for her performances and the fact that she finally had reached the pinnacle of her career. These were the obvious reasons, for her to stay where she was. In addition, the French people and the Moulin Rouge were very good to her. Lastly, she had made a little girl's dream, come true.

It was now late April and Erin knew that the Moulin Rouge and the other cabarets in Paris, and those throughout France and Europe, for that matter, would be closing in a couple of months, for their summer 'Holiday'. Well, actually the summer 'Holiday' season in Europe, was July and August. Therefore, Erin would sing through May and June and then she thought, that Jimmy and her would get married, the first week in July.

She smiled to herself as the thought, that finally getting married and marrying her prince, was everything a little girl could want. Jimmy's personality, when he was around people, had changed one hundred percent. He was now very warm and outgoing. He no longer hid from society, trying to keep everyone at arms length, since he got his mask from Mr. Degas. He literally, was a changed man.

He still though, was very jealous of Erin, whenever they were around other men, whom she enjoyed. Erin had total control over Jimmy and she knew it. Not that Jimmy didn't have a mind of his own, but now that he had a finance and he no longer had to hide himself, from the public, he just seemed totally happy and contented.

After returning to the Moulin Rouge, Erin had discussed her new contract with Messieurs, Demuiré and de Hugo, and told them of her desire to only work, one more year, as she and Jimmy had other plans. Both gentlemen weren't too happy with Erin's decision, but they had no choice, but to accept Erin's wishes. They drew up a new contract and Erin and Jimmy both signed it. Both executives felt, that who knows, Erin could change her mind later on, as women so often do, and so they left the door open.

CHAPTER 63

❀

Marriage
-Scarface's Long Arm-

Erin and Jimmy got married in Saint Michael's-Angel's Catholic church, in the small village of Villenueve, in the province of Seine-Et-Marne. It was supposed to be a small wedding with Erin's closest friends from the Moulin Rouge and from Montmarte, but it turned out, that thousand of her fans, also turned out for her wedding. Jimmy rented a small French sports car and they took off for Switzerland, after the wedding ceremony was over.

Unbenounced to either Erin or Jimmy; but there standing in the wedding crowd, was another person, who through his Sicilian Mafia family in Sicily, had been sent by Al Capish, to kill, both Erin and Jimmy. The man wore a long black leather coat and had on his head, a typical black French beret, which covered a black shock, of his greasy hair. He carried a small black doctor's valise. The long black arm of Al 'Scarface' Capish was still very evident, even in Europe. After all, it was through the French port of Marseilles, that most of Capish's drugs, left for the United States.

Evidently, Al Capish still felt that Erin had tricked him, as he had heard from one of the chorus girls at the Kit Kat club, after she was tortured, that she had told Erin how to fool Al, into thinking that she had a very bad case of syphilis as he saw, when Erin took off her panties. He also had one of his assassins, murder the old lady, Maude O'Malley, alias, Mademoiselle Fife le Roach, who was the tattoo artist, responsible for tattooing Erin's genital area, which looked to the average 'john', like she had a severe case of syphilis. The old lady who lived in a small basement apartment, in South Chicago; Erin would have been saddened, had she known.

There is a Mafia-Sicilian saying which is the corner stone of the Italian Mafia credo and those words are, *La Vendetta*, which says; '*Sul sangue di mia madre, prenderò la mia vendetta*' 'On the blood of my mother, I will get my revenge'.

Jimmy and Erin left the small village that same morning and were on their way to Bern Switzerland. Jimmy wanted to take a short detour and drive across Marne, France first, outside of the small French village of Sézanne, as that is where he was so terribly wounded and where, so many of his buddies, were slaughtered by the German machine gun fire, in the battle of the Marne.

Jimmy had spotted a small roadside cemetery and he pulled the car off on to the shoulder of the road and stopped. Both he and Erin got out and they walked over to the cemetery. An iron gate protected the cemetery entrance and it had a lock on it. Jimmy looked at Erin with a sad look as he said, "Damnit, we've come all this way, only to find the cemetery locked." Erin had spotted a small house located in the rear of the small cemetery and she said to Jimmy,

"Perhaps the caretaker lives there?" As they both walked toward the little house, they heard a noise behind them, as a large black sedan raced by. It looked like the driver was in a hurry to get somewhere, as he was driving extremely fast. They saw him glance in their direction; slow down and then he picked up speed and went on his way. Jimmy said,

"Some of these damn Frenchman, drive too fast." As they approached the stairs, leading up to the front door of the old house, an old lady, who looked to be in her nineties, opened the front door a crack and she said in French,

"*Mademoisille et Monsieur, est-ce que je peux vous aider s'il vous plaît*"? 'Mademoisille and Monsieur, may I help you please?' Erin said,

"*Nous sommes si désolés pour vous ennuyer, mais le portail au cemetary est verrouillé et mon mari cherchait le concierge, voir s'il ouvrirait le portail, pour que nous regardions le grave.*" 'We're so sorry to trouble you, but the gate to the cemetery is locked and my husband was looking for the caretaker, to see if he would open the gate, so that we might view the graves.' The old lady thought for a minute and then she said,

"*Mon mari est mort récemment et je non plus long peut ouvrir le portail de cemetary, mais je vous permettez d'utilise ma clef, si vous promettez de le retourner me*". 'My husband has recently died and I no longer, can open the cemetery gate, but I will let you use my key, if you promise to return it to me'. Erin said,

"*Vous remercier beaucoup et oui, nous retournerons la clef à vous après nous verrouillons le portail*" 'Thank you very much and yes, we will return the key to you, after we lock the gate.'

Neither Erin nor Jimmy, had noticed when they were talking to the old lady, that another car sped by them, as though that car, might be following the black car, that had passed by them, only a few minutes earlier.

Jimmy and Erin walked around the small country cemetery and Jimmy saw several of his American buddy's graves, which were buried there. He took off his hat and he said a prayer. Erin watched Jimmy, and she could see that he was upset, as she noticed a small tear, escape from his right eye. Erin squeezed Jimmy's hand, as they walked back to the old ladies house, after locking the cemetery gate.

Storm clouds began to gather in the eastern sky, which before had been bright and sunny; it quickly darkened, as though a storm was coming in from the French Alps. Thunder could be heard in the distance, with flashes of lightning, lighting up the eastern sky. It started to rain and after giving the key to the cemetery gate, back to the old lady, Erin and Jimmy made a dash for their car. By the time they got the doors opened to their car, they were both drenched. While it was only late afternoon, but with the darkening sky, it looked like it was midnight. Jimmy drove very slowly, until he spotted on his left, a small inn. The sign outside which was barely visible in the driving rain read, '*L'Horloge de Coucou: le Pain & le Petit Déjeuner*' 'The Cuckoo Clock: Bread & Breakfast'. Jimmy said to Erin,

"Sweetheart, I think we should see if they have a room, as driving in the dark, on these treacherous mountain roads, is too dangerous" Erin agreed with him and Jimmy pulled into a small parking space, in front of the small inn, which had only room for three or four cars. Because of the driving rain, Jimmy and Erin failed to notice the large black sedan, which was parked two spaces over from theirs and next to their sport's car, was a small sedan.

CHAPTER 64

❀

A Sicilian Vendetta

-Murder-

As Erin and Jimmy stepped into the small foyer, of the *'L'Horloge de Coucou: le Pain & le Petit Déjeuner'. The* Cuckoo Clock: Bread & Breakfast Inn', they noticed a large man standing by the front desk, reading a newspaper. With his swarthy face and very Italian facial features, Erin felt a cold chill run up her spine. He was dressed in a long black leather coat and he wore a black beret, over his mass of black shaggy hair. He glanced at both Jimmy and Erin, and Erin could see him ogle her and lick his lips, with what looked to her, with one eye. Erin thought he was about to speak to them, but he didn't, as he seemed to think better of it. Erin asked the desk clerk, if he had a room for the evening.

"*Le Monsieur, est-ce que vous avez une salle pour le deux de nous, pour ce soir?*" 'Mr., do you have a room for the two of us, for this evening?'

"*Oui je fais*". 'Yes I do,' answered the clerk. The guest rooms, and there were three of them, were all located on the second floor. The proprietor lived with his family, on the first floor. Both Erin and Jimmy went upstairs to their room and opened the door. The small room was very cozy from Erin's standpoint and it had a small fireplace. Jimmy made a fire and then he said to Erin,

"Erin darling, I'll go get our suitcases from the car." Jimmy walked back down stairs and nodded to both the clerk and to the man in the black leather coat, who was still standing and reading his newspaper. It was still raining quite heavily, although the wind had subsided somewhat. Jimmy got both suitcases out of the trunk of the car and as he was already soaking wet, he figured, what's a little more wetness. After he came upstairs, he looked in the mirror, as he was so used to his new mask, that he had forgotten to cover it, in case of rain. However, after inspecting it in the mirror, it didn't look like it was any worse for wear. Evidently he thought, that the four coats of varnish that Mr. Degas had brushed on the mask, made his mask, impervious to water.

Erin was already in the bathtub, when Jimmy returned and while he waited for her to finish bathing, he sat on the edge of the bed, thinking about his good fortune in marrying Erin and Mr. Degas, who created a mask for him. Jimmy had always believed in Devine Providence and he therefore never questioned his faith. Life seemed to be turning around, or so he thought. He heard a noise coming from the adjoining room, as he noticed, that their room had two adjoining doors, which could be made into a suite of rooms, should a large family require larger accommodations. He walked over to one of the doors and he listened for a moment. Evidently who ever was in the adjoining room, was settling in for the evening, as he heard no more noise coming from that room.

Jimmy went back to attend to the fire which was dying out, when he sensed someone behind him, as he half turned, he was knocked unconscious by a vicious blow to the head, with some kind of a blunt object. The person who knocked Jimmy unconscious, took the bed sheets off the bed and tied both Jimmy's hands and his feet and then he lifted Jimmy and placed him in a small guest chair facing the bed. He then wrapped another sheet around Jimmy and the chair, so Jimmy could not move.

Jimmy's head wound was bleeding heavily and the blood was running down the back of his head and into his shirt. Erin was just about finished with her bath and was putting on her 'peignoir', after putting a small drop of perfume, between her breasts. As she opened the bathroom door, she felt a hand wrap itself around her mouth, as she struggled to see who was trying to gag her. She managed to break free of this person for a second and as she turned, she saw it was the man in the black leather coat. She was just about to scream, when he hit her with the back of his hand, and knocked her across the bed, unconscious.

While Erin was unconscious, the man proceeded to take Erin's peignoir off and he tied her, spread-eagled to the bed. Erin was stark naked. Her hands were tied to the wrought iron bed-head and her feet were tied to the foot portion of the bed. Erin was just now starting to come around. Her jaw, where the gangster had hit her, was red and beginning to swell. Her left eye was starting to close. Erin looked around the room and she spotted Jimmy tied up and sitting in a chair, facing the bed, with his head, hanging down. Evidently, this creep wanted Jimmy to view what he was about to do to Erin, before he murdered her. Jimmy however, was still out cold, or else he was pretending that he was. Finally, after taking off his shoes, pants and his shorts, He walked into the bathroom and got a glass of water, which he threw, into Jimmy's face. Jimmy began to come too, and he was mumbling incoherently. Jimmy could see Erin, hogtied to the bed, with her legs spread wide apart. The man had stuffed gags, in both Erin's and Jimmy's mouths, so that they couldn't cry out. The gangster said to Erin and Jimmy in Italian,

"*Lo voglio' il se di sapere, che gli sciocchi nessuni con Al Capish, il padrino. Il La faida, è la fondazione del codice di Mafia di Scilian delle nostre leggi, e nessuno, mai rompe quella legge, senza pagare le conseguenze. Non importa come lungo porta, il braccio lungo del Mafia, lo troverà e l'uccide.*" 'I want you'se' to know, that no one fools with Al Capish, the Godfather; the *La Vendetta* is the foundation of the Sicilian Mafia code of law, and no one ever breaks that law, without paying the consequences. No matter how long it takes, the long arm of the Mafia, will find you and murder you. ('*La Mano Nera*'—The Black Hand).

Jimmy was now taking stock of their predicament and trying to figure out, in his desperation, just how he and Erin might survive this animal and his *La Vendetta*. It looked hopeless, as he could not move and Erin certainly was helpless, being hogtied to the bed as she was. The Mafioso gangster climbed on top of Erin; as Erin tried to avoid his garlic and onion smelled, foul mouth breath, with his two-day beard. His hairy legs and body, gave Erin the creeps, she felt like a gorilla was making love to her. Erin could feel his arousal and she spit in the gangster's face. The mobster first wanted to rape Erin, in front of Jimmy, several times and then proceed to cut up her face, with a razor, he had laid on the nightstand, before cutting her throat.

With that, he hit Erin once again in the face, this time with his fist. Erin was knocked unconscious. A quick movement behind him, startled the gansgster, as a garrote was placed around his neck and was being tightened with such force, that the gangster's eyes were starting to pop out of his eye sockets. His face was turning purple and his tongue was protruding from his mouth. He began to drool, as Bill John, was exerting excruciating pressure, in order to kill this dago son-of-a-bitch. The gangster tried in vain, to pull off the garrote, but Bill was too strong for him. Both Erin and Jimmy couldn't believe their eyes, as they both wondered, where did Bill come from. The gangster, whose voice was becoming hoarse, whispered in Italian,

"Oh il mia di mamma, son-o-a-la femmina, come ha borbottato un Mary di Grandine." 'Oh mama mia, son-of-a-bitch', as he tried to mumbled a Hail Mary, as he slipped into unconsciousness and with his last gasp, died.

When Bill was sure the gangster was dead, he pulled him off of Erin, who was crying and shaking from her ordeal. Bill put Erin's robe around her, as he held her in his arms for just a moment, and then he untied Jimmy.

Both Jimmy and Erin were both in a state of shock and for a few minutes, were unable to comprehend just what had happened, as it happened so fast.

Bill then said to them both, "Look, neither of you are in any shape to help me carry this big gorilla downstairs, so what I will do, is throw him out of the second story window. I will then quietly walk down stairs, and carry him out to his car. I will then try and get rid of him and his car. I should be back in just about a half hour or so."

Bill went to the bedroom window, the one window that didn't have its counterpart on the first floor, which was a blank wall, thus hoping to avoid anyone downstairs, from seeing what was going on. He lifted the big gangster up and placing his feet on the window ledge, he pushed him out. Bill doubted that anyone could hear him fall, as the storm seemed to intensify and the only noise to be heard, was the rain hitting the small inn's red clay tile roof.

He then blew a kiss to Erin and smiling at Jimmy, he cautiously crept downstairs. No one was in the lobby, so he quietly opened the front door and he walked around the kitchen side of the inn to the back yard, trying to avoid the bedroom windows on the first floor. He picked up the gangster and he carried him out to his black sedan. Bill had emptied the pockets of the gangster, before he threw him out of the window. He saw on the gangster's passport, that his name was Salvatore P. Luciano and his hometown was, Palermo, Sicily. He had a P.O. box for an address. Bill thought to himself, I will give the folks back in Palermo a surprise, as he laughed to himself. He started the big black sedan, with the Mafia gangster seated in the passenger seat. He backed out of the parking place, without turning on his lights and then he proceeded up the highway, about a mile.

Before it started to rain yesterday afternoon, Bill in his plan, had driven back and forth on the highway, several miles, to see if he could find a place to dispose of the body of this Sicilian gangster and his car, should events turn out favorably for him. He noticed a short forestry service road entrance and to him, it looked like it was a road used by the French forestry personnel, as the sign on the gate read; "Il francese, il Ministero di Strada di Foreste-Revisiona." 'French-Ministry of Forests-Service Road'.

It was gated and the muddy road was very narrow with deep ruts. The road hugged a ledge, which evidently the French forestry people had bulldozed, so that they could gain access to the forest, which surrounded this side of the mountain.

He doubted that the road was used very often, as weeds had grown in some of the ruts. Perhaps he thought, that some forestry personnel might use it once or twice a year. After driving a quarter mile or so in the dark, he switched on the car's headlights and he drove slowly along the highway, to try and make sure he didn't miss the entrance to this forestry service road.

Finally, as he turned a corner, the headlights from the car, shown on the gate. He drove up to the gate, and shut off the headlights. He had a small jack handle, which he found, in the trunk of his rented car and he easily broke off the rusted lock on the gate. He got back into the car and he drove into the forest area on this slippery clay road, just out of sight of the main highway.

His headlights hardly penetrated the darkness and the rain, with the windshield wipers running on high. Finally he found the spot he was looking for, one which didn't have boulders placed alongside the road edge, to help stop any cars or trucks, from accidentally, driving off the mountain and plunging down, into the deep rocky crevasse below. He turned off the headlights and he walked around the car to the passenger side, he opened the door and he grabbed the gangster's head in one arm, as he pulled his skinning knife from under his shirt and he scalped the Mafia gangster. He began at the man's forehead, and in a sort of pulling and slicing motion; he took off, the gangster's shaggy black, greasy hair scalp, in one swift motion.

There was little blood of course, as the man's heart had stopped a while ago and when that happens, the blood tends to travel down to the feet. Placing the wet scalp on the ground, he walked back around the car, turning the steering wheel toward the road's edge and he put the gear shift, in first gear and after releasing the clutch, the car jerked, as it inched toward the cliff side of the road, which dropped down, over a thousand feet into a gorge. He listened, to see if he could hear when the car hit bottom. Finally, he thought he heard it hit the rocks below. Then the gasoline tank exploded, and the car was consumed in flames. He doubted that anyone would find the car, let alone the body, as the fire probably burned the man to a crisp. Bill then raised his arms to heaven, while clutching the man's scalp in his right hand, as he let out a sort of blood curdling, war whoop, as he carried his grisly souvenir in his hand, allowing the rain to wash off what little blood, was still clinging to the scalp. Bill's intention was to mail this gangster's scalp, back to the gangster's home, in Palermo, Sicily, as a warning to the Mafia, that two could play their game.

CHAPTER 65

❁

The Hospital
-A Scary Drive-

Bill walked back to the inn, down the mountain road and then he tied the gangster's scalp to the rear bumper of his car. He opened the front door of the inn and walked quietly up to the room, where Erin and Jimmy were staying. He opened the door and both Erin and Jimmy were holding each other, as they sat on the bed, shaking. Erin had treated Jimmy's head wound as best she could, by tearing a piece of cloth from her slip, to mop up the blood which was still seeping from his head wound. Erin knew that Jimmy needed professional medical help and soon, as he seemed to talk incoherently, about what had just taken place and he couldn't seem to focus his eyes on anything.

Bill went to his own room for a few minutes, to get clean dry clothes and then he returned to Erin and Jimmy's room. After looking at both Erin's facial scrapes and Jimmy's head wound, Jimmy said to Erin,

"We must get Jimmy to a hospital as soon as possible. I looked into his eyes and his pupils are dilated, which gives me the impression, that Jimmy is either suffering from a concussion or worse, a fractured skull." Bill thought for a minute and then he said to Erin, "Can you drive." Erin answered him by saying,

"No, I can't, I've never driven any kind of a car, ever." Bill thought for a minute and then he said,

"Well, there's no time like the present to learn. Jimmy can you shift gears, while Erin steers?" Jimmy tried to think about Bill's question and then he shrugged his shoulders, as he couldn't seem to concentrate on the meaning of Bill's words. Bill moved his head from side to side, as he looked at Erin, with a worried look on his face.

Finally Bill said, "Look we've got to do something, as we can't just stay here and hope that Jimmy, somehow will get better, as he needs medical help now." Bill then said to Erin, "I will assist Jimmy to your car and help with the luggage, meanwhile, you pay the bill for both your room and mine. I'll settle with you later." He went on,

"What we'll do about your car is this; Erin, you will steer, keeping to the left side of the road. In Europe, most countries drive on the left side of the road, while I'll drive a few hundred feet ahead of you, just in case you can't stop for some reason, I can stop your car, with mine. I believe that Jimmy, out of a sort of rote, will know when to shift gears and he will tell you when to push in the clutch, so that you can move the gear shift lever.

Now if push comes to shove and you can't seem to use the clutch, and Jimmy can't tell you when to push in the clutch, then providing you can move the shift to first gear, you can drive all the way into that small village, where you and Jimmy got married, in first gear. I believe that there is a small hospital located in that same village."

"Oh and further, if the clerk asks you where did the man in the black leather coat go, tell him that he wanted to get an early start and he left his room payment with you, okay?"

Erin said, "Fine."

CHAPTER 66

❁

St. Michael's Hospital
-Erin and Bill-

Erin paid for the room for the man in the black leather coat, her room and Bill's room and she said to the clerk," *"Au revoir et vous remercier, vous avez une Auberge charmante."* 'Goodbye and thank you, you have a lovely Inn.' The clerk smiled as he said,

"Vous remercier la Madame." 'Thank you Madame.'

Bill put Jimmy into the passenger seat of his small sport's car and Erin sat in the driver's seat, scared to death. Bill then said to Jimmy,

"As Erin has never driven a car before, you will have to tell her when to push in the clutch with her left foot, so she can shift gears at the proper time. Jimmy sort of smiled, as though he couldn't quite comprehend what Bill was saying. Jimmy's eyes were still dilated. Bill then decided that Erin would have to drive to the village in first gear, as he now realized that Jimmy didn't understand, what he wanted him to do. Bill opened Erin's door and he showed her the gas pedal, the clutch and the brake pedal, on the floor, telling her that the gas pedal would make the car go faster. Then with his right foot, he placed it on the clutch, pressing down and then he put the car in first gear. Immediately, Jimmy's little sport's car began to move.

Bill hurriedly jumped in his car and he took off, passing Erin until he got a few hundred yards ahead of her and then he slowed down, so that she could catch up. He watched Erin carefully through his rearview mirror, as she struggled with the steering of the little sport's car. Erin seemed to catch on fairly fast, as she now could keep the car in her own lane, whereas before, she had been swerving all over the road. Although, the swearing of the French drivers passing her, kind of unnerved her, as she now had a long line of cars waiting for a chance to pass her on this curvy mountain highway. European drivers are known for their fast and impatient driving, with no road manners what so ever. Erin didn't understand what the finger she was getting from these irate drivers, meant. Erin was doing the maximum speed in first gear, which was just about ten miles per hour, with the little engine screaming.

Smoke was now coming out of the radiator, as Erin's driving in first gear, was overheating the engine. Bill hoped that they could reach the hospital, before the engine froze up. Bill had remembered when he left the village of Villenueve that the small hospital was right on the outskirts of the village. He could see the cross on the top of the hospital's bell tower. He motioned with his hand out of the window, for Erin to follow him into the hospital's, small parking lot. Bill almost came to a stop, as Erin struggled to turn the steering wheel, in an effort to follow Bill into the parking lot.

Bill could tell that Erin didn't remember, which pedal to push for the brake, as he saw her looking down at the floor, and he was hoping that she wouldn't put her foot on the gas pedal first, before he had time to stop her. Therefore, he let her car's front bumper, bang into his rear bumper, as he applied his brakes, until her engine coughed, sputtered and then died, as it could no longer move foreword, against Bill's braking action. They both got out and Bill hurried back to Jimmy's car, to help him get out, as he, Erin and Jimmy, went into the hospital's emergency room. The nun on duty said, *"Manquer de le et les monsieurs, quel est le problème?"* 'Miss and Mr.'s, what is the problem'?

Erin explained that her husband, Jimmy O'Brien had fallen down the stairs and he hit his head on the cement sidewalk. She though that he might have a concussion. The nun then called a doctor who happened to be passing the nurses station. *"Le médecin, est-ce que vous regarderez cet homme, comme sa femme pense qu'il pourrait avoir un concussion, par suite de lui tomber sur une façon de promenade de ciment?"* 'Doctor, will you look at this man, as his wife thinks that he might have a concussion, as a result of him falling on a cement walk way?'

The French doctor looked into Jimmy's eyes with a small light. He asked Jimmy to move his eyes from side to side and then he muttered something under his breath. He then told the nun, *"La soeur, s'il vous plaît mettre ce malade dans la salle 107, comme je crois aussi, qui il ou a un concussion très sévère autrement, un crâne fracturé."* 'Sister, please put this patient in room 107, as I agree, that he either has a very severe concussion or else, a fractured skull.' Erin looked at Jimmy, with a worried look on her face. Bill then said,

"There, there, Erin, don't give up, as Jimmy is a very strong person and I'm sure that the doctor's, can relieve the pressure on his brain." This doctor and several more, came into Jimmy's room for their observations of Jimmy and consulted with each other, what best to do about his condition. Finally, a course of action was decided on, after making some preliminary tests. A nurse-nun came in and she wrapped Jimmy's head in a cold towel, which had been made cold, by placing it in an icebox. For the moment, a series of hot and cold compresses would be applied to Jimmy's head and he was given herbal medication, to thin his blood.

After three days, Jimmy responded favorably enough from his treatment, for the doctor to tell Erin, that Jimmy was suffering from a rather severe concussion and as far as he could tell, he did not have a skull fracture. Erin smiled with the doctor's good news. It was on the fourth day, when the doctor told Erin, that Jimmy could be released from the hospital, that same afternoon, after lunch. Jimmy was in a very good mood, laughing and teasing Erin and Bill. He didn't have much recollection of what happened to him. Erin and Bill decided that they wouldn't tell him, until they reached Erin's hotel in Montmarte.

They arrived in Montmarte that same evening. Jimmy could now drive the car and that was quite a relief for Erin, who didn't think that she could drive Jimmy's car any further, as she was scared to death of driving.

CHAPTER 67

❦

A Strategy
-Erin, Jimmy and Bill-

After registering, Erin and Jimmy went straight to their room, while Bill said that he was going to sit in the bar for a short while, to sort of unwind, as his adrenalin, was starting to peter-out, and he was exhausted. Beside the need to relax and unwind, Bill's main purpose for wanting to have a drink, was to case the bar area and it's patrons. Bill felt uneasy, as he knew that where there is one Mafia gangster, there are usually more, hanging around.

He also felt, that when Salvatore Pasquale Luciano, didn't show up at a predetermined rendezvous, somewhere in Switzerland, his partner's course of action, would be to back track his partner's trail, to find out why, if he could. Hits of this importance, could not fail, or else, one or all of these Mafia hit men, assigned to this hit, would be held accountable. Al Capish didn't accept failure or excuses.

Bill didn't see anyone who might fit the unsavory description of a Mafia hit man. However, before he went upstairs to bed, he had almost forgotten about the scalp, tied to the bumper of his car. He went out into the parking lot and found that it was still hanging there, none the worse for wear. He put the scalp in his pocket. He then took the elevator upstairs to his room, and he went to bed. Bill got up early and he knocked on Erin and Jimmy's door. Erin came to the door, as she put her finger, next to her mouth, telling Bill, that Jimmy was still sleeping. Erin and Bill sat on the couch in Erin's sitting room, while they discussed what had happened to them both, over the past twelve months or so.

Bill was flabbergasted at how well Jimmy's mask looked. Fact is, at first, he had completely forgotten about Jimmy's war wound, the mask was that real looking. Erin asked Bill how he knew that she and Jimmy had gotten married. Bill answered,

"I was there in the church." He went on, "After I had heard that Jimmy had quit the South-Chicago Iron & Bridge Company, as he and their management had a sort of disagreement, over their hiring practices. Jimmy accused them of being in bed with the union, he didn't want any part of any company, which was in cahoots with a union, no matter what the reason was, and you know how principled Jimmy was." He continued, "Well after Jimmy left his company, I lost tract of him. I figured that you and Mrs. O'Sullivan would keep in touch with one another and so I called her. It was Mrs. O'Sullivan who told me of your pending marriage to Jimmy and where the marriage ceremony was to take place and when." He went on,

"I thought that if I could get to your marriage in time, that perhaps I could be Jimmy's best man. Well the ship I was on ran into a huge storm and suffered severe damage, severe enough, that she was taking on water. Therefore, instead of going directly to Le Havre, France, we had to dock in Liverpool, England for repairs." He continued, "The entire ship's passengers, whose destination was France, were all put on a smaller ship and we're taking to Le Havre, France. By the time I got to your wedding, you guys were just taking your marriage vows. So while I didn't get to be yours and Jimmy's best man, I at least got to see you both, get married." He went on,

"It was at the wedding, that I spotted this gangster, who I had a hunch, might attempt to put a hit on you. Therefore, I followed him, as he followed you and Jimmy." Jimmy finally got out of bed, as he heard Erin talking to someone in the sitting room. He came out of the bedroom, with just a towel wrapped around his waist. He shook Bill's hand and they both hugged.

Jimmy said to Bill,

"I'm sorry you didn't get here in time, as I would have liked to have had you, as my best man." Bill repeated for Jimmy, what he had told Erin about the mishaps he had, in trying to reach the small village of Villenueve. He also related his story of how and why; he was able to foil the Sicilian hit man, from killing both Erin and you. Bill then said,

"You know us Indians Jimmy" Jimmy then said to Bill,

"How many times Bill, has it been, that you have saved either my life or Erin's?" Bill laughed as he said,

"What are friends for?" Bill seemed at a loss for words for a minute when Jimmy said,

"Spit it out, what's on that evil mind of yours? I can tell by the lack of an expression on that stoic face of yours, that something's bothering you." Finally Bill spoke,

"I don't like to be the bearer of bad news, but I feel obligated that because you both are my friends and I care about what happens to you, I believe, that I should tell you both, of just how serious a problem you have, especially Erin." He went on, "I'm sure you both were looking forward to a nice long European honeymoon, during the so called European 'Holiday', and Erin pretty much had put behind her, those problems she had with Al Capish and his band of animals." He continued, "With Al Capish and his Sicilian gangsters, they never forget, as *La Vendetta* is the basis of their blood relationship. They swear an oath in blood, that the Mafia family, is above anybody's individual family and is above any allegiance, which they might have sworn to, in their individual country. As a member of the Mafia, you don't question any orders given to you, by a Mafia chieftain or Don. If a contract is 'let', to murder someone, you murder that someone, cause if you fail, then you take the place of the intended victim and you are first tortured and then murdered. They make no exceptions." He went on,

"Just about every country on earth, has Mafia, as part of their subterranean culture, that is, the Mafia, just about controls everything that is illegal, from smuggling illicit drugs, prostitution, gambling, extortion and the so called white slave markets, of the far East. Their control also extends into the labor unions in the United States. They are a ruthless band of murderers; theirs is a secret society; *'la societá segreta'*. If instructed to murder their mother, sister, father or brother, they question no one, but they carry out this gruesome task." He continued,

"I don't personally know everything that went on between Erin and Al Capish and I don't need to know, but what ever it was, that allowed Erin to break Al Capish's murderous hold on her, he has never forgiven her. For that in his mind, is making a fool out of him and no one gets away with that. The Mafia, murders, threatens, extorts and intimidates. They corrupt police departments, government officials at the local and state levels, and their evil influence, reaches into the highest levels of the United States government, itself. They are like a cancer, kill one part and it grows somewhere else in the body politic." He went on,

"You may not know it, as the French papers pay little or no attention, to what goes on in America, but Alphonse Capish was sent to Alcatraz Federal prison in August of this year. However, that doesn't mean that he has lost his power; he still is king of the rackets and the Godfather of organized crime.

"I don't mean to scare you Erin or you Jimmy, as I said before, you two are my closest friends in all the world and I would do nothing to hurt either of you. However, it would be my advice to you both, to get out of 'Dodge' so to speak, as quickly as possible. I'm sure, that while you're in Europe and considered foreigners, you would not have the protection that you would have by law enforcement, if you were back in the states, nor would you have the area to hide in, that the United States could afford you both, in it's immense size." Bill stopped speaking for a moment, after Jimmy said,

"Boy Bill, you sure are painting a very scary picture for both Erin and myself. Is it your feeling, that even though you got rid of that Sicilian hit man, that there are others, waiting in the wings so to speak, to murder us?" Bill then said,

"Jimmy, there is no question about it, as we speak, some Mafia hit man has been searching for that guerilla, that I killed back in that French, bread and breakfast and if he doesn't find him, he'll report back to his higher ups and they will assign another hit man to do the job. Its never ending with these people, until they extract their revenge, through La Vendetta; *"La Mano nera;"* 'The Black Hand'. It's their justice system and it had been used, by all of the Roman Emperors. Honor, even though these people in its truest sense, have none, but it is the backbone of the Mafia." Erin then put her two cents, in,

"Bill, Jimmy and myself, have just signed an extension of my contract, for me to sing at the Moulin Rouge for another year, beginning this September and I don't know how we can break it, without getting sued?"

Bill then said, "Well, I think that both you and Jimmy should return to Paris and the Moulin Rouge, explaining to the powers that be, of your predicament and perhaps they'll understand and let you out of your contract. After all, Erin, you are the rage of Paris and I doubt seriously, that they would want, any negative publicity, when it comes to you and your adoring fans." Jimmy nodded his head in agreement.

CHAPTER 68

The Syndicate

-A Reprieve-

All three friends returned to Paris and they found an open door in the rear of the Moulin Rouge, where they all entered. Bill said to both Erin and Jimmy,

"Look, I'll be moseying along and I'll meet you both later, oh lets say about five p.m. at the *'Le Parisian Gai'* 'The Gay Parisian'. I believe that it's located over on *'134-le Grand Boulevard'.* 'The Grand Boulevard.' Which is located, just about a block south of here and one block west, if my memory serves me right." Jimmy then said,

"Your memory, ha, were you ever there?" Bill answered Jimmy in this way,

"While you were convalescing state-side after the war, I was on leave in Paris for two weeks and believe me, this was one of my favorite watering holes, plus it had gorgeous dancing girls at; *'dix cents une danse.'* 'Ten cents a dance,' back then, if my memory serves me right." Erin laughed with Bill, who was trying to re-live those days, back in Paris, after the close of World War 1. Jimmy patted Bill on the back and Erin gave him a kiss, as Bill walked back out of the stage door entrance.

Erin and Jimmy walked along the darkened back corridors of the Moulin Rouge, hoping to find somebody there. Finally, Erin spotted what looked like a guard, she walked over to him, and she said to the man in French,

"Est-ce que Andre, est n'importe quel de la direction dans?" Andre, is any of the management in'? The guard answered Erin,

"*Oui, Mademoiselle Erin, un des directeurs asseyent dans son bureau.*" 'Yes, Miss Erin, one of the managers is sitting in his office'. Erin and Jimmy continued walking, until they reached the elevators. Erin knew that all of the executives, had offices up on the third floor and so she punched number 3, on the elevator control panel. The old elevator kind of lurched, as it began its slow ascent to the third floor. Jimmy opened the mechanical door, using the door-opening lever.

As Erin looked down the dimly gas lit corridor, she spotted a brighter light and she figured that some executive was in his office. As Erin and Jimmy approached the well lit office, they could hear giggling and Erin sensing what was going on, grabbed Jimmy by the sleeve, holding him back. She then sort of tippytoe'd down by the office door. Evidently, a chorus girl and Messier Demuiré had just finished making love on his desk, as Erin knocked on his office door. She could hear some scurrying, as apparently, the chorus girl was retreating to his private bathroom, he had in his office and he was straightening up the top of his desk. Messier Demuiré said, "*Entre s'il vous plaît, je suis si désolé comme je n'ai prévu personne.*" 'Come in please, I'm so sorry, as I didn't expect anyone.'

"*Ah, Mademoiselle Erin, quel la surprise de pleasant, que est-ce qui vous apporte et votre mari à mon burea.*" 'Ah, Mademoiselle Erin, what a pleasant surprise, what brings you and your husband to my office'?

Erin began by telling Messier Demuiré about their escaping, one of Al Capish's hit men up in the French Alps and their fear, that there would be more attempts on their lives. Mr. Demuiré seemed to understand their plight as he said,

"Well Erin, do you wish to have an adjustment made to your recent contract, or do you wish to cancel it altogether, as I can understand your feelings." Jimmy then said,

"Messier Demuiré, what are the penalties, if we would like to cancel Erin's contract altogether?" Messier Demuiré than adopted a more pensive facial expression as he said,

"Before I answer you Messier O'Brien, I would expect that as far as you both are concerned, you probably believe that myself and Messier de Hugo own the Moulin Rouge." He went on, "Well that is far from the truth, as we more or less act as so-called front men for the Moulin Rouge operation, here in Paris. However, the Moulin Rouge is a syndicate, that is, besides Messier de Hugo and myself, the Moulin Rouge is owned by many more individuals; some known to the general public and others who are, shall we say, anonymous and wish to remain so." He continued,

"Some of these investors, operate out of their own countries, that is those partners in the Moulin Rouge, are not all Frenchman and some operate, lets say, a little above the law, as he winked at Erin and Jimmy. That is to say, such investors are influenced by world events, such as the 'Great Depression', going on in the United States, which has now begun in Europe. In addition, he said, political considerations also, affect the syndicate." He went on,

"Without saying anymore about these outside pressures, Messier de Hugo and I, as representatives of the Moulin Rouge and the syndicate, which owns this cabaret, have decided that we would tear up your contract, should you wish us to do so." He continued,

"Because of your immeasurable performances, here at the Moulin Rouge and with our deepest appreciation for you, we have decided to give you six months, so called severance pay and wish you well."

Erin and Jimmy were sort of speechless at Messier Demuiré's offer. Neither of them expected such an offer, as both thought that they would have to pay some gigantic penalty, in order to cancel their contract with the Moulin Rouge. Jimmy's quick mind now took over, as he thought to himself, *'I wonder if the Mafia, for reasons known only to themselves, decided that Erin with her massive popularity and with her huge fan base, it would be smarter to just severe ties with Erin, and not pursue Al Capish's vendetta toward her. Jimmy thought further; perhaps smarter heads had prevailed, and had persuaded Alphonse Capish, to back away from trying to murder Erin?*

Jimmy felt and the Mafia knew, that by murdering Erin, it would certainly backfire and bring down many governments, on the heads of the Mafia and the syndicate itself. The one thing the Mafia didn't need, as strong as it was around the world, was any bad publicity and Erin's death, could act, as a sort of catalyst, in that it could stir public opinion, against the Mafia and organized crime itself.

Messier Demuiér had a cancellation document on his desk, which he asked both Erin and Jimmy to sign, as well as himself, as representing the Moulin Rouge Enterprises. Thus, Erin's glorious career seemed to have come, to an abrupt ending, at least in Europe. With a look of sadness and relief on their faces, both Erin and Jimmy, acting as Erin's manager, signed this document, releasing both of them from any criminal redress. Shaking Messier Demuiré 's hand, both Erin and Jimmy, left the Moulin Rouge, Erin with a look of sadness and Jimmy with a look of relief.

Then Erin said to Messier Demuiré,

"*A vous en désordre et votre ami, en désordre de Hugo, je manquera vous les deux, pour vos plusieurs bienveillances montré me, pendant que j'a chanté à votre magnificient. J'aussi manquera, tout mes ventilateurs et amis, qui j'a fait ici au Moulin et dans la Ville de Lumière et amour, Paris et l'amour ils a tout montré me; Je vous aime tout!*"

'To you Messier Demuiré and your friend, Messier de Hugo, I shall miss you both, for your many kindnesses shown to me, while I sang at your magnificent cabaret. I will also miss, all of my fans and friends that I have made here at the Moulin Rouge and in the City of Light and love; Paris and the love they have all shown to me. I love you all'!

Messier Demuiér kissed Erin on the mouth and on both of her cheeks and Jimmy on both of his cheeks. Messier Demuiér had a small tear, fall from his eye, as he said to himself, *'only once in a lifetime, shall the City of Paris and I, ever see such a talent, as Mademoiselle Erin O'Hara, cross our paths; for we truly, were the fortunate ones.*'

CHAPTER 69

❀

Au Revoir à la France
-Erin, Jimmy & Bill-

When Bill left Erin and Jimmy at the Moulin Rouge, he deliberately walked in the alleys, behind several Chapeau, 'hat' stores, to see if he could find in their trash, a box of some sort. He was also looking for, some scrap wrapping paper, which the store might have thrown out, for one reason or another. He wanted to wrap and ship the scalp, to the home of, that Mafia hit man, who Bill had scalped, back in the French Alps. Finally, he found what he was looking for.

He took out his fountain pen, after he placed the scalp in the discarded box, which had some scuffmarks on it, together with some pieces of soiled paper, which he used as packing material. He found some old pieces of string, which he wound around the box and tied it tightly. He then printed the name of, Salvatore P. Luciano, his post office box number, Palermo, Sicily, on the box. He had placed in the box, pinned to the scalp, a small necklace with the evil eye on it. He knew just how superstitious the Italians and Sicilians were, regarding such an evil omen. He found a *'bureau de poste'*, a 'post office', where he mailed the package. Bill smiled to himself, as scalping that hit man, gave him terrific satisfaction and piece of mind.

Bill then walked over to the *'Le Parisian Gai'*, 'The Gay Parisian', and entered. He walked over to the bar and he ordered a drink. He figured that probably Erin and Jimmy would be gone, the better part of the afternoon, and so he thought, he would order a sandwich and a beer, which he did, after he finished his Martini. The waitress, a cute little thing said to Bill, after she brought him his sandwich,

"*Monsieur, est-ce que vous souhaite asseoir dans la cabine ou reste à la barre?*" 'Mr., do you wish to sit in the booth or remain at the bar?' Bill's French wasn't too good, so he kind of guessed at what the waitress was telling him, and he said,

"*Le bien-aimé, j'aimerais un les deux.*" 'Sweetheart, I would like a booth'. The waitress smiled at Bill's attempt to communicate with her in French, so she said,

"Messier, I believe that I speak better English, than you do French, so lets you and I, speak English or American, as you yanks prefer." Bill laughed at this cute and perky little French waitress and so he sat in a booth, toward the back of the cafe and bar. From his booth, he could see the front door and where he could see Erin and Jimmy, when they came in. The waitress wasn't very busy and so she struck up a conversation with this peculiar looking yank, with a ponytail.

Bill had told her about when he first came into this place, which was, a few years ago while on leave, shortly after the war ended and what a nice time he had had.

The waitresses name was Angelique, Angelique Cosette. She said that she had lost three brothers in the war and her older sister was married and living in Bordeaux. "What is your name, Messier?" Bill answered.

"My name is Bill John." Angelique thought about Bill's name, and then she said,

"Messier Bill, you have two first names, how come?" Bill tried to explain why, but she couldn't understand. Finally, Angelique said,

"Messier Bill, I get off from work shortly and I thought that you might like to have a drink 'or so' with me?" It was 'or so', that caught Bill's attention as he said,

"I'm expecting to meet friends in a little while here and perhaps you would like to join us?" Angelique thought for a minute and then she said,

"Oui, I would very much like to meet your friends."

It wasn't more than twenty minutes, when Bill spotted Erin and Jimmy entering the cafe. Bill whistled and waved his hand. Erin and Jimmy walked over to the booth, where Bill was sitting, with a cute young lady. Bill got up as he said,

"Angelique, I would like you to meet, two of my dearest friends, Erin O'Hara and Jimmy O'Brien. Erin and Jimmy, meet Angelique Cosette, the love of my life." Everyone laughed, although Angelique's face turned red. Angelique then said,

"'I'm so happy to meet Bill's closest friends, although either Bill is a little drunk, or else he is a little presumptuous, telling you that I am the love of his life, when we just met."

Erin could sense in Angelique's statement, that she liked Bill a lot, but she didn't care for him telling his friends, of their close association, when she had just met Bill. Each ordered a sandwich and a bottle of warm beer.

Angelique kept watching Erin, as though she knew her and then finally she said, *"Pardonne Mademoiselle, mais aren't vous le chanteuse célèbre de l'Escroc de Moulin, Mademoiselle Adrienne de la Durequex?"* 'Pardon Mademoiselle, but aren't you the famous chanteuse of the Moulin Rouge, Mademoiselle Adrienne de la Durequex? Erin smiled as she said,

"Why yes I am, how did you know?" Angelique answered her,

"Je parlerai anglais dans répondre à vous, pendant que vous parlez français assez bons, il vaudriez mieux je pense, qui nous tout a parlé anglais. Oui, j'a fait a vu vous au Moulin un soir quand me et mon trois est venu voir vous, après votre image et le réexamine vous a reçu, par le français presse. Je pourrais ajouter, vous étiez prodigieux." 'I'll speak English in answering you, while you speak pretty good French, it would be better I think, that we all speak English. Yes, I did see you at the Moulin Rouge one evening with my girl friend, after your picture and the rave reviews you received, by the French press, interested us. I might add, you were *'prodigieux'*, 'stupendous'. Erin had a big smile on her face, as she said to the young waitress,

"Thank you for your kind comments and I'm glad that you enjoyed my performance." Bill then asked Erin,

"How did it go with the executives of the Moulin Rouge this afternoon?"

"Much better than I could have expected, right Jimmy?" was Erin's answer. Jimmy then said,

"While I agree with Erin, I still feel that there was more to our meeting with Messier Demuiré, than Messier Demuiré told us." Bill then asked,

"What do you mean, there was more to the meeting than what Messier Demuiré told you?" Jimmy thought for a minute and then he said,

"Let me try and explain what I mean, as well as how I felt about our meeting. It had occurred to me while Messier Demuiré talked to us in a rather vague sort of way, that my thinking was at the time, and still is, that the syndicate that he referred to several times, has ties with the Mafia. I now believe that it was they, who decided to pull the chain on Erin, and call off their *La Ven-*

detta. With her massive and adoring following, they felt that if any harm came to her, the world's attention would be unbelievably relentless in pressuring the authorities, until that is, the person or persons, involved in murdering Erin, were brought to justice and they felt that they, the Mafia, couldn't stand the negative press." He went on,

"But Erin and I both believe that it's now time, to say *'au revoir',* 'goodbye'. As we both believe in Devine Providence and we both feel that we should return to the good old U.S. of A." Bill looked at them both and then he said,

"When are you planning on leaving?" Jimmy looked at Erin as he said,

"Sometime this week; just as soon as we can make reservations both for the train from Paris to Le Havre and for our ocean liner, back to New York."

Angelique who had been listening intently to their conversation, but didn't comprehend what the trio was talking about, had a sort of hurt look on her cute face, with the mentioning of Erin and Jimmy, returning to America. *'What about Bill'*, she thought, *'would he also be going back'*? Bill who was sorting out in his mind what Jimmy had just said, and was watching the expression on Angelique's cute face, piped up as he said,

"I'll be sticking around here for a couple of more weeks, as I'm beginning to enjoy the sites." Angelique had a big smile on her face with Bill's good news, as she felt deep down, that he was attracted to her, as she was to him. Bill then added,

"Lets keep in touch and I think Erin, that we should use Mrs. O'Sullivan, as our sort of go between, as I know that you write to her often."

CHAPTER 70

❧

Le Normande
-Shipboard Honeymoon-

Erin and Jimmy said goodbye to both Bill and Angelique at the train station in Paris, as they boarded their train for Le Havre. Erin had tears in her eyes as she gave Bill a big kiss and a hug and she hugged little Angelique and gave her a sweet kiss. Jimmy shook bill's hand and he gave Angelique a kiss on her cheek.

They arrived in Le Havre's train station, about eight thirty a.m. and then took a shuttle bus to the port of Le Havre. As they got off of the shuttle bus, they could see the huge ocean liner, Le Normandie, the pride of the French fleet, sitting out at the far end of the harbor in deeper water. They would have to take a 'lighter' out to the huge ship, as the harbor at Le Havre, wasn't deep enough to accommodate the draft of this huge ship, considering the high and low tides.

After a ship's steward, located their room and brought their luggage in, Jimmy tipped the steward. Erin then gave Jimmy a big smooch, as she said,

"You know sweetheart, with our honeymoon cut short by that Mafia hit man, this seems like a fitting continuation of our honeymoon; may it never end." Jimmy smiled at her and swatted her on her rear end, Erin laughed as she said, "Careful Jimmy, that's the pot of gold." Both Erin and Jimmy were tired, it seemed like with all of the excitement brought on by that Mafia guerilla, and Erin's singing gig at the Moulin Rouge, they had been kept in a heightened state of mental anxiety. They now could unwind and so they both fell asleep on the bed, fully clothed.

Outside of one storm, the crossing of the Atlantic Ocean was very calm and uneventful and they arrived in New York, eight days later. As they sailed into New York harbor, Both Erin and Jimmy, looked at the Statue of Liberty, wondering just how their own parents and grandparents felt, when they too, looked at this magnificent monument, to the world's immigrants and especially their own Irish ancestors.

It was almost noon, when the giant French luxury liner birthed at one of the piers, in New York harbor. Jimmy flagged a taxi and the taxi took them to the Knickerbocker Hotel, where they had made reservations by wireless, from the ship, earlier. Erin said that she would like to see New York and take in a couple of Broadway shows. After about three days, Jimmy said to Erin,

"Sweetheart, I think it's about time for us to be moving on. New York is just too big for my liking, with its 'pushy shovy' people and its dog eat dog, mentality. He thought to himself, *'New Yorkers certainly are different from us midwesterners, where good manners are still important."* Jimmy then said,

"Erin honey, is there any reason, that you might want to visit Chicago, if not, I think we should take the train to Cincinnati, Ohio and make inquiries about getting employment, on one of those large river boats?" Erin thought for a minute and then she said,

"While I would like to have visited with Mrs. O'Sullivan up in Niles, Illinois, but for now, its not that important. "Fine", said Jimmy; "We'll catch a train tomorrow morning for Cincinnati."

CHAPTER 71

Cincinnati, Ohio
-The Island Queen-

Both Erin and Jimmy had found employment on the giant Ohio, riverboat-paddle wheeler, the Island Queen, as Mr. Wallace was more than happy, to have Jimmy return, as the companies legal council, for Hayes, Pickering & Haffendorf Ltd., who were owners of a fleet of riverboats, which traveled the Ohio and Mississippi rivers.

Mr. Pickering and his wife had traveled the continent of Europe this spring and found time to see the famous and risqué floor show, at the famous Moulin Rouge, where Erin just happened to be singing. He of course fell in love with Erin. His wife noticing the peculiar body movements of her husband, and the gaga expression on his face, acting like a school boy with his first crush, realized that he had fallen madly in love with Erin, for just a moment though, as she would soon remind him of who he was married to, by twisting his ear.

So there was no question about it, once Mr. Pickering heard from Mr. Wallace, that Jimmy O'Brien and his wife Erin, were seeking employment and with Mr. Wallace telling him that Erin used to sing at the Moulin Rouge in Paris, as the famous chanteuse, Mademoiselle Adrienne de la Durequex. Mr. Pickering was delighted, as he had seen her perform in Paris at the Moulin Rouge, although Mr. Wallace didn't know that. Not only for his own personal reasons, but he knew that with her singing on the companies riverboats, business would probably quadruple.

Mrs. Ella Mae Pickering, the wife of Mr. Pickering, while being a good church going southern Christian woman and a member of the Ladies Christian Temperance Society, of Ft. Thomas, Kentucky, had to snicker to herself, when she saw the scantily clad chorus girls of the Moulin Rouge, as they danced with no underpants. While she protested to her husband and pretended to look away, but she never the less, enjoyed the show, as much as her husband Jedidiah did, as she peeked over her fancy Chinese fan, with her slightly flushed and perspiring face, as she kept crossing and uncrossing her legs involuntarily, as the floorshow reached it's conclusion.

As a prim and proper southern matron or belle, no woman would step outside her door, without a fan. Both from a practical standpoint, for hitting flies and brushing away gnats, but for using it occasionally, as a foil, so to speak, to peek over every now and then, with a sort of a flirtatious glance, while flickering her eyes, at Titus Roscoe Beaudrieu 11, whenever she happened to see him on the street.

Mr. Beaudrieu was the town banker and a pillar of southern society, as it were and quite handsome. He also was recently widowed. It was said, that his wife died of alcohol poisoning, as she became a so-called closet drinker. She had a craving for Bordeaux French wine. She didn't realize that wine was very insidious, in that it slowly seduces its victims, by numbing their brains and creating a chemical dependency. With her bottle of wine, she not only had found a close friend, but a crutch as well, to sort of lean on, when life seemed too much for her, to bear.

Her drinking they say, was caused by her husband's infidelity. He also was known to gamble some and to frequent those gambling and pleasure palaces, over in Covington, Kentucky. As I said, Mrs. Pickering always carried her Chinese silk fan, a gift from her mother for her sixteenth birthday. It brought back to her mind, memories of when she was a young girl and when she often borrowed one of those racy ten-cent romance novels, from under her grannies bed, to read out behind the barn.

She would then enter a world of fantasy, where shady roué's would have their way with her and she would lie in the tall grass, perspiring, with a flushed face. While she knew deep down, that such impure thoughts weren't good for a young lady to think about, but that was a time, she relished and she often in her own mind, traveled back in time, in order to re-live those wicked moments, of forbidden pleasures.

She and Mr. Beaudrieu had separate bedrooms. He mother had warned her about men and their never satisfied appetite for sex. Almost like animals, therefore, she always locked her bedroom door at night.

CHAPTER 72

❦

Southern Tour

-A Rousing Success-

With much fanfare and with an introduction befitting a queen, Erin O'Hara's, second American tour de force had begun. Her first tour began in the speakeasies and the seedy bars of Chicago and of course, included the magnificent gentlemen's club; The Bombay Club and finally ended in the French Pavilion at the world famous Toulouse Lautrec café, at the Chicago's Worlds Fair; 'A Century of Progress'. Although her career reached its zenith at the Paris, France café, of the same name. This American river tour or engagement was really Erin's finale farewell tour, although it wasn't billed as such.

Erin had already told Jimmy, that the riverboat tour would be her last, as she wanted to settle down somewhere and raise a family, preferably in Chicago, as she had a sentimental love for the Windy City, even though it was there, that she was hurt so badly as a child and as a young woman, both mentally and physically.

With Erin's decision to settle in Chicago, Jimmy figured that he would resume his old law practice. Their riverboat tour, took them to all of the major southern cities that resided on either the Ohio or Mississippi rivers

The old south fell in love with Erin O'Hara and drew Erin to its bosom, and she fell in love with the old south. Erin no longer sang under her stage name of Mademoiselle de la Durequex, but was simply billed as 'Erin O'Hara, the Irish Beauty'.

After performing in two tours on the Island Queen, Erin and Jimmy left the riverboat and went north to Chicago. Erin had been trying to get pregnant, but couldn't and she didn't know why. *'Was Jimmy infertile, or did she have a problem'?* Erin and Jimmy after establishing residence on Chicago's 'Gold Coast', went to see an internationally famous Gynecologist, Doctor Cornelius X. Walsh. Dr. Walsh was also a product of Canaryville and after examining Erin and running many tests on her, he finally in collaboration with several other doctors, came to the conclusion, that Erin had been so badly beaten as a child, that her reproductive organs had been damaged and she could no longer conceive.

This was heartbreaking news for Erin, who had always wanted a large family, but she realized that God works in mysterious ways.

CHAPTER 73

❦

Adoption

-St. Vincent's Orphanage-

It was on an early fall morning when both Erin and Jimmy, had made an appointment with the Mother Superior of St. Vincent's orphanage in the south side of Chicago. The morning air had a crispness to it and Erin was bundled in her mink coat, to ward off the chilly fall, Chicago weather. Erin had not realized, that the Mother Superior of St. Vincent's orphanage was none other than, sister Angela Clare of St. Teresa's parochial school and Erin's former music teacher and mentor, as Jimmy had made the appointment to see about adopting a child, if they could.

They both walked into the foyer of the orphanage and asked at the front desk about their appointment with the Mother Superior. The sister who sat at the front desk told them that the Mother Superior's office was just down the hall and to their right. They walked down the hall and knocked on the door. Erin didn't notice the name printed in gold leaf letters on the office door.

A voice inside said, "Come in please." As Erin and Jimmy opened the door, there sat a nun who seemed very familiar to Erin, though the nun was a lot older, but Erin was sure that she knew her, but couldn't place her for a moment. When sister Angela looked up at Erin, there was no question in her mind, that standing before her, was little Erin O'Hara, the pride of her music class, back at St. Teresa's. Sister Clare broke out in tears as she hugged and kissed Erin, who was still unsure as to whom this nun was. Finally, after a lengthy hug, Erin said,

"Sister, are you sister Angela Clare, of St. Teresa's?" With an affirmative nod by Sister Clare, Erin burst out in tears, as she hugged and kissed her former music teacher, who was directly responsible for her fabulous career. After several hours of conversation and with Sister Clare admitting that she was a rabid fan of Erin's, she showed Erin her rather large scrapbook, following Erin's career.

After asking both Erin and Jimmy, just what kind of a child they were looking for. Erin said,

"We both thought that for our first child, a boy would be nice."

"Well, at the moment, we don't have a baby boy that fits your description, however, what we do have and I think that you both would be interested in, are two beautiful, identical twin baby girls. I'm sad to say, that the mother died giving birth to these beautiful little girls, as she lay in an alley, on the cold wet red bricks, hemorrhaging." A passer by heard her screams and tried to get some help for her, but by the time the police arrived, she had died. But the two beautiful little baby girls are just fine." She continued,

"The mother, a recent fifteen year old Irish immigrant, was raped by a no good Irish drifter as far as we can tell, whose name I won't give you, as its not important. She had told the passer by, who tried to get help for her, before she died, that she wanted her baby girls, to be raised with the names of her choosing; Irish names. She evidently felt that her babies would be girls, or else she hoped that they would be." Sister Clare had a smile on her face as she said,

"God works in such mysterious ways, that sometimes, I am awe struck by what he is doing." Erin and Jimmy hadn't given a thought about a girl, let alone two baby girls. They certainly hadn't figured on such an event, as they both kind of had it in their minds, that they would like a baby boy, at least for their first child. They both now turned their thoughts, about raising two little girls, whose teenage mother had died, giving birth to them. Perhaps God was offering her a way to make amends so to speak, for her sinful life?

Erin's mind now wandered back to Canaryville, where her mother had died, giving birth to her and her tyrant for a father. She tried to see in her mind's eye, if she could, just what this little and frightened teen-age Irish girl, looked like, all alone in a strange country and probably scared to death, after having been raped and become pregnant, by an Irish drifter. *Was she petite, was she a blonde or did she have red or black hair. What about her parents, were they dead or alive? If they were alive, what part of Ireland did she come from?* So many unknowns, but Erin now felt a sort of empathy, for this little unwed mother and her two babies. Sister Clare said,

"Erin, neither you or Jimmy are obligated to adopt these two babies, but I think that at least, you should see them before you make up your minds, one way or the other." Erin nodded, as did Jimmy. They both left Sister Clare's office and followed the nun to the nursery. Sister Clare walked directly to two little bassinets, which sat side by side, with pink bows attached to them. She reached into the first bassinet, and picked up the first baby, and she handed her to Erin. She then picked up the second baby and she handed her to Jimmy. Erin noticed that both girls had black hair and green eyes, which made her smile. Both Erin and Jimmy responded to the warmth and the crying of these two little angels, as they both snuggled against Erin and Jimmy's bodies, seeking warmth and security.

Sister Clare was no dummy. She knew that once Erin and Jimmy cuddled these two little babies, that their decision as to whether or not they might consider adopting them, was now a moot point. Erin and Jimmy had fallen in love with these two little precious and beautiful babies. Sister Clare with a rather stern look on her face said,

"As I mentioned to you before, should you decide to adopt these two baby girls, their mother according to the man who found her and who summoned help said, that before she died, as she held the man's hand, that she would like her babies to have the names of two of her sisters back in Ireland." She continued, "Now I can't hold you to keep this little mother's wishes, of you naming her babies with the names of her sisters if you don't like their names, but I would like you to a least to consider them, as a sort of tribute to this poor unfortunate girl, who was nothing more than a child herself." Erin then said,

"Well, what are the two names?" Sister Angela thought for a minute and then she said,

"The oldest or the first baby to be born, was to be named Kiera the second baby or the youngest, is to be named Léan, which is the Irish name for Helen. Both Erin and Jimmy looked at one another and they both spoke simultaneously as they said,

"Fine, those names seem perfect for these two beautiful little darlings." Sister Clare smiled as she said,

"Then so be it, God has chosen the parents for these cute baby girls. We can return to my office, where I'll need you both to sign some papers, giving you both legal status as parents, of Kiera and Léan O'Brien."

CHAPTER 74

The Proud Parents
-Kiera & Léan-

After giving, a generous donation to St. Vincent's Orphanage, Erin and Jimmy kissed sister Angela, as they took their two babies, their bassinettes and all the baby paraphernalia, so necessary in handling these two newborns, to their car. As Jimmy took off down the street with Erin holding both babies in her lap, the O'Brien's were beaming with pride and happiness.

After arriving at their Gold Coast apartment, both Erin and Jimmy spent the next two weeks learning how to change diapers, burping the twins, heating milk bottles and more importantly, walking the floor each and every night, trying to get the twins to adapt to a more favorable schedule of waking and sleeping, at least more favorable to their parents. Both Erin and Jimmy were exhausted, as the twins seemed to enjoy their parent's frustration and tiredness.

After several weeks had gone by, the O'Brien's took their newborns for a visit to their adopted grandmother, Mrs. Mary O'Sullivan, up in Niles, Illinois. Mrs. O'Sullivan of course, became the doting and loving grandmother of the twins. Often Erin and the twins would spend a weekend or so, at Mrs. O'Sullivan's tourist home visiting her, while Jimmy was adding more and more clients to his already booming law practice.

Mrs. Sullivan had kept in contact with Bill John and she reported that Bill John had married that cute little perky French waitress, Angelique Cosette in

Paris, France and Bill and Cosette, had opened up a hardware store in Cincinnati, Ohio.

The End

978-0-595-37046-7
0-595-37046-2

Printed in Great Britain
by Amazon